DATE DUE

FINA

Ace Books by Greg Cox

(Based on DC Comics Miniseries)

INFINITE CRISIS

52

COUNTDOWN

FINAL CRISIS

FINAL CRISIS

Based on the DC Comics Miniseries

GREG COX

ACE BOOKS, NEW YORK

THE BERKLEY PUBLISHING GROUP
Published by the Penguin Group
Penguin Group (USA) Inc.
375 Hudson Street, New York, New York 10014, USA
Penguin Group (Canada), 90 Eglinton Avenue East, Suite 700, Toronto, Ontario M4P 2Y3, Canada
(a division of Pearson Penguin Canada Inc.)
Penguin Books Ltd., 80 Strand, London WC2R 0RL, England
Penguin Group Ireland, 25 St. Stephen's Green, Dublin 2, Ireland (a division of Penguin Books Ltd.)
Penguin Group (Australia), 250 Camberwell Road, Camberwell, Victoria 3124, Australia
(a division of Pearson Australia Group Pty. Ltd.)
Penguin Books India Pvt. Ltd., 11 Community Centre, Panchsheel Park, New Delhi—110 017, India
Penguin Group (NZ), 67 Apollo Drive, Rosedale, North Shore 0632, New Zealand
(a division of Pearson New Zealand Ltd.)
Penguin Books (South Africa) (Pty.) Ltd., 24 Sturdee Avenue, Rosebank, Johannesburg 2196,
South Africa

Penguin Books Ltd., Registered Offices: 80 Strand, London WC2R 0RL, England

This is an original publication of The Berkley Publishing Group.

This is a work of fiction. Names, characters, places, and incidents either are the product of the author's imagination or are used fictitiously, and any resemblance to actual persons, living or dead, business establishments, events, or locales is entirely coincidental. The publisher does not have any control over and does not assume any responsibility for author or third-party websites or their content.

Visit DC Comics online at www.dccomics.com or at keyword DC Comics on America Online.

PRINTING HISTORY
Ace trade paperback edition / July 2010

Library of Congress Cataloging-in-Publication Data

Cox, Greg, 1959–
    Final crisis : based on the DC Comics miniseries / Greg Cox.—Ace trade paperback ed.
        p.   cm.
    ISBN 978-0-441-01857-4
    1. Heroes—Fiction.   2. Good and evil—Fiction.   I. DC Comics, Inc.   II. Title.
    PS3603.O9F56 2010
    808.8'0352—dc22

                                                                        2010010551

PRINTED IN THE UNITED STATES OF AMERICA

10 9 8 7 6 5 4 3 2 1

ACKNOWLEDGMENTS

My fourth DC Comics novelization, following *Infinite Crisis*, *52*, and *Countdown*, was just as enjoyable as the first three. As always, I have to thank all the talented comic book writers, artists, and editors who gave me so much to work with, including Grant Morrison, Eddie Berganza, and Adam Schlagman. Anyone who enjoys this novel should definitely check out the original *Final Crisis* comic miniseries as well. It's well worth your time.

I also want to thank my editors, Christopher Cerasi and Ginjer Buchanan, for signing me up one more time and making sure I had all the materials I needed to complete this book in a timely fashion. And my agents, Russ Galen and Ann Behar, for ensuring that all the contractual details went smoothly. Here's hoping this won't really be the *final* Crisis. . . .

In addition, I took full advantage of various fannish resources, including the helpful staff at my local comic book shop, Captain Blue Hen Comics in Newark, Delaware, as well as some amazingly useful fan websites that analyzed *Final Crisis* in painstaking detail. I particularly appreciated the thorough efforts and annotations of Douglas Wolk, Gary Greenwood, David Uzumeri, and the Mindless Ones.

Last but not least, I could not have written any of these books without the support and encouragement of my girlfriend, Karen Palinko, who has sculpted many exquisite statues and action figures for DC Direct, and our busy four-legged family: Alex, Churchill, Henry, Sophie, and Lyla.

This novel was primarily adapted from the *Final Crisis* comic miniseries, originally published in seven issues by DC Comics (July 2008 to March 2009). Additional material was adapted from *Final Crisis: Submit* (December 2008). These comic books were created by the following people:

EDITOR
Eddie Berganza

ASSISTANT EDITOR
Adam Schlagman

WRITER
Grant Morrison

ARTISTS
Christian Alamy
Drew Geraci
JG Jones
Doug Mahnke
Jesus Merino
Tom Nguyen
Carlos Pacheco
Rodney Ramos
Norm Rapmund
Marco Rudy
Walden Wong

CHAPTER 1

NORTH AMERICA.
40,000 YEARS AGO.

A herd of frightened deer stampeded past the startled youth. Ordinarily, Anthro would have tried to bring down one of the deer with his bound stone axe, but at the moment fresh meat was the last thing on his mind. The sinewy youth stood transfixed amidst the grassy veldt beneath a clear blue sky. His long, knotted brown hair blew in the wind. A crude flint knife was tucked beneath the waist of his deerskin loincloth. Handmade moccasins protected his feet from rocks and thorns. Despite the hot summer sun beating down upon his bare skin, he felt a chill run down his spine. His keen brown eyes gaped in awe. He raised his axe defensively.

"Man," a voice named him.

The word emanated from the wondrous and terrifying apparition before him: a gleaming figure who looked like nothing that Anthro had ever seen in all of his ten-and-seven summers. Although the unnatural being had the shape of a man, his skin and garments were as smooth and white as polished shell. Shining silver patterns covered his face and form like war paint. His opalescent features bore a contemplative expression. He reclined upon a floating throne fashioned from a strange glossy blue substance. The stars themselves adorned the throne, blinking and flashing even in the middle of the day. The full moon shone behind the figure's hairless head as though captured from the heavens. A halo of shimmering silver light arced above the back of the throne, even as the finely crafted seat hovered impossibly over the surrounding brush, held up by nothing but empty air. Trembling, Anthro grasped that he was in the presence of a god.

"I am Metron."

The words and language were unfamiliar to Anthro, but their meaning was somehow clear to him. Although tempted to flee, he stood his ground, less than five paces away from the stranger. His fists tightened around the haft of his axe. Fear clutched his heart, which pounded wildly beneath his chest, but the seated god made no move to strike him dead. Instead Metron gazed serenely upon the mortal youth, his slender fingers steepled beneath his chin. His inscrutable visage offered no hint of his intentions. Glowing white eyes, devoid of pupils or irises, locked onto Anthro, who could not look away. The boy's mouth felt as dry as bone.

"Have no fear," Metron said. "Here is knowledge."

The stranger raised his right hand and held out one finger. Anthro yelped and jumped backward as, without warning, a bright orange spark leapt from the god's finger to a nearby shrub, which suddenly ignited into flame. A crackling blaze engulfed the bush. Thick black smoke billowed into the sky. The smell of burning leaves and branches filled the air. Anthro felt the heat of the flames upon his face and skin, and backed away warily.

The sudden blaze momentarily distracted him, and when he turned to look back at the god, he was amazed to see that Metron was gone. Both the god and his starry throne had vanished as though they had never existed. Anthro searched the horizon, which stretched out around him for as far as the eye could see, but spied no trace of the stranger. A single clap of thunder boomed from the cloudless sky.

Anthro rubbed his eyes, half convinced that the god had been nothing more than a dream or vision, but then the wind shifted, blowing the smoke toward him. He approached the blaze cautiously, captivated by the dancing red and yellow flames. The light from the fire seemed to ignite something deep within him. He knew he should flee from the flames, before they consumed him as well, but instead he stared at the burning bush in rapt fascination. New ideas and possibilities raced through his mind.

What if . . . ?

The screams of the dying thrilled the caveman's savage heart.

Vandar Adg, undying leader of the Blood Tribe, led his men into battle against their enemies, who had been caught by surprise by the twilight raid. He bellowed ferociously as he hammered his foes with the jawbone of a sabertooth he had once killed with his bare hands. The tiger's pelt was draped over his massive shoulders. A belt of human skulls, strung together on a leather thong, girded his waist. Merciless black eyes peered out from beneath his sloping forehead and protruding brows, and a dense black beard bristled from his brutish features. Matted black hair hung down his back, and the hot blood of his victims splattered his shaggy chest and face.

As it should.

Crushing the skull of an oncoming warrior with a single blow, he took a moment to savor the carnage all around him. The Bear Tribe's peaceful camp, nestled in a wooded valley surrounded by rocky hills, was now the home of war. Angry shouts, along with cries of pain, echoed across the camp, as the men of the Bear Tribe fought tooth and nail to defend their mates and children from the invaders. They hacked and jabbed at the howling cavemen with axes and spears, while the raiders stuck to clubs of bone and heavy wood. The dead and dying littered the ground, awash in spreading pools of gore. Bones were shattered and flesh was torn. The smell of spilled blood made Vandar Adg's mouth water.

Despite the fading sunlight, he found it simple to tell the combatants apart. His own warriors looked like him, with thick, stocky bodies and bulging brows and jaws. Their opponents were a newer breed of man, with flat faces and scrawny bodies that made Vandar Adg sneer in disgust just looking at them. Ageless and immortal, he was old enough to remember when the world had belonged to his own kind alone. He found it hard to believe that this race of weaklings had managed to survive at all, let alone that they now threatened to overrun the woods and plains unless he wiped them all out, one clan after another. The world was too small for two breeds of man. One had to die.

He looked forward to feasting upon the fallen.

Peering about in the fading sunlight, he spotted an aged warrior standing guard in front of a flimsy shelter made of stitched animal hides. An ornate necklace of polished shells and teeth marked him as Ne-Ahn, the chieftain of the Bear Tribe, as surely as his grizzled features and magnificent silver mane. He barked out orders to his men as he gripped the haft of his war-axe with both hands. The skull of a mighty cave bear, the tribe's sacred totem, was mounted above the closed entrance of the tent behind him. The trophy warned that the spirit of the bear also defended the shelter.

But Vandar Adg feared neither beast nor spirit. Grinning in bloodthirsty anticipation, he charged toward the gray-haired chieftain. A younger warrior rushed between them, attempting to block the huge cannibal's path, but Vandar Adg snatched the sharpened spear from the man's grasp and kicked him brutally in the gut. The fighter toppled backward, clutching his stomach, and Vandar Adg speared him through the chest with his own weapon. Bright red froth sprayed from the man's lips as he convulsed upon the ground before falling still. Leaving the spear jutting from his victim's ribs, Vandar Adg stomped over the body on his way to confront Ne-Ahn.

To the honor of his ancestors, the old man showed no fear as he spied Vandar Adg heading toward him, bloody jawbone in hand. Ne-Ahn's wrinkled face suggested that he had seen many tens of winters, which still made him countless generations younger than his deathless adversary. Ancient scars, covering almost every inch of his wiry frame, attested to the aged warrior's valor and endurance. He faced death with the steady nerves of one who had done so many times before. Only once did he glance fearfully back at the tent behind him.

Vandar Adg wondered what he was hiding.

Letting out a defiant whoop, the chieftain swung his axe at Vandar Adg, who ducked beneath the blow and grabbed onto the old man's throat with his free hand. He yanked Ne-Ahn off his feet so that his legs dangled above the ground. Vandar Adg's powerful fist squeezed tightly, crushing the chieftain's windpipe. A strangled gasp escaped the man's lips before he went limp in the invader's grasp. The axe slipped from his fingers, and his bulging eyes glazed over.

Vandar Adg grunted in satisfaction. Tossing the lifeless carcass aside, he strode forward toward the chieftain's tent. He would add Ne-Ahn's skull to his belt later; for now, the defenseless shelter called to him. The mounted bear skull bared its bony fangs, but he paid it no heed. Painted handprints, belonging to the man he had just killed, adorned the tanned hides covering the entrance to the tent. Curious to discover just what Ne-Ahn had been guarding, he pulled aside a hanging flap of hide to expose the old man's treasure.

A young female, ripe for the picking, crouched anxiously inside the tent. Bright red hair, the color of fall leaves, fell past her shapely shoulders. A buckskin loincloth and vest did little to conceal her lithe figure and tender flesh, which was invitingly smooth and taut. Striking chestnut eyes widened in alarm as he barged through the doorway, and she gasped out loud.

A leering grin stretched across his bestial countenance. Bloodlust gave way to a different sort of hunger. Despite his contempt for these flat-faced new men, he was developing a definite taste for their women. This one looked fresh and supple enough to bear him many healthy children.

Eager to claim his prize, he reached for the female, who refused to be taken without a fight. The keen edge of a flint knife flashed in her hand as she jabbed the blade deep into his meaty chest. The blow might have killed a lesser man, but not Vandar Adg; ever since he had first bathed in the eldritch light of a fallen star, countless ages ago, death had held no power over him. He had seen vast sheets of ice advance and retreat across whole oceans and continents over the course of his immeasurably long lifetime, yet still he remained, as invincible as ever. Age and disease could not sap his strength. No beast or man could slay him.

Nor this foolish female.

A sharp pain seared his chest as the blade pierced his flesh, but the injury merely angered him. He plucked the useless blade from his chest and tossed it away. Snarling, he smacked the girl across the face so hard that her teeth rattled, then seized a fistful of her hair and hauled her out of the tent. Still fighting, she kicked and shrieked and struggled to get free as he dragged her through the dirt behind him. An anguished cry tore from her throat as she glimpsed the chieftain's body.

Was the girl the old man's daughter or his mate? Vandar Adg neither knew nor cared. Ignoring her strenuous protests, he saw that his men had all but conquered the weaker Bear Tribe. The mangled bodies of the new men were strewn about the camp. Although most were dead, a few of the fallen warriors still whimpered in pain before their skulls were crushed by an enemy club. As the wounded were put to death, others among the raiding party followed their leader's example by ransacking the ravaged camp for women and other trophies. Now was the time to enjoy the spoils of their victory. Tonight they would feast well—on the flesh and marrow of the new men.

Such was the way of the Blood Tribe.

Squealing, the red-haired female fought to escape him. She dug her bare heels into the ground and grabbed onto a leafy bush, refusing to let go. Her fingers clung frantically to the trunk of the bush as she screamed to the heavens for deliverance.

Vandar Adg found her struggles amusing. Wrapping an arm around her waist, he impatiently wrenched her away from the bush and slung her over his shoulder. Her tiny fists pounded uselessly against his back as she kicked and clawed and thrashed like an enraged sabertooth. He admired her spirit. Breaking it would be a pleasure.

But before he could enjoy her, startled gasps and exclamations broke out behind him. Puzzled, he turned to see his men shouting and pointing at a stony ridge. A bright orange glow rose from behind the top of the ridge, as though the sun itself was creeping up on them. Vandar Adg blinked in confusion, while his men backed away in alarm. Both hope and fear showed upon the brutalized faces of their captives.

A heartbeat later, the rising glare exposed the form of a youthful Bear tribesman, who stepped defiantly onto the crest of the hill. His right arm held aloft a wooden branch that ended in a blazing ball of fire. Flames crackled about the burning brand, which the flat-faced stripling held as fearlessly as he might a spear or axe. He stood silhouetted against the purple sky, holding back the fall of night with the fiery . . . *thing* . . . in his hand. Wide-eyed cavemen jabbered fearfully.

Vandar Adg's jaw dropped. His bloodshot eyes were agape. He could barely comprehend what he was seeing. Fire was a menace, set loose at times by lightning and angry gods, which all men feared and stayed far away from.

He had witnessed many a wildfire over the ages, and been burned badly on occasion, but . . . fire in the hands of man? A mere *boy*?

This was something new.

For the first time in millennia beyond counting, fear gripped the immortal's heart. He let go of the squirming female, dropping her onto the blood-soaked earth. Her brown eyes shone with relief and recognition as she spotted the stripling upon the ridge. She whispered a name before scrambling away from Vandar Adg, who barely noted her departure. The terrifying sight before him had driven the lust from his loins.

How was this possible?

The youth gave Vandar Adg and his raiders no time to overcome their shock. The arm bearing the burning brand swept down, setting aflame the shrubs and grasses at the base of the ridge. To the cavemen's horror, a wall of fire rushed toward them, consuming everything in its path. The glare from the conflagration turned twilight into day. Smoke blew against Vandar Adg's face, choking him. The scorching heat seared his skin and he threw up his hands to shield his face from the sparks and flames. Howling in terror, his men fled the camp in a panic, abandoning their captives, who ran for safety themselves.

Vandar Adg hesitated only for a moment before joining the chaotic exodus. Glancing back over his shoulder, he caught one last glimpse of the nameless youth standing astride the barren ridge, gazing down implacably upon an inferno of his own creation. The fleeing immortal realized that he had underestimated these new men and the changes they were bringing. He vowed that he would not make that mistake again.

The doomed camp went up in flames.

CHAPTER 2

Dan Turpin struck a match.

As the stocky ex-cop lit his cigarette and tossed the match aside, it struck him that fire was probably mankind's first big mistake. *Like everything else the sad, stinking human race ever thought of, we take a good idea and use it to kill ourselves.*

A balding bruiser of a man way past retirement, Turpin took a drag on the cancer stick as he ambled along the docks down by the waterfront. A rumpled tan trench coat was draped over his burly frame. His weathered features wore a chronically sour expression. Towering steel cranes perched over dilapidated wharves, while busy stevedores unloaded the freighters anchored along the piers. Seagulls circled and cawed overhead. A salty breeze, blowing off the harbor, did little to improve his disposition.

Formerly a member of Metropolis's elite Special Crimes Unit, Turpin no longer carried a badge, but that didn't stop him from pounding the pavement as a private eye these days. He was three weeks out on the trail of six missing children. Bright kids, gifted kids, who went out one day and never came home. At this late date, Turpin had little hope of finding the kids alive, but who knew? There was still a chance that one or more of the children might still be kicking. And if not, then whoever was responsible needed to get what was coming to them.

His investigation led him to a deserted wharf adjacent to a run-down warehouse. Chain-link fences guarded wooden pallets piled high with miscellaneous crates, bales, and bags. Smoke rose from one of the timber crates. A look of disgust came over Turpin's bulldog face as he recognized the stomach-turning stench of burning flesh.

Oh hell . . .

He squeezed through a ragged tear in the fence, the rusty metal tines snagging on his coat, and headed toward the crate for a closer look. The top of the crate was smashed clean through, as though it had been struck by a falling meteor. The nauseating odor, which raised unpleasant memories of his wartime experiences as a Boy Commando, grew stronger and more oppressive with every step. Bracing himself for the sight of a child's torched remains, he stepped up onto the edge of a pallet and peered down into the splintered crate.

"What the hell?"

There was a smoking body lying inside the box all right, but it didn't belong to one of the missing kids. Instead, to his surprise and relief, Turpin found a battered figure sprawled atop boxes and boxes of cheap toy ray-guns from China. The man's bright red uniform, which was fashioned from a strange unearthly fabric, was torn and scorched, like he'd come through some sort of fiery accident. Fresh cuts and third-degree burns scarred his exposed face and skin. Broken limbs jutted at unnatural angles. A high-tech computer gadget, strapped to the victim's left shoulder, was now just a charred mass of fused crystals and burning circuitry, and a futuristic silver helmet rested next to the body. Bright arterial blood soaked the crushed cardboard boxes beneath the figure, who appeared tall and muscular enough to give Superman a run for his money. Not that his brawny physique seemed to have done him much good. From the look of things, the vic had crashed to Earth after getting walloped somewhere up above the clouds. For all Turpin knew, the guy had fallen straight from orbit.

Just my luck, he thought sourly. *I go looking for some stolen kids and I find a super muk-muk lying in the garbage.*

He'd had his fair share of run-ins with costumed heroes and villains during his stint with the S.C.U. As far he as he was concerned, most of them were nothing but trouble. It took him a moment to place a name to the demolished face before him.

Orion, he recalled. *One of those so-called New Gods from outer space.*

Was the injured spaceman still alive? Turpin leaned over the edge of the crate and reached down to check for a pulse. His meaty fingers brushed Orion's throat—and he yanked them back in pain. "Oww!" Flesh sizzled and smoke rose from his reddened fingertips, which suddenly stung like the blazes. Touching the god's blistered flesh had been like grabbing onto a red-hot coal, and Turpin sucked on the injured fingers in a futile attempt to ease the pain. He would've killed for a bucket of ice to plunge his hand into.

His startled exclamation roused Orion, who startled Turpin by sitting up abruptly. Bloodshot brown eyes glared fiercely. "Heaven . . . cracked and broken . . ." he snarled through cracked, busted lips. His short red hair was singed and disheveled. Ugly burns and bruises marred his rugged features, and blood leaked from a broken nose. He seized Turpin's lapels with both hands, dragging the ex-cop toward him until their faces were only inches apart. Smoke rose where his fingers clung to the trench coat, and crimson spittle sprayed Turpin's face. *"You!"*

Turpin tried to pull away, but Orion's grip was too strong. "Get your hands offa me!"

"They did not die!" the spaceman shouted urgently. Bulging veins throbbed upon his brow and throat. The heat from his body felt like a blast furnace. Rage contorted his ravaged countenance. He spit out a mouthful of broken teeth. *"He is in you all . . . !"*

The outburst (warning?) exhausted the last of Orion's strength. His fingers let go of Turpin's coat and he toppled backward into the pulverized plastic ray-guns. Swollen eyelids closed for good as he sagged limply atop the bloodstained cargo. His raspy voice faltered, so that Turpin could barely hear the war god's final cryptic utterance:

"Fight . . ."

A grotesque death rattle punctuated the word and Orion's body fell still. His chest stopped heaving as his labored breathing surrendered to silence. Turpin didn't need to risk scorching his fingers again to know that Orion had gone wherever New Gods went when they kicked the bucket. He had a dead space alien on his hands.

What the hell was talking about? the surly detective wondered. He patted down his smoking lapels before they set the whole coat on fire. *Who is in who again?*

Turpin had seen plenty of stiffs before, but a chill ran along his spine as he stared down at Orion's smoldering corpse. A sudden wind whipped up the litter around his feet, and a shadow passed over the grisly scene. Turpin glanced up to see what was blocking the sun. Just for a second, he thought he glimpsed an ominous figure hovering in the air high above the wharf: a black knight, in gleaming ebony armor, standing astride a pair of . . . floating black skis?

"Huh?" He rubbed his eyes, convinced that he must be seeing things. When he looked again a heartbeat later, the surreal image had vanished along with the mysterious shadow. Turpin scratched his hairless dome in confusion. He wiped Orion's bloody spit from his face. Was it just his imagination, or had there really been an armored bozo skiing through the sky like some sort of alpine Angel of Death?

Like this crazy world wasn't already screwy enough.

DETROIT.

Scarlet lightning slashed through crimson skies as roiling black clouds churned violently above the city. Although it had been bright and sunny only minutes before, a sudden storm transformed afternoon into twilight. Howling winds whipped through the high-rise buildings overlooking the Riverfront. The sky was the color of freshly spilled blood.

"Hey, John! You have to check this out!"

The tenth-floor windows of Shining Light Architecture offered a spectacular view of the tempest raging outside. John Stewart looked up from his drafting table, where he had been designing a new state-of-the-art homeless shelter, to see his co-workers standing at the windows, gaping at the storm. "The weather's gone nuts!" Howie Bernstein exclaimed. Sheets of rain lashed the reinforced glass windows.

"Hold on a second," John replied. A trim black man in his late thirties, dressed in casual office wear, he was distracted by a vibration on his right ring finger. There didn't appear to be a ring there, but appearances could be deceptive. He got up from the table and headed for a supply closet nearby. "I have a message coming in."

He stepped into the closet and closed the door behind him. An emerald glow emanated from the power ring on his finger as it flashed into visibility. Answering its hail, he willed it to report.

"LANTERN STEWART 2814.2," the ring addressed him. Its voice was sexless and robotic. "1011 IN PROGRESS."

"1011?" John had never heard that code number before. "What the hell's a 1011?"

Whatever it meant, it clearly demanded his attention. He turned the ring's light on himself, erasing his civilian attire to reveal the skintight green and black uniform underneath. Emblazoned on his chest was the insignia of the Green Lantern Corps, an interstellar police force composed of the bravest beings from thousands of different worlds and civilizations. John was one of two Earthmen assigned to this particular sector of space. He assumed his partner had just gotten the same call.

Better get on the way, he thought. One of the advantages of being the head of his own firm was that nobody could complain if he took long breaks and business trips without warning. A glowing emerald aura surrounded his uniformed body as he silently phased through the walls of the skyscraper and took off into the stormy sky outside. The driving rain vaporized against his protective force field. His ring informed him that he was needed in Metropolis, so he flew east at supersonic speed. Emerald light suffused his dark brown eyes as the ring converted his willpower into energy. His power ring, which matched the insignia on this chest, glowed brightly upon his finger.

"My backup on the way yet?"

"LANTERN JORDAN 2814.1 HAS BEEN ALERTED," the ring assured him. "HIS RING IS NOT RESPONDING AT THIS TIME."

John wondered what was keeping Hal. He hoped his partner wouldn't be long. He had a bad feeling about this call, starting with the incarnadine elemental fury all around him. As he soared through the turbulent winds and lightning, he was troubled to discover that the freak storm, which was getting worse by the moment, seemed to extend all the way from Detroit to the East Coast. The unnatural red tint of the atmosphere worried him; he hadn't seen the sky this color since the last Crisis. As he understood it, crimson storms like this often meant that the interdimensional barriers between parallel universes were breaking down, causing the raw energy of the Multiverse to bleed into separate realities.

That was *never* good. . . .

METROPOLIS.

A multilane suspension bridge overlooked the waterfront. Turpin peered down at the wharf from the bridge's pedestrian walkway. The huge steel girders and cables stretching above him provided only meager protection from the fierce wind and rain. Jagged bolts of lightning slashed across the sky. Traffic across the bridge had halted as commuters parked their cars and got out to watch the spectacular electrical display from the elevated vantage point. Tugging his soaked trench coat closed against the weather, Turpin knew he ought to find someplace warm and dry. *Let the space cops handle this,* he told himself. *This is outta my league.*

Sure enough, an emerald glow heralded the arrival of a Green Lantern, who came swooping down from the stormy sky toward the crime scene below. Spectators on the bridge shouted in excitement at the hero's arrival. Digital cameras and cell phones captured his descent for posterity. Turpin squinted, but couldn't make out which Green Lantern it was. There had been at least five of them over the years, and that was just counting the humans. He couldn't keep track of them all.

"We used to fight in the alleys," he muttered. "Guys these days fight in the clouds."

A woman wearing a fedora and a black leather jacket joined him on the walkway. She leaned against the painted metal guardrail. Long black hair spilled from beneath her hat, and the brim of the fedora shadowed her face. The rugged jacket looked like something a biker might wear.

"Progress?" she asked.

"You tell me." He turned to look at her. "Wait—didn't the Question used to be a guy?"

A flash of lightning momentarily dispelled the shadows, revealing that the woman before him was conspicuously missing a face. A blank expanse of smooth bronze skin stretched from her forehead to her chin, and only a pair of indentations and one small bump hinted at where her eyes and nose should have been. She had no mouth or lips at all.

"Lung cancer," she replied. Her husky voice held a slight Spanish accent. She nodded at the burning cigarette in Turpin's hand. "From smoking."

"Lightweight," he cracked, then regretted it right away. The Question's body stiffened, and he could practically feel her glaring at him from somewhere behind her featureless visage. He wouldn't have thought it was possible to scowl without a face, but somehow this dame was pulling it off. He tossed the cigarette onto the pavement and ground it out beneath his heel. "Sorry! I'm sorry!"

He wondered how the faceless woman was related to the previous Question, a vigilante/detective who used to work out of Hub City. He'd had the same creepy No-Face thing going on, but he'd also fed Turpin some good leads back in the day. So far this new chick was turning out to be a reasonably useful informant too. She was the one who had tipped him off that there was something fishy going on down by the docks, even if he still wasn't sure what the connection was between a dead super hero and some missing kids. *Hope I didn't piss her off too much with that "lightweight" crack.*

"What you got for me?" he asked.

"A question, you ignorant old fart." She sounded distinctly annoyed, but at least she was still speaking to him. "What did your six have in common, apart from being poor and smart? Any evidence of meta-gene activity, for instance?"

Meta-gene? Turpin was no scientist, but he knew that was supposed to be the genetic marker responsible for giving certain people superpowers under the right circumstances, like when they were exposed to weird chemicals or radioactive meteors or whatever. At least, that was the theory. Turpin had no idea if there anything to it, or if it was just scientific gobbledegook some egghead had dreamed up to land a hefty pile of grant money. As far as he knew, though, none of the missing kids were future candidates for the Teen Titans or Infinity Inc. They were bright kids, sure, maybe even prodigies, but they didn't fly or walk through walls or anything like that.

He shook his head.

"Somebody's targeting meta-humans," the Question insisted. "I keep turning up links to this place." She fished a postcard out of her jacket pocket and handed it to Turpin. Thunder boomed overhead as she edged away from him. "You be careful in the shadows, Danny boy."

She looked like she was making an exit, but Turpin still had plenty of questions. "Why are you helping me anyway?"

The Question didn't answer him. Instead she vaulted over the guardrail. "Hey!" Turpin exclaimed. *"Hey!"* He leaned over the rail, fearing that she had jumped to her death, only to see her land nimbly on the roof of a warehouse several feet below. She darted across the rooftop, then dropped out of sight. Turpin scanned the docks, but didn't catch another glimpse of her. She was gone.

"Damn super muk-muks."

Grumbling, he examined the card she'd given him. It turned out to be an ad for some sort of trendy nightspot called the "Dark Side Club." The name of the club was printed in ornate Gothic type against a stark black background. An address in Manhattan was listed on the flip side of the card, along with the admonition "Members Only." *Guess I'm heading to the Big Apple.*

Right after he got out of the rain.

A dome of emerald energy protected the crime scene from the elements. News-copters hovered overhead, braving the inclement weather, as John Stewart gave the site a preliminary once-over. Broken windows in the warehouse adjacent to the docks suggested that this was hardly the most salubrious stretch of the waterfront. An enormous poster, plastered on one side of the building, provided a welcome splash of color in the squalid locale. The faded poster depicted a man in a garishly colored circus costume breaking free from countless chains, locks, and handcuffs. Huge block letters identified the performer as Mister Miracle! The World's Greatest Escape Artist!

That would be the second *Mister Miracle,* John realized. *Shilo Norman, not Scott Free.* John had caught the original Mister Miracle's show at The Palace years ago, and this new guy was supposed to be even more impressive. *Didn't he escape from a black hole a while back?*

A bright green flare, burning its way through the seething clouds overhead, brought John's attention back to the matter at hand. He peered up through the dome to see his partner, Hal Jordan, descending from the sky. His uniform was similar to John's, although Hal sported a green domino mask over his face and white gloves over his hands. He was a handsome, cocky white guy, with wavy brown hair, who liked to risk his life as a test pilot when he wasn't defending the cosmos as a Green Lantern. He and John had watched each other's backs through plenty of rough scrapes over the years. John trusted Hal with his life.

"What kept you, flyboy?" John ragged him. "Blonde or redhead?"

"Deep and dreamless," Hal insisted, despite his well-deserved reputation as a ladies' man. He phased through the energy dome to join John on the wharf. "What's the story?"

"Cooling rapidly." He scanned the battle-scarred body lying amidst the ruins of a shattered crate, but his ring detected no signs of life. "You ever hear of a 1011 before? Apparently, it doesn't happen often."

"1011?" Hal's brown eyes widened behind his mask. A small scar cut diagonally across his left temple. "Deicide?"

John was impressed that Hal recognized the code number. Then again, his partner had a few years' seniority on him. "That's right. Somebody just murdered a *god* on our watch." He stepped aside to give Hal a better view of the corpse. "Recognize him?"

"Orion!" Hal looked over at John in surprise. "The warrior god of New Genesis," he said, referring to the distant homeworld of the more benevolent New Gods. He shook his head in amazement. "A-number one cosmic hard-ass."

"Yup," John confirmed. He and Hal had fought beside—and against—the New Gods on several occasions, most notably during that "Cosmic Odyssey" a few years back. John winced at the memory. That had been a bad one. A rookie mistake on his part had cost them an entire world. He *still* had nightmares about it. *I don't want to think about what could have done this to somebody like Orion.*

Unfortunately, that was their job.

A grave expression came over Hal's face. He was obviously taking this just as seriously as John was. "I'll report to the Guardians on Oa," he said, raising his ring to his lips. "You alert the Justice League."

The Guardians of Universe, the founders of the Green Lantern Corps, were a race of incredibly ancient, immortal beings who watched over the cosmos from their citadel on the planet Oa, located at the very center of the universe. John stood by as Hal's ring projected holographic images of three of the Guardians into the air above them. Possibly the oldest intelligent beings in the galaxy, the Guardians were dwarfish blue humanoids whose diminutive stature belied their incalculable power. Manes of snow-white hair added to the magisterial dignity of two of the male Guardians, while another boasted a smooth, hairless cranium. A stylized image of a Green Lantern adorned the front of their flowing scarlet robes. Their characteristically solemn faces grew even more somber upon news of Orion's death. Concern furrowed their imposing brows.

"Seal the crime scene to the planet's Lagrange point," the first Guardian instructed. "No one must enter or leave the gravity well."

"Dust for radiation prints," the third added. "Interrogate all potential suspects."

"1011 requires a vast energy expenditure," the second Guardian noted. "Locate the weapon."

John was impressed, and troubled, at how hands-on the Guardians were being regarding this incident. Usually, they trusted their Green Lanterns to use their own discretion when it came to policing their respective sectors. The Guardians preferred to concentrate on the Big Picture instead. *So how big is this?*

"This is a matter of utmost concern. Lantern Jordan 2814.1," the first Guardian stressed. "The gods of New Genesis and Apokolips have long been locked in a stalemate. The death of Orion suggests that the balance of power may have shifted toward evil. A special-operations Alpha Lantern Unit is on its way. Prepare to receive them."

"Special operations?" John echoed. The Alpha Lanterns were something new in the millennia-long history of the Corps: an elite squad of cybernetically enhanced Green Lanterns whose powers and authority outstripped ordinary Green Lanterns like him and Hal. The Guardians had instituted the Alpha Lanterns only a few months ago, in the wake of a devastating interstellar war that had almost destroyed the entire Corps. This was the first time they had ever been dispatched to Earth.

John wasn't sure how he felt about that.

The Guardians' images blinked out of existence as they terminated the transmission. He and Hal shared a worried look. If even the Guardians were going into crisis mode, just how hairy was this going to get?

A worrisome thought occurred to John. "You know," he reminded his partner, "these New Gods? They come with bad gods too."

CHAPTER 3

METROPOLIS.

The Bakerline Municipal Landfill was located in the outer boroughs of the city. Despite the fancy name, the place was still just a garbage dump. Heaps of refuse rose like sand dunes amidst its acres. Discarded mirrors jutted from the trash, reflecting the rising sun. Yesterday's storm had finally blown over, but the accumulated debris was still soggy beneath the feet of the four teenage heroes rushing through the dump. The humid morning air stank of mildew and decay.

"Keep up, Sparx!" Empress called out to her teammate. The armored heroine raced up the side of a massive trash pile, her boots slipping and sliding on the damp cardboard and spongy mattresses beneath her feet. She wore a red satin tunic and loincloth over a tight-fitting suit of golden chain mail. A topknot of bright purple hair crested a polished helmet that covered her entire face. A gilded baton was gripped in her right gauntlet. Her eager voice held a Jamaican accent. "It's just over this rise!"

"I'm coming! I'm coming!" Sparx replied. White-hot electricity sparked and crackled around her head and shoulders, and her luminous white skin shone as bright as an incandescent bulb. A dark blue leotard, long gloves, and thigh-high boots clung to her shapely figure. The zigzag hems of her garments warned the world that she was literally a living lightning bolt.

She caught up with Empress at the crest of the heap, where her flashing eyes immediately zoomed in on a futuristic throne half buried in the surrounding refuse. Even tilted at an angle and coated with grime, the chair stood out amidst the discarded dressers and medicine cabinets piled around it. Sparx caught a glimpse of her radiant profile in the cracked mirror of an overturned dressing table. She looked just as excited as she felt.

"There!" Empress said triumphantly. She lifted the visor of her helmet to reveal a jubilant dark-skinned face. "You believe me now? My visions told me we'd find it here."

Sparx had never doubted her. Empress came from a long line of voodoo priestesses whose spiritual gifts were nothing to sneeze at. Sparx had learned to take her friend's psychic visions very seriously. According to Empress, the throne was known as a Mobius chair and it had once belonged to one of the New Gods. "But if it's literally from another world, a higher reality . . ." Her mind boggled at the implications. "I mean, this is a totally major launch for the League of Titans!"

Forming their own brand-new super-hero team had been a bold move, but this discovery proved they had made the right call after all. *They* had found this bizarre, possibly dangerous, alien artifact, not the Doom Patrol or the Challengers of the Unknown or any of the more established groups. Just wait until their parents found out. She couldn't wait to tell her friends and family back in Ontario. *We've hit the big time at last!*

Sparx glanced back over her shoulder at the remainder of their team, who were dragging behind. "C'mon, Mas y Menos!" The twin Guatemalan heroes, whose names roughly translated to "Plus and Minus," wore white bodysuits with red accents, along with matching crash helmets and goggles. One brother wore a plus sign on his chest; the other sported a minus sign. Despite the super-speed they shared whenever they were in contact with each other, they hesitated at the bottom of the slope, as though reluctant to clamber up the smelly pile of rubbish. Sparx cheered them on. "Go, League of Titans!"

"Si podemos!" they shouted back in unison.

Then, without warning, it all went wrong. . . .

A sinister figure, whom she immediately recognized as the diabolical

Doctor Light, rose from behind the Mobius chair. His tight black costume bore a spiky white sunburst on the chest, and a long white cape flapped behind him. Polished lenses studded his belt, and a finned helmet crowned his head. A black goatee gave his vulpine features an even more satanic cast. The nefarious scientist, who specialized in the criminal application of optics, was a particularly nasty adversary of the Teen Titans and the Justice League. Rumor had it he had once assaulted the Elongated Man's wife.

"Watch out!" Sparx shouted, but it was already too late. Before she could fire an electrical blast at the villain, a pair of brilliant yellow laser beams shot from his upraised palms. The rays bounced off the mirrors scattered around the chair, which Sparx suddenly realized had been placed there all too strategically. *It was a trap—and we walked right into it!*

A searing blast of heat struck her at the speed of light. A scream erupted from her lips and she collapsed onto the soggy garbage. A second scream, ringing out almost simultaneously, informed her that Empress had been hit as well. She heard her friend hit the ground only a few yards away, even as she writhed atop the trash in utter agony. Her entire nervous system felt like it was on fire. The sparks cascading along her hair flickered weakly. Barely clinging to consciousness, she struggled to keep her eyes open.

"Ha!" Doctor Light cackled mercilessly as he stepped out from behind the Mobius chair. He stroked his goatee in smug self-satisfaction. "The first unsuspecting victims of the blindingly obvious team of Doctor Light and Mirror Master!"

Mirror Master? The injured heroine was puzzled by the evil scientist's remark, until mirror images of another villain emerged from a pair of propped-up Venetian mirrors, like Alice stepping through the Looking-Glass. The newcomer's padded green cowl clashed with his ugly orange jumpsuit. A wide green belt held a variety of pouches and holsters. Despite the pain scrambling her thoughts, Sparx recalled that Mirror Master was a charter member of the Flash's infamous Rogues Gallery.

"Aye, that was pure dead brilliant," he crowed. His thick Scottish accent practically required subtitles. "The eejits dinnae see us comin'."

To her dismay, she saw that Mas y Menos had fallen victim to the villains' ambush as well. Each version of Mirror Master tossed one of the twins onto the ground. Hundreds of small jagged shards of glass were embedded in the boys' skin, as though they had run headfirst into a hail of flying mirror fragments—which they probably had. Their white costumes had been torn to shreds, and dark red blood streamed from countless nicks and cuts. Sparx prayed that meant Mas y Menos were still alive. . . .

I could cauterize those wounds, she thought desperately, *if that blast hadn't short-circuited me . . . !*

But she could barely move, let alone come to her teammates' rescue. Her skin crawled as she heard Doctor Light walk over toward her and Empress. His beady blue eyes gleamed salaciously as he leered at the helpless teenage heroines. "Gad!" he exclaimed. "They're *asking* for it in these outfits!"

Pervert, Sparx thought angrily. Playing possum, she resisted the urge to spit at his feet. *Keep your hands off me, you creep!*

"Aye, awright," both Mirror Masters said impatiently. They stepped through one mirror and came out another as a single being. He smirked at Doctor Light. "We're not a bad team, but let's keep our heads in the game." Ignoring the defeated heroes, he inspected the Mobius chair. "What's this piece a' junk for anyway?"

"Something Libra wants," Doctor Light said with a shrug.

Libra? Sparx thought. *Who the heck is Libra?*

Through blurry eyes, she watched the villainous duo finish arranging a ring of mirrors facing the chair. The mirrors focused multiple beams of light onto the throne, causing it to levitate up out of the trash. Doctor Light adjusted the controls on his belt and the beams grew bright enough to make Sparx's eyes water. To her amazement, she saw the chair begin to shimmer like a mirage, then slowly fade away.

"Look here, McCulloch," Doctor Light addressed his cohort. "I was having a word with the Reverse-Flash earlier, and he implied that you were the sort of man who might be able to lay your hands on certain . . . you know . . . pharmaceutical requisites. . . ."

Mirror Master nodded knowingly. "Aye, aye, whit yeh wantin'?" He flashed a gap-toothed grin at the other villain. "I've got a wee bittie Peruvian Flake that'll straighten oot the fin on yer heid nay bother."

"No, no!" Light protested. "Do I look like some pathetic *junkie*?" His shifty eyes darted about nervously. He looked sweaty and uncomfortable. "If you must know, I have a date with Giganta and . . . well, Arthur Light never likes to let a lady down. Especially one of such intimidating proportions."

"Giganta?" Mirror Master chortled loudly. One of Wonder Woman's oldest foes, the colossal femme fatale could grow to over fifty feet tall. "The monster wummin?"

"Enough," Light said irritably, "or I'm never teaming up with you again." He sounded as though he regretted bringing the subject up in the first place. "How about we just finish teleporting the chair to Libra and keep our personal lives personal?"

Lying on the ground nearby, Sparx found the entire conversation skeevy in the extreme, but at least it kept the two villains from noticing that she wasn't out cold like the rest of her team. *Keep on talking,* she urged them silently, as she tried to muster the strength for one good lightning-blast. Her head was throbbing, and her limbs still felt as limp as overcooked spaghetti, but she gritted her teeth and tried to focus past the pain. Faint blue sparks sputtered around her fingertips.

Just give me a few more minutes. . . .

The villains stepped back to observe the Mobius chair's gradual disappearance. By now all that was left of the alien throne was a faint afterimage floating in the fetid air. Sparx had no idea who this "Libra" was, or what he needed the chair for, but she knew she had to stop this if she could. Biting down on her lips to keep from gasping, she painfully hoisted herself up onto her hands and knees. She crawled stealthily toward Doctor Light, until she was only a few feet away from him. Lightning arced between her outstretched fingers as she got ready to give him a jolt he'd never forget. If she was lucky, she might even have a little juice left over for Mirror Master.

You're going to pay for hurting my friends, she vowed, *even if takes every last volt!*

"We're working for Libra now," Doctor Light declared, "and what Libra wants, Libra gets."

Sparx took a deep breath. Her fingers flared brightly.

He spun around and stamped down hard upon her head. The insulated sole of a white rubber boot ground her face into the trash. The coppery taste of blood filled her mouth only seconds before a total blackout knocked out all her power. The last thing she heard was his nasal voice gloating over her defeat.

"Remember?"

KEYSTONE CITY.

"Call me Libra," the stranger said. "I balance the scales. I even the odds."

He stood at the end of a long rectangular conference table in the back room of an abandoned strip club in the bad part of town. A hooded gold cloak was draped over his head and shoulders, and a dark blue mask covered everything on his face except his intense blue eyes. Copper studs, resembling the standardized weights used to balance scales, adorned his indigo costume, thick gold gloves, and knee-high gold boots. His left fist gripped a long metal staff crowned by a symbolic set of hanging scales, and a sharp, four-bladed spear-point waited at the opposite end of the staff. The seventh sign of the zodiac was inscribed upon his chest.

"Let's face it," he addressed a skeptical audience. "The Secret Society of Super-Villains is a toothless shadow of its former glory. Despite your individual talents, you folks have been through hell. Time and again you've been defeated, demoralized, and humiliated . . . but I'm here to help you change all that. Because make no mistake, there is a God!" His voice rang out in exultation as he preached to his illustrious guests like an evangelist of evil. "A New God in whose Unholy Name the bad men can offer up their prayers—and He *will* answer! And here is His Book!"

He slapped his palm down atop a massive leather-bound tome resting on the table before him. Legend had it the so-called Crime Bible was written in blood upon human skin. Also known as the Black Book, the tome had been adopted as a sacred text by outlaws and cultists throughout the world. Libra stretched out his arms in benediction.

"Here is the Great News! And all who follow me in His Name will be granted their heart's desire!" His fervent gaze swept the room, falling briefly on each of the scowling faces looking back at him with varying degrees of suspicion and resentment. "You want a 'hero' killed? We can do it! You want better powers? Sign on the dotted line and they're yours! Believe in Him, that's all He asks. And that, my friends, is only the beginning of my bid for leadership of this august organization." He raised his staff like a perverse Moses about to part the Red Sea. His ardent voice reached a fever pitch. "Do I hear a *Hallelujah*?"

Despite his exhortation, neither applause nor cheers greeted the end of his sermon. Instead, the others muttered darkly among themselves until Lex Luthor rose to his feet at the opposite end of the table. Superman's arch-enemy wore his trademark green and purple war suit. A glossy enamel overlay enhanced the high-tech body armor, which incorporated exclusive LuthorCorp designs along with black market alien technology. Luthor's bald dome shone beneath the flickering fluorescent lights in the ceiling. He made no attempt to conceal his overweening arrogance and contempt.

"I've heard your stump speech before," he informed Libra, "and I'm still not impressed. You may have dazzled the rank and file with your overblown oratory, but the rest of us?" He gestured at the other luminaries in the room. "Do we look like the sort of people who'd be inclined to follow orders?"

Seated around the table was, with one notable exception, the elite of the super-criminal community. A veritable legion of doom that included:

Vandal Savage, immortal enemy of the Justice Society of America.

Ocean Master, Aquaman's estranged half brother and perennial rival for the throne of the undersea kingdom of Atlantis.

Talia Head, daughter of Rā's al Ghūl and heir to her father's League of Assassins.

Dr. Thaddeus Bodog Sivana, infamous mad scientist and sworn nemesis of Captain Marvel.

Gorilla Grodd, a super-intelligent simian from Gorilla City in Africa.

The Human Flame, a small-time inventor and bank robber whose main claim to fame was being handily defeated by the Martian Manhunter several years ago.

Frankly, Luthor had no idea why Libra had bothered to invite the latter to this top secret summit meeting. The Human Flame, aka Michael Miller, was just an ex-con with a gimmick, not an A-list super-villain like the rest of the assembly. The fact that Libra had included such a worthless specimen in the proceedings was reason enough to doubt the hooded stranger's judgment, at least as far as Luthor was concerned. *I wouldn't even hire Miller as a flunky*, he thought. *My old henchman Otis was a genius by comparison.*

"Luthor's right," Vandal Savage agreed. His sloping brow and prognathous jaw hinted at his Neanderthal roots, while a tailored black Nehru jacket demonstrated just how far he had come from his caveman days. "You invite us to some deserted fleshpot in the heart of Flash territory, then expect us to hand over the reins of the Secret Society? We are organized supercrime specialists. . . ."

"I don't want to take your place at all," Libra interrupted him. He settled back into what appeared to be the fabled Mobius chair of the New Gods, or at least a convincing facsimile thereof. He rested the upper half of his staff against his shoulder. "But, please, people have been waiting fifty thousand years for Vandar Adg to crush civilization beneath his boot heel. Excuse me if I stifle a yawn. . . ."

Savage rose angrily from his seat. "I am not averse to the taste of human flesh, sir!"

"Spoken like a true gentleman," Libra replied sarcastically. He lounged upon his chair, not at all intimidated by Savage's feral outburst. "Who says I'm human, anyway?" He faced down the other villain's challenge with glib assurance. "It strikes me that your enemies fight and win again and again because they truly believe their actions are in accordance with a higher moral order. But what happens in a world where Good has *lost* its perpetual struggle against Evil?"

He paused to let that provocative notion sink in. "In return for your participation in my grand experiment, I can absolutely guarantee each and every one of you your heart's desire." He flipped through the pages of the Crime Bible, as though seeking inspiration in its sanguinary verses. "How's that sound?"

Luthor was unswayed by Libra's empty promises. "My 'heart's desire'? I don't imagine that is within *your* power to deliver."

"What do you want me to say, Lex?" Libra reached over and patted the arm of the Human Flame, who was seated on his left. "Mike here believes in me. He wants the Manhunter from Mars dead just as much as you dream of dancing on Superman's grave."

Luthor was offended by the very comparison. Miller's homemade "crime suit," complete with built-in flamethrower, looked like a kid's science project compared to his own state-of-the-art war suit. Metal nozzles protruded from the cast-iron red vest protecting the Human Flame's portly torso. His padded helmet, safety goggles, and work gloves appeared to have been acquired from his neighborhood hardware store. He wore a baggy white sweater under his metal vest, and his ill-fitting red trousers needed pressing. A fuzzy brown mustache carpeted his upper lip. Double chins bobbed as Miller nodded enthusiastically whenever Libra spoke. To Luthor's infinite annoyance, the porcine oaf was busy snapping pictures of the meeting with his cell phone. For his scrapbook, no doubt.

"You imagine this half-wit, this *nonentity*'s hate matches mine?" Luthor leaned forward, resting his steel-shod knuckles on the tabletop. "You presume I have no creed?" He glowered venomously at Libra. "My creed is *Luthor.*"

"Hey! Hey! Mr. Luthor!" Mike protested. "You don't understand. Libra's serious. He's the real deal!"

Luthor decided he had heard enough. Miller's insipid blathering wasn't even worth replying to. Turning away from the table, he headed toward the exit. With any luck, the rest of the quorum would soon follow his example. He doubted that the likes of Sivana, Talia, and the others would fall under Libra's spell the way the Human Flame had. All of them had better things to do than waste their time on this impertinent pretender.

"Don't leave, Lex," Libra called out from his chair. His mocking tone was just as insolent as before. "Can't we murderers, madmen, and masterminds work in harmony just this once, to achieve something none of us ever has before?"

Luthor paused and looked back at the table. As much as he hated to admit it, he was more than a little curious as to Libra's true identity and motives. Despite his best efforts, he had been able to uncover frustratingly little information regarding the hooded interloper. Unconfirmed reports suggested that Libra, or someone employing the same alias, had once tangled with the Justice League many years ago, but beyond that, the stranger's file was far too skimpy for Luthor's liking. He didn't enjoy being in the dark. "What's in it for you?"

"An end to the age of super heroes." Rising from his throne, Libra brandished his spear-tipped staff in one hand while cradling the Crime Bible in his other arm. The point of the spear abruptly burst into flame. "A full-on, no-kidding Twilight of the Gods. That ambitious enough for you?"

He beckoned with his staff and, right on cue, two more villains entered the chamber via a side door, dragging a battered-looking prisoner between them. Luthor immediately recognized the newcomers as Doctor Light and Effigy. The latter was an unstable juvenile delinquent who had been endowed with pyrokinetic abilities by some meddlesome aliens. Bright yellow flames blazed atop his head, making him look like a human candle, and a dark red jumpsuit encased his slender physique. Rippling heat waves emanated from his body, causing Arthur Light's narrow face to drip with perspiration beneath his finned helmet. Luthor felt the temperature in the room rise dramatically as startled gasps came from the criminal legends seated around the table. Ocean Master gulped down a glass of water.

Luthor hadn't expected to see either Light or Effigy here, but what really startled him was the identity of their captive. J'onn J'onzz, the Martian Manhunter, slumped between the two villains, his scuffed blue boots dragging on the floor behind him as his captors physically hauled the alien champion toward Libra. Beetle brows and sunken red eyes betrayed J'onzz's extraterrestrial roots, along with his olive green skin. A voluminous blue cape hung in tatters from his broad shoulders. Intersecting straps formed a large red X across the chest of his scorched indigo uniform. Dark green bruises mottled his inhuman countenance, and chartreuse blood dripped from his smashed nose and lips.

"Heh," Light cackled. "He's still groggy from the pyro-tranquilizers."

Luthor recalled that fire affected the Martian the same way kryptonite affected Superman. The hero's vulnerable state elicited no sympathy from him. Luthor's never-ending battle against the Man of Steel was enough to turn him off alien do-gooders forever. He savored the Manhunter's obvious discomfort in Effigy's presence. Whimpering in pain, J'onzz shrank from the burning villain's touch.

"Keep him that way," Libra instructed. Placing the Crime Bible safely back onto the table, he hefted his staff with both hands. The flaming spear tip was poised to strike. The entire shaft glowed like molten lava. "I'd hate to take this one on in a fair fight."

Luthor had to agree. At his best, his superhuman strength and invulnerability undiminished by mere combustion, the Martian Manhunter's powers rivaled Superman's and then some. At the moment, however, he looked as weak and defenseless as a lamb being led to the slaughter. His captors shoved the alien down onto his knees in front of Libra.

"Holy crap!" Mike exclaimed. His piggish eyes bulged behind his safety goggles. "Can everybody see this?" He held up his camera phone, frantically trying to capture the dramatic moment. He puffed out his chest. "This, friends and neighbors, is what happens to anybody who messes with the Human Flame!"

"Amen," Libra said.

Without further ado, he drove his burning spear deep into the Martian Manhunter's back. The impaled hero screamed in agony as the fiery point of the spear emerged from his chest. Convulsing, he groped frantically for the shaft protruding from his back, but it was already too hot to touch. Spreading flames ignited his alien flesh and costume. Engulfed in flame, the dying hero cried out the name of his long-lost Martian bride:

"M'yri'ah!"

His burning corpse collapsed onto the floor. The smell of roasted Martian filled the room, and both Grodd and Vandal Savage licked their lips. Talia placed a silk handkerchief over her nose and looked away.

All right, Luthor conceded. *That impressed me a* little.

CHAPTER 4

NEW YORK CITY.

On the television set, the ruins of the blasted city had a sickly radioactive glow. The peaks of shattered skyscrapers jutted at odd angles from heaps of rubble and melted metal slag. Armored sentinels, riding large mutant hounds, patrolled the barren wasteland. Barbed-wire fences and watch-towers guarded the perimeter of the ruins, which had once been a thriving urban metropolis before a toxic explosion destroyed it exactly two years ago. A caption running along the bottom of the screen identified the transmission as "LIVE FROM BLÜDHAVEN."

"A dead city! A suppuratin' wound on the flank of an idle nation!" Reverend G. Godfrey Good railed from the TV. The militant black preacher, who had only recently risen to prominence, stood behind a podium that had been set up right outside the borders of the restricted disaster zone. A foot-high tower of hair, as white as the clerical collar beneath his chin, rose above his cherubic face. The impressive hairdo made Don King's tonsorial trademark look like a crew cut. His fervid brown eyes shone brightly behind a pair of wire-frame glasses as he wagged a disapproving finger at the world's alleged indifference to the appalling postapocalyptic landscape behind him. "My heart goes out to the suffering citizens of benighted Blüdhaven. Another year gone, and not one day closer to salvation. Make no mistake, the message rings clear! If you're poor, if you're homeless, you can rassle the mutations out of your *own* backyard!"

"Aw, shut your trap," the bartender muttered. Using his remote, he muted the sound on the large flat-screen television set mounted beneath the ceiling of the smoky downtown tavern. He went back to pouring some cheap rotgut into Turpin's glass. "You ask me, that stinkin' city had it coming."

"Maybe," Turpin admitted. Even before it got nuked by the Secret Society during the last Crisis, Blüdhaven had been a cesspool of crime and corruption. But that was ancient history now; he had other things on his mind these days.

Like six missing kids.

He glanced around the squalid dive, which catered to the sort of low-life scum he used to bust on a daily basis. A jukebox blared in the background, competing with harsh laughter and angry curses. Hardened ex-cons played pool or lobbed missiles at the dartboard, while a world-weary waitress dodged grabby hands. A ceiling fan churned the stuffy air, which reeked of tobacco and other controlled substances. Turpin perched on a stool in front of a long wooden bar, keeping an eye on the scene via the cracked mirror behind the bartender. Obscene graffiti was carved into the surface of the bar, next to multiple cigarette burns. A pair of yuppie tourists, who had obviously taken a wrong turn, stuck their heads into the tavern, then hurriedly retreated. *Smart move,* Turpin thought.

Ordinarily, he wouldn't be caught dead in a sleazy blood-bucket like this, but sometimes you had to go trolling among the bottom-feeders if you wanted to get the straight dope on what was going on in the underworld. He fished the Question's postcard out of his pocket, looking it over one more time while he waited for the local stoolie to make contact. He nursed his drink slowly, much to the annoyance of the surly barkeep. Turpin was tempted to ask for a glass of milk just to piss the guy off.

"You Turpin?"

He spun around on his stool to find the Tattooed Man standing behind him. As his alias implied, elaborate designs had been inked on nearly every inch of Mark Richards's face and arms—and probably the rest of him as well.

The muscular ex-Marine wore a white tank top and baggy, low-rise jeans, the better to show off the brightly colored snakes, spiders, bats, cobwebs, barbed wire, knives, bullets, bombs, pit bulls, and throwing stars embellishing his dark brown skin. Military dog tags dangled on a chain around his neck, and an unlit cigarette was tucked behind one ear. His shaved skull made room for more tattoos.

"'Bout time you got here," Turpin grumbled. Word was, Richards worked as a hit man these days, but he'd been keeping a low profile since escaping from a prison planet a few weeks back. As it happened, he owed money to somebody who owed Turpin a favor, and it was time to collect.

Richards glanced around uncomfortably, as though he didn't like being seen with Turpin. "Not here," he said in a low voice. "Outside."

Works for me, Turpin thought. He followed the crook out the exit and lit himself a fresh cigarette. It was well past midnight and a gibbous moon shone over the Bowery. The grimy streets and sidewalks were nearly deserted, smart New Yorkers knowing better than to visit this part of town after dark. Old newspapers, candy wrappers, broken glass, cigarette butts, and discarded syringes littered the pavement. Graffiti defaced the metal shutters protecting the neighborhood businesses, which mostly consisted of liquor stores, bars, and porn shops. The few cars that zipped past on Jones Street did so quickly with their doors and windows tightly shut. Low-rent hookers congregated on the corner, shouting lewd come-ons to the passing vehicles. Winos and junkies huddled on the stoops, lost in their own private deliriums. Raucous laughter brayed from a nearby alley, and the sidewalk rattled beneath Turpin's feet as the Z train rumbled past underground.

"All right," Richards said, once they were out of earshot of the bar. He looked up and down the street to make sure no one was watching them. A tattooed scorpion crawled up his arm. "Let's get this over with, bud."

Turpin didn't like his tone. "I ain't your 'bud.' Call me that again and you'll be chowing down on your last, best hope of fathering an heir to the Tattooed Man fortune."

"Whatever." Richards didn't argue the point as he guided Turpin through the Bowery to their destination. They jaywalked across narrow streets and alleys, dodging the occasional speeding taxi. Richards took pains to avoid the glare of the streetlamps. "So, you know much about what goes on at the Dark Side Club?"

In theory, the Tattooed Man had pulled strings to get Turpin a face-to-face with the big shot running the mysterious nightspot, a local kingpin known only as "Boss Dark Side." The detective hoped Richards could deliver; otherwise, he had come a long way for nothing. He kept his guard up, just in case the no-good skel was planning a double cross. "Lemme guess. Something sad and stupid with whips and leather?"

"Heh," Richards chuckled. A Chinese dragon detached itself from his shoulder and flapped briefly around his head before settling back onto his skin. "You'll see."

They arrived at the address in question, which belonged to a converted brownstone at the corner of Morrison and A streets. No sign gave away the name of the club. The only identifying mark was a symbol inscribed over a pair of heavy double doors; it took Turpin a second to place the icon as the Greek letter omega. Heavy iron bars guarded the windows, and closed metal shutters hid whatever was going on inside. Unsavory characters loitered on the sidewalk in front of the building, eyeing Turpin suspiciously.

A pair of thuggish bouncers flanked the entrance to the club. One of them was a stony-faced bruiser with greasy brown dreadlocks and muscles that positively screamed steroid abuse. Despite the muggy temperature, he was decked out in black leather biker gear. A diamond-encrusted medallion in the shape of the letter K added a vulgar touch of bling to his outfit. His companion was a slightly leaner blond guy wearing a tight white T-shirt and khaki trousers. He had a sly, furtive expression. Both men brandished heavy wooden baseball bats. Neither of them looked like sports fans.

Richards conversed briefly with the men, then stepped aside to let Turpin approach the entrance. The tattooed felon turned to leave. "You're on your own now," he informed Turpin. "I'm done here."

Turpin figured as much. "Yeah," he said gruffly. "Go get another pretty picture scribbled onto your sorry hide. A butterfly maybe. Or a unicorn."

Richards shot him a dirty look before disappearing back into the grungy back alleys of the Bowery. Turpin wasn't sorry to see him go. He'd got what he'd wanted from the reputed hit man: access to the exclusive milieu of the Dark Side Club. The rest was up to him.

"You heard the man," he told the bouncers. "Take me to your leader."

Wordlessly, the goons opened the door and escorted him inside. Dim lighting obscured his view of the club's interior. Matte black paint coated the walls, soaking up what little illumination leaked from the curtained doorways opening up off the foyer. Throaty gasps and ecstatic whimpers of pain escaped from behind the black velvet drapes, along with the tinkling of champagne glasses and the occasional crack of a lash. Weird atonal music, of the sort that grated on Turpin's nerves, played over the Muzak system. A coat-check girl, wearing a ribbed corset and a black latex bondage mask, offered to take Turpin's coat. Her bare arms and cleavage had a peculiar plastic sheen. Brusquely declining her services, he wondered whom Dark Side had paid off to keep this joint from being raided. *I'll bet Vice would have a field day here.*

His sullen escorts led him up a spiral staircase to a private lounge on the top floor, where he found their boss seated on a leather couch behind a low, felt-covered coffee table. A middle-aged black man in a tailored gray suit, Boss Dark Side was silhouetted against the elaborate Art Deco mural covering the wall behind him. A polished mahogany cane was stretched across his lap, and tinted glasses concealed the man's eyes. The single Angle-poise lamp on the table barely dispelled the heavy shadows cloaking the far corners of the room. Off to one side, something rustled behind heavy velvet curtains.

"Ahhh, there you are," Dark Side greeted him without getting up. He had a deep bass voice that sounded a bit on the raspy side, perhaps from spending too much time in his own smoky club. He coughed hoarsely. "Tell me, Mr. Turpin, have we met?"

Not that the detective knew of, although something about the seated club owner seemed oddly familiar. Turpin decided to take charge of this interview right away. "Call the goons off," he barked, sneering at the muscle-bound losers violating his personal space. He removed the cigarette butt from his lips. "I'm an old man. These guys would hate to have their asses handed to 'em by an old man."

The big guy with the dreadlocks bristled and looked like he wanted to call Turpin out right then and there, but his boss held up his palm to restrain him. Dark Side chuckled, as though amused by the detective's attitude. "Kalibak. Kanto," he addressed the goons. "Outside."

The bouncers reluctantly exited the lounge, leaving Turpin alone with the club owner. He squinted at the other man. "'Boss Dark Side,' huh?" He didn't believe for a moment that was the man's real name. As aliases went, the portentous moniker struck Turpin as more than a little ridiculous, like this slick hoodlum thought he was Darth Vader or something. He looked Dark Side over dubiously, unimpressed by what he saw. Now that his eyes were adjusting to the gloomy lighting, he could tell that the other man was in pretty bad shape. Beads of perspiration glistened on Dark Side's hairless cranium, and deep fissures creased his sweaty face. His complexion had an unhealthy grayish cast. Even sitting down, his breath was ragged. "Guess I expected someone younger," Turpin said.

Dark Side rose unsteadily to his feet, leaning upon his cane. "Bodies . . . they wear out quickly here. Mortal flesh oxidizing in the combustion of time." He dabbed at his brow with a silk handkerchief. A silver tiepin matched the omega symbol above the club's entrance. "And me, I was hurt in a fall, you might say. But it's what we endure that makes us strong, don't you think?"

"My father used to say the same thing," Turpin muttered. "So you wanna tell me how come the trail of my missing kids leads right to you?"

Dark Side made no effort to divert the gumshoe's suspicions. "How could it not?" He limped out from behind the table until he and Turpin were only inches apart. His dark suit blended with the shadows, which almost seemed to be creeping in on them. "As for the children . . . I gave them to Granny."

Granny who? Turpin wondered. His fists clenched at his sides.

"Humanity's best hope for the future," Dark Side mused aloud. "Its young. Its life force."

He removed his glasses to reveal a pair of soulless red eyes that glowed like Perdition itself. In his day, Turpin had dealt with every kind of sociopath and deviant, from child molesters to serial killers, but Dark Side's infernal gaze was enough to make even the jaded ex-cop shudder. There was no trace of mercy or compassion or even humanity in those crimson orbs. Pure evil radiated from his eyes. Hatred without emotion, utterly cold and destructive.

"There was a War in Heaven," Dark Side declared. "And I won. Your future belongs to *me* now."

Turpin found it impossible to look into the monster's unbearable red eyes. A chill ran down his spine, followed by uncontrollable rage at the heartless abomination before him. "What did you do to those kids, you sick bastard!"

He grabbed onto Dark Side's shoulder and drew back his fist.

"Remove your hand."

Dark Side seized Turpin's wrist, squeezing it so hard the bones scraped against each other. The detective grunted in pain as, with shocking strength, the crippled crime boss removed Turpin's hand from his shoulder, while calmly answering the other man's query.

"We taught them to say the Equation," Dark Side explained, refusing to release his grip. "How to be stunted, malformed slaves." He dragged Turpin across the room toward the velvet curtains. "Come closer, Turpin. I can use you."

He forced the detective to the ground before finally letting go of his wrist. Grimacing in agony, Turpin found himself prostrate on the carpet. He clutched his injured wrist, which was already turning black and blue. He didn't *think* it was broken, but it probably needed an X-ray, assuming he got out of here alive.

"There," Dark Side said. "It's best that you see the New Model Human from your knees."

He drew back the drapes to reveal what Turpin had heard rustling behind the curtains only minutes before. The missing children, plus several more whose disappearances must have gone unreported, shambled out into the murky light. Turpin barely recognized the kids, whose childish faces had been hideously transformed. Horrible dead eyes, whose incarnadine glow matched Dark Side's own luciferous orbs, gazed out from pallid, pasty faces that lacked even the slightest hint of innocence or individuality. Dark bags sagged beneath their sunken eyes, and pointed teeth peeked out from between their lips. Drool dripped down their chins as they shuffled toward Turpin like zombies.

He recoiled from the awful sight. The stolen children, none of whom looked more than ten years old, weren't even human anymore. "No. . . ."

"They are beyond salvation," Dark Side intoned, as though to crush any hopes Turpin might nurse of somehow reversing the kids' ghastly condition. He beckoned them onward. "Come, children. Show him what you have learned about Anti-Life."

CHAPTER 5

WASHINGTON, D.C.

Inside the Hall of Justice, situated on the capitol's grassy Mall not far from the Lincoln Memorial, the world's greatest heroes held an emergency meeting. Superman, Batman, Wonder Woman, Green Arrow, Black Canary, Red Tornado, Firestorm, Vixen, Hawkgirl, and John Stewart sat around a stainless steel table emblazoned with the world-famous seal of the Justice League of America. A large bronze bas-relief of Justice herself dominated one wall, while high glass windows looked out over the sparkling blue reflecting pool outside. Both John Stewart and Wonder Woman had contributed to the design of the JLA's headquarters, whose graceful architecture incorporated both earthly and extraterrestrial materials.

Superman rose from his seat to address his teammates. The bright red S on his chest was one of the most famous—and trusted—symbols in the galaxy. "As most of you know, the New Gods are a race of warring alien deities from the far end of the universe. The good gods, such as Orion, dwell on the distant world of New Genesis, while their evil counterparts rule over the desolate planet Apokolips." Rumor had it that the New Gods had recently departed this plane for good, but apparently that wasn't the case. "The fact that even the Guardians of the Universe are taking this matter very seriously ought to give you some indication of the power levels we're dealing with here."

"Evil gods, evil people," Batman said grimly. He had a zero-tolerance policy for bad guys, regardless of their planet of origin. His forbidding black cowl and cape stood in sharp contrast to Superman's own brightly colored uniform. A black bat adorned his chest, and opaque white lenses in his cowl concealed his eyes. "Different universe, same dumb." He slid a folder across the table. "I've prepared a detailed dossier for those of you who haven't encountered these beings before."

"Unfortunately," Superman added, "Orion's death suggests things have escalated to a whole new level. The prophecies of the New Gods always foretold that Orion would die in the final battle between New Genesis and Apokolips. The discovery of his body raises the possibility that such a battle has begun—or has already been lost."

Wonder Woman spoke up. A ruby-inlaid tiara nestled atop her lustrous black hair, and a golden breastplate and girdle reflected her Amazon heritage, as did her exotic Greek accent. "If the evil gods have been reborn on Earth, it's imperative that we find them before they strike."

"Agreed," Superman said. "These are celestials capable of cracking the planet in half and enslaving billions." He took a deep breath before making the emergency official. "Justice League Condition Amber."

EARTH.
SECTOR 2814.

Three hundred miles above the spinning blue planet, four Alpha Lanterns placed Earth under quarantine. Cosmic surgery, performed by the Guardians themselves, had amplified their abilities far beyond those of mere ordinary Green Lanterns. Each Alpha Lantern wielded *two* power rings, and their individual lanterns had been surgically implanted in their chests, replacing their hearts, so that they no longer needed to recharge their rings periodically. Cybernetic modifications made them the best of both worlds, combining the drive and willpower of organic beings with the ruthless logic and efficiency of machines. Featureless green masks concealed the robotic countenances that had supplanted their previous faces. Emerald force fields encased their bodies, shielding them from the vacuum of space, as their rings wove an intricate lattice of glowing green energy around Earth's atmosphere, sealing the planet off. The thin green skin would allow nothing more than sunlight, gravity, and the usual electromagnetic emissions to pass through the barrier.

"Alpha Lantern Kraken," the leader of the squadron reported back to the Guardians on Oa. The female Lantern had survived one of the Corps's toughest assignments, rescuing a fellow officer from dread Apokolips, before being promoted to the Alpha Lanterns. A hinged jaw gave her faceplate a vaguely insectile aspect. A two-piece suit of emerald armor exposed her bare blue midriff, and a severe indigo haircut framed her intimidating visage. Tiger stripes marked her azure mask like war paint. Her glowing yellow lenses, without pupils or irises, contemplated the spinning globe below. "Crime scene secured."

THE CITADEL OF NIL.
NEXUS OF REALITIES.

"Behold, New Earth," the Monitor declared. "The foundation stone of all existence. The prime element of the Multiversal Orrery that sustains us all . . ."

Hermuz and his fellow Monitors watched from afar as the Alpha Lanterns completed their work. From their perspective, Earth-Zero appeared as a small blue globe, no larger than a child's ball, at the base of a towering helix of alternate Earths. Over fifty such globes were enclosed within the Orrery, an immense multistory mechanism whose intricate workings maintained the delicate balance of fifty-two separate realities, each subtly different from the rest. The interconnected globes were suspended within a clear metallic liquid that helped to protect the Orrery's fragile components from corrosion and infection. Cathedral windows allowed the Monitors to observe the interior of the vast apparatus from their floating platforms and elevated catwalks. Cables and conduits ran from the base of the tower, and laser pointers spotlighted potential sources of disturbance. At the moment, only Earth-Zero was enveloped in a shimmering green radiance.

To Hermuz's relief, the Alpha Lanterns' actions did not appear to have undermined the overall integrity of the Orrery. He leaned upon the rail of his levitating observation platform as he inspected the readouts on the platform's holographic instrument panel. "New Earth is secure. The Bleed drains are intact." His gaze shifted to a disturbing gap in the helix. "The Orrery has survived repair after suffering the loss of moving part Earth-51."

"Excellent news," Rox Ogama replied. His fellow Monitor stood beside Hermuz on the platform. Both men were tall, humanoid beings in futuristic silver and purple armor, charged with overseeing the Multiverse. Flowing red capes were affixed to their gleaming metallic shoulder-plates, and electronic circuitry blinked upon their golden wristbands. Although all fifty-two of the Monitors had sprung into existence at the very dawn of this latest Creation, time flowed at different rates in their respective universes so that Ogama appeared several centuries younger than Hermuz. Silver had not yet infiltrated his thick black muttonchops, and his florid pink face was that of a middle-aged mortal in his late forties. Parallel cornrows traversed his cranium. He turned toward his friend, a dour expression upon his face. "But what of young Uotan? I hear he is to face absolute sanction for his failure." Ogama shook his head. "When did we become so severe?"

"Such are the times," Hermuz said dolefully. A neat black beard, along with a receding hairline, distinguished him from his fellow Monitor. Concern deepened the creases of his craggy features. "But that is for the High Council to decide . . . and the rest of us to bear witness to."

Dozens of Monitors gathered in the main auditorium. They packed the bleachers and galleries facing the dais, their individual appearances reflecting the distinctive nature of their respective universes. Variations in age, race, and gender distinguished the diverse immortals from each other. The hubbub of many whispered conversations echoed off the imposing marble walls of the hall as they murmured softly to each other. Among the solemn assemblage, one young female Monitor was more distraught than the rest.

Weeja Dell wrung her slender hands together as she waited anxiously for the sentencing to commence. Her beloved had already been condemned by the High Council; now all that remained was to hear what dire punishment they intended to impose. Rows of braided black hair graced her smooth pink dome, converging toward a ponytail at the back of her head. Anguish contorted her lovely features, and her striking green eyes glistened wetly.

Perhaps it is not too late, she prayed. *Perhaps the Council will show mercy.*

A hush fell over the auditorium as the lights dimmed. The brilliant orange glow of a teleportation beam lit up the dais as the prisoner suddenly appeared before the assembly. Nix Uotan stood before his peers, trapped inside a translucent yellow force field. Shackles bound his wrists and ankles, and his control gauntlets had been deactivated. A stiff black Mohawk crested his handsome brow. His youthful face, so brave and unashamed, tugged at Weeja's heart. Worried turquoise eyes sought her out in the bleachers until their anguished gazes met.

Here I am, my love. You are not alone.

Tahoteh, eldest of the Monitors, stepped up to a lectern overlooking the dais. Eons of faithfully tending to the Orrery, as well as his own native universe, had turned the older Monitor's beard to silver. His stentorian voice rang out over the auditorium. "Nix Uotan. Your failure shames us all. Not since Mandrakk, the Fallen One, was cast down into darkness has a Monitor so betrayed his trust."

The name of the dark one elicited a shudder from the assembly. Once the brightest and most brilliant of their ancient race, Mandrakk had developed an insatiable hunger for the very stuff of existence. The primordial Eater of Life, he had been banished to the blackest shadows of the Multiverse eons ago. Ancient prophecies spoke of an endless night when he would return to prey on all creation. Weeja could not believe that Tahoteh could even dream of comparing her beloved Nix to such an unspeakable evil, and yet the magistrate continued to denounce the shackled youth: "There is only one punishment for a Monitor whose negligence endangers the Orrery of Worlds."

"The destruction of Earth-51 was beyond my power to avert," Nix insisted. "Malign forces from beyond my universe conspired against me. I suspect sabotage. . . ."

Tahoteh cut off Nix's defense, denying the accused Monitor one last chance to plead his case. A mysterious plague, possibly imported from another continuum, had all but destroyed life on Earth-51, at the same time that Nix had been lured away from his duties by an apparent threat to the Multiverse. By the time he'd returned to his Earth, the damage had been done.

It's not his fault, Weeja thought. *Others took advantage of his heroic nature.*

She searched in vain for any sign of mercy upon the magistrate's face.

"The sentence is exile," he decreed. "You will be stripped of your duties and powers and Word of Attention. You shall live out your days as a mortal germ . . . and die to feed the Orrery."

The severity of the sentence elicited gasps from the audience. Such a punishment had never been imposed upon a Monitor in the entire history of the Multiverse. To live as a mortal? It was unthinkable—and unbearably cruel.

Rox Ogama, Monitor of Earth-31, rose to speak on Nix's behalf. He had been known to dissent with the Council before. "But consider his youth, Prime Monitor. . . ."

Tahoteh was unmoved. "His inexperience will not restore Earth-51 to the Orrery. We cannot risk his carelessness endangering another universe in our care." He rapped the lectern with his gavel. "The sentence stands."

"No!" Weeja leapt to her feet, unable to keep silent any longer. "It's not his fault!"

"Silence!" Tahoteh admonished her. "We are the Monitors, ancient and wise. Our wisdom is beyond question!"

A holographic display panel materialized above the lectern. Moving swiftly to carry out the sentence, Tahoteh manipulated the controls. Nix Uotan convulsed inside the force field as an intense golden light flooded his prison. No mere teleporter beam, the coruscating effulgence ate away at his very being, which began to dissolve into the ether. "I'll find a way back to you, Weeja Dell!" he shouted frantically. His fists pounded against the force field. "I promise I'll find a way baaaaack. . . ."

His voice trailed off as the last vestiges of Nix Uotan blinked out of sight.

"Justice is done," Tahoteh proclaimed from the podium. "May the Orrery endure!"

Weeja could bear no more. "I can't be part of this!" Sobbing, she stumbled out of the galley, desperate to get as far from the auditorium as possible. Unconcerned with the spectacle she was making of herself, she shoved past her fellow Monitors, many of whom looked scandalized by her outburst. *Let them gape and gossip,* she thought bitterly. *What do I care, now that my love has been banished forever?*

"Forgive me, Weeja Dell," Ogama called out as she fled the chamber. "I tried to speak in his defense."

For what little good it did, she lamented. Ogama's words had been too little, too late. *All hope is lost. Our dreams are shattered.*

She ran blindly through the melancholy corridors of the citadel until she came at last to a high balcony overlooking a sullen copper sea. Waves crashed against the everlasting foundations of the citadel, many stories below. Intricate celestial clockwork, composed of numinous beams of amethyst light, ticked by overhead as a swollen red sun slowly sank beneath the horizon, bathing the rocky coastline in ruddy twilight. The crumbling ruins of an ancient civilization poised precariously on the high basalt cliffs extending beyond the citadel. Exhausted, Weeja collapsed against the cracked marble ramparts. For a second, she considered throwing herself over the edge. Only a profound sense of duty stayed her from seeking oblivion upon the foam-splashed rocks below. If she took her life, who would look after the universe in her care?

"Weeja Dell, wait!"

An older Monitrix caught up with her on the balcony. Above her elegant features, Zillo Valla wore a high, flared headdress, which fanned out like a silken halo. An ocean breeze caused her scarlet cloak to flap behind her as she joined Weeja at the parapet. Sisterly concern shone upon her face.

"Why?" Weeja asked despairingly. The sheer injustice of it all tore at her soul. "Nix tried to *save* the Orrery, not to harm it. Others plotted against him. Why would no one listen to him?" Tears streamed from her eyes. The ache in her heart shocked her in its intensity; she had never experienced anything like it before. Her voice descended to a whisper. "And why do I care so much?"

"Listen to me, Weeja Dell," the other woman said. "We Monitors were faceless once, when the Multiverse was young and every Earth was identical. But as their histories diverged, so did our separate paths and identities. We now have names and stories. There are heroes and villains, secrets and lovers. . . ."

Her sympathetic tone made it clear that she knew full well of the special bond that had formed between Weeja and Nix, a passionate connection that they had barely begun to explore before calamity transformed their budding romance into a tragedy.

"It's true," Weeja confessed. "I never *felt* anything before." She tasted salt upon her lips. "Now I'm . . . crying?" She looked to the other woman for counsel. "What has become of us?"

Zillo Valla regarded her soberly. "Ogama fears we have become contaminated by contact with the obscure life-forms that grow within the workings of the Orrery. Through them, Time has entered our timeless realm. Beginnings and endings."

Such as the beginning of my love for Nix, Weeja thought, *and the end of the happiness we found together.* "What shall we do, then, sister? How can I endure this?"

"Consider our divine engine, our celestial fountain of interlocking universes. All existence depends on its survival." Zillo Valla placed a comforting hand upon Weeja's shoulder. "Save your love for the Orrery."

Unseen by either woman, Rox Ogama spied on the tender scene from the shadows of an arched doorway. Eavesdropping on their conservation, he was pleased to hear that neither woman seemed to suspect the part he had played in Nix Uotan's downfall. Weeja Dell, in particular, appeared to be too caught up in her own turbulent emotions to grasp the larger picture.

Just as he intended.

He lifted his gauntlet to his lips and spoke softly into the built-in communicator. "Attentions wander," he reported to his unspeakable master. "Nix Uotan, our only obstacle, is gone." All was proceeding according to plan. "We're on. . . ."

METROPOLIS.
EARTH-ZERO.

At first, he couldn't even remember who he was.

Nick Ustan sat upright in his bed, confused and disoriented. His head pounded with the mother of all hangovers. He massaged his aching scalp, feeling his scruffy black Mohawk beneath his fingers, as he groggily awoke to the reality of his cheap rented digs in Queensland Park. Astronomical posters of the sun, moon, and solar system were tacked to the plaster walls of his bedroom. Unwashed laundry was strewn about the bare wooden floor. A plywood bookcase held an extensive collection of used books, magazines, and comics. A clock radio sat on the dresser next to his bed. A television set sat silently atop a plastic milk carton. Peeling white paint coated the radiator. Tangled sheets shrouded the lower body of the lanky black teenager. Sunlight filtered through a set of cheap bamboo blinds, and a car alarm blared loudly outside.

"Aww man . . ."

For a few minutes, as he blinked the sleep from his bleary eyes, bits and pieces of a half-forgotten dream clung to his consciousness. There had been a giant machine the size of a church steeple, like a complicated clockwork mechanism, but with spinning blue globes instead of gears. And a girl . . . Hadn't there been a girl? With sad green eyes and braided black hair? If he concentrated, he could almost see her face. . . .

He tried to hang on to the dream, but the blaring car alarm, as well as the pressing demands of the waking world, drove the memory from his mind. Rubbing his eyes, he glanced at the digital display on the clock radio. His heart sank.

"9:15? I am in such deep . . ."

His voice trailed off as his gaze fell on his own hands. They looked *wrong* somehow, as though he had never seen them before. But that was ridiculous, wasn't it? He'd had the same hands for eighteen years now.

So why did he feel like nothing was as it should be?

Lowering his hands, he tried to shake off the peculiar mood he was in. He was going to be late for work if he didn't get a move on. Tossing aside the sheets, he got out of bed. The uncarpeted floor felt reassuringly solid beneath his bare feet. He reached for the remote on the bed stand and clicked on the TV set facing the end of the bed. Perhaps a dose of the morning news would snap him back to reality?

The twelve-inch screen blinked to life. An attractive blonde wearing a black leather jacket appeared before a microphone. Nick recognized her as Black Canary, the current spokesperson of the Justice League of America. Her striking blue eyes were rimmed with red, as though she had been crying. Her husky voice cracked as she read a prepared statement in front of the JLA's imposing headquarters in Washington, D.C.

". . . a valued friend and comrade . . ."

"Screw that!" Green Arrow shoved his way into the frame. His forest green cap and quiver of arrows made him look like a modern-day Robin Hood. A green domino mask failed to conceal the unchecked fury in his blazing emerald eyes. His blond mustache and Van Dyke beard quivered as he ranted into the mike. "Whoever did this to J'onn will suffer, you hear me! They will suffer!"

The camera pulled back to reveal a throng of reporters attending the press conference. Wooden police barriers held back a crowd of civilian spectators, many of whom clutched flowers or homemade signs of support. An impromptu shrine, piled high with stuffed animals, floral tributes, and boxes of Oreos, had been erected in front of the building's rectangular reflecting pool. An insert in the upper left-hand corner of the screen displayed the brooding features of a green-skinned alien champion as an anchorman's voice solemnly brought new viewers up to speed:

"Live from JLA Headquarters in D.C.: the super-hero community reacts to the horrific murder of J'onn J'onzz, the Manhunter from Mars."

Nick couldn't believe his ears. The Martian Manhunter was *dead*? The shocking news dispelled all thought of his own lingering unease. This was majorly serious. J'onn Jonzz was right up there with Superman and Wonder Woman when it came to defending the planet from the most catastrophic of threats. And now somebody had wasted him? Nick's blood ran cold. First, Orion, now this? What the hell was this world coming to?

CHAPTER 6

NORTH AMERICA.
40,000 YEARS AGO.

The sun was sinking into the sea as Anthro knelt upon the sandy beach. A plucked chicken roasted upon a spit above a nearby campfire. The tantalizing aroma of cooked meat wafted past the youth's nostrils, but he ignored the rumbling of his stomach. His bow and arrows leaned against a piece of driftwood, and a crude stone wheel rested atop the sand, awaiting further blows from the boy's chisel. Gentle waves lapped at the shore.

Many moons had passed since the mysterious god had taught him the use of fire, yet new ideas and discoveries constantly filled Anthro's mind. Many nights, as he lay in his tent beside his mate, Embra, the racing of his thoughts kept sleep at bay. Since their chieftain's death, the Bear Tribe had looked to Anthro's strength and cunning to keep them safe and fed, but at times the youth had to go off by himself to be alone with the clamorous notions crowding his skull. When he returned from one of these hunting trips, he often brought back more than just fresh game. Sometimes he had found another way to make all their lives easier.

Many of the tribe now held him in awe. Some even called him shaman. . . .

The lure of the roasting chicken failed to distract him from his reverie.

Lost in a trance, he used a pointed stick to trace a pattern in the sand. He let his restless spirit guide his fingers. Not until he finished the sketch did he recognize it as the same pattern that had marked the god's shining visage. He wondered what magic the rune held.

A brilliant glare lit up the beach, and Anthro looked up in surprise. To his amazement, the sun, which had been sinking to his left only heartbeats before, was *now rising to his right*. But that was not all that changed. His eyes widened in fear and wonder as he saw that the familiar coastline had been replaced by a startling new vision:

A colossal female idol, many time the size of any man or beast, lay partly buried beneath blackened mounds of ashy debris. Her pitted skin and garments were fashioned from a slick, hard substance Anthro had never seen before. Carved skins were draped over the mammoth figure. Her right arm held aloft the likeness of a burning torch, while her other arm cradled an immense tablet bearing strange, indecipherable markings. Spikes radiated from her crown. A greenish patina hinted at ages of neglect and decay. Her towering form had tilted halfway over, so that it threatened to come crashing down onto the scorched and lifeless rubble below her.

In the distance, beyond the broken idol, Anthro glimpsed a baffling view of what he could only guess was an abandoned campsite of the gods. Gigantic structures, composed of the same weathered substance as the huge idol, rose before a smoky black dawn. Their twisted skeletons and gaping wounds suggested that some terrible cataclysm, such as a raging forest fire or angry volcano, had befallen the heavenly campsite. Sunlight glinted off broken shards of some strange transparent amber. A hot wind blew smoke and ash against Anthro's face, and he choked on the noxious fumes.

"You!"

A blond-haired youth emerged from the shadow of the toppled goddess. He ran across the ruins toward Anthro, shouting at the top of his lungs in a language the cave boy had never heard before yet somehow understood. The stranger's corn-colored tresses streamed behind him. Instead of a loincloth or skins, a short garment of woven blue fabric covered his loins and upper thighs, and a leather pouch was belted to his waist. His bare chest and arms were deeply tanned. He looked no older than Anthro himself.

"Metron gave you a weapon against the gods!" the boy yelled urgently. He ran as though pursued by a rampaging herd of shaggy long-tusks. "We need it now!"

He reached out to Anthro, who instinctively extended his own hand. Their fingers stretched toward each other, only instants away from touching. Desperate blue eyes searched Anthro's face for the answer to a question Anthro couldn't begin to comprehend. All he knew was that whatever the other boy needed, it was a matter of life and death. He grunted in confusion.

Then, abruptly, the vision ended.

Disoriented, Anthro found himself back in the fading twilight of the lonely beach. He looked all around him, but the running boy, the giant idol, and the distant wasteland had all vanished from sight. Nothing but empty air awaited his outstretched fingers. It was sunset once more, and he smelled his chicken burning.

For a moment, he thought that perhaps he had simply woken from a strange and perplexing dream, but when he brought his hand to his face, he felt a coating of heavy gray ash upon his skin. The dusty coating was proof that what he had just experienced was no mere dream. It had been an omen, perhaps even a warning, from the gods.

And the blond-haired boy had been their messenger.

Anthro did not know what the vision meant, but he knew he had to be prepared. His finger moved across his face, tracing the mask of Metron upon his own thoughtful features. He prayed that the sacred markings would protect him and his people from what lay ahead.

No matter *what* the gods had in store.

CHAPTER 7

TOKYO.
NOW.

The gigantic monster rampaged through the city streets. Over seventy feet tall, the scaly red tentaclosaur stomped along the Ginza, leaving a trail of destruction in its wake. Screaming men and women, clutching their bawling offspring, ran away from the towering beast in panic. Its ponderous tread flattened abandoned cars and trucks. Barbed tentacles, the size of swinging construction cranes, lashed out at the defenseless buildings blocking its path. Rubble rained down on the streets and sidewalks below as flashing neon signs exploded into showers of sparks and broken glass. Fallen debris clogged escape routes, and shattered peaks of torn asphalt jutted like fangs from the ravaged pavement. Billowing clouds of smoke and dust blotted out the sun. The beast's deafening roar drowned out the high-pitched shrieks of the fleeing refugees. The distant slopes of a snowcapped mountain, rising majestically on the horizon, drew the creature onward, heedless of the devastation it was inflicting on the hapless city.

"Fushikuraje was old and tired," Rising Sun recalled, as decades-old newsreel footage of the behemoth's onslaught played on a screen behind him, "but his efforts to reach the Monster's Graveyard left the city in ruins."

The middle-aged Japanese super hero sat behind a desk on the set of his eponymous talk show. Although no longer a young man, he still fit comfortably into his trademarked white silk uniform. A crimson sunrise was emblazoned patriotically upon his chest, and a raised collar framed his distinguished features. Strands of gray infiltrated his dark brown hair and mustache as he proudly looked back on his glory days:

"Luckily for us all, in my day we rolled up our sleeves and got the job done." On the screen behind him, his younger self, glowing with harnessed solar energy, was joined by a coterie of heroic figures. A masked warrior in futuristic indigo armor, an oversized robot with steam-hammer hands, a speeding alien android on roller skates, and a green-haired youth in a turquoise wet suit were only a few of the colorful adventurers who aided Rising Sun in his valiant efforts to curtail Fushikuraje's earthshaking pilgrimage. "In my day, Ultimon, Hammersuit, Cosmo Racer, Junior Waveman, and the other noble champions of Big Science Action *earned* their status as Japanese heroes!"

The pride in his voice turned to contempt as he sneered directly into the camera. "Not like today. When have any of these new young wasters ever faced a monster bent on turning all of Tokyo into a radioactive toilet? Tell me that! What do they ever do except lounge around in their trendy nightclubs drinking cocktails and smoking?" He snorted in disgust. "Super heroes? Posers, I say!"

His angry jeremiad was greeted by hoots and derision in one of the very clubs he mocked. ACTION COMICS was the hottest new nightspot in Shibuya, catering to the young, the hip, and the impossibly glamorous. Gorgeous teenage boy and girls, clad in the latest super-hero-inspired fashions, crowded the booths and dance floor, after waiting for hours to get past the hulking bouncers outside. Cartoon sound effects and word balloons were painted in Day-Glo colors upon the walls. Neon lit up the smoky atmosphere. Japanese pop tunes blared above the laughter, pickup lines, and general hubbub. Rising Sun's indignant features filled a wall-sized plasma TV screen. The conservative hero-turned-commentator was a figure of fun to the carefree teens partying at the club. The louder he ranted, the more they laughed at him. Didn't he realize how ridiculous he sounded?

"Hah!" Big Atomic Lantern Boy guffawed. The stocky adolescent hero hung out with his friends in a roped-off VIP lounge overlooking the main floor. A metallic gold iron lung, liberally adorned with manga-styled reproductions of Green Lantern's insignia, encased the boy's barrel-shaped torso. A circular porthole in his chest offered a glowing X-ray view of his ribs and lungs, and a bright green effulgence radiated from the porthole. His round head protruded from the top of his stiff metal collar, and a solitary black topknot curled atop his shaved cranium. He turned to his friend and chortled again. "That's you, Heino! He's talking about *you*!"

Heino Okata, better known as Most Excellent Superbat, held court in the VIP lounge alongside his fellow young heroes. A slender youth with the cheekbones and brooding air of a teenage pop star, he was a self-styled icon in the making. His flamboyant costume was an inspired mash-up of World's Finest super-fashions. Jagged spikes, inspired by the spurs on Batman's gauntlets, jutted from both sides of his bright blue cowl. His golden collar was modeled on Superman's belt, and a Utility Belt was slung across his chest like a sash. The abstract yellow shapes covering his crimson tights appeared totally random until you realized that they were actually the negative spaces from Superman's famous S-shield repeated in irregular patterns across his lean frame. The ends of his blue scalloped cape were clipped to his wristbands. He leaned back against a red velvet couch and sipped on a martini. A scowl showed beneath the gilded bat-shaped mask covering the upper half of his face. "Pfahh."

Shiny Happy Aquazon sounded equally offended by Rising Sun's cranky dismissal of their generation. "What does he know about us anyway?" The amphibious young merwoman wore a one-piece emerald bathing suit over a fishnet body stocking. Her aquamarine tresses betrayed her familial connection to the legendary Junior Waveman, and her chartreuse skin gleamed healthily. Swim goggles were perched above her brow. A miniature harpoon launcher was strapped to her hip. "I once saved the life of an injured porpoise!"

Well-Spoken Sonic Lightning Flash nodded in agreement. The visor of his bubble helmet was raised to make drinking easier. His yeti-sized rubber running boots rested on the low velvet table before them. Shy Crazy Lolita Canary Girl, who was barely a foot tall, perched upon his shoulder. The doll-sized heroine wore a Japanese schoolgirl's uniform, complete with pleated skirt and very loose socks. Dyed blonde pigtails complemented her pixieish features, and her angelic golden wings fanned the air.

"Rising Sun is a stupid old man," Most Excellent Superbat declared. He raised his glass in an ironic toast to the increasingly apoplectic older hero, who continued to fulminate on the screen before them.

"Japan has always had a proud tradition of super-heroism, with special distinction in the field of monster-hunting. But these feckless youngsters make a laughingstock of us all." Rising Sun shook his finger at his unappreciative audience. "It shames us that the noble calling of super hero has become nothing more than a gimmick!"

Superbat rolled his eyes. "All my life I've wanted to be a gimmick," he said defiantly, while his costumed entourage hung on his every word. "The transformation of man into merchandising! Spirit into toy!" He shook his head disparagingly at the screen. "When will he realize that being fantastic is a superpower in itself?" Confident in his own superior relevance, he shrugged off the old hero's petulant ranting. "Something will happen to put Super Young Team on the map. We'll show him. We'll save the world our own way!"

Caught up in his own pithy rhetoric, he initially failed to notice that his companions, and indeed the entire club, were no longer paying attention to him. He looked up from his drink to discover that all eyes had turned toward a newcomer who had just entered the club. Wide-eyed teens, both superpowered and otherwise, gazed in awe at a massively muscled older man wearing only slacks, sandals, and a plain black T-shirt. His shaved skull reflected the neon glow of the club's interior. Cell phones and cameras feverishly captured his arrival. Canary Girl's wings fluttered in excitement. A tiny hand was clasped over her mouth as she pointed eagerly with the other.

"Sonny Sumo-san!" Superbat exclaimed. He leapt to his feet. "We are not worthy!"

The legendary wrestler strode toward the bar, ignoring the tumult his unexpected appearance had generated. A crowd of adoring fans parted to let him through. His muscles bulged beneath the tight black shirt; he was twice the size of the hero-worshiping boys and girls flocking to get a better look at him. A deep bass voice that made Darth Vader sound like a castrati addressed the bartender.

"Water. Ice. In a tall glass."

The bartender filled Sonny's order, then looked up in alarm, not because of Sonny Sumo's intimidating presence, but in response to the clanking metal monstrosity that followed Sonny into the club. A towering robotic samurai forced its way through the crowd to come up behind Sonny. Built-in weapons bristled upon its lacquered exoskeleton, and glowing red lenses glared from its leering steel faceplate. Heavy iron boots pounded against the floor as the fearsome cyborg loomed over the mortal wrestler.

"SONNY SUMO," an amplified electronic voice rang out. "MEGAYAKUZA CHALLENGES YOU!"

Sonny calmly sipped his water. He didn't even turn around.

A steel-shod fist hammered the bar. "DID YOU HEAR ME, SONNY SUMO?"

"I fight for money." Sonny tapped his empty glass to ask for a refill. "Talk to my manager. Maybe you'll get a chance to face me in the ring . . . where there are rules to prevent me from killing you." The bartender nervously poured fresh water into the glass. "Take my advice, friend. Don't provoke me."

"I AM NOT YOUR FRIEND!" Megayakuza raised his hands. Flickering metal nozzles were embedded in his palms. "I AM MEGAYAKUZA!"

Brilliant orange flames jetted from the cyborg's hands, setting Sonny's back on fire. His T-shirt went up in flames, while the bartender frantically hustled the nearest liquor bottles away from the conflagration. The stomach-turning smell of baked flesh pervaded the smoky atmosphere of the club as Sonny's exposed skin blackened and blistered.

Sonny calmly drained his glass dry.

Megayakuza extinguished his flamethrowers before he set the entire club ablaze. Bayonet attachments folded into offensive positions from latched compartments in his forearms. The sharpened blades caught the glow of the flames licking Sonny's skin.

"NOW WILL YOU FACE ME, COWARD?"

Moving with blinding speed, Sonny spun around and drove the empty glass right through Megayakuza's armored chest and out his back. Sparks erupted from the cyborg's ruptured cuirass. Static squawked from his mouthpiece as his servomotors froze up. The lights behind his crimson lenses shorted out, and a wisp of smoke escaped his eye sockets before he toppled backward onto the floor.

Sonny yanked back his arm. Splintered titanium ribs scraped his skin.

He placed the cracked glass back on the bar. No longer empty, it now contained a pulpy purple heart that appeared to be half organic, half mechanical. A greasy black lubricant dripped onto the polished woodwork, and more goo slimed Sonny's beefy arm. The charred remnants of his T-shirt clung to his blistered torso.

A stunned hush fell over the entire nightclub. Even Superbat and his fellow celebrities could only watch agape as Sonny stepped over Megayakuza's lifeless remains and headed for the men's room to freshen up. The last lingering flames upon his back flickered out.

A silhouette of a man in a cape marked the entrance to the lavatory. Sonny shoved the door open. A handful of startled teenagers, who had missed out on the excitement, looked up in surprise at the sight of the scorched and smoking sumo champion. "Beat it," he said gruffly.

The young men hastily vacated the facilities.

Over in the VIP lounge, Superbat overcame his dumbfounded amazement to recognize a priceless opportunity when he saw it. "Atomic Lantern Boy, go! Get his autograph!"

"Say it's for your sister," Aquazon suggested, shoving the hesitant teen forward. Her turquoise eyes gleamed with enthusiasm. "But she daren't go into the men's toilets!"

Sonny's back stung like the blazes. Leaning over a porcelain sink, he splashed cold water onto his face and shoulders. Steam rose from his roasted body, and ugly burns and blisters defaced his flesh. A mirror above the sink reflected his pained, world-weary expression.

All I wanted was a night out, he thought. *Was that too much to ask?*

The door swung open and a boy in a clunky green and yellow outfit poked his head into the restroom. "Excuse me, Super-Sumo-san. . . ." He gulped nervously. "Autograph?"

Sonny gripped the sides of the sink. "Maybe another time."

"It's not for me," the boy persisted. "My sister has—"

Pain frayed the limits of Sonny's patience. "Another time!"

To his annoyance, he heard the door swing open wider. Footsteps approached him from behind as a peculiar pinging noise intruded on his suffering.

"Didn't you hear me?" he barked. "I said out!"

But when he looked in the mirror he saw the footsteps belonged not to the sheepish autograph hound, but to a confident-looking black man in a natty white suit. Sunglasses concealed the man's eyes, and a stylish fedora capped his head. He appeared not at all intimidated by Sonny's size and/or celebrity. Sonny thought the man looked familiar, but couldn't quite place him. *Some big-name rapper or pop star?*

"Sonny Sumo." He spoke Japanese with an American accent. "My name is Shilo Norman. Onstage, they call me Mister Miracle."

Right, Sonny thought. *The escape artist.* He hadn't recognized the man out of his garish circus costume.

The pinging noise, which seemed to emanate from beneath the American's tailored jacket, grew louder. A strange tingling sensation rushed over Sonny's smarting skin as his blistered flesh healed instantaneously. He lifted a hand to his face and felt smooth, unblemished skin.

"That sound," he murmured. "I know that sound." Long-forgotten memories stirred at the back of his brain. "And my skin . . ."

Shilo Norman fished a small device, which resembled a sleek, modern smartphone, from his jacket's inner pocket. He held up the gadget. "Motherboxxx led me to you. She's about the only thing left after the war, see? There was a cosmic war . . . and the powers of evil won."

What war? Sonny thought. *What's he talking about?*

"I know how this sounds," Mister Miracle continued. "But can't you *feel* how the world has changed since the turn of the century? They're *here* among us now."

Who *is?* Sonny wondered, baffled by the stranger's ominous pronouncements. *And what does this have to do with me?*

Shilo read the confusion on Sonny's face. "I was kind of hoping you might be able to help me put some kind of team together."

"Wow!"

The startled exclamation came from the starstruck boy in the doorway, who was still lurking in the background. Glancing over at the door, Sonny

saw that the youth had been joined by a handful of equally wide-eyed
friends, including a young man who was dressed like some sort of bizarre
Batman and Superman hybrid. The costumed teens cautiously pushed their
way into the restroom.

"Does this count as another time?"

CHAPTER 8

METROPOLIS.

"Bedazzle. Bedlam . . ."

Nick Ustan paged through a paperback dictionary, reciting each word one by one. A spiral notebook was spread out in front him. Sketches of imaginary super heroes, including Nazi versions of Superman and Supergirl, filled the pages of the notebook. Colored pencils were scattered atop the table of a booth at the back of a downtown Belly Burger franchise. An orange polyester uniform marked Nick as yet another Belly Burger employee, currently enjoying a fifteen-minute break from the cash register. The smell of french fries and greasy burgers clung to his uniform and skin.

"Cathexis. Cathode."

"Hey, Nick!" A blonde girl in a matching uniform slid into the booth across from him. "Me and Shirley were just talking about dreams and stuff. You ever dream in color?"

Nick lifted his nose from the dictionary. "Every night. And the colors always seems bright—purer—than they are in real life." His gaze turned inward. "But strange and weird too. Like last night, I was being judged by these super-people who built this machine made out of parallel universes. And they sentenced me to some kind of exile here on Earth and . . . that's when I woke up."

"Whatever," Celeste said, already bored. She shook her head. "You're such a stoner."

"Not really." Nick tried to explain what he meant to the indifferent cashier. "Sometimes I just feel like I belong somewhere else, that's all." He paged through his dictionary. "Like one day I'm gonna find the magic word that will take me home. . . ."

Celeste shrugged. She pulled out her cell phone to check her text messages. "Just remember, your break's over in five minutes."

Nick went back to his dictionary, determined to make every minute count before he returned to another three hours of mindless fast-food drudgery. *There's gotta to be more to life than this,* he thought. *There* has *to be.*

"*Criminal. Crimson. Crinkle . . .*"

GOTHAM CITY.

The Mad Hatter was a mess.

The dwarfish villain was sprawled on the carpet of the seedy rented apartment that served as his current "headquarters." His green frock coat was splattered with crimson, and his cockeyed bow tie had been yanked out of shape. His usually prodigious nose had been flattened, and blood and snot streamed from his nostrils. A blackened eye was swollen shut. Broken teeth gnawed at a fat lip. Tears gushed down his quivering cheeks as he whimpered in pain.

"That was me askin' nicely," Turpin snarled.

Fists clenched, he loomed over the battered lunatic. Creepy Victorian dolls, mostly of golden-haired little girls, cluttered the shelves. A stuffed white rabbit was propped up on the sofa, and the shards of a broken teapot littered the floor. Turpin couldn't remember precisely how he'd gotten here—he'd been having trouble with blackouts lately—but the Hatter had obviously fallen on hard times since escaping from Arkham Asylum a few weeks back. His trademark top hat lay trampled upon the carpet. Loose springs and circuitry spilled from its broken top. Without his hypnotic chapeau, the Hatter was helpless against the vengeful ex-cop.

Tough, Turpin thought.

He grabbed the Hatter's lapels and hauled him up onto his knees. "Please!" the sniveling Hatter stammered. "Stop hitting me! I—I only made the prototypes . . . the mind . . . m-m-mind control hats. . . ." He threw up his white-gloved hands to protect what was left of his face. "I . . . don't know where they took the children. . . . I don't . . ."

"Liar."

His knee came up to meet the Hatter's face. The brutal blow mashed whatever had remained intact within the villain's broken nose. The Hatter squealed like a boiled rabbit. Turpin smirked in satisfaction. Who knew the sound of breath whistling though smashed cartilage could be such a turn-on?

"You're gonna tell me where those kids are, you hear me?" Tossing the Mad Hatter aside, he rummaged through the nearest closet, which was packed to overflowing with cardboard hatboxes. He yanked them open one after another, hoping to find some clue to the missing children's whereabouts. Derbies, berets, sombreros, beanies, fedoras, trilbies, and every other variety of headgear went flying over his shoulder as he searched in vain for a fresh lead.

Wait a second, a voice at the back of his head piped up. *Didn't I find the kids already?* A disturbing vision of blank eyes and drooling lips flashed briefly across his mind before slipping away again. *Damn blackouts,* he thought. *What the hell is* wrong *with me?*

A low moan alerted him that the Mad Hatter was making a break for it. Giving up on the closet, he watched the brutalized villain feebly drag himself into the bathroom. Turpin stomped over and kicked the door open before the pathetic skel could even try to lock him out. He found the Hatter hunched over the toilet, retching into the bowl.

"Where do you think *you're* going?" Turpin snarled. The Hatter's wretched state and inability to defend himself only stoked the volcanic anger that seemed to be growing inside Turpin with each passing moment. He wrenched the toilet seat from its moorings and smacked the Hatter viciously across the back of the head with it. The stained porcelain ring cracked against the villain's skull. "Tell me where I can find those kids, or I'm gonna give you brain damage with a friggin' toilet seat! How's that gonna look when they make the movie of your life, creep?"

Turpin caught a glimpse of himself in a cracked bathroom mirror. His craggy face looked roughly hewn from crumbling stone, and his skin was dry and gray. Homicidal rage burned within his sunken eyes. The harsh fluorescent lights made his head hurt. Swollen veins throbbed beneath his skin. He looked as sick as he felt. Like he was stewing in poison.

I feel so angry all the time. Can't even think straight.

"B-blud . . ." The Hatter was curled up in a fetal position on the grimy tile floor, his hands shielding his head. He spit out a mouthful of broken enamel. "B-Blüdhaven."

Figures, Turpin thought. He turned away from the Mad Hatter in disgust, leaving the bloody wreckage on the floor. *Should've known it.*

All roads lead to Hell.

MARS.

Despite the quarantine imposed on Earth, the Guardians had granted the Justice League a special dispensation to return the Martian Manhunter's body to his native planet. An emerald dome, generated by John Stewart's power ring, shielded the funeral party from the Red Planet's inhospitable environment. Beyond the dome, a rust-colored desert landscape stretched for miles in every direction. Weathered stone mesas were buffeted by swirling clouds of fine dust. Olympus Mons, the largest volcano in the solar system, rose impressively on the horizon. The sun seemed small and very far away.

"J'onn J'onzz was my friend," Superman declared. He stood before a sealed casket generously bedecked with flowers. His head lowered in mourning, he delivered the eulogy while his fellow heroes listened in silence. Past and present members of the JLA, along with representatives from the Teen Titans, the Outsiders, the Justice Society, the Birds of Prey, and most every other active super-hero team were gathered beneath the protective dome. Wonder Woman dabbed at her eyes with a tissue. Batman glowered ominously. Skeets, Booster Gold's robot sidekick, levitated above the heads of Booster and the new Blue Beetle. Black Canary choked back a sob. Green Arrow placed a comforting arm around her. Mister Terrific, Stargirl, Hal Jordan, Kyle Rayner, Red Tornado, Vixen, Wildcat, Black Lightning, Alan Scott,

Geo-Force, Hawkman, Hawkgirl, Firestorm, Metamorpho, Gypsy, Fire, Ice, Red Arrow, Flash, Snapper Carr, Zatanna, and many others were also in attendance. Superman liked to think that J'onn would have been touched by the turnout.

"Always there, always strong, always reliable," he praised their departed friend and ally. "J'onn was someone I could confide in. Someone who understood was it was like to lose a world and find another." His throat tightened. "We'll all miss him . . . and pray for a resurrection."

Outside the dome, the dry red soil waited to receive the last of its sons.

KEYSTONE CITY.

"Well, gentlemen?" Libra asked. "Convinced?"

As before, the hooded enigma sat at the head of the table in the back room of the abandoned strip club. This time, however, a larger assortment of super-criminals had responded to Libra's summons. A-list masterminds like Talia Head and Gorilla Grodd rubbed shoulders with costumed hoodlums and psychopaths like Weather Wizard, the Shadow Thief, and Killer Frost. Lex Luthor was dismayed by Libra's glowing clout in the super-villain community.

"The Martian was an easy target," he sneered. "Hurt Superman and perhaps I'll take you more seriously."

"Say what you like, Luthor," Clayface gurgled. A mass of amorphous brown sludge, the shape-changing monstrosity slouched in his seat. His lumpy countenance only vaguely resembled a human face. Gaping nostrils took the place of a nose, and petrified teeth filled a jagged gash of a mouth. His phlegmy voice sounded like he was gargling mucous. "Libra delivered for the Human Flame." Beady red eyes glanced over at Miller, who sat beaming at Libra's left hand. "And I'm next on the list, so no screwing this up for me!"

Libra leaned back against Metron's captured throne. His lance rested against his shoulder. "So let me get this straight," he asked Luthor. "You're saying if I hurt Superman, you'll join me?"

Luthor hedged, reluctant to commit himself. "Well . . ."

The meeting broke up shortly thereafter, after another of Libra's pretentious sermons on the inevitable triumph of evil. Luthor led an exodus of villains into the dismal parking lot behind the building. A highway overpass concealed the infamous assemblage as each departed in their own distinctive fashion. Sivana boarded a spherical hovercraft of his own design while Effigy caught a ride in Killer Frost's converted ice-cream truck. Deathstroke drove off in a sleek red sports car paid for by the proceeds of his last few contract killings. A miniature tornado lifted Weather Wizard off the pavement as Amazo launched himself into the air like Superman. Clayface oozed through a rusty sewer grating. The Shadow Thief, flattened to two-dimensionality, slid silently up the side of one of the concrete columns supporting the overpass.

A chauffeured black Rolls-Royce waited for Luthor, but first he felt a need to vent to Vandal Savage. "Look at them!" he said, referring to the gullible felons making their getaways. "That preening snake oil salesman has opened the Secret Society's doors to dangerous Z-list wannabes. Even that reptile Sivana agrees that we have to make an alliance against Libra's ambitions. Can we count on you, Savage?"

"I have walked the Earth since the morning of time," the ageless Neanderthal replied. An antique rapier rested in a scabbard against his hip. Tailored silk attire belied his prehistoric origins. "I've seen so many little men squandering their little lives on petty power struggles that bring meaning to otherwise futile existences." He drew the sword from its sheath. "If he promises me an end to boredom, I'll take it."

That was *not* what Luthor wanted to hear.

The Human Flame watched as Luthor slammed the door of his limo shut before being driven away. The arrogant arch-villain had obviously been trying to stir up trouble. "Ignore him, boss," he advised Libra, who lurked in the doorway of the strip joint's back entrance. "Zillionaire suits like Luthor expect the world on a silver platter."

"Even Luthor will come around when he sees what I do next," Libra promised, sounding unconcerned by Lex's scheming. "But I'm not the boss, Mike. You'll know all about it when the boss shows up."

Mike wondered who he meant, not that it really mattered to him. "All I know is you're the guy who put the Human Flame back on the map after I lost all those years in prison." He gave Libra an enthusiastic thumbs-up. "I owe you big-time."

"Mmm, yes." Libra patted Mike on the back and guided him back toward the murky doorway. A cold wind whipped up the trash littering the parking lot. Now that the other villains had gone their myriad ways, he and Mike had the club entirely to themselves. "Why don't we go back inside and talk about . . . well, what you owe me."

CHAPTER 9

HALL OF JUSTICE.
WASHINGTON, D.C.

The Justice League's morgue was three doors down from its infirmary. Orion's lifeless body floated above a computerized autopsy table incorporating advanced Kryptonian and Thanagarian technology. A force field maintained a sterile atmosphere around the levitating cadaver. Diagnostic scanners projected three-dimensional X-ray images of Orion's internal organs onto a nearby screen. The dead god's helmet rested on a stainless steel counter nearby.

"J'onn Jonzz is dead. Orion is dead." Wonder Woman took stock of recent events. "The Justice League no longer has access to the instantaneous mind-to-mind contact J'onn's telepathic skills provided. . . ."

"Say no more," Superman said. His grim expression matched Diana's assessment of their strategic losses. "The global superhuman community is on priority alert." He turned to the World's Greatest Detective. "Batman?"

The Dark Knight scrutinized the scans of Orion's remains. "According to my sources, the Secret Society has taken credit for J'onn's murder. It was an execution, organized-crime style." His gruff voice suggested that he expected nothing less from their foes. "Orion is something else, but I've asked the Flash to investigate some potential leads that could link the killings."

Before he could elaborate, footsteps sounded in the corridor outside.

Batman's keen ears identified two distinct treads, one familiar to him, the other unknown. He scowled at the interruption.

"Someone's coming," Wonder Woman said. "Green Lantern?"

Hal Jordan entered the morgue, accompanied by an alien Green Lantern unfamiliar to Batman. A smooth azure faceplate concealed the woman's features. Luminous yellow lenses covered her eyes, and a mane of dark indigo tresses framed her mask. A brilliant emerald glow emanated from a circular portal in her chest, and a bare midriff exposed taut blue skin. Batman instantly noted the stranger wore *two* power rings, not just one.

That was new, and more than a little disturbing.

"Guys," Jordan introduced the stranger, "my superior officer, Alpha Lantern Kraken."

She glanced around disdainfully. "More members of the local crime-fighting club, Jordan?" She strode into the morgue as though she owned the place, like an FBI agent reluctantly forced to deal with a bunch of small-town cops. Her voice had a cold mechanical ring to it. "How much do these extracurricular distractions compromise your ability to protect this entire sector, I wonder. When did you last spend significant time on Heliopolis, M'Brai, Athmoora, or any of a thousand other inhabited worlds under your jurisdiction?"

Jordan stood up for himself. "Earth has a habit of attracting serious trouble." He nodded at Orion's corpse. "As you can see. The victim here is of celestial origin."

"Then it's important that we work quickly before the body sublimes back to the Source," Kraken replied, referring to the mythical realm from which the New Gods supposedly drew their power—and to which they were said to return upon their deaths. "Unfortunately, this backwater planet lacks the technology to accurately determine the cause of a god's death."

Batman disagreed. "He was shot." His gloved finger pointed out the evidence on the holographic scans. "The internal trauma's consistent with the blast pattern of a bullet detonating inside Orion's skull." He stepped aside to let Kraken get a better view of the display. "What kind of bullet remains to be seen, since it left no other trace of its passage."

Superman confirmed Batman's findings. "X-ray him again, Lantern Kraken. You'll see."

"Someone shot a god and left no exit wound?" Kraken turned her back on the scans, dismissing their theory out of hand. "I think not."

Batman was irked by the alien's attitude. "I maintain he was shot. That's why I instructed one of your officers to reexamine the crime scene for a bullet." He couldn't resist needling the arrogant Alpha Lantern a bit. "John Stewart is another valued member of our 'crime-fighting club.'"

Kraken took the bait. She wheeled about indignantly. "*You* instructed Lantern Stewart 2814.2? On whose authority?"

Wonder Woman reached out to restrain the other woman. "Sister . . ."

"I am *not* your sister." A crackling burst of emerald energy repelled Diana's fingers. "I am in charge of this investigation! By order of the Guardians of the Universe who police countless worlds, including this one."

A vigilante at heart, Batman was not about to let Kraken—or the Guardians—pull rank on him. "I don't remember voting them into the League."

Jordan stepped between Batman and Kraken, attempting to play peacemaker. "Batman, guys. Alpha Lantern Kraken is one of the best investigators in the Corps. I'm sure we can all work together."

"This a job for trained professionals," Kraken insisted. "And I believe your duty shift is over, Jordan." Her icy tone made it clear that his presence, and diplomatic overtures, were neither desired nor appreciated. "We'll call you in the morning."

METROPOLIS.

A miniature green bulldozer tore up the pavement where the Dumpster containing Orion's body had once been. Wooden crates and pallets still surrounded the crime scene. A glowing emerald outline, floating several feet above the floor of the wharf, indicated the placement of the body. Moonlight peeked through clouds overhead, and a salty breeze blew off the bay.

John Stewart crouched behind the toy-sized emerald bulldozer, directing its actions with his power ring. He fought back a yawn. He'd been to Mars and back today, and it was nearly midnight. Still, he didn't want to turn in until he'd thoroughly inspected the murder site one more time. *If Batman says there's a bullet here, then I'm going to find it.*

"Cordon's secure," Opto309v reported as he descended from the sky. The alien Green Lantern from Sector 2260 was Stewart's designated backup tonight, while Hal and Kraken met with the Justice League. Although humanoid in size and shape, Opto sported a pair of floppy antennae that resembled the ears of a beagle. His leathery red skin looked positively barbequed. A pair of horny barbs jutted from his chin. The domino mask concealing his face was probably unnecessary given that the nearest other member of his species was hundreds of light-years away. "Found anything yet?"

"Maybe." The bulldozer scooped another pile of rubble into a small green wheelbarrow. "The ring detected a trace energy signature it couldn't identify. Whatever it is, it's been buried in this concrete foundation for fifty years or more. Which makes it an unlikely candidate for the murder weapon," Stewart conceded, "but I decided to dig it out, just to make sure. . . ."

"You hear that?" Opto's antennae twitched. Stewart couldn't hear anything, but that wasn't too surprising; the alien's auditory faculties were much more finely tuned than his. Opto took to the air to investigate. "Tell me when I get back."

Confident that the other Green Lantern had his back, Stewart kept his eye on the bulldozer's excavations, which finally yielded results. One last scoop of debris exposed a bullet-shaped object composed of a smooth translucent material. An eerie violet glow radiated from the interior of the bullet, which appeared to contain some sort of intricate bioorganic skeleton. The arcane filaments seemed to be made of equal parts bone and circuitry.

"CAUTION," his ring alerted him. "UNIDENTIFIED THEOTOXIC MATERIAL."

Theotoxic? As in fatal to gods?

"All right." A thin green aura protected his fingers as he reached cautiously for the bullet. "What do we have here?"

"GUARDIAN ARCHIVES IDENTIFICATION: RADION . . . EMERGENCY . . . EMERG—"

The ring's report was cut off by a squawk of static, and a wisp of green smoke escaped the ring before its light went out.

"Ring?" Stewart stared in confusion at the ring. He had recharged it right after he had gotten back from Mars; it should have still had plenty of power. He moved his hand away from the mysterious bullet. "Why have you stopped—?"

A volley of glowing emerald spikes slammed into him, nailing him to the side of a heavy wooden crate. He cried out in pain as the spikes impaled his palms, wrists, thighs, ankles, and gut. Crucified, he gazed up in shock at his attacker, who wore a familiar green uniform.

"My God. *You!*"

The faint metallic ringing was probably nothing, but Opto figured it couldn't hurt to check it out. This was his first visit to Earth so he wasn't entirely sure what constituted a threat or not. For all he knew, the tinny peals came from some deadly native predator, like the venomous bell-snakes of Refelcta Prime.

A massive steel suspension bridge overlooked the waterfront where the New God's body had been found. Opto's keen ears and antennae led him to the very top of the bridge, where he was startled to discover the source of the ringing: a green plasma construct of a windup toy Guardian clanging a pair of tiny metal cymbals.

The alien blinked in confusion. Was this some sort of bizarre Terran joke? If so, he didn't get it.

The construct evaporated before his ears. The annoying echoes faded away, to be replaced by an agonized scream from the wharf below. Despite his unfamiliarity with this planet, there was no mistaking the sound of another sentient being in torment.

"Lanternjohnstewart?"

Opto flew away from the bridge.

"Say good-bye to your eyes," his attacker warned from only a few feet away.

A pair of emerald spikes hovered before John Stewart's face, poised to strike. A hostile power ring glowed ominously upon an outstretched hand. Stewart strained against the missiles pinning him to the crate. Despite the searing pain and shock, he tore his right fist free of a rotting timber plank and slammed it into the palm of his backstabbing opponent, who was taken aback by Stewart's unexpected resistance. The blow disrupted his enemy's concentration. The blinding spikes blinked out of existence.

"Johnstewart!"

Opto's voice chased the traitor away.

COAST CITY.

Hal Jordan slept soundly in his apartment near the airfield. His power battery rested atop a wooden dresser. Drawn drapes kept out the lights of the city. The door to his clothes closet was ajar, and an aviator's jacket hung on the back of a chair. Despite his reputation as a ladies' man, he had his bed all to himself.

"Green Lantern Hal Jordan 2814.1!" A cold inhuman voice, along with a sudden emerald glare, roused him from sleep. He sat up to find an entire contingent of Alpha Lanterns standing at the foot of the bed. Kraken, Boodikka, Varix, and Chaselon glared at him ominously. Kraken's right-hand ring projected a blinding green spotlight onto him. She held up a bloodstained uniform with her other hand. Blinking before the glare, it took Jordan a second to recognize the uniform as one of his spares. "I'm placing you under arrest for the murder of a New God and the attempted murder of your partner!"

"Whuh?" Groggy and wearing only a pair of khaki boxer shorts, Jordan couldn't quite grasp what was happening. The scar on his temple itched; he couldn't remember how he'd gotten it. He instinctively raised his own ring to defend himself, but all he could muster was a puff of wispy green smoke before the ring shorted out entirely. He stared at the lifeless ornament in surprise. "What the hell?"

"Your power ring and badge have been suspended for the duration of this inquiry," Kraken declared. Her glossy faceplate flipped up to reveal the robotic mechanical visage underneath; like the rest of her elite division, she was part machine now. "No Lantern escapes the Alpha Lanterns!"

Against his will, his ring flew from his finger into Kraken's open hand.

He had been stripped of his weapon.

WASHINGTON, D.C.

"Look, I was never Jordan's biggest supporter," Batman admitted, "but this just doesn't scan." He and Superman strode through the corridors of the Hall of Justice. The sun was rising outside, but the dawn did little to lift his mood. If anything, the big picture was getting steadily darker. "Don't tell me you trust Kraken."

As ever, Superman tried to see the positive side. "If she's wrong, and I'm sure she is, it shouldn't take us long to prove Hal's innocence." He stepped out onto the plaza in front of the building. Sunlight glittered upon the surface of the reflecting pool. His cape fluttered in the breeze. "I only need an hour or two. I know you can hold the fort until I get back."

"I hope you're right," Batman said. Nocturnal by nature, he clung to the shadow of the central arch, declining to step into the light.

"Doctor Mid-Nite and Wonder Woman are with John now," Superman reminded him, "administering Purple Ray treatments." With luck the healing powers of the violet radiation, which had been developed by the Amazons of Paradise Island, would help the comatose Green Lantern recover from his grievous injuries; unconscious since Opto309v had found him, Stewart had so far been unable to name his attacker. "If we assume Kraken's wrong, we still have a god-killer at large." He glanced in the direction of Metropolis. "But if I don't show my face as Clark Kent at the *Daily Planet*, I blow my secret identity out of the water."

Batman watched as Superman took off into the sky. He shook his head, questioning his friend's priorities at this critical juncture. Not for the first time, he was grateful that billionaire playboy Bruce Wayne didn't have a day job.

"Superman, Superman," he muttered before heading inside. He marched briskly back to the morgue, where he found Kraken inspecting Orion's remains once more. "Alpha Lantern Kraken," he said gruffly. "We need to talk about Jordan."

He was startled by the state of the corpse. The levitating cadaver looked surprisingly immaterial, more like a mirage than a corporeal form. Coruscating sparks flaked away from Orion's body before evaporating into the ether.

You could literally see through the floating remains. "What's happening to Orion?"

"I already told you," Kraken said brusquely. "The body of a god is mostly energy. It sublimes without a trace." She turned to face him, her hands upon her hips. "And as for Jordan, this is not the first time he went rogue. He was once possessed by Parallax, the Fear-Thing. Many thousands died as a result."

"I remember." Batman could hardly forget the incident. In a moment of weakness, after his beloved Coast City was devastated by an alien attack, Hal Jordan had apparently gone mad and turned against the Guardians, the Green Lantern Corps, the Justice League, and the entire universe. Although he had eventually freed himself from the psychic parasite that had infested his mind, it had taken Jordan a long time to regain the trust of his fellow heroes. Batman had only recently come around to fully accepting him as an ally again.

Had Jordan truly gone berserk again? It was possible, Batman supposed, but something about this didn't feel right. The evidence against Jordan struck him as flimsy and circumstantial. So why was Kraken in such a hurry to pin these attacks on her fellow Lantern?

He stepped forward to confront her, but, before he could say anything, Kraken faltered, seemingly overcome by a sudden weakness. She tottered unsteadily and clutched her head. A moan escaped her mandibles, and beads of sweat broke out upon her bare arms and midriff.

"Are you all right?" Batman asked.

"Help me!" she blurted, her voice cracking. Her haughty demeanor vanished, replaced by sheer desperation. She didn't even sound like the same person anymore. "She's eating my mind alive. . . ." She held out her left hand. The unmistakable impression of a power ring had been driven into her palm. "Tell them our weapons don't work. . . . Tell them . . ."

She stiffened abruptly, shaking off her temporary infirmity. "No!" Her voice regained its icy timbre. She caught Batman staring suspiciously at her open palm. "Why are you looking at me like that?"

Behind the opaque white lenses of his cowl, Batman's eyes widened at the telltale ring-print as his trained mind instantly put the pieces together. "Black Alert!" he shouted, activating the building's computerized security system. "Seal the Hall of Justice! Get me backup, now!"

He grabbed onto Kraken's left arm.

"Don't you *dare* touch me!" she protested. Crackling green flames ignited along the length of her arm, but Batman refused to let go. Nomex insulation in his glove protected him from the flames, at least for the moment.

"John has one hell of a right hook, doesn't he?" He realized now who had really attacked John Stewart. *This was all a frame-up!*

Kraken did not deny her guilt. "Stewart is critical. Wonder Woman cannot leave him . . . but Doctor Mid-Nite is already responding to your alarm." The blind physician was also a skilled crime fighter, but that didn't seem to concern Kraken—or whatever malevolent entity had apparently possessed the Alpha Lantern's body. Both her power rings flared like balefire. "He will arrive in exactly thirty-five seconds, but even he, to his eternal, punishing regret, won't reach you in time."

A pair of glowing emerald centipedes, the size of moray eels, sprang from her twin power rings. The wriggling constructs attacked Batman's neck from both sides, their stingers penetrating the thick reinforced fabric to pierce the skin beneath. He grunted in shock as they injected a potent neurotoxin into his veins.

The venom struck like lightning. He swayed backward, surrendering his grip on her arm. His face contorted in agony as a phosphorescent green froth spilled down his chin. His legs buckled and he collapsed onto his knees. He raised his fists, hoping to put up a fight despite the debilitating effects of the poison coursing through his system. His head throbbed painfully, and his limbs felt like lead. His heart was pounding faster than the Flash's boots. He tried to speak, to warn Kraken that the Justice League would track her down no matter what, but only an inarticulate groan escaped his clenched jaws. Nausea twisted his gut into knots.

A booming sound shook the morgue. At first, Batman thought it was just his head ringing, but then he realized that the din was actually coming from inside the room. Surgical instruments rattled in their trays, and the overhead lights flickered on and off. "Do you hear that sound?" she exulted. "Like thunder?" Her evil centipedes retreated back into her rings. "Are you afraid at last?"

A shimmering vortex opened up behind her, like a spinning tunnel stretching into infinity. Batman recognized it as one of the secret pathways the New Gods had used to traverse the cosmos. Bioorganic tendrils extended from the mouth of the vortex, anchoring it in space-time. Staring into the roaring tumult within the tunnel would be enough to induce vertigo in the strongest soul, even if you weren't already fighting against a sickening poison. He averted his eyes to keep from vomiting.

"Did you think the gods would tread lightly when they came among you?" Kraken was silhouetted before the gaping maw of the vortex. Her arms were raised in unholy triumph. "Into the Boom Tube with you, my sweet. A new plaything for Granny."

Granny?

Batman struggled to make sense of it all, but his weakened mind and body betrayed him. He toppled forward onto the floor, landing prostrate at Kraken's feet. The eldritch tendrils reached out for him.

"The life you knew is over," she decreed. "You are mine now!"

CHAPTER 10

BLÜDHAVEN.

Sneaking into the decimated city had proven easier than expected. Nobody, not even the homeless refugees camped outside the forbidden zone, really wanted to get back into the blasted, radioactive wasteland. A sickly silver glow radiated from the broken pavement and melted skyscrapers. Torched vehicles clotted the deserted streets. Greasy puddles filled gaping potholes and craters. Diseased flowers, their florid purple blooms obscenely overgrown, sprouted from scorched asphalt. A foul miasma hung over the desolate scenery. No one in their right mind would want to linger here, let alone creep in uninvited. Nevertheless, Turpin clung to the towering piles of debris as he made his way on foot across the rubble. He was getting closer to the missing kids; he could sense it. The last thing he wanted was to get picked up for trespassing before he found them.

I've come too far to turn back now.

Galloping footsteps disturbed the silence, and sizzling laser blasts soon sliced through the noisome air. Turpin ducked behind an overturned semitruck to avoid being spotted by a trio of Atomic Knights riding huge mutant Dalmatians. The armored sentries, who patrolled the toxic ruins, appeared to be in pursuit of a giant mutated cockroach. They called out urgently to each other as they fired at the fleeing monster with their nuclear lances. Turpin had to wonder what lamebrained government egghead had dreamed up the Atomic Knights program.

They couldn't have just sent in the Marines or something?

He waited until the knights and their disgusting quarry were safely past before creeping out into the open again. A chittering squeal in the distance hinted that the zealous knights had bagged the beast. Turpin quickened his pace in case they turned back his way again. The shattered, uneven landscape was tough going, and he was breathing hard before he got too far. He dabbed at his sweaty brow with a fraying handkerchief. He felt like he was burning up inside.

The whirr of chopper blades alerted him to the approach of a S.H.A.D.E. helicopter. Search beams scoured the wreckage ahead of the chopper, closing in on Turpin, who found himself caught in the middle of a crumbling outdoor park or plaza. Vultures sipped from the brackish waters of a charred marble fountain. A decapitated bronze statue lay on its side. Turpin looked around frantically for someplace to hide.

"Psst!" a hushed voice called out to him. "Over here!"

Huh? Turning toward the voice, Turpin spotted a lone figure lurking in the entrance of the Bismark Avenue subway station. A towering white Afro was perched atop the man's head, and a clerical collar bobbed beneath his fleshy chin. A priestly cassock seemed out of place in this hellish milieu. Exuberant brown eyes shone brightly behind a pair of eyeglasses. He beckoned urgently to Turpin. "This way, my friend!"

The spotlight was closing on the detective fast. *Any port in a storm,* he figured as he hastily accepted the stranger's invitation. He darted beneath the eaves of the doorway only seconds before the chopper passed by overhead. Turpin let out a sigh of relief before taking a closer look at his rescuer.

"Wait a second." Turpin placed the minister at last. "I seen you on TV." At that sleazy dive in NYC, among other places. "Good. Reverend Godfrey Good, right?"

The flamboyant preacher looked pleased to be recognized. "Gotta love TV." A broad grin spread across his well-fed face. "Oh, great one! Hallelujah! I knew I'd find you here!"

The man's effusive greeting baffled Turpin. *Great one?* Had Good mistaken him for someone else, or was he simply out of his mind? "Just who do you think I am, Reverend?"

Good smiled slyly. "All will be revealed," he promised, before holding a finger to his lips. "But let us not tarry here any longer lest the unbelievers chance upon us."

Turpin heard the copter make a second pass above them. *Probably not a bad idea,* he conceded. He let the preacher lead him down into subway tunnels below the city. Phosphorescent greenish gray moss, growing profusely upon the tiled walls and concrete supports, gave them just enough light to navigate by, once his eyes adjusted to the gloom. Walking along the abandoned subway tracks was unnerving, but he guessed that it had been at least a few years since any trains had come speeding through these tunnels. The once-lethal third rail was long dead.

He avoided stepping on it anyway.

Their footsteps echoed hollowly in the concrete catacombs. The stuffy air smelled of rot and mildew. Rats—or what he hoped were merely rats—scurried away at their approach. Blind, deformed lizards splashed in the puddles between the rails. Turpin stepped carefully to avoid sinking an unwary foot into one of the stagnant pools. Gnawed human bones had been flushed down into the tunnels along with the rest of the trash. Insects scuttled through the empty eye sockets of a skull. A loose jawbone crunched beneath the soles of his shoe.

Looks like the end of the world came early around here.

Reverend Good seemed to know where he was going. After a short, uncomfortable trek through the subway system, they reached the entrance of a cavernous subterranean bunker deep beneath the city streets. Rusty pipes and cables ran along the ceiling like swollen veins. Humming turbines generated enough electricity to power arrays of harsh halogen lights. Faded block letters identified the location as "Command-D."

Some sort of top secret military installation?

Dead soldiers and scientists were strewn about the facility, beside the corpse of an unlucky Atomic Knight and his canine steed. Rats and other scavengers had picked the bodies down to bony scaffolding. Yellow hazmat suits were torn to shreds. Bullet holes riddled the puke green concrete walls.

Discarded shell casings testified to the ferocity of the fighting that had gone on here, apparently not too long ago. From the looks of things, Command-D was no longer in the hands of the U.S government.

So who *was* running the show now?

Good gestured proudly at the carnage. "See how selflessly we have prepared this pit of human suffering and sickness as a cradle for your rebirth." He chuckled gleefully as he stepped casually over the bodies of the dead. "We've already won. And they don't even know!"

"What the hell are you talking about?" Turpin barked, gazing in horror at the aftermath of a massacre. The deranged preacher wasn't making any sense. "This was about kids. Missing kids." He balled up his fists. "You want the same treatment I gave the Mad Hatter?"

"But you already met the children," Good insisted, "back in New York." He jogged Turpin's faulty memory. "Blank, mindless eyes? Sharp little teeth?"

Ghastly images flashed across the ex-cop's feverish mind, like snapshots from a half-forgotten nightmare: *Malformed children shuffling out from behind a velvet curtain. Pallid, pasty faces. Drooling lips. Dead eyes.*

Had that really happened?

Turpin clutched his head. Trembling fingers kneaded his throbbing skull. "What are you talking about? What *is* this place?" He reeled backward, unable to process what was happening to him. "The air out there, it must be screwing with my head. . . ." A tinge of hysteria entered his voice. Spittle sprayed from his lips. "What the hell's going on here?"

"We, sir, are the gods of Apokolips," Good answered calmly, "manifesting in all our bleak glory to bring about the final crisis of Man." He took hold of Turpin's arm and guided him farther into the bunker. "Come in, come in. All is begun." He sounded eager to show the detective what lay beyond the entrance. "They've even grown a new body for your son Kalibak the Cruel."

Turpin vaguely remembered fighting an alien monster named Kalibak years ago in Metropolis, but what did that have to do with all this craziness? He felt something warm and wet trickling from his ears and raised a hand to his left earlobe. His fingers came away red and sticky. His brains felt like they were leaking out his ears. "My *son* . . . ?"

Good tugged on his arm, drawing him forward into a squalid underground cell block. Dozens of children and teenagers were caged behind sturdy iron bars. Many of them reminded him of the ghoulish faces from his fragmentary flashbacks. Zombie eyes gazed mindlessly at him from pallid, sagging faces. Idiotic grins greeted the men's approach. Other prisoners reacted more normally; they sobbed and whimpered within their cells, distraught and frightened. Desperate boys and girls rattled the bars of their cages.

"Mister!" A teenage boy with long blond hair, wearing nothing but a pair of ragged denim cut-offs, reached frantically through the iron bars. His blue eyes were wide with fear. "Mister, they're making slaves out of us!"

Reverend Good confirmed the accusation. "They are destined to become subhuman degenerates, living, breeding joylessly, and dying in agony to serve the eternal, all-consuming Fire Pits." The ghastly prospect overjoyed him. "Hallelujah!"

"Oh God . . ." Turpin couldn't believe his eyes. His whole world seemed to have gone insane. He drew his Colt pistol from beneath his trench coat, but lacked the strength to use it against Good. His bleeding ears proved there was something seriously wrong with him. The fever raging inside his head sapped his ability to resist; suddenly it was all he could do to keep standing, let alone fight back against the callous preacher. His cracked, granite features were frozen in a mask of abject horror. "You can't get away with this. . . ."

"It's wrong to pity the weak," Good chided him. He guided his disoriented charge past the cell block through a pair of swinging double doors into a larger chamber that appeared to be some sort of huge laboratory/operating room. Sprawling metal catwalks looked down on the ugly industrial workshop. Freakish medical monstrosities floated in liquid-filled tubes mounted to lead-lined walls. Freshly spilled blood and viscera puddled on the floor around an unsanitary-looking steel operating table. A smell like a butcher shop assaulted Turpin's senses, but Good acted perfectly at home in this high-tech charnel house. He called out to a pair of figures huddled around the operating table. "Mister Simyan and Mister Mokkari will back me up on that. Won't you, boys?"

The two men looked up from their labors. "Great one!" one of the surgeons hailed Turpin. The man's gaunt, sallow face was smeared with greasy makeup, giving him the look of a deranged transvestite. Blurry black swirls resembled badly done tattoos or war paint. His green surgeon's smock was stained with red, his rubber boots splashing through spreading pools of gore. His head was shaved smooth. He held up a viciously long hypodermic needle.

His brutish companion was even more outré. Thick black hair was swept back to expose the sloping brow and prognathous jaws of a missing link. Bristling muttonchops carpeted the sides of his face, and a monocle magnified a sullen, bestial eye. His yellow teeth were filed into points. Clad in olive green scrubs like his collaborator, he snipped at his patient with a pair of serrated surgical scissors. *That has to be Simyan*, Turpin realized. The ape-man's name fit him like a bloody glove.

"Rejoice!" Mokkari crowed. "The Evil Factory is open for business!"

He stepped away from the operating table to reveal a scene straight out of *The Island of Doctor Moreau*. A hybrid monstrosity, with the brawny body of a muscleman and the head of a tiger, was strapped to the table. Fresh sutures revealed where the grafts had taken place. An oxygen mask was affixed over the Tiger-Man's snout. Its yellow eyes rolled in their sockets, and a low growl rumbled from behind the mask. Claws suddenly sprouted from his hands and feet.

"No," Turpin muttered in disbelief. What had begun as a routine missing-persons case was getting more nightmarish by the moment. His stomach turned. "This ain't right. . . ."

He spotted a third figure standing in the shadows beneath the catwalk: a blue-skinned alien woman wearing a skimpy suit of green metallic armor. A smooth blue mask was affixed to her face, and a lambent emerald glow radiated from her chest. She looked like a Green Lantern, but Turpin sensed that she was not here to rescue anyone. Instead she stepped forward to stroke the Tiger-Man's head. It purred beneath her touch.

Reverend Good chuckled in approval. "Where the New Gods fell, what chance have Earth's primitive strongmen against all the armies of Apokolips?" He steered Turpin around a large sparking generator. "See, we've started rounding them up already!"

To his dismay, Turpin saw Batman himself trapped inside some kind of futuristic iron maiden. A burnished steel clamp covered the Dark Knight's lower body, and his outstretched arms were encased within the parted halves of the gleaming metal sarcophagus, so that only his head and upper torso were fully visible. A globular helmet was suspended above his cowled head. Syringes loaded with bubbling green chemicals were embedded in the helmet, with the needles pointed inward toward Batman's skull. Plastic tubing connected the syringes with a cylindrical steel vat behind the iron maiden. The Dark Knight slumped helplessly inside the diabolical torture device.

"Oh God, oh Jesus." Turpin staggered backward in shock. If Good and his cohorts could do this to Batman, what hope did the rest of them have? His growing despair fed the fever consuming his mind. He could practically hear an alien voice laughing mirthlessly inside his skull. Boss Dark Side's leering visage surfaced briefly from his memory. The awful truth could no longer be denied. "There's someone in my head. . . ."

Someone—or something—incalculably evil.

His hushed murmur roused Batman, who turned toward Turpin. "They're coming to get us all!" he shouted as he strained futilely against his bonds. "Warn the Justice League!"

The helmet—with its multiple needles—descended onto Batman's head. The syringes pumped their foul contents into the Dark Knight's brain. His body spasmed as he foamed at the mouth.

"Warn everyone!"

CHAPTER 11

METROPOLIS.

"This is great stuff, Kent," Perry White enthused, doling out a rare word of praise. The irascible editor in chief of the *Daily Planet* waved a sheet of freshly printed copy in the air. His shirtsleeves were rolled up to his elbows, and an unlit stogie was clenched between his teeth. "The Martian Manhunter obit almost had me weeping until I reminded myself that an editor's heart is cold as ice."

Clark was barely listening. Distracted, he stared out the window at the city below. Sunset painted the streets and skyscrapers red. Batman had been missing for hours now, and he was still no closer to finding out what happened to him. He had scoured nearly the entire planet with his telescopic vision without any luck. *Where are you, Bruce?*

"What's the matter?" Perry asked, noticing the usually mild-mannered reporter's troubled expression. "Feeling the chill right through my shirt?"

Clark's shudder was no act. "Like someone walked over my grave, Mr. White."

He compulsively scanned the city as he strolled out of Perry's office into the *Planet*'s busy bullpen. Rows of cubicles stretched between him and the elevator banks. Framed front-page headlines, mounted on the walls, commemorated the newspaper's illustrious history. His fellow reporters tapped away at their computers while working the phones. Deadlines kept everyone moving briskly.

The familiar hubbub did little to ease Clark's mind. *Orion, J'onn J'onzz, John Stewart, Batman . . . We're being picked off one by one, and we still don't even know who we're fighting yet.* Neither Superman nor Clark Kent had been able to get to the bottom of this mystery. *Why do I feel that the worst is yet to come?*

He wondered if Lois might have any fresh leads. His wife was leaning against Jimmy Olsen's cubicle holding up a CD. "This is everything on the missing kids story," she announced, handing the disk over to Jimmy. A pink blouse and pencil skirt flattered her attractive figure. "If you could get this downstairs to press for me, I'd be really grateful."

"Sure thing, Ms. Lane." Jimmy rummaged beneath his desk for a moment before taking the CD. He dashed for the elevators.

Clark's brow furrowed. He peered over the tops of his horn-rimmed glasses. "Jimmy?" Still preoccupied with Batman's worrisome disappearance, it took Clark a second to realize that something wasn't quite right here. "Wait a minute. . . ."

Hadn't he just seen Jimmy downstairs on the sidewalk outside the building?

The elevator doors closed on "Jimmy." Clark's X-ray vision saw through the doors to reveal the freckle-faced cub reporter dissolving into a heap of animated sludge. An evil grin stretched across a gloppy, half-formed visage.

Clayface!

The metamorphic felon was one of Batman's oldest foes. What was he doing in Metropolis—and poking around under Jimmy Olsen's desk?

A huge explosion took out the top floors of the Daily Planet Building. The ferocious blast blew out the windows, raining broken shards of glass onto the streets of Metropolis. Smoke and ash billowed up into the sky. A searing fireball shattered Clark's glasses and burned away his civilian attire, revealing his bright blue and red Superman costume underneath. He realized too late that Clayface had planted a bomb right beneath his very nose.

"Lois!" Superman shouted. *"Lois!"*

The newsroom had been reduced to rubble. Burning sheets of paper wafted through the choking haze. His super-vision penetrated the thick black smoke. To his horror, he saw Lois's hand stretching upward from a pile of debris. Blood trickled down her wrist, and her wedding ring was covered with soot. He could barely hear her heartbeat.

"No!"

Two generations of Flashes raced through the streets of Keystone City, leaving a pair of scarlet blurs behind them. The wind generated by their passage whipped up copious amounts of litter. This wasn't exactly the most salubrious part of town.

". . . so he asks me to read through the entire Internet," Wally West griped as he ran at over a hundred miles an hour, "looking for any 'unusual' activity around the time J'onn was murdered." A yellow lightning bolt was emblazoned on the chest of his skintight scarlet uniform, and a pair of streamlined golden wings ornamented the sides of his cowl. Thick-soled yellow boots pounded the pavement dozens of time per second. "Thank you, Batman!" he said sarcastically. "And thanks for tagging along, Jay."

Jay Garrick, the original Flash, had no trouble keeping up with his younger successor. His old-school uniform consisted of a winged silver helmet, a crimson shirt bearing the traditional Flash lightning insignia, blue trousers, and red pirate boots. Graying temples and timeworn features gave away how long he'd been in the super-hero game.

An abandoned strip club loomed before them. *Live Girls!* read the dilapidated marquee, above curvaceous neon silhouettes. *Nude! Wild! Nude!*

"Why here?" Jay asked. The run-down building tugged at his memory. "You know, this is where Barry and I met all those years ago."

Barry Allen, Wally's uncle, had been the Flash between Jay and Wally. He had perished heroically during the so-called Crisis on Infinite Earths. Jay still missed him. He knew Wally did too.

"At a nudie bar?" Wally raised an eyebrow. "Nobody told me *that* when I was Kid Flash!"

Wally had started out as a teen sidekick before taking over as the Flash after Barry's death.

"It used to be the Keystone City Community Center," Jay explained. Vibrating their molecules, they phased through the locked door of the dingy lap dance venue before skidding to a halt in a back room at the rear of the club. Half-empty drinking glasses and overflowing ashtrays suggested that the room had recently hosted a meeting. Jay paused to take in the sordid setting. Girlie pictures, of the sort that had been confined strictly to French postcards in his day, were pinned to a cork bulletin board. Cobwebs gathered in the corners of the ceiling. Dried green blotches stained the carpet. The musty air smelled of tobacco and . . . a gorilla? "Good old Barry. At least he never lived to see it all go to hell." He shook his head at the times, which seemed so much darker and more oppressive than his own heyday. "And now poor J'onn J'onzz . . ."

Wally circled a conference table. Cigarette burns scarred its surface. "A tracking station recorded a seismic pulse around the time we think J'onn's heart exploded." He gestured at the room around them. "The epicenter was here."

A sudden vibration shook the premises. "What's that?" Jay asked. "A subway?"

Wally shook his head. "I just turned the whole place out while you were blinking." He lifted a leather-bound tome from the table. "Traces of Martian blood and this phony 'Crime Bible' thing."

Jay was impressed by Wally's speed. He hadn't even seen him move. *He's faster than I ever was.*

"Oh yeah, and *that*." Wally pointed at the bizarre blue throne at the head of the table. The ornate chair, which resembled something from an old *Flash Gordon* serial, seemed out of place in the grimy back room. "Plastic and wire pretty much, but it looks like the Mobius chair the New God Metron used to travel around in."

Metron had been a cosmic explorer, Jay recalled, devoted to the eternal pursuit of knowledge. He was supposed to be one of the *good* New Gods. Jay found the whole notion faintly sacrilegious. His skin crawled as he glanced around the disreputable meeting place. *This place gives me the creeps.*

Wally scratched his chin as he contemplated the chair. "Okay, I think we may be onto something. . . ."

"What's on your mind?" Jay asked.

"Well, Batman came up with a pretty wild idea, which I'm kind of running with." He put down the Crime Bible. "We're talking god-weapons, right? Imagine a bullet fired backward through time."

"Do I have to?" Jay missed the days when the Fiddler robbing a bank was the worst he had to deal with. "Wally, I *hate* anything having to do with time-travel in all its forms."

He reached out to examine the chair, only to be repelled by a violent burst of energy. He stumbled backward and would have landed on his rear had not Wally grabbed onto him at super-speed. The two Flashes stared in alarm as the "Mobius chair" emitted a blinding glow from the circular halo atop its back.

Wally nodded, as though this was all making sense to him. "What if this is where the god-bullet breaks into time?" He spoke rapidly as the ideas came racing out of him. "The shell travels back through time, kills Orion, and passes through him into the past where it finally buries itself in the concrete fifty years ago." He squinted at the incandescent throne. "And that thing there is the scope of a higher-dimensional gun."

"You sure about that?" Jay asked. "'Cause it's pointing straight at us, son."

A loud thrumming noise rattled the club. Glasses bounced atop the table-top. A pinup calendar fell off the bulletin board. Coruscating beams of blue white light issued from the halo . . . or scope if Wally was right about the device. Tendrils of electricity sparked around the chair.

"My God!" Wally exclaimed, edging away from the line of fire. He shielded his eyes with his arm. "That *noise!*"

The floor trembled beneath their feet, and an ordinary chair toppled over. "It's like the end of the world!" Jay blurted. Regaining his balance, he stepped to one side. Despite the alarming phenomena, however, he noticed something oddly familiar about the tremors shaking the room. "Those vibrations, Wally! Don't you recognize those vibrations?"

It can't be, he thought, peering into the glare. *Not after all these years . . .*

"Wally! Jay!" A voice Jay had never expected to hear again called out urgently from the dazzling effulgence before them. Barry Allen, perhaps the greatest Flash of all, came racing out of the light, pursuing a glowing trans-lucent bullet. His crimson costume was almost identical to the one Wally had adopted in his honor. His outstretched fingers reached desperately for the whizzing bullet. "Run!"

So startled was Jay to see his deceased comrade in the flesh that it took him a split second to realize that Barry was not alone. Just as the Flash chased after the time-traveling bullet, he was simultaneously being pursued by an ominous figure in gleaming ebony armor. The black knight swooped after Barry on a pair of sleek midnight skis. Curved silver blades tipped both ends of his ebony ski poles. The frantic look on Barry's face made it clear that he was racing nothing less than Death itself.

"Run!" the Flash cried out again. *"Run!"*

CHAPTER 12

NEW YORK CITY.

The Dark Side Club was no longer open for business. Metal shutters covered the windows. No light peeked out from behind the closed front door. The omega symbol inscribed on the door foretold the End of All Things—or so the Frankenstein Monster feared.

The monster, who had long ago adopted his creator's name as his own, led a team of S.H.A.D.E. operatives on a midnight raid of the brownstone. Over seven feet tall, he towered above his mortal lieutenants, who also worked for the Super Human Advanced Defense Executive, a covert agency that protected mankind from paranormal threats. The agency had drafted Frankenstein into its service not long after his most recent resurrection.

Crude sutures revealed where his patchwork body had been stitched together. His pallid green flesh smelled like a rotting corpse. Tarnished copper electrodes jutted from his temples. He wore a dark wool peacoat over a faded nineteenth-century cavalry officer's uniform. A broadsword was strapped across his back, and an antique steam-pistol was clutched in his grip.

His backup sported more contemporary arms and attire. S.H.A.D.E. was printed in white block letters upon their SWAT gear. Automatic rifles covered the monster as he approached the club's unlit entrance. Contrary to his depictions in the media, he moved with surprising speed and agility. His mother, the lightning, flashed above the Bowery.

A heavy leather boot kicked the front door open. He barged into the club, followed by a team of gun-toting agents in helmets and body armor. The club appeared to be deserted, but his mismatched ears heard light footsteps upstairs. He raced up a spiral staircase to a private lounge on the top floor. "Freeze!" he barked as he threw open the door. Embalmed vocal cords rendered his voice hoarse and scratchy. As always, it hurt to speak.

Flashlights mounted to the rifles of the SWAT team behind him lit up the plush chamber, exposing a shriveled corpse propped up on a leather couch. The body, which was in an advanced stage of desiccation, belonged to an elderly man wearing tinted glasses and an expensive suit. A polished mahogany cane rested in the crook of his arm. A silver tie-pin was fashioned in the shape of an omega.

Boss Dark Side? Frankenstein regarded the wizened cadaver quizzically. The reputed crime lord was supposed to be a much younger man. . . .

A faceless woman stepped out from behind a velvet curtain. An implant in his skull, which gave him instant access to the S.H.A.D.E. database, identified her as Renee Montoya, the Question. A trench coat and fedora signified her status as a private investigator.

"That's right," she said, unconcerned by the multiple guns targeting her. "Ask the question. What kind of gangland killing leaves a man mummified?"

"He said 'freeze!'" Agent Clerval reminded her. The SWAT team spread out to block the exits.

A burst of thick white smoke filled the lounge, fogging the beams of the flashlights. The Question leapt into the midst of agents, lashing out at them with her fists, elbows, knees, and feet. An almost balletic display of martial artistry sent her stunned assailants sprawling. Agent Clerval smashed onto a felt-covered coffee table in front of the couch. A stray shot took out an overhead lamp. Sparks and glass rained down from the ceiling. Swirling fumes added to the confusion.

Frankenstein did nothing to obstruct the Question's escape. He was more concerned with the unnatural state of Dark Side's body. He was in no need of replacement parts at the moment, but even if he had been, he would have eschewed any donations from this particular corpse. The crime boss's body appeared to have rotted away from the inside. Bending over the withered remains, the monster sensed the lingering remnants of a profound evil. Not since he had defended reality from the ravenous hordes of the Sheeda had he felt such an abomination bearing down upon mankind.

This contagion is not of this Earth.

The Question paused in the doorway on her way out. "Ask yourself this," she advised the monster. "What happened to Danny Turpin?"

Then she was gone. The fading smoke resolved into the shape of a question mark. Cursing agents scrambled to their feet, massaging their ringing skulls.

"Leave it," a bodiless voice commanded via their earpieces. Frankenstein recognized the smooth cadences of Father Time, the immortal head of S.H.A.D.E. "We'll pick up Montoya on the street." Time spoke directly to the monster via the implant in his skull. "Frankenstein, report."

The monster turned away from the body. Sunken red eyes surveyed the lounge. "Sir, over here!" Agent Moritz called out. She pointed at an abstract black-and-white mural on the far wall. A glowing silver handprint moved across the wall, searing an ominous message into the artwork. The floating cursor resembled the pointing-hand graphic employed on modern computer screens, except that it was the size of an actual human hand. The scorched letters flared up brightly as the moving finger etched them into the wall, then faded away as the hand moved on. *Shades of Omar Khayyam*, the literate monster thought.

"I have no idea what we're looking at," Moritz admitted. She lowered her weapon and took off her helmet. Awe shone on her painfully human features. The light from the burning letters played across her face. Her fellow agents gazed at the eerie spectacle as though in the presence of something divine. "We getting this on camera?"

Agent Lavenza scanned the wall with a handheld sensor. "Emissions are off the dial," he said in a hushed voice. Tears leaked from his eyes.

"Father Time," Frankenstein croaked. "Can you see?" He leaned forward to read the warning manifesting before their eyes. "The letters disappear once written, as in a book a ghost were author of." Although born of science, the monster knew a miracle when he saw one. "A prophecy."

The message spelled out by the digital hand was not a comforting one: KNOW EVIL.

WASHINGTON, D.C.

"Hold that thought, Frankenstein." Father Time twirled a pocket watch as he faced an array of glowing monitors in S.H.A.D.E.'s secret headquarters in the nation's capital. Reborn every New Year's, he currently took the form of a dapper young black man wearing a pin-striped suit, bowler hat, spats, and domino mask. He turned his attention from the transmitted images of the Dark Side Club to a different screen bearing the image of a stern-faced Middle Eastern man with a neatly trimmed mustache and goatee. "Excuse me, Taleb. My New York team just found the Ark of the Covenant or some damn thing downtown."

"I'll order a crate," Colonel Taleb beni Khalid replied dryly. As the Black King of Checkmate, the United Nations' top intelligence agency, he was the closest thing Father Time had to a peer. A chessboard motif framed Khalid's lean visage. "Pay attention, Time. The situation in Blüdhaven is slipping through our fingers. Some local warlord has set himself up in an experimental weapons bunker. He's killing anyone who gets too close to Command-D." The Israeli-Arab spymaster shook his head dourly. "American citizens don't need to know that anarchy has erupted inside their country's borders, do they?"

Time was inclined to agree. Blüdhaven had been a problem ever since the Secret Society of Super-Villains had dropped a humanoid chemical weapon on it two years ago.

"I need your most expendable agents," Khalid stated. His dark eyes glittered. "And we need to talk . . . after you've explained to Ms. Montoya her role in the future of global law enforcement."

NEW YORK CITY.

The Question walked briskly away from the Dark Side Club, heading downtown toward the East Village. A puff of chemical smoke dissolved the glue beneath her mask. She peeled away the blank Pseudoderm to expose the face of Renee Montoya, late of the Gotham City Police Department. She thrust the wadded-up mask into her coat pocket, then shucked her hat to further alter her appearance. Chances were, Frankenstein and his goons were too busy investigating Boss Dark Side's bizarre demise to chase after her, but she didn't intend to make it easy for them if they did.

The fact that she had just met Dr. Frankenstein's infamous monster barely fazed her. After working homicide in Gotham, then chasing the Crime Bible all over the world as the Question, it took more than that to rattle her. She'd rather face Frankenstein than the Joker any day. . . .

The lights of lower Manhattan stretched out before her. Even though New York was famed as the City That Never Sleeps, she had the nocturnal sidewalks pretty much to herself. Streetlamps cast her shadow on the frosty pavement. She looked forward to crashing at her favorite B&B in the Village. After that workout with the S.H.A.D.E. agents, she was too tired to even think of hitting any of the local gay bars.

Was Meow Mix even open at this time of night?

An unexpected flash of lightning drew her gaze upward. Her dark brown eyes widened at the sight of a fireball falling from the sky like a comet. For an instant, she flashed back to the rain of meteors that had pummeled Gotham during the last Crisis. She had lost her partner, Crispus Allen, that night. . . .

The blazing missile crashed through the top floors of a multistory office building that Renee prayed was unoccupied at this late hour. Glass and masonry exploded from the northern face of the tower as the comet arced toward the streets below. It hit the ground with an earthshaking impact that Renee felt from over a block away. A cloud of dust and smoke rose from ground zero.

Oh my God! Renee's cop instincts kicked in as she ran toward the scene. Despite the hour, she found a crowd of horrified onlookers gathered around the impact site. She shoved her way through the bystanders to reach the edge of a smoking crater in the middle of Fifth Avenue. To her amazement, she found a young blonde woman lying at the bottom of the crater. A charred black cape was draped over her battered figure, and her scorched red skin was scraped and bleeding. A pitiful moan revealed that the girl, who looked to be about sixteen years old, was still alive—despite falling hundreds, if not thousands, of feet.

Renee immediately took charge. "Don't just stand there!" she barked at the spectators. "Somebody call an ambulance!"

She scrambled down the sides of the crater to reach the girl's side. Lying in a fetal position amidst the rubble, the blonde stirred feebly. Soot and scars obscured her identity, making it hard for Renee to figure out who she was.

Supergirl? Power Girl?

"*Ich . . . ich . . .*" the blonde murmured weakly . . . in German? "*Ich bin . . . Uberfraulein?*"

Renee didn't get it. Why would Supergirl be speaking German?

"Sssh!" she comforted the girl, whoever she was. "It's okay. Help's on the way." To her relief, she heard sirens heading toward them. Renee guessed that half the emergency vehicles in town were on their way. Uberfraulein's crash landing had been hard to miss.

"*Nein!*" Renee's soothing words failed to calm the injured girl, who tried unsuccessfully to get to her feet. She rolled onto her back and Renee gasped in surprise. Instead of the expected S-shield, a swastika was emblazoned on the girl's chest.

She's a Nazi?

Aryan blue eyes stared up at the sky in fear. Her youthful face was scratched and torn. "*Ist der . . . der Himmel blutungen . . . die Holle . . . ist hier. . . .*"

"What's she saying?" a bystander called out to Renee.

Heaven is bleeding, she translated silently. *Hell is here.*

Renee stood up, unsure what to make of all this. A heavy hand landed on her shoulder as the muzzle of a gun pressed against the nape of her neck.

"Renee Montoya?" The gruff voice sounded like it belonged to one of the S.H.A.D.E. agents she had trashed earlier. "Almost didn't recognize you with your face on." Armed troopers closed in on her from both sides. Laser-sights placed multiple red targeting dots over her heart. "You're coming with us."

She didn't see that she had much choice.

CHAPTER 13

METROPOLIS.

Nick's boss was not happy.

"This is very easy to explain," Mr. Podrasky said from behind his desk at Belly Burger. His orange polyester shirt matched Nick's, except for the Manager button pinned to his chest. He glowered at the young cashier. "You're scaring the crap out of people."

I didn't mean to, Nick thought. "But . . ."

"But nothing!" Podrasky threw up his hands. "Our customers expect burgers with fries. Bizarre, unsettling questions? No."

Nick tried to defend himself. "I just wondered if anyone else felt the graviton impacts increasing?"

"Gravitons?" Podrasky pinched his nose, as though he felt a migraine coming on. "Even the stupid word is annoying." He pointed toward the door of his office. "You know what you are? You are no longer employed at this outfit!"

Nick knew he should be upset about losing his job, but he found it hard to care. Instead he was tempted to ask the older man what he thought of the bizarre cave paintings Cave Carson and his team of daredevil spelunkers had recently uncovered in the New York City subway extension, the ones that matched the crop circles that had been appearing mysteriously all over England the last few days. Somehow, though, he suspected that Mr. Podrasky cared about as much about that strange recurring pattern as he did about gravitons. . . .

The teenager left his Belly Burger cap behind as he exited the fast-food restaurant for good.

KEYSTONE CITY.

They ran. By God, they ran.

Three generations of the Flash raced after the luminous time-bullet while being pursued by the skiing Black Racer. Jay Garrick struggled to keep up with his younger counterparts, while Barry Allen, newly restored to life, was out in front. Barry reached frantically for the zooming bullet as though hoping to avert its fatal course.

If anyone can do it, Jay thought, *Barry can.*

Wally was right behind Barry. The Speed Force crackled around them. Jay was caught up in the other Flashes' slipstream as they ran backward through the time, so many thousands of times faster than the speed of sound that it was impossible to talk to each other; their words simply couldn't catch up.

Leaving Keystone behind, they reached Metropolis in a heartbeat. Orion appeared before them, looking as though he had just fought the battle of his life. At this point in the past, the alien war-god was still alive, if only for an instant more. Barry made one last grab at the lethal bullet, but even he was too late. Eldritch poisons churned inside the projectile's core. It exploded inside Orion before traveling farther into the past.

Orion's helmet was blown off his head. A concentric pulse radiated from his body, rippling the very fabric of space and time. He crashed into a wooden crate along the waterfront, and Jay cursed in frustration. Orion had been assassinated right before their eyes, despite Barry's desperate attempt to change history.

They couldn't slow down, though. Glancing back over his shoulder, Jay saw the Black Racer right behind them. The ebony embodiment of Death hovered briefly in the air above the murdered god before taking off after the three Flashes again. His bladed ski poles jabbed at the empty air beneath him. His visored helmet concealed his face. Was he after all of them, Jay wondered, or just Barry for escaping death before?

There was no way to know and little margin for error. Out of the corner of his eye, Jay briefly glimpsed a balding, middle-aged bruiser in a trench coat stumbling onto Orion's body before they left the crime scene behind, heading back toward the present. The brutal velocity began to take its toll on the older hero. A stitch stabbed at his side. He was breathing hard. The sun and stars arced across the sky as the Flashes raced the Black Racer across time. Jay wasn't sure he was going to make it. He felt himself falling behind.

The black skis passed above him.

KEYSTONE CITY.

"I ran out of steam on the return curve," he explained later. "Only just made tonight before my knee gave out." He clutched a steaming cup of hot coffee. Joan Garrick, his wife, sat beside him on the couch. "I felt that . . . thing zipping right overhead in an ice-cold rush, going too fast to stop for me, while the others accelerated, red-shifting beyond the speed of light, and the last thing I saw . . ." He smiled at the memory of Barry and Wally pulling ahead of the Black Racer as they disappeared into tomorrow. "It's a little-known fact that Death can't travel faster than the speed of light."

An extended family of Flash wives and children were gathered around him, hanging on his every word. Linda Park, Wally's beautiful young wife, had her arms around her two young children, Jai and Iris. Time paradoxes and hypercharged metabolisms complicated their ages, but the girl appeared ten years old, the boy around eight. Iris Allen, Barry's widow, sat on the other side of Jay, fighting tears. Her trembling hands were clasped together as though in prayer. She was still wearing her wedding ring, even after all these years.

"They said he was dead," she whispered, shaken to the core by Jay's story. Her eyes were moist and her voice caught in her throat. "All this time, and

I knew, knew it wasn't for good. He'd *never* been outsmarted before, not my Barry."

She looked urgently at Jay. "And it's not Barry from the past or a parallel Earth, is it? Not this time."

Joan smiled warmly at the other woman. The wives of the Flashes shared a special bond, like the spouses of the early NASA astronauts. They had always been there for each other. "Tell her, Jay."

"It *was* Barry Allen," Jay stated confidently. He draped an arm around Iris, almost as overcome with emotion as she was. His own throat tightened. "I'd know that aura anywhere. On my soul, Iris, I saw your husband alive."

FLORIDA.

The Hall of Doom was hidden away in the swampy depths of the Everglades. Lurking alligators guarded the dome-shaped headquarters of the Secret Society. Its camouflaged green exterior was capable of sinking beneath the murky depths of the lagoon to avoid detection. A pair of oval windows with half-drawn metal shutters resembled the hooded eyes of some vast reptilian predator rising from below. Mosquitoes buzzed above the turbid waters. Snails oozed up the sides of mossy cypresses.

"This is for me?"

Inside the headquarters, Mike Miller, aka the Human Flame, looked over the upgraded new armor Libra had just bestowed upon him. A chrome-plated Kevlar breastplate fit over a suit of gray steel mesh. A metal gorget and matching pauldrons armored the throat and shoulders. A black leather belt held pouches for arms and ammo. Similar suits hung on racks in the Society's locker room. There was enough armor to equip a whole gang.

"Boss, you're way too generous," Mike protested. "In fact, it's starting to come over kinda gay, if you don't mind me saying." Worried that he might have said too much, he hastily made amends. "I mean, it ain't that I'm ungrateful." A flamethrower rested at his feet. His goggles hung around his neck. "Nobody ever did nothin' for Mike Miller before. . . ."

"Mike, Mike." Libra sounded more amused than offended by the other man's discomfort. "A new hideout. A new uniform. It's all part of your commitment to a higher purpose." He gestured grandly at the burnished steel suit, which was laid out on a metal bench in front of Mike. "Go on. Try it out."

Mike lifted the helmet from the bench. A crimson visor shone like blood against the polished steel faceplate; it kind of reminded him of the killer robots on that old TV show. "Pretty cool, I gotta say, but I'm still sentimental about the old crime suit." Copper nozzles studded the chest-plate of his homemade armor. He raised the helmet above his head. "I can hear a voice. . . . Is there a radio playing in there?" He eyed the intimidating headgear hesitantly. "That might be kinda distracting."

"A voice? What's it saying, Mike?" Libra came up behind him. "Listen close." Without warning, he grabbed the helmet and shoved it down onto Mike's head. He raised his own voice, which turned cold and mocking. "You hear it now, Mike? That's the Anti-Life Equation, you pathetic, ignorant failure!"

"No . . . *nuhhh* . . ." Mike's muffled voice escaped the helmet. "I don't want this . . . !" He clawed at the helmet's sides, but Libra held it in place with both hands until Mike's struggles subsided. His feeble mind quickly succumbed to the helm's insidious message, and his arms dropped stiffly to his sides. "*Ugghh.*"

Lex Luthor decided he'd seen enough. He stepped from the shadows of a nearby doorway, where he had been eavesdropping on the other villains' disturbing encounter. His personal bodyguard, Mercy Graves, accompanied him. The tall blonde woman wore a black chauffeur's uniform and was rumored to be a renegade Amazon from Paradise Island. Luthor trusted her as much as he trusted anyone—which was barely.

"Lex!" Libra acted surprised by the bald mastermind's arrival. "What a time for you to spring up out of nowhere. The Society's not meeting for another three hours. . . ."

Precisely, Luthor thought. He liked to keep his adversaries off balance.

Libra's gloved hands came away from the Human Flame's helmet. "Mike here almost choked to death. But he's fine now." Brandishing his lance, Libra turned to face Luthor. "You finally decided to take my leadership bid seriously, huh?"

"I don't know *who* you are," Luthor admitted, his arms crossed atop the lapels of his Saville Row suit. He had left his high-tech war suit behind to demonstrate that he didn't need the world's most advanced body armor to intimidate this pretender. "But somehow you stopped Superman in his tracks. He hasn't answered a single emergency call for eighteen hours."

Libra chuckled softly, as though at a private joke. Beside him, the Human Flame hoisted the tanks of his flamethrower onto his back. "So, let's just say you owe me."

"No," Luthor insisted. "Let's just say yours is a threat we intend to neutralize." As far as he was concerned, anyone who could take Superman out of commission, even for less than a day, was too dangerous to be allowed free rein.

Unconcerned, Libra draped an arm over the shoulders of his armored acolyte. "You remember Mike, don't you? 'Half-wit' Mike. 'Nonentity' Mike." He threw Luthor's scornful words back at him. "Well, Mike's become part of something *much* bigger than you now."

The Human Flame lurched forward. Fire spurted from the muzzle of his flame-gun. "Judge others," he said robotically. His voice now lacked both doubt and humanity. "Enslave others. Anti-Life justifies my hatred."

Mercy stepped between Luthor and his foes. She dropped into a defensive crouch. But before she could lash out at the Human Flame, a half dozen locker doors banged open to reveal armed soldiers in identical steel armor. Their gleaming helmets matched the one fastened securely over Miller's head. Bloodred visors hid their eyes. Sophisticated energy-rifles targeted Mercy and Luthor, who realized that he had made a rare miscalculation. Libra was obviously prepared to resist any coup attempt. His faceless foot soldiers spread out to surround the rebellious billionaire and his outnumbered bodyguard.

It seems, Luthor mused, *I should have worn my war suit after all.*

"In less than twenty-four hours," Libra bragged, "the ability to make decisions will be forcibly removed from the inhabitants of this planet, Lex, so I would treasure this once-in-a-lifetime offer." He waltzed boldly up to Luthor. "Join us, like Mike, with a Justifier helmet on your empty head. Or renounce science, swear an oath on the Crime Bible, and pledge your service to the Master of All Evil." Declining to name said master, Libra laid a hand on Luthor's shoulder. "The Day of Apokolips is at hand, sir, and I am only its prophet." Zealous blue eyes peered out from behind the sinister evangelist's indigo mask.

"Choose."

CHAPTER 14

METROPOLIS.

The Intensive Care Unit of Metropolis Memorial Hospital struck Clark as even colder and more sterile than his own arctic Fortress. Blinking medical equipment monitored Lois's vital signs. An oxygen mask was fastened over her face. Plaster casts encased her broken arms and legs, and a neck brace supported her head. Almost a day had passed since the explosion at the *Daily Planet* and his wife still hadn't regained consciousness.

"The doctors say it could have been much worse, Mr. Kent." Jimmy Olsen—the *real* Jimmy Olsen—fidgeted uncomfortably a few feet away from Lois's bed. He tugged on his trademark bow tie. "Perry's still on life support, Dirk Armstrong lost a leg, and Adele from Human Resources died." Jimmy looked hopefully at Lois. "At least Superman got the shrapnel out of her heart."

"I know," Clark said. He sat at his wife's bedside, gently grasping her hand. His gaze was fixed on Lois, never looking away. His invulnerability was no match for the guilt stabbing his heart. "But I was *there*, Jimmy. If I'd just suspected what was happening, if only I'd been fast enough!"

Jimmy laid a comforting hand on Clark's shoulder. "Not even Superman could have reached that bomb in time."

The young photographer had no idea how ironic his words were. *Probably just as well*, Clark thought; life was complicated enough right now without Jimmy knowing his true identity.

"You know what?" Jimmy added. "I think you and Ms. Lane should have some time alone." He glanced at the hypersonic signal-watch on his wrist. "Superman hasn't been seen since yesterday. Maybe I'll try to track him down."

Clark wished he could tell Jimmy not to waste his time. "I guess Superman has problems of his own, Jimmy." He didn't look up as his friend headed for the door. "I have to stay with my wife."

Jimmy's footsteps receded down the hallway outside, leaving Clark alone with Lois. He leaned forward in his chair and gently stroked her bandaged head. His heat vision was the only thing keeping her struggling heart beating. He was tempted to whisk her away to the Hall of Justice, despite the risk to his secret identity, but, judging from Batman's mysterious disappearance from the morgue, the Hall's security may have been seriously compromised. Besides, Wonder Woman had already confirmed that Lois's injuries were beyond even the Purple Ray's ability to repair. Everyone had done what they could. Now all he could do was stay by her side for as long as it took.

"I'm sorry you're in so much pain," he whispered softly, tears running down his cheeks. "It's all because of me." He lifted her limp fingers to his lips. Her fragile skin was worryingly cold. "Lois, dear Lois. I'd do anything to take your pain away."

"Anything?"

An unexpected figure spoke from the doorway: a green-skinned youth wearing a long violet coat over a slick purple jumpsuit. Mussed blond hair was pushed away from his high forehead. A metallic gold belt circled his waist. His literally futuristic attire was made of fabrics that wouldn't be invented for centuries.

Superman blinked in surprise. "Brainiac 5?"

The Coluan super-genius was a direct descendent of Superman's alien arch-foe; thankfully, he shared only his ancestor's computerlike intellect, not the original Brainiac's heartless nature. A valued member of the Legion of Super-Heroes, Brainiac 5 helped defend the United Planets of the thirty-first century from all manner of threats and villainy. Which meant that he was presently a thousand years before his time.

"The future needs you, Superman," Brainiac declared, stepping into the hospital room. He shut the door behind him. "The entire space-time continuum needs you." He consulted a chronometer on his wrist. "You need to come with me to the thirty-first century!"

"But . . . Lois," Clark protested. He removed his glasses. "If I don't stay with her, she'll die. My infrared massage is all that's keeping her heart alive."

Brainiac 5 nodded. "I anticipated that response." He extracted a tiny vial from the inner pocket of his jacket. A luminous red fluid glowed within the vial. "This substance is *ultramenstruum*, a rare substance distilled from the very Bleed that separates the fifty-two universes from each other."

"The Bleed?" Clark had heard the term before, but only vaguely understood what it meant. Didn't it have something to do with the red skies?

"As crystals grow in solution," the human computer explained pedantically, "so have exactly fifty-two alternate universes emerged within the Bleed. Only my twelfth-level intellect was capable of extracting a minute portion of *ultramenstruum* for this crucial mission. I believe it is capable of healing your wife, just this once."

Superman assumed Brainiac 5 knew what he was talking about. He usually did, at least where matters of future science were concerned. "Aren't you tampering with history by saving Lois?"

Brainiac 5 snorted. "If you don't come with me, Kal-El, there won't be *any* history, past or future. It's that important." He handed the vial over to Clark. "Hurry. Time is on the verge of fracturing even as we speak."

For the first time in hours, Clark allowed himself a flicker of hope. He accepted the vial from Brainiac 5 and carefully uncapped it. The aroma that reached his nostrils was like nothing he had ever smelled before. More intoxicating than the finest champagne or ice cream, it seemed to hold an infinite number of olfactory possibilities at once; it was the pungent essence of sheer abstract potential. Praying silently, he gently removed the oxygen mask from Lois's bruised face and poured the scarlet elixir down her throat.

The effect was instantaneous. Lois's eyes flickered open and she gasped out loud. Superman heard her shredded heart resume beating, growing stronger by the moment. Lois sat up and looked around. "Clark?"

Clark resisted an urge to jump for joy, all the way to the moon. The elixir had done all Brainiac 5 had promised and more. *Thank you, Brainy!* he thought. *I'll never forget this!*

Lois touched her lips, as though the unearthly taste of the Bleed still lingered there. An anxious look came over her face as she took in her surroundings. "That explosion!" She clutched Clark's arm. "Perry? Jimmy?"

"They're fine," he assured her. He took her in his arms, holding her gently so as not to damage her fragile humanity. There would be time enough later to update her on all the particulars of the disaster. For now, he just wanted to hold her close. "Thank heavens you're okay. I was afraid I'd lost you forever."

She grinned back at him, then kissed him deeply. "No chance of that, Smallville. Not when I still have a story to write." She patted her hospital gown, searching in vain for a pocket. "I don't suppose you have a pen on you?"

Clark knew right then that Lois was her old self again. He quickly found her a pen and pad at super-speed, returning to the hospital room in less than a second. Curtains and old magazines were rustled by a sudden breeze. "I can't wait to read it."

"Ahem." Brainiac 5 cleared his throat impatiently. Clark and Lois turned his way. "I'm sorry to interrupt this touching scene, but we're running out of time. *Time* is running out of time. We need to go. *Now.*"

Lois squinted at their alien visitor. "Clark? What's he doing here?" She recognized Brainiac 5 from Superman's previous encounters with the Legion of Super-Heroes. An elegant eyebrow arched quizzically. "Please tell me I haven't been out of commission for a thousand years!"

"Just the longest day of my life." Clark reluctantly tore himself away from her. "But I'm afraid I have to go. There's some sort of Crisis in time." Tugging open his shirt, he changed from Clark Kent to the Man of Steel. "I have to tell you, Brainy, I'm not comfortable leaving my own era at a time like this. Batman is missing. The *Planet* was bombed. . . ."

"I can return you to this very moment," Brainiac 5 promised. "One of the advantages of time-travel."

Superman trusted Brainiac 5 to keep his word, as he always had before. This was hardly the first time the Legion had called upon Superman. Still, he glanced back at Lois with a worried look on his face. Whoever had instigated the attacks on J'onn J'onzz, John Stewart, and the *Planet* was still out there. "Do me a favor, Lois. Contact my cousin. Have her take you and Jimmy to the Fortress. I'll feel a whole lot better knowing you're all safe while I'm away."

"I'll do that," Lois agreed. Clark knew she had Supergirl on her speed dial. "Don't worry about me." She shooed him out the door with a wave of her hand, trying to be strong yet believing in her husband completely. "Go. Do what you have to do. Just don't keep me waiting."

I never will, he thought. *No matter what.*

"All right, Brainy. Let's go."

The future was waiting.

WASHINGTON, D.C.

"No Lantern escapes the Alpha Lanterns!"

The Alpha Lanterns escorted Hal Jordan through the corridors of the Hall of Justice. Glowing emerald chains, generated by the power batteries embedded in the alien Lanterns' chest, shackled Hal's arms to his sides. Heavy emerald stocks were locked around his throat. A scab covered a small scar on his temple.

"I know you never seem to get tired of saying that, Boodikka," Hal said to a tall female Lantern wearing a winged helmet, "but like I told you, I'll come quietly."

Wonder Woman, Black Lightning, and Alan Scott, Earth's original Green Lantern, looked on as their comrade was forced to endure a "perp walk" before their eyes. Diana refused to let this travesty of justice go unchallenged.

"He didn't do it," she protested. "There's no motive. No conclusive evidence." She appealed to Kraken's sense of fairness. "Are you determined to ignore the possibility of the evil gods' involvement?"

"Evil gods!" Kraken scoffed. "None of you can find any trace of the distinctive cosmic emissions we associate with so-called celestials." Glancing back over her shoulder, she regarded Wonder Woman as she might an annoying gnat. "I answer to the Guardians of the Universe, not you. Jordan's guilt will be established in tribunal on Oa." She raised a hand to forestall any further objections. "Alpha Lanterns are bonded to the great Power Battery, which renders our judgments infallible."

Diana doubted that. As she knew from experience, even the gods and goddesses of Olympus could be fallible at times. Why should these imperious extraterrestrials be any different?

She appealed to Hal. "Tell them! Something's wrong. . . ."

"Diana, I don't know why, but I can't remember where I was when Orion was killed or when John was injured." He shrugged. "I can't argue with these guys. Let me talk to the Guardians. I'll be fine."

Diana admired his faith in the Guardians and the Corps. *I pray it is not misplaced.*

"Don't worry about Earth," he assured her. "Only Green Lanterns in or out now."

That didn't stop John from being attacked, she thought worriedly. *Or Bruce from disappearing.*

She was sorely tempted to liberate Hal by force, but knew that was not what he would want. Hal had devoted his life to the Green Lantern Corps. He deserved a chance to regain his standing among them, even if that meant facing judgment on distant Oa.

Against her instincts, she let the Alpha Lanterns depart with Hal in a brilliant flash of green light. Her fellow heroes looked no more pleased by this appalling turn of events than she was.

"Ridiculous," Black Lightning declared. A former Olympic athlete and U.S. Secretary of Education, Jefferson Pierce was a tall black man of noble countenance. His head was shaved smooth, and a blue domino mask was affixed to his features. The jagged lightning bolts adorning his dark black and blue uniform symbolized the supercharged electrical abilities at his command. Among other things, he could hurl thunderbolts like Zeus himself.

"I tried to make them see reason," Alan Scott said, "but I'm a Green Lantern in name only." Unlike the far-flung members of the Corps, the older hero's powers were mystical in origin; he drew his enchanted green flame from a magical meteorite that had been fashioned into a lamp by ancient Chinese artisans. His distinctive raiment bespoke his independence from the Corps. Instead of a variation on the usual Green Lantern uniform, he wore a voluminous purple cloak over a red tunic and green trousers. A high purple collar framed his face, and a brown leather belt girded his waist. A purple domino mask protected his identity. Although he had been fighting for justice for over forty years as a member of the Justice Society of America, eldritch energies had kept him surprisingly fit for a man of his years. His blond hair held no trace of gray or silver. Only his weathered mien and worldly air testified to his age and experience. He glanced over at Diana. "You're still convinced Darkseid is involved?"

Darkseid was the dreadful ruler of Apokolips, home of the evil New Gods. He was said to have perished not so long ago, but Diana was skeptical. Like Circe and Ares and her other ancient enemies, true evil never died.

"Someone murdered a New God," she observed, "and dumped his body on Earth. Superman is at the bedside of his injured wife. Batman is missing. . . ."

Bruce's mysterious absence troubled her. She had been only a few rooms away, tending to the injured John Stewart, when the alarm had gone off at the Hall of Justice. By the time she and Doctor Mid-Nite had investigated, there was no sign of Batman in the morgue, and no indication of what had happened to him. Kraken later claimed that she had left Batman there a few minutes earlier, but Diana had her doubts. Alas, all security footage and recordings had been inexplicably wiped clean. *Bruce's handiwork*, she wondered, *or someone else's?*

"It is suspicious," Alan agreed. "There just isn't enough evidence to convince the meta-military agencies operating under the Checkmate umbrella." Alan had deep connections to the world's intelligence community, which was one of the reasons she had asked him to swing by the Hall of Justice today, in hopes that his sources could shed some light on the deepening mystery. "They decided to prioritize the latest breakdown of authority in Blüdhaven. Perhaps we should too."

Blüdhaven. Diana's porcelain brow furrowed in thought. The devastated city had been an ongoing problem ever since the "Infinite Crisis." Was the timing of this latest disturbance just a coincidence, or could it be part of a larger conspiracy?

The lantern emblem on Alan's shirt reminded her of their most recent setback. "We all know Hal Jordan didn't do it." They strolled down a corridor toward the Hall's communications hub. "You ask me why I feel certain the evil gods are involved. Intuition. Will that do?"

Alan did not dispute her. "Diana, in the past, we could always count on the good New Gods to defend us against their evil counterparts. Without their knowledge, their warriors and technology, we'd be at a frightening disadvantage. We'd need to start training an army." He stroked his chin thoughtfully. "Hmm. Did I ever tell you how President Roosevelt helped us assemble over fifty mystery men and women as the All-Star Squadron back during the war?"

"My mother told me about it," Diana replied. Her mother, Queen Hippolyta of the Amazons, had fought to defend democracy during the Second World War. "Article X? The draft for super heroes?"

Alan nodded. "We called them 'mystery men' back then, but . . yes."

They entered the monitor room. Glowing videos screens, tracking situations across the planet, covered the walls. A young red-haired woman sat before an impressive control panel, prescription glasses aiding her shrewd blue eyes. A metal wheelchair did nothing to diminish Barbara Grayson's skill and confidence. Although she had once fought crime as Batgirl, she now went by the codename "Oracle." As such, her computer skills were unparalleled.

Alan greeted Barbara. "Without J'onn J'onzz, you'll be the hub of our communications, Oracle." He gestured at the sophisticated apparatus around them. "We've set you up with the best equipment money can buy. You may not be able to serve on the front lines, but you'll be indispensable to our preparations."

"Hey!" she objected to the older man's mildly patronizing tone. A hands-free phone headset cradled her scalp. "They also serve those who have a huge network of contacts." Her fingers danced across the keyboard in front of her. "Trust me, the word has gone out. . . ."

Diana hoped it was not too late.

FAWCETT CITY.

Feeling discouraged, Freddy Freeman slumped in an easy chair in front of a silent TV. A pair of metal crutches was propped up against the side of the chair. Due to a childhood injury, the dark-haired youth required the crutches whenever he was simply Freddy and not the heir to the powers of Shazam. News magazines were scattered on the floor of his bachelor apartment, their alarming headlines catching his eye.

The whole world seemed to be going to Hades.

Lost in thought, he didn't even look up as a seven-foot-tall Bengal tiger padded into the living room, carrying a teapot and two cups on a silver tray. The imposing feline wore a tailored green suit with a striped silk tie that matched his natural coloring. Whiskers sprouted from his snout. A tantalizing aroma arose from the teapot.

". . . legendary tiger tea," Tawky Tawny purred, "given to me as a gift on my last adventure." Large orange paws delicately poured Freddy a cup. "See what you think of this while I tell you all about it."

Freddy appreciated his friend's obvious attempt to distract him from his troubles, but it was going to take more than a cup of tea and an amusing anecdote to ease his mind. "I keep thinking I've made such a mess of things, Tawny. Billy's gone. Mary's disappeared. . . ."

As Captain Marvel Jr., Freddy had once fought beside his friends, Captain Marvel and Mary Marvel. But everything changed when the wizard Shazam, who had endowed all of them with their powers, died a few years ago. Billy Batson, aka Captain Marvel, had been forced to take the wizard's place at the Rock of Eternity, absenting himself from Earth, while Billy's sister Mary had lost her own powers in the process. Unable to accept the loss of her special abilities, Mary had set out on a dangerous quest to regain her lost powers, no matter what. Freddy had not seen or talked to her in months, but he had heard disquieting rumors that she had gotten mixed up with some very bad magic. . . .

"I made a promise to protect the world," Freddy said sadly, "to keep the darkness at bay, but what's become of the Marvel Family?" A sip of tea warmed his throat, but did little to lift his spirits. "Maybe I should just say my magic word and change to somebody stronger than me . . . and never change back. My *other* self never has the doubts I feel. He won't stop until he's brought Mary back home and made everything okay."

After the wizard's death, Freddy had been forced to undergo a series of arduous trials to prove himself worthy of his former gifts. Now, as he got an encouraging nod from Tawny, he stood and spoke the wizard's name once more.

"Shazam!"

METROPOLIS.

Supergirl clutched a computer printout in one hand while she bent to pet her cat with the other. Her bright red, blue, and yellow costume resembled that of her celebrated cousin's, right down to the flowing red cape and the world-famous S on her chest. Her long golden hair dangled before her eyes as the purring ginger cat rubbed its head against her crimson boots. A short blue miniskirt and cropped top showed off her bare legs and midriff. Kara Zor-El was only seventeen years old by terrestrial reckoning.

The cluttered apartment reflected the diversity of the Kryptonian teenager's interests. A guitar leaned haphazardly against an end table while a half-finished painting of Argo City rested on an easel. A sewing machine rested on the kitchen table, designs for new costumes strewn about the floor nearby. Bookshelves sagged beneath the weight of dozens of interesting volumes on a wide variety of topics. Postcards from around the world were magnetized to the fridge. Oracle's emergency e-mail was still displayed on the screen of her laptop.

"I'll be back soon, Streaks," she promised the cat. "I have to go pick up Lois and Jimmy, and take them to the Fortress. Be good. And don't you *dare* pee in my laundry basket again!"

STAR CITY.

"A *draft* notice?"

Oliver Queen indignantly crumpled the piece of paper in his hand. He was stretched out on a rumpled king-sized bed, wearing nothing but a pair of Lincoln green boxers. A blond mustache and goatee failed to conceal his exasperation. Sweat glistened on his hairy chest. A picture window offered a striking view of snowcapped mountains.

"What about tracking down J'onn's murderers?" he protested. "If they want me, I have a JLA signal device in my belt buckle."

"*I'm* drafting you, Oliver." Dinah Lance zipped up the front of her Black Canary costume, depriving her husband of yet another spectacular view. Her wavy blonde hair was provocatively mussed. Black fishnet stockings flattered her limber legs, which had kicked many a bad guy's butt. She tossed him his Green Arrow suit and a quiver of arrows. "Get up."

Oliver grudgingly climbed out of bed and pulled on his working clothes. "If anybody falls for this authoritarian, militaristic crap, it'll prove I'm absolutely right about absolutely *everything*!"

Black Canary let him rant. She had heard it all before, and loved him anyway.

WASHINGTON, D.C.

Alan Scott had to admit that Oracle had really delivered. Only a few hours had passed since President Thorne had invoked Article X, but already the Hall of Justice was playing host to the largest assemblage of heroes Alan had seen since Black Adam last declared war on the entire world. The Justice League, the Justice Society, the Teen Titans, the Outsiders, and the Shadowpact had all answered the call. He looked out over a sea of brave, determined faces. Even Detective Chimp looked ready to do his part.

"I'm proud of you," he said, addressing the crowd. "All of you. Let's see any enemy stand against *us*."

If only they knew where the enemy was . . .

CHAPTER 15

TOKYO.

Storm clouds piled ominously above Narita Airport. A private jet waited on the tarmac as a stretch limo parked several yards away. Shilo Norman and Sonny Sumo emerged from the limo and walked toward the plane.

". . . three days later," Shilo said, regaling Sonny with the tale of his greatest escape, "I crawled out of my own grave. The whole world thought it was Mister Miracle's biggest stunt ever, but it was real." He sounded like he could still barely believe it himself. "What I did was impossible."

"For a man perhaps," Sonny replied. "Maybe not for Motherboxxx."

Shilo raised the phone-sized device. Sonny leaned forward, cocking his head as though listening to Motherboxxx. It seemed to him that he could almost hear something from the mysterious gadget, just at the very fringe of perception. It was like the box was talking straight to his unconscious mind, bypassing his more skeptical forebrain.

"You starting to believe me?" Shilo asked. "Just when I have to leave Japan?"

They paused on the way to the plane. "I believe you believe," Sonny admitted, "and I can't deny there's something special about that box of yours." His massive arms were crossed atop his chest. A fresh black T-shirt replaced the one scorched by Megayakuza. "I'll be thinking about what you said. Maybe

I can just about buy the idea that the powers of evil have got their hooks into the world. But what makes you think a sumo wrestler and an escape artist are the ones to fight back? Showbiz people?"

"I don't think we have a choice." Shilo tucked Motherboxxx back into his jacket pocket. Tinted glasses hid whatever fear he might have been feeling. "I don't think anybody does right now. Seems to me we're all going to have to fight this war sooner than later."

Sonny didn't like the sound of that, but, before he could reply, Motherboxxx began pinging in alarm. Sonny looked back to see a squadron of armored soldiers closing in on them. Creepy metal helmets, with bloodred visors, hid their attackers' faces. One of them lifted a rocket launcher onto his shoulder.

"Shilo!" Sonny shouted urgently. *"Down!"*

They threw themselves onto the pavement just as the rocket whizzed overhead, striking the jet. A fiery explosion blistered Sonny's back anew, the shock wave hurling them away from the smoking wreckage. Shrapnel whistled through the air, barely missing them. Burning jet fuel produced a cloud of choking black smoke. Sonny's ears were ringing.

The men scrambled to their feet. They saw the armored terrorists rushing toward them, heedless of the smoke and flames. "Who the hell are these people?" Shilo exclaimed, coughing on the fumes. His hat had blown off his head, exposing his smooth brown scalp. The device in his jacket was pinging like mad. "Motherboxxx is going nuts!" He looked around in confusion. "Where's airport security?"

Not where we need them, Sonny thought. He barreled into the oncoming terrorists like a linebacker, knocking them aside. Shilo hurried after him, away from the trashed jet, which wasn't going to be flying anywhere now. Sonny's sheer bulk momentarily overwhelmed their faceless assailants, but he knew that they didn't stand a chance unless they got away from here soon. They were unarmed—and badly outnumbered.

"Mister Miracle, super escape artist!" he called out even as he bulldozed through their enemies. He crushed one terrorist beneath his armpit, while a fist the size of sledgehammer knocked another bad guy's helmet loose. More terrorists piled on him from behind. Sonny wasn't sure, but he suspected that the armored goons were trying to take them alive. "This would be a good time for a miracle!"

As if on cue, a pair of blinding headlights shone through the smoke. Sonny heard a powerful engine revving. Shaking off a mass of clinging terrorists, he raised his arm to shield his eyes as the headlights came zooming toward them.

"That works," he conceded.

Shilo shook his head. He ducked beneath the swinging fist of a terrorist and flipped his attacker onto the tarmac. He squinted at the approaching lights. "That has nothing to do with me."

Then *who*?

A snazzy silver sports car burst through the spreading flames. Its streamlined aerodynamic design boasted chrome trim and a domed windshield. Glowing blue hubcaps spun like pinwheels. The car squealed to a halt only a few feet away from the embattled performers. A stocky young man wearing a glowing green breastplate, whom Sonny vaguely remembered from the nightclub, stuck his head and shoulders up through the vehicle's open sunroof.

"We waited and waited for your autograph, Super-Sumo-san!" Big Atomic Lantern Boy shouted by way of explanation. "Finally we could wait no more! Jump aboard!"

Sonny and Shilo didn't need to be told twice. Fighting off their pursuers, if only for a moment, they clambered into the getaway car, where they found a whole crew of garishly costumed boys and girls crammed into the car's wide bucket seats. Now that they had succeeded in capturing Sonny's attention, he belatedly identified their rescuers as some of those new celebrities/super heroes who were so inexplicably popular with Japan's youth. He recognized their faces and outfits from the covers of various tabloids and gossip magazines.

Burning rubber, the car took off down the runway with Sonny and Shilo aboard. "I can't believe it!" Shiny Happy Aquazon squealed. Chartreuse pigtails bobbed vigorously. Her harpoon gun jabbed into Sonny's side. "I'm really in the Wonder Wagon with Mister Miracle!" She fished a smartphone from her waterproof utility belt. "I have your picture here on my phone!" she promised Shilo. Webbed fingers poked at the phone's keypad. "Really, it's somewhere right here!"

"Don't forget Sonny Sumo!" Atomic Lantern Boy reminded her. He squeezed into the backseat between Sonny and Well-Spoken Lightning Flash. A tiny winged girl hung on to the latter's helmet for dear life.

Behind them, the armored terrorists piled into an open flatbed truck and took off after them. Bullets bounced off the rear of the "Wonder Wagon" as the gunmen opened fire with automatic rifles. Sonny realized that the war Shilo had spoken of had caught up with them, and then some. *I'm in the middle of this now, whether I like it or not.*

He extracted his own phone from his pocket. Bullets shrieked past him as he dialed his manager. "You heard me right," he shouted over Morrie Shimura's indignant protests. Gunfire punctuated every syllable. "Cancel my fight with Killotron tonight." He glanced back over his shoulder at the determined terrorists. "I'm on a mission from the gods."

"Listen to me," Shilo said urgently to the driver of the vehicle, ignoring the cell phone Aquazon was thrusting in his face. He rode shotgun beside Most Excellent Superbat, having commandeered the passenger seat up front. "You kids saved our lives and that's cool, but you can't get mixed up in this." He was obviously worried about the frivolous young people's safety. A glance in the rearview mirror confirmed that the truckload of terrorists was rapidly gaining on them. Bullets sparked off the Wagon's impervious body. Concrete barricades blocked their path directly ahead; they were running out of tarmac. "Superbat—whatever you call yourself—we need to get off this runway and locate the authorities."

Behind the wheel, Superbat scoffed at the notion that he and his friends were ill-prepared to handle a crisis of this magnitude. "Excuse me. We *are* the Super Young Team." He shifted gears and, without warning, the Wonder Wagon tilted backward, throwing Sonny back against his seat, *and took off into the sky.* Rockets flared from the flying car's undercarriage, leaving twin contrails behind them, as the Wonder Wagon climbed toward the heavens. Its wheels flipped into a horizontal position, parallel to the ground below. Their luminous rims spun like jet propellers. Peering out through the window, Sonny was amazed to see the airport—and then all of Tokyo—shrink away beneath them. Within seconds, they were soaring above the clouds.

Hundreds of feet below, the terrorists' truck crashed into the barricade, and a fireball engulfed the vehicle.

Superbat shifted gears again. The Wonder Wagon leveled off at an altitude of approximately twenty thousand feet. He turned and smirked at Shilo.

"We've done this sort of thing before."

BLÜDHAVEN.

The blasted city was even worse than Wonder Woman remembered. She was shocked at how little progress had been made at rebuilding the disaster site, or even tearing down the ruins. Displaced families filled the impoverished refugee camp on the outskirts of the city. Weathered tents and trailers housed the homeless survivors of the catastrophe. Campfires burned in rusted metal barrels. Weary, hungry people huddled around the fires.

"We'll find you and your mother a much better place to live," Diana promised a pigtailed little African-American girl named Jayla. She bent down to give the courageous five-year-old a hug. "I promise."

"But what about everybody else?" Jayla asked, showing an admirable concern for the welfare of her neighbors. Diana made a mental note to see to it that Paradise Island contributed more to the relief efforts. Her mother, Queen Hippolyta of the Amazons, would surely consider it a worthy cause.

Jayla's mother looked on from a few feet away. "Reverend Good says we all got to have faith, but I'm still waiting for faith to buy us a ticket out of this garbage dump." She peered wistfully across the polluted Avalon River dividing the camp from the devastated waterfront beyond. Her ill-fitting secondhand clothing showed signs of wear, and grief and hardship had aged her beyond her years. "Our home is back there."

"Yeah, well, nobody's going home in Blüdhaven for a long time," Sergeant Gardner Grayle of the Atomic Knights responded. He pointed across the river. A barbed wire fence marked the perimeter of the restricted zone. "Official cleanup still only stretches as far as the whaling museum over there on Renfield, and there are only 125 of us knights patrolling the wall."

A trio of knights had met Diana at the border. Their medieval-looking armor protected them from the toxic mists wafting across the polluted river, and their tinted visors let them see past their crested helmets. The giant mutated Dalmatians they rode snuffled at the plastic feed barrel.

Wonder Woman surrendered Jayla back to her mother. "Nevertheless, I'd like to go in a little way."

She had no way of knowing for certain that the troubles in Blüdhaven were linked to Orion's death, J'onn's murder, and the other distressing events of the last few days, but, once again, she was inclined to trust her intuition. Hunches were often concealed messages from the gods, to be disregarded at one's own peril. Right now every fiber of her being was telling her that the font of their recent woes lay hidden somewhere within the blighted wasteland before her.

"We're required by federal law to accompany you into contaminated territory," Grayle stated. He made one last attempt to dissuade her. "You sure you don't want to wait for the S.H.A.D.E. supertroops to get back from reconnaissance?"

According to Grayle, a team of government operatives had already preceded her into the city. Diana wondered what S.H.A.D.E. might know that she didn't.

She shook her head. "We may not have time for that, Sergeant."

Grayle and his fellow knights knew better than to attempt to obstruct her. They rode their canine steeds alongside her as they made their way past the outer barriers. Only a single concrete bridge still crossed the river into Blüdhaven. Wonder Woman and the Atomic Knights had the multilane bridge to themselves before setting foot on the toxic soil beyond. Diana's boots stirred up clouds of ash and dust. She didn't want to think about how much of those ashes had formerly been flesh and blood. A noisome miasma hung over the ruins.

Blüdhaven had truly gone the way of ancient Pompeii. . . .

Sergeant Grayle led the way. "Command-D is a gene weapons test site they built under cover of the rubble at Chemo Ground Zero. Some local crime lord's holed up in there, and Uncle Sam has too much invested in the research, so air strikes are out, super-soldiers in." His oversized Dalmatian padded gracefully through the debris. "These pony dogs of ours are a direct result of Command-D research."

A female knight rode up beside Diana. "Excuse me, I don't mean to interrupt, but this is such an honor. You've been such a total inspiration to me." A scarlet plume crested her helmet as she introduced herself. "Marene. Marene Herald."

"I'm proud to have you at my side in this graveyard, Marene." A frown came to Diana's lips as her blue eyes pierced the noxious mists. The smell of freshly spilled blood assaulted her nostrils. "Hold! What is that ahead?"

Dead men were strewn across the debris. They hung lifelessly from tilted streetlights, or lay sprawled across the gore-soaked rubble in various stages of dismemberment. Shattered bones jutted from ruptured rib cages. Severed heads and limbs littered the landscape. Loose entrails spilled from disemboweled corpses.

Marene gagged audibly. She raised a gauntlet to the mouth of her helmet. "Oh my God," she gasped. "You ever seen a man turned inside out before?"

"Yes," Diana said. "Unfortunately."

The dead men wore identical striped uniforms. Grayle rode forward to inspect the bodies. "S.H.A.D.E. operatives." He peered at the bloodied face of the nearest corpse. "This guy said his name was Replika." The knight looked around at the sundered remains. "I think they're *all* him. . . ."

So they are, Diana realized. Although the grisly state of the carnage had initially obscured this fact, closer inspection revealed that the scattered victims were all the same man. Clones, or some sort of duplication ability? She wondered if there were any copies still breathing.

Before they could search for survivors, however, Diana's ears alerted her to the sound of something flying toward them from deeper within the ruins. Looking up, she spotted a solitary figure descending from the sky. An alarmed pony dog reared up on its hind legs.

"Back up!" she warned the knights. "Someone's coming."

The figure landed atop a nearby pile of rubble. Diana's eyes widened at the sight of a buxom young woman in a black latex leotard, cut high on her hips. Stubble dotted her scalp, which had been shaved bald except for a pair of knotted pink pigtails. A thunderbolt-shaped cutout on her chest exposed cleavage of grotesquely exaggerated proportions. A black cape with dark red trim flapped about her shoulders. Thigh-high black boots rested atop ten-inch stiletto heels, and magenta circuit diagrams adorned her glossy black corset.

"*I did it,*" the newcomer giggled. "It was bad me." She rested her hands on her hips as she posed brazenly atop the debris. "Hey there, pretty Princess Diana. Guess what?"

Wonder Woman barely recognized the girl. "Mary Marvel? You look . . . different."

That was an understatement. The Mary Marvel she recalled had been a heroic young woman of unusual charm and innocence. A trifle naïve, perhaps, but nothing like the smirking siren facing them now. This new Mary made Circe look like a vestal virgin. *I'd heard there had been trouble,* Diana thought, *but I never imagined anything like* this. . . .

"What's happened to you?"

Mary shrugged. "It's simple, really. I just couldn't stand being wholesome and plain and boring one second longer." She flaunted her obscenely enlarged décolletage. "It's amazing what they can do at the Flesh Farm at Command-D." She looked amused by Diana's shocked expression. "Don't worry, you'll see for yourself soon enough. . . ."

Without further ado, she launched herself at Diana at lightning speed. Razor-tipped gloves slashed at Diana's face, but the Amazon princess deftly twisted away from the blow, so that the claws only grazed her shoulder. Even still, Mary's attack left deep gouges across Diana's bare skin. Blood ran from the wounds.

But the carnage had only begun. Mary's explosive trajectory carried her straight through Marene Herald, ripping the female knight in two before either Diana or the other knights even realized what was happening. The upper half of Marene toppled onto the ground, leaving the rest of her still seated in her saddle. The valiant knight was now just a pair of legs in stirrups, a stick-up shard of spine. A random slice of Mary's claws decapitated the dead woman's steed as well, and the headless Dalmatian crumpled to the ground. Blood-soaked armor clattered against the rubble.

No! Diana thought, shocked at Marene's abrupt demise. It had all happened so fast!

The other knights were still wheeling about in confusion. They waved their energy-lances in the air, unable to keep up with the blinding speed of Mary's attack. Diana wasn't even sure if they realized Marene was dead yet. The surviving dogs howled in fear.

"Wha—?" Grayle exclaimed. "Moving . . . too . . . fast!"

Mary gave them no time to mourn. She circled back in midair and grabbed onto a handful of Wonder Woman's luxurious black tresses.

"Oh God!" Grayle gasped, transfixed by the sight of Marene's bisected remains. "Oh my God!"

"Yes!" Mary gloated. She yanked Diana's face toward her outstretched claws.

Wonder Woman jerked her head back, sacrificing a lock of hair. An Amazon bracelet, forged from shards of Zeus's own shield, deflected Mary's claws. "Hola!" Diana challenged her foe as her warrior's training came to her aid. Matching Mary's superhuman speed and strength, Wonder Woman punched Mary squarely in the face, liberating a tooth from the other woman's gums, before shattering Mary's right elbow with her own. The injured girl swore profanely, blood spraying from her lips.

By the gods, Diana thought. *She doesn't even sound like Mary Marvel anymore.*

Her broken arm dangling uselessly, Mary snarled and struck back with her left. Magical lightning crackled down the length of her arm as it pistoned forward at the speed of sound. Wonder Woman caught the punch in her palm. Incandescent blue sparks erupted from the collision.

Time to end this, she resolved. *Before anyone else gets hurt.*

Crushing Mary's fist in her grip, Wonder Woman forced the corrupted heroine to her knees. Mary's girlish face contorted with pain and rage, while in the background, the surviving knights turned angrily toward the murderous superwoman.

"Marene's dead!" one of the knights cried out in despair. He cradled the dead woman's upper torso in his arms. Her blood splattered his forged steel cuirass. He glared at Mary through his translucent visor. "She killed my sister!"

The knights aimed their energy-lances at Mary. "Step aside, Wonder Woman!" Sergeant Grayle ordered.

"No!" Diana shouted. It was doubtful that the knight's weapons could even hurt Mary, yet Diana still hoped to forestall any further violence. Despite Marene's tragic end, Wonder Woman knew there had to be more here than met the eye; Mary Marvel was no killer. "Please, Mary," she entreated. "Tell me what's happened to you!"

Mary grinned horridly through her pain. "I do what Darkseid tells me now!" She laughed in Wonder Woman's face. "They've been hiding in human bodies, you stupid bitch! You're too late!"

"In human bodies?" Diana didn't need her golden lasso to know that Mary was telling the truth. She swiftly grasped the full implications of the revelation. "Eternal Hera, *that's* why we couldn't find them!"

Mary chuckled evilly. "You screwed up! In five minutes, the Anti-Life Equation goes global . . . and the whole world is ours!"

The Anti-Life Equation? Diana stepped back in horror. The Equation was said to be a mystic formula that granted its possessor absolute power. Darkseid had been searching obsessively for it since time immemorial. *Is it now at his disposal?*

"Like I said, don't worry." Mary wrested her fist free from Wonder Woman's grip. "You'll be working for Darkseid too."

The appalled Amazon braced herself for combat, but Mary made no effort to continue their battle. Instead she merely opened her fist to reveal a shattered glass vial atop her palm. The Greek letter omega was etched upon a glass fragment. Eerie green fumes rose from the broken vial.

"We needed a delivery system," Mary said smugly. "We needed a disease carrier."

The septic fumes invaded Diana's bloodstream through the gashes in her shoulder. A sudden fever rushed over her, sapping her strength. The infected wounds stung like hellfire. The doleful ruins seemed to spin around her. She dropped limply to her knees, even as Mary Marvel rose to her feet once more. Their positions reversed, Mary gazed down at the faltering Amazon in malignant triumph. The Atomic Knights' laser blasts bounced harmlessly off her latex-clad frame. Mary spit in Diana's face.

"And that's *you*, Wonder Woman."

WASHINGTON, D.C.

Alone in the JLA's communications center, Oracle kept watch over the world. An electronic chime alerted her to an incoming transmission from an undisclosed location in the Swiss Alps. Mister Terrific's face appeared upon one of the myriad screens facing the wheelchair-bound hacker.

"Oracle," Michael Holt addressed her. A T-shaped black mask was affixed to his features. The African-American hero was said to be the third-smartest man in the world, although nobody could agree on who the first two were. A valued member of the Justice Society, he also served as the current White King of Checkmate. "This is Mister Terrific at the Castle. Can you check on something?"

"Way ahead of you," she replied. "Something really weird is happening."

A progress bar on the computer screen directly in front of her tracked another transmission that had just registered on her radar. "DOWNLOAD FIFTEEN PERCENT COMPLETE," her software reported ominously. The bar was darkening from left to right.

"Michael . . . Can I call you Michael?" Oracle said. "It looks like someone in Blüdhaven just sent an e-mail to every single address on the planet Earth." She knew how crazy that sounded. "This isn't possible. . . ."

Like the ultimate spam, the message bypassed the JLA's own security filters to land directly in her in-box. She wondered if she dared open it, then realized the question was academic. "Oh crap! It's opening itself!"

Her fingers danced across the keyboard as she hastily tried to erect a firewall against the invasive e-mail. "Michael, alert the troops, while I try to do something from here!"

The spam blew through her defenses like they weren't even there. To her horror, she saw that the same transmission was simultaneously spreading to every TV screen, radio receiver, public address system, cell phone, PDA, and GPS unit on Earth. In-flight movies, scratchy subway loudspeakers, department store Muzak systems, and even comic book message boards were being hijacked to transmit the insidious mass-mailing. The Greek letter omega flashed across nearly every screen in front of her.

"VIRUS UPLOADING," her computer reported.

The progress bar was almost black.

"We have to shut it down," Oracle realized. "We have to kill the Net!"

Theoretically, that was impossible, but both the JLA and Checkmate had access to advanced extraterrestrial technology that left mere Earthly science in the dust. One of the advantages of having Kryptonians, Thanagarians, Rannians, Martians, and other high-tech aliens on your side. Oracle prayed that would be enough.

"Pull the plugs!" she shouted urgently. One by one, the omega sign took over the screens. She shoved herself as far away from her main screen as she could without actually losing touch with the keyboard. "Oh God. Pull the plugs before it's too late!"

It was exactly 5:30 P.M. Eastern Standard Time.

The moment the world cracked open.

CHAPTER 16

KEYSTONE CITY.
LATER.

Bursting through time, the Flashes skidded to a stop right where they had started, in front of that abandoned strip club in the bad part of town. Friction left a trail of smoking blacktop behind them. Litter blew past their ankles.

"Wow!" Wally West gasped, catching his breath. Even for the Fastest Men Alive, that had been quite a run. He wasn't sure, but he thought they'd overshot the present, ending up a few weeks in the future. Glancing back over his shoulder, he was relieved to see no trace of the fearsome Black Racer. Apparently they had outrun Death.

For now.

The thought reminded him of his uncle's miraculous resurrection. Wally looked over at Barry Allen, who was squatting on the sidewalk up ahead, resting his legs. So much had happened, and so quickly, since Barry's return that Wally hadn't really had a chance to process the fact that his long-lost uncle was truly alive again.

"Barry?" He stepped hesitantly toward the other Scarlet Speedster, half afraid that this would all turn out to be some heartbreaking trick or illusion. "Is it really you?" He came up behind the seated figure. Visions of Barry's funeral flashed through his brain. "Talk to me, Uncle Barry."

Barry stared at his own reflection in a greasy puddle. "We couldn't save Orion, Wally." He sounded confused, distracted, like an amnesiac gradually regaining his memory. "His murder had already happened. So *why*?" He seemed just as baffled by his unlikely resurrection as Wally was. "I was dead. Why did I have to come back?"

He stood up and looked around. A concerned expression quickly came over his face. "Wally, what have they done to the world?"

Good question, Wally realized. Glancing about, he saw that Keystone City had changed dramatically for the worse. All the shops were closed and boarded up. Weeks' worth of rotting garbage was piled high on the sidewalks. Flames flickered on the horizon. The air reeked of smoke and decay. Barbed wire fences barricaded nearby alleys. Rats rooted openly through the gutters. Obscene graffiti had been spray-painted over the curvy silhouettes in front of the strip club. Threatening-looking aircraft patrolled the sky, scouring the streets below with harsh white searchlights. The sky itself was a churning red maelstrom that reminded Wally uncomfortably of the Crisis that killed Barry so many years ago. Granted, this was a seamy neighborhood, but how could things have gotten this bad this *fast*?

A newly erected billboard answered their questions.

Live for Darkseid, the sign read. Die for Darkseid.

"Darkseid," Barry whispered, tapping into some sort of memory from the Great Beyond. "Darkseid's falling, dragging the whole universe down as he goes. The entire structure of existence." His blue eyes widened in dismay as he somehow grasped the enormity of this latest Crisis. "The whole Multiverse, Wally!"

To be honest, Wally was still trying to get over the whole back-from-the-dead thing. "Barry." He reached out and took hold of his uncle's shoulder. Barry felt reassuringly solid, not like a mirage or a ghost at all. "Listen to me. You were *dead*, Barry. We never got over it." He searched his mentor's face for some understanding of just how much this moment meant to him. "Do you have any idea how I'm feeling right now?"

His heartfelt entreaty got through to the other man. "An unknown force just reverse-engineered me to life out of a blizzard of faster-than-light particles," he explained. "I'm sorry if I seem a little abstract." A familiar smile broke out across his face and he clasped his nephew in a vigorous hug. "The

Curse of the Flash Family," he laughed. "Everything gets done on the run and life happens in the rearview mirror." The genuine warmth in his voice convinced Wally once and for that this really *was* Barry Allen, back again. "My God, it's good to see you, Wally."

The second Flash let go of Wally. He stepped back to take a better look at his former sidekick. "The costume suits you." He then surveyed the awful future they had wound up in. "Guess things got out of hand 'round here pretty rapidly, huh? Hope you're ready to save the world like we used to."

A distressing thought suddenly occurred to Wally. "I have a wife and kids." *Linda. Jai. Iris.* "I have to find them in all this."

"They made it to safety," Barry promised. "Flash fact."

Before he could explain how he knew that, a series of tremors—almost like giant footsteps—shook the pavement beneath their boots. Broken windows rattled in their frames. The rats scurried for cover. The Flashes spun toward the noise, and found themselves confronted by a shocking tableau.

A quartet of costumed women blocked the street behind them. Three of them were mounted atop immense armored hellhounds. Drool spilled from the dogs' slavering jowls, and their rubbery black lips peeled back to expose savage yellow fangs. Bloodshot eyes glared at the Flashes. The fourth woman had no need of a steed; over sixty feet tall, she towered over the nearby buildings like a monster from a 1950s drive-in movie. An ape-mask concealed her features, but Wally immediately identified her as Giganta, one of Wonder Woman's arch-enemies. A skull and crossbones was printed on her sloping brow. Bushels of wild auburn hair cascaded past her massive shoulders. A brown leather harness encased her Brobdingnagian figure. It was her mammoth boots that had rocked the asphalt.

Wally recognized the other women as well, but only barely. Wonder Woman sat astride a huge white mastiff, brandishing a bloodstained spear. Ivory tusks sprouted from the porcine mask covering the bottom half of her face, so that she resembled some sort of ferocious boar-woman. A gilded dog collar was fastened around her throat. The pitted bronze shield she held bore an embossed omega symbol. Dull red eyes held no trace of her usual wisdom and humanity, and sweat glistened upon her oiled thews.

"Diana?!" Wally whispered.

Flanking her atop their own rabid mounts were Catwoman and that new

Batwoman from Gotham City. Like Wonder Woman, both women had also been transformed in disturbing ways. Catwoman's purple latex body suit looked even more like S/M gear than usual; a kinky panoply of cinched leather straps and buckles bound her tightly into the costume. Razor-sharp barbs tipped her trademark whip. She hissed angrily at the Flashes.

And as for Batwoman . . . well, Wally hardly knew this new heroine, who had only recently made her debut in Gotham, but he doubted that she usually fought crime with a ball-gag in her mouth and a deadly looking laser pistol in her grip. A mane of curly red hair was piled above her bat-winged mask like she'd just been jolted with electricity. A scarlet bat-symbol was impressed upon the chest of a black rubber suit, although her scalloped cape was missing. Her head was cocked oddly to one side, giving her a slightly brain-damaged affect that didn't gibe with the skilled urban vigilante she was reputed to be. Her dilated ruby eyes rolled vacantly in their sockets and a muffled cackle escaped her gag as she stared at the Flashes.

What's happened to her? Wally thought. *What's happened to all of them?*

He had a bad feeling about this. . . .

Wonder Woman pointed her spear at the Flashes. "Super heroes," she growled from behind the boar-mask. *"Kill."*

Metal spurs dug into the flanks of her mega-mastiff, urging the dog forward. The Female Furies galloped at the shocked heroes. Wonder Woman led the way, waving her lance above her head as Catwoman cracked her whip. Batwoman fired rays of sizzling red destruction from her pistol. Giganta loped after them, dragging her knuckles upon the pavement like an ape. City blocks trembled beneath her ponderous tread.

"Ride, Furies! Ride!"

Ordinarily, Wally would have trusted Wonder Woman with his life, but obviously things had changed. Realizing that there was no reasoning with the distorted heroines, the Flashes fled from the Furies in a blur of motion. Still exhausted from their headlong sprint through time, they couldn't shake their pursuers as easily as they might have before. The hellhounds and their Amazonian riders chased after the Flashes with surprising speed. The omega on Wonder Woman's shield flashed like a police car's signal light—or maybe a tracking device. Giganta's redwood-sized legs carried her entire blocks in a single stride.

"Kill runny men!" she grunted. "Eat them up!"

As they raced through the city, with the Furies hot on their heels, Wally was dismayed to see that the evidence of Darkseid's reign extended far beyond the squalid neighborhood of the strip club. All of Keystone appeared to have gone to hell. Dead-eyed citizens wandered the sidewalks like mindless drones. Statues and memorials had been overturned. Churches, libraries, and museums had been reduced to burnt-out husks. Thick black smoke billowed from the chimneys of ugly factories and crematoriums. Obey Darkseid! a stadium marquee exhorted. Your Life Is Anti-Life.

A deserted construction site loomed before them. Barry signaled Wally to head for the yard. They vibrated through a chain-link fence, only a few blocks ahead of the Furies. Moving at super-speed, Barry unwound a length of steel cable from a heavy metal drum. "Grab the other end," he called out to Wally.

Although it had been years since they had last teamed up as the Flash and Kid Flash, Wally instantly grasped what Barry had in mind. He hastily wrapped his own end of the cable against an upright steel girder—and waited for the nightmarish hunting party to catch up with them.

I hope this works, he thought. He couldn't risk leading the Furies to his family. *We need to give them the slip before we can check on Linda and the kids.*

The Flashes didn't have to wait long. Within seconds, Wonder Woman and the others came charging toward the construction site. They tore through the fencing like it wasn't even there, trampling it beneath the paws of their rabid mounts. Catwoman's lash cracked like a gunshot, and Giganta pounded her chest like King Kong. Wally ducked a blast from Batwoman's laser's pistol.

Only Wonder Woman spotted the trap before them. "Halt!" she shouted. She pulled back hard on the reins of her hound, which reared up onto its hind legs. Slobber sprayed from its snapping jaws. Wonder Woman fell behind her predatory sisters. "Stop!"

But her frantic command came too late. Sheer momentum carried the other Furies forward into the taut hawser cable strung across the site. Batwoman and Catwoman pitched forward, thrown from their saddles. Giganta tripped over the cable and lost her balance, plummeting toward the ground like an overturned skyscraper. The Flashes sprinted in opposite directions to get out of the way of the falling giantess. A half-finished building was flattened beneath her colossal body. The impact was seismic in proportions.

It worked, Wally exulted. *The bigger they are . . .*

Barry gave him a thumbs-up from across the yard. Wally waved back at him, then realized that Wonder Woman had not fallen for their snare. She hefted her spear and aimed it at Barry. An electronic voice emanated from her shield:

"SUPER-SPEEDWAVE. TRACKING . . ."

She can still see us, Wally realized. *No matter how fast we are.*

"Barry! Watch out!"

She flung the spear at Barry. Runners of arcane energy crackled along its length. "Die!" she growled. *"Die!"*

Alerted by Wally, Barry dodged the lance a split second before it would have impaled him. Nearby, the other Furies started to stumble to their feet. Batwoman spit out her ball-gag, which had been loosened by the collision, and gnashed her teeth like an enraged vampire.

"Go, Wally!" Barry shouted. "Run!"

Before the Furies could recover fully from their tumble, the Flashes disappeared like twin streaks of scarlet lightning. Adrenaline gave Wally a second wind, allowing them to leave the fiendish hunting party for good. He still found it hard to accept just *whom* they were running from.

"That was really her, Barry," he said in horror, unable to comprehend what could have transformed his friend so dreadfully. "It was Wonder Woman."

Barry nodded grimly. He had known Diana even longer than Wally. "Like I said, the entire Multiverse is avalanching into oblivion. We have to save everyone." Taking the lead, he headed for Central City at hundreds of miles per hour. "We start with family."

CHAPTER 17

WASHINGTON, D.C.

"Quiet!" the Tattooed Man hissed at his son. "Don't let them hear you."

Mark Richards tugged the dreadlocked teenager behind a rack of ski jackets, out of view of the sports shop's shattered front window. They hid inside the abandoned retail outlet, while red-eyed zombies shuffled by outside. The lights were off inside the store; Richards counted on the murky shadows to help conceal them from the brainwashed storm troopers patrolling the streets. Ever since the Anti-Life Equation had gone global, turning pretty much the whole world into a police state, keeping one's head down was all that mattered. It pissed him off that his boy hadn't figured that out yet.

"But I heard them all turn away," Leon protested. Only thirteen years old, he already thought he knew better than his old man. A wrinkled black T-shirt advertised some new rap album. The elastic of his boxer shorts showed above the waist of drooping jeans, which were at least two sizes too big for him. He toted a sniper rifle they had just looted from the hunting department. Fresh ammo weighed down the pockets of his sagging jeans. "They're chasing somebody else!"

"Sssh!" Richards grabbed Leon by the neck and slammed him into a nearby checkout counter. A tattooed scorpion twitched irritably on his forearm. "They're chasing us, boy! They've got Justifiers *everywhere*!"

The Justifiers were the jackbooted enforcers of the new regime. They used the Anti-Life Equation to "justify" their brutal treatment of anyone who defied Darkseid's will. Richards and his family had been ducking the soldiers for what felt like weeks now. *I never thought I'd miss the damn Justice League,* the tattooed hit man thought, *but this is frigging* Dawn of the Dead *territory.*

"Ow!" Leon pulled away from his father's grip. "Get your hands off my throat!"

Richards let go of the teenager's neck. He hadn't meant to squeeze so hard; he had just wanted to shake some sense into the boy. Didn't Leon realize how dangerous things were now?

Angry tears welled up in Leon's eyes. "I heard them," he insisted stubbornly.

Richards crept over to the window, his dog tags jangling around his neck. "Yeah, maybe you're right after all." He peered out the window, barely recognizing the city outside. The omega symbol was on every wall and billboard. Derelict cars rusted at the curbs. The formerly busy streets were devoid of traffic. Thick black smog blotted out the sun as blank-faced pedestrians trudged along the sidewalks. No one laughed or cursed or spoke. A levitating armored gunship cruised above the desolate avenue, its searchlights shining down on the hapless people. Richards spotted a bright electric flash above the gunship. "Something's going on up ahead!"

A figure in a skintight blue and black uniform leapt from an upper-story window onto the top of the gunship. A canvas bag was slung over the man's shoulder. Electricity sparked along the gray metallic hull of the ship, while the costumed daredevil rode atop the vessel like a whale rider. Richards recognized Black Lightning from past run-ins with the Justice League. He'd been on the receiving end of the hero's trademark shock treatment before. It had hurt like hell.

Leon raised his rifle and took aim at the airship, whether to defend or attack Black Lightning, his father wasn't sure. He squinted through the gun's scope.

"Put that down," Richards barked. He grabbed hold of the rifle's barrel and shoved it toward the floor. "You see the colors he's wearing. All that glow and crackle?"

"Yeah, I know." Leon reluctantly lowered the weapon. "All my life you've been telling me how much I have to hate super heroes." He didn't sound entirely convinced. Leon's intense brown eyes watched Black Lightning take on the looming gunship single-handed. "But he's not one of *them* under that suit, not one of Darkseid's thugs. He's some dude like us."

Speak for yourself, Richards thought. *That do-gooder is nothing like me.*

Black Lightning's electrical assault disrupted the gunship's navigational systems. Taking a nosedive, it crashed into the street. The impact threw Black Lightning from his perch atop the vessel. He slammed into the blacktop, only seconds before the downed aircraft exploded behind him. His rough landing was enough to make Richards wince in sympathy, until he remembered getting zapped by the selfsame hero the last time Black Lightning and his JLA buddies busted his chops. A fireball erupted only a few yards away from where the man lay dazed upon the asphalt. Bright orange flames licked at his heels.

Leon looked anxiously at his father. "We can't just watch!"

Richards felt his son's accusing gaze upon him. Inked snakes and spiders squirmed uncomfortably atop his skin.

"Crap," he swore before clambering out of the broken window. He couldn't believe he was actually risking his neck for a goddamn super hero. Leon scrambled after him. Richards felt the heat of the blaze against his face. "I should have brought your sister."

They sprinted down the pavement, but they weren't the only ones after Black Lightning. A squadron of Justifiers poured out of the burning gunship. Ominous steel helmets covered their faces. Scorched armor protected them from the flames. They brandished high-tech energy-pistols that put Leon's old-fashioned rifle to shame.

"Alpha target acquired," the largest of the Justifiers announced mechanically. Reptilian green scales covered his brawny torso in lieu of body armor. His scaly hide and size marked him as Killer Croc, one of Batman's most savage foes. From the looks of things, he had taken a big gulp of Libra's Kool-Aid. His voice was harsh and guttural. "Superhuman code designate: 'Black Lightning.' Electrical field manipulator, level 12."

Heedless of the spreading conflagration, the Justifiers marched toward the fallen hero. Their steel-toed boots pounded heavily against the pavement. "Wear the helmet!" they intoned. "Be like us! Be justified!" They targeted

Black Lightning with their sidearms, all the while chanting like brain-dead cultists. Killer Croc lumbered forward, bearing an empty helmet in his huge webbed claws. "Life is a question! Anti-Life is the answer!"

Against his better judgment, the Tattooed Man came to the hero's rescue. He stripped off his grimy wifebeater, revealing the living tattoos covering every inch of his upper body. Animated knives and throwing stars sprang at the unsuspecting Justifiers. Razor-sharp points found the chinks in the soldiers' armor. Blood spurted onto the asphalt.

"Warning!" a wounded Justifier cried out. "Superhuman designate unknown!"

Richards peeled a broadsword off his back. "Designate this, bastards!"

An entire arsenal of angry tattoos flew off his skin. Vampire bats flapped at the startled soldiers, snapping at their arms and legs with bloodthirsty fangs. Cartoon bombs and sticks of dynamite exploded at their feet. Cobwebs snarled the Justifier's helmets, blinding them. Rattlesnakes and cobras injected them with inky venom. Croc lunged at the Tattooed Man, only to find a length of barbed wire tangled around his legs. He toppled headfirst onto the pavement, hitting the ground like a scaly bag of potatoes. Richards drove the disoriented storm troopers back with his sword, even as Leon pulled Black Lightning to safety. The stolen rifle was strapped across the boy's scrawny shoulders. "I got your back, Dad!"

The stunned hero moaned in pain.

You're welcome, Richards thought sourly. *This has gotta be the dumbest move I've ever made.*

He was already regretting it.

Black Lightning awoke to the sound of an angry voice.

"It's the Four Horsemen of the Apocalypse on the streets," the voice groused. "Invasion of the body snatchers, space Nazi Anti-Life fire and brimstone. And Mister Justice League here makes us a target."

He's talking about me, Black Lightning realized. Opening his eyes, he found himself lying on a cot in some sort of basement or furnace room. A naked lightbulb, hanging from the ceiling, cast the only light in the room. A large oil-burning furnace chugged in the corner. The size of the burner suggested it was intended to heat an entire building, not just a private residence. Unpacked boxes of school supplies and a heap of damaged desks practically screamed "grade school" to the groggy hero, who had once taught high school in Metropolis. Not entirely sure how he'd gotten here, he kept still as he tried to take stock of his situation. *Is that the Tattooed Man talking?*

He vaguely remembered the villain coming to his rescue before. . . .

"You all know how I feel about these people," Mark Richards snarled at his family, who stood around him, looking tense and frightened. A Glock semiautomatic pistol was tucked into his waistband. "I had my way, we'd kill and eat the bastard."

"Mark!" An attractive African-American woman, whom Black Lightning assumed was Richards's wife, Michelle, rebuked her husband. She clearly didn't want to hear that kind of talk in front of their kids.

"I'm only saying he's trouble," Richards said. "Costumes equal trouble. Special powers club never brought nobody nothing but grief."

According to the JLA's files, the former Marine had acquired his living tattoos in the remote Balkan kingdom of Modora, where he had mastered the arcane art of "sin-grafting." The restless illustrations supposedly embodied the sins of all the men he had killed, both in war and in his new career as professional assassin. It was all a bit mystical for Black Lightning's tastes, but there was no denying the Tattooed Man's singular ability. Those tats were more than just ink.

The teenage boy spotted him stirring on the cot. "Dad?" He pointed at Black Lightning.

Richards squinted at the supine hero. "I think he's moving."

Guess there's no point in playing possum anymore, Black Lightning thought. He sat up, swinging his legs onto the floor, only to be overcome by a sudden wave of dizziness. He grabbed onto the edge of the cot to steady himself until the queasiness passed. *Remind me not to crash an enemy aircraft again.*

He took in the scene through his yellow-tinted goggles. The Tattooed Man and his family were standing over by the furnace. The latest edition of the *Daily Planet*, now an illegally published samizdat, lay in a bag at Richards's feet. He flipped through a copy of the newspaper. A defiant banner headline read: "BLÜDHAVEN, HERE WE COME!"

Black Lightning feared that Richards was going to feed the papers to the furnace. "Don't do that," he said. "Don't just burn those papers. People struggled hard to make them."

"What's that?" Richards scowled. The tattoos on his arms and neck bristled. "You think we don't read? I'm just some dumb 'super-villain' wiping his ass on the printed word—that's the first thing you think?" He stomped toward Black Lightning, his fists clenched. Thorns sprouted from his knuckles. "I just saved your life, and I get judged?"

His wife got between Richards and Black Lightning. "Mark," she pleaded, trying to calm him. The kids, a teenage boy and girl, watched uncomfortably from the sidelines.

"I'm sorry," Black Lightning said, not wanting to provoke the man. "Thanks for the assist. I was on my way to the Hall of Justice when a Justifier brigade appeared out of nowhere. Jumping out of the window onto that gunship was the only viable escape route." He surveyed the furnace room. Canned food and ammunition were stored on the shelves. "You and your family have done pretty well to survive this long in a world that doesn't even belong to us anymore."

"The world never belonged to people like me, superstar." Richards backed off, but kept the chip on his shoulder. He hurled the newspaper onto the floor. "What else is new?"

Black Lightning rose from the cot and straightened his shoulders.

"Why the hero pose?" Richards mocked him. "You leaving?"

"We're *all* leaving," Black Lightning said, taking charge of the situation. "Pack only essentials. If you stay here, Justifier patrols will almost certainly find you in a matter of hours."

The daughter, who looked to be about seventeen years old, glanced nervously at her dad before speaking up. A plastic headband held a pile of curly black hair in place. A white belly shirt and low-rise jeans looked like standard high school apparel. "My bag's been ready for days," she volunteered.

"Laurel?" The Tattooed Man gave the girl a startled look. "What? Where did all this come from?" He glared at his family. "You all decided on something without talking to me?"

Visibly embarrassed by her dad's attitude, Laurel Richards retrieved a blue carryall bag from the corner. "My dad really hates super heroes," she explained.

Yeah, I got that impression, Black Lightning thought. He peered at the girl's overstuffed luggage. A stuffed teddy bear was crammed into a mesh side pocket, alongside various notebooks and CDs. "You can probably leave most of that stuff," he suggested. He nodded at the heap of junked desks. "This is a school, right? Is there a bus?"

The bus was parked in a garage at the rear of the school. Racks of tools lined the auto shop. Spare tires were piled against one wall. Grease and motor oil stained the hard concrete floor. The bright yellow school bus looked like it was in pretty good shape, but the Tattooed Man still wasn't convinced they needed to evacuate. He glowered at Black Lightning.

"We survived two weeks on our own without you or any of your JLA buddies," he protested, even as the hero climbed into the driver's seat. Richards's hand rested on the grip of his pistol. "Didn't you hear me? The battery's dead."

That was the least of their problems. "Stand back," Black Lightning warned, before sending a jolt of electricity through the steering wheel into the battery. "I can spark her up."

"No," Richards insisted. "We're safe here." His muscular body blocked the door of the bus, keeping his family outside the vehicle. "We got everything we need to survive here until it's over."

Black Lightning spelled it out for him. "This won't be over until each and every one of us chooses to resist. Darkseid is remaking the world in his image, using our technology, our people, as building blocks. There are more and more Justifiers all the time. It's time to leave."

"Don't tell me what to do!" Richards growled. "I can take care of my own family!"

His wife disagreed. "But we're not safe here, Mark. We're trapped. Waiting to die, waiting to be eaten by whatever the super heroes couldn't stop this time."

"Aw, Michelle," Richards muttered. His shoulders sagged in defeat. "Not you too."

Black Lightning was grateful for the woman's intervention. "Listen to your wife, Mr. Richards." He climbed inside the bus and revved its engines. "Saddle up."

A door crashed in at the front of the school. Soldiers loudly ransacked the building. Heavy footsteps pounded toward the garage. Killer Croc's guttural voice called out from far too nearby. "Come out! Come out, wherever you are! Justify your lives to Darkseid!"

"Hell," Richards swore. Giving in, he stepped aside and let his family pile into the bus. The kids strapped themselves into the seats. The Tattooed Man helped his wife aboard before climbing into the bus himself. "Damn storm troopers found us after all."

Black Lightning wished he hadn't been proven right. "Everybody!" he shouted as he hit the gas. "Hold on tight!"

The bus smashed through a wooden garage door into the parking lot beyond. A chain-link fence enclosed the lot. Black Lightning didn't ask Richards to unlock the gate; he drove right through it instead. The Justifiers already had their scent. Speed, not stealth, mattered now.

They bounced over the crumpled fence onto an empty avenue. It was a cold, black night. Sulfurous clouds of thick black smoke obscured the stars. Searchlights swept across the sky. A monumental bust of Darkseid, newly erected atop a nearby brownstone, gazed out over the city. Behind the wheel, Black Lightning quickly oriented himself. New names, like "Armagetto Avenue" and "Fire Pit Alley," had been scrawled over the street signs, but he thought he knew where he was. He turned onto "Darkseid Drive," heading for the highway. The sooner they got beyond the Beltway, the better.

"Oh. My. God," Laurel gasped a few seats behind him. Glancing in the rearview mirror, Black Lightning was dismayed to see a squadron of Justifiers chasing after them astride giant mastiffs the size of ponies. The slavering hellhounds pursued the bus with frightening speed, rapidly eating up the distance between them and their prey. The armored soldiers riding the pony dogs fired flamethrowers at the rear of the bus. A blazing burst of heat scorched the back windows.

"Get down!" Richards shouted at his wife and kids. He hauled himself down the length of the bus and yanked the Glock from his jeans. He shot out the wide rear window, then fired at the mounted Justifiers right behind them. "Trouble!" He shook his head in disgust. "What did I tell you?"

Leon joined his father at the back of the bus. Crouching beside him on the rear seat, he shot at the Justifiers with a handgun of his own. The sharp report of the gunshots added to the chaos. The boy swore under his breath.

"Watch your language!" his dad corrected him.

Pausing to reload, Leon tossed a gun to his sister. Laurel fumbled awkwardly with the weapon. "The safety, remember!" the boy yelled. "It won't work without the safety."

The girl stared in horror at the weapon in her hands. "I can't," she confessed. "I just can't. . . ."

Black Lightning didn't blame her. He hated guns too.

Especially in the hands of teenagers.

The hellhounds pulled up alongside the speeding bus, closing in on them from both the left and the right. Michelle and Laurel ducked for cover as the dogs' riders opened fire on the vehicle. Sizzling energy-blasts blew out the side windows. "Die!" the Justifier on the right commanded. "Die for Darkseid!"

Black Lightning searched the road before him. Up ahead, the elevated thoroughfare overlooked I-395 below. A concrete barrier guarded the rocky slope leading down to the lower expressway, which led north out of the city. He swung the wheel hard to the right.

The side of the bus slammed into the Justifier and his canine steed. They went somersaulting over the railing. Black Lightning floored the gas pedal.

Laurel peered over the back of the driver's seat. Her eyes bulged as she realized what he had in mind. "Mom!" she blurted. "Hold on tight!"

The bus crashed through the concrete barrier, shattering its front headlights. The jarring impact almost tossed Black Lightning from his seat, but he held on to the wheel with all his strength and kept his foot on the gas. Overworked shock absorbers took a beating as the bus careened down the slope onto the highway below. The bumpy ride tossed the passengers about. The Tattooed Man smacked his head into the ceiling.

He gave Black Lightning a dirty look. "Everything going according to plan up there, super hero?"

"Sit down!" Black Lightning barked, like a school bus driver admonishing an unruly student. An incandescent glow lit up his eyes. "Shut up! I'm concentrating."

Unfortunately, they weren't out of the woods yet. A fleet of patrol cars, the omega symbol freshly painted on their hoods, picked up where the dog cavalry left off. Sirens blaring, they chased after the fleeing bus.

Just as the cars were catching up with them, however, bright blue sparks crackled all along the exterior of the bus. Lightning arced from the bus to strike the patrol cars, which were flipped over onto their sides by the galvanic storm. Upside down or on their sides, the capsized cars skidded across the blacktop before colliding into streetlights and fire hydrants. Flames burst from beneath their hoods. Dazed Justifiers scrambled out of the burning vehicles. They were too shaken up to even try firing back at the escaping bus.

Unfortunately, the unleashed lightning had also set the bus on fire. Yellow paint blackened and peeled. Black smoke smelled of burning rubber. "What the hell was that?" Richards bellowed. He grabbed onto the window frame, only to be jolted by a flash of residual electricity. Tattooed barbs retreated from his singed fingertips. "We're on fire! What did you do?"

"I can make electricity dance like Beyoncé," Black Lightning snapped. His eyes still sparked behind his yellow goggles. "You want more?"

The Third Street tunnel appeared before them. Dark, impenetrable shadows filled its open mouth. *Thank God,* Black Lightning thought as he hit the brakes. *We're almost here.*

The blazing bus squealed to a halt. He jumped from his seat and kicked open the door. "Everybody out!" he hollered. "Before the tank goes up!"

He and the Tattooed Man hustled the civilians out of the bus. The flaming vehicle lurched to one side as its melting tires sagged onto their hubs. The front of the bus looked like it had lost a head-on collision with Superman. Choking black fumes filled the fugitives' lungs.

"That was intense!" Laurel squealed as Black Lightning helped her onto the pavement. She clung to her bulging carryall as though her future depended on it. "Is everybody okay?"

Richards hurried his daughter along. "Move."

Flames engulfed the bus right behind them as they dashed from the torched school bus toward the gaping maw of the tunnel. "Far end of the tunnel is no-man's-land," Black Lightning shouted to the others on the run. "A disputed territory Darkseid's forces haven't managed to lay claim to yet. My daughter Anissa is there with a S.H.A.D.E. emergency relief division. A chopper is waiting to ferry you to Watchtower Three."

Anissa Pierce, better known as Thunder, was a super heroine in her own right, having inherited her meta-human abilities from her father. Black Lightning had contacted her to arrange this rendezvous shortly before being ambushed by the Justifiers earlier. He had no doubt that she was waiting for him at the other end of the tunnel.

The glow from the burning bus lit up the entrance, partially dispelling the murky gloom beyond. Discarded cars clotted the narrow lanes, forcing the party to squeeze between them. Rats gnawed on rotting human corpses. The smell of death pervaded the tunnel. Black Lightning hung back, guarding the rear of the exodus, while Richards and his family rushed ahead. Weighed down by her overstuffed bag, Laurel started to lag behind. "Catch up, princess!" Richards called out to the girl. "Leave the bag!"

"I'm okay!" she insisted, unwilling to abandon the precious remnants of her former life. Stumbling, she fell forward onto her knees. Loose CDs and journals spilled onto the pavement. She frantically scooped them back into the bag. "I'm coming!"

Hostile energy-blasts suddenly ricocheted off the concrete walls. Glancing back, Black Lightning saw a pack of Justifiers chasing after them on foot. A high-voltage barrage drove them back, but probably not for long. Zapping all those police cars had taken a lot out of him; he was running low on juice. *I need a chance to recharge.*

A particularly determined soldier made it past the lightning. Sparks electrified his armor, but did not deter him. He took aim at the kneeling girl.

"Anti-Life Justifies my pain!" he declared. "Justify *yours*!"

The Tattooed Man spied his daughter's danger. "Laurel!"

Boomerangs, shrunken heads, and flaming skulls sailed at the Justifier, knocking his gun from his hand. The man went down screaming, buried beneath an avalanche of ferocious tattoos. Bat-winged imps jabbed at him with pitchforks while a rabid wolverine snapped at his limbs. A flock of ravens pecked at his visor.

Laurel looked away in horror.

"It's okay," Richards comforted the sobbing girl. He took her in his arm and led her away from the nightmarish spectacle. "Everything's okay. Daddy's tattoos got him."

More Justifiers advanced down the tunnel. Black Lightning started shoving the abandoned cars together. "We need a barrier to buy us some time." Grunting in exertion, he called out to the Tattooed Man. "How about you set your shoulder to the wheel, Richards?"

"See, this is what I'm talking about!" the surly villain griped. He turned Laurel over to his wife before wheeling around to confront Black Lightning. "You giving out orders like it's all natural!" He watched his family scurry down the tunnel toward safety. "Why waste time on this when we only got a hundred yards to go?"

"Because without this, we won't make the hundred yards." Black Lightning nodded at the oncoming storm troopers. "Take a look."

Richards peered past Black Lightning. The Justifiers were closing in on them fast. Killer Croc was in the lead, his mammoth frame silhouetted against the blazing bus. Energy-blasts tore through the parked automobiles.

"Crap," Richards muttered. He joined Black Lightning behind an empty SUV. Working together, they flipped the heavy gas-guzzler onto its side, forming a crude barricade between them and Darkseid's soldiers. He glared intently at the faceless scumbags menacing his family. "Okay, here's where we say 'no' to all that."

Something in the villain's decisive tone encouraged Black Lightning.

How about that, he thought. *Maybe the Tattooed Man has finally seen the light.*

The two men crouched behind the overturned SUV. Red-hot laser beams fried the air above their heads. Black Lightning locked eyes with his unlikely ally.

"You have to promise me something, Mr. Richards," he said urgently. "There's something I need you to memorize. A circuit."

A circuit? Richards eyed the hero dubiously. *Now what was he on about?*

"I don't care what you think about me," Black Lightning said, even as their mutual enemies closed in on them. "This isn't just some turf war between my side and yours. Our world, our entire reality, is transforming into the broken, deranged expression of an alien will, and we *all* have to fight it!" He held up his hand. A peculiar symbol was scrawled in what looked like Magic Marker on the back of his glove. "I want you to look at this drawing. Don't forget. Symbols have power, as you should know better than most!"

Richards didn't want to hear it. Black Lightning sounded like his old drill sergeants back in the Marines, filling his head full of talk of duty and fighting for one's country. But that was before he was captured by those Modoran rebels and tortured within an inch of his life. He was the Tattooed Man now, and he only looked out for his own.

"Shut up!" he snarled. "Keep your crazy talk to yourself!"

Black Lightning wouldn't let up. "Listen, Richards. This is vital intel that needs to get to the JLA. If I don't make it, because your family's safety took priority, it's up to you to get the job done." He shoved the marked-up glove in the other man's face. "You got that?"

A shot rang out, winging Black Lightning in the arm. Blood spurted from the wound. At first Richards thought that one of the Justifiers had gotten a lucky shot, then he realized that the bullet had come from behind him. He spun around to see his son standing a few yards back, holding his smoking pistol with both hands. The boy gulped. He stared numbly at the wounded super hero. He looked like he might throw up.

Leon? Richards stared aghast at his son. *He shot Black Lightning?*

"Put that goddamn thing away!" he snapped. He yanked the gun from the boy's trembling grip. "What the hell were you thinking?"

Guilt and confusion were written all over the boy's face, as vividly as the tattoos on his father's body. "I—I heard you fighting!" he stammered. "I did it for you, Dad!" Tears streamed down his face. "I did it for *you!*"

Richards knew that was nothing but the truth. *I taught him this,* he realized. *This is all my fault.*

"All of you, run!" Black Lightning sagged against the exposed underside of the SUV, clutching his arm. Blood streamed down his side. His dark face had an ashen cast as he gritted his teeth against the pain. He hurled a stray thunderbolt at the advancing Justifiers with his good arm. The electrical blast seemed weaker than before. "I can hold them off for a few more minutes. Now, go!"

The Justifiers were almost upon them. Killer Croc snatched up a discarded motorcycle and heaved it at the SUV. It crashed against the barrier like a missile. The Justifier behind Croc held out an empty helmet. "Submit!" he commanded. "Submit to Anti-Life!"

The Tattooed Man grabbed his son and ran.

"Don't forget, Richards!" Black Lightning called after them. "It's up to you now!"

"That's the last we saw of him," Michelle Richards said. She sat between her children aboard the S.H.A.D.E. chopper. Emergency blankets were draped over their shoulders. Leon's face was buried in his hands. Laurel sobbed against her mother. Michelle looked up at Anissa Pierce. "I'm sorry about your father. He was a good man."

Thunder wore a black and yellow uniform that mimicked her father's colors. Curly dark brown hair tumbled past her shoulders. Golden lightning bolts embellished the front of her costume, as well as the lobes of her ears. Michelle thought she could see the family resemblance.

"We have to go back!" the young heroine demanded. She got in the face of the S.H.A.D.E. commander. Troopers in Kevlar body armor filled the benches inside the copter's passenger compartment. She shouted over the whir of the rotors. "Put us down. I need to go back for my dad!"

"Negative, Thunder," the CO said firmly. "We need all our metas for the Omega Initiative." He turned toward Michelle. "Speaking of which, what happened to your husband, Ms. Richards?"

Michelle lifted her chin. "He didn't come with us. He said he had something to do. A choice he had to make." Her throat tightened and she dabbed at her eyes with a tissue. "You see, he finally realized what I always knew. Mark Richards was never a villain, not really." She drew her children close to her. "He was a super hero all along."

She prayed that someday she could tell him how proud of him she was.

CHAPTER 18

WASHINGTON, D.C.

An army of Justifiers laid siege to the Hall of Justice. Their steel helmets and armor eradicated their former identities as they assaulted the JLA's headquarters with rifles, hammers, battering rams, and pounding metal gauntlets. A blast of intense heat and light momentarily repelled the mob, long enough for a single battered figure to be thrown through its open doors. The doors slammed shut behind the newcomer. A powerful force field, generated by thirty-first-century technology borrowed from the Legion of Super-Heroes, hummed back into place. Bursts of energy flashed across the surface of the invisible field wherever the Justifiers' weapons smashed against it.

Okay, Ray thought. *That's one delivery taken care of.*

A second later, he bounced off the League's orbital satellite on the way back to the Hall. His body literally transformed into light, he used the reflective underside of the space station to beam himself through the force field two hundred miles below. He shimmered briefly in the Hall's main foyer before solidifying back into flesh and blood. A bright gold helmet, with a fin-shaped crest, hid his face. Gold trim accented his black leather uniform, and a striped flap crossed the front of his jacket. A flared collar fanned out behind his head. Two heavy leather satchels, bulging with freshly printed newspapers, were slung over his shoulders. He dropped the bags onto the tile floor of the foyer.

"Holy crap, kid!" Green Arrow greeted him. He finished bolting the front doors from the inside. A control panel to the right of the doors reported on the current status of the force field. A quiver of arrows was strapped to Oliver Queen's back, and his customary green hood shadowed his features. "That was a close one! I thought you just needed to turn into a beam of light to get past the field."

"Easy for me," Ray Terrill conceded, "but *that* guy's solid." He pointed at the sprawled figure he had hurled through the doors moments before. A tough-looking black guy wearing a ragged tank top and torn blue jeans, the tattooed stranger looked like he'd been through the wars. Ray had spotted him trying to fight his way through the mob outside to reach the safety of the shielded headquarters. A timely solar blast had given the man the break he needed to get to the entrance. "No way was I leaving him to the Justifiers."

"Yeah, well, you just rescued the Tattooed Man," Green Arrow griped. He placed a verdant boot on the fugitive's chest, pinning him to the floor. He notched an arrow to his bow and aimed it at the man's heart. "He's a Trojan horse for the bad guys! Probably led 'em straight to us!"

The man came to and squirmed beneath the archer's heel. Tattooed rattle-snakes uncoiled from his shoulders, rearing up to threaten Green Arrow. "Like hell, I did! And I got a name. Mark Richards, all right? I'm an Anti-Life survivor!" He glared up at the suspicious hero. "You want the word from Black Lightning or not?"

That got Green Arrow's attention. "Black Lightning? What would he be doing with Secret Society cannon fodder like you?" He poked Richards in the chest with the point of his arrow. "This had better be good."

"Super heroes!" the Tattooed Man snarled. He clearly had a chip on his shoulder, besides the inky rattlers. "It's the end of the world and you still act like you own it!"

Nevertheless, the snakes retreated back onto the Tattooed Man's skin. Green Arrow eased off and let Richards clamber to his feet. "Don't try anything funny," Queen warned, keeping the known felon in his sights. "Come with me. I think the others are going to want to hear about this." He looked over at Ray. "You too, kid."

Green Arrow marched Ray and the Tattooed Man into the Justice League's gleaming conference room. A handful of heroes and civilians were gathered around a stainless steel round table. As they entered, Black Canary was handing a glass of water to Oracle. Ray couldn't help noticing how tense and tired everyone appeared. Two anxious-looking women were seated nearby. A pair of costumed kids—a girl and a boy—was playing tag around the table. Ray dragged his lumpy bags behind him. The Tattooed Man glanced around like he was casing the joint.

"Pretty bird!" Green Arrow called out to Black Canary. His mood seemed to lift somewhat at the sight of his wife. "The Resistance has company!" The relentless pounding of the army outside had managed to penetrate the solid steel walls around them. "Time to move out before Darkseid's mind-control cops move in."

He took a moment to introduce everybody. Lowering his bow, he gestured at the two women in civilian clothing: an attractive young Asian woman in her midtwenties and an older woman with gray hair and a worried expression. "Ray, T-Man . . . Linda and Joan, the 'Flash Widows Club.'" That was a joke, Ray assumed, or at least he hoped so. The two children came running over to see them. "Linda's kids, Jai and Iris." Queen turned toward Oracle, whom the Ray had dealt with before. "Barbara was in hiding, holding down the fort here at HQ, when the rest of us rolled into Washington under the cover of darkness."

The little boy, who wore a formfitting yellow uniform and mask, gazed up at the newcomers. "The Ray!"

His big sister, Iris, wore a matching yellow costume. Her long red hair presumably came from her father's side of the family. "Cool! Have you seen our dad?"

"I heard that the original Flash"—he glanced over at Joan Garrick—"evacuated a whole town, single-handed, in minutes, but that's all I know." He wished he could offer Linda and her kids some comforting news regarding the modern Flash, but nobody had seen Wally West since before the world went to hell. Was he still fighting the good fight somewhere, or was he one of *them* now? More than a few heroes had already been converted to superpowered Justifiers.

Remembering why he was here in the first place, Ray tugged open one of his bags and pulled out a folded newspaper. The ink came off on his gloves. "You seen the new edition of the *Planet* yet?"

Jai's eyes bulged. "It still comes out?"

"They have a printing press in Superman's Fortress of Solitude." He felt bad about not delivering any papers here before. "To be honest, we thought the Hall of Justice was under occupation."

Black Canary claimed the paper, which was only four pages long. The front page featured a color photo of a team of Resistance fighters bravely holding their thumbs up. The motley crew was comprised of U.S. soldiers, Atomic Knights, Checkmate agents, S.H.A.D.E. commandoes, and a few renegade super heroes and villains. A belligerent headline proclaimed "BLÜDHAVEN, HERE WE COME!" The article below was credited to James Bartholomew Olsen.

"The *Planet*'s all we've got now," Dinah Lance commented, "now that all electronic media are broadcasting Anti-Life twenty-four hours a day." She lifted her gaze from the newsprint. Weary black circles shadowed her striking blue eyes. Last the Ray had heard, she was still the current leader of the Justice League. "Give me some good news, Ray. What happened to the Blüdhaven strike force?"

The Ray gulped uncomfortably. He was afraid someone was going to ask that.

"Umm . . ."

CHAPTER 19

BLÜDHAVEN.

The pestilential landscape above Command-D had become a slaughterhouse. The butchered remains of the strike force were strewn about the rubble like broken toys. Carrion birds picked at the bloody carcasses of dead pony dogs. Atomic Knights, Checkmate foot soldiers, and other fatalities had been left to rot where they fell, alongside a few sadly expendable super heroes. Negative Woman slumped lifelessly against a shattered concrete pillar, her blonde hair obscuring her bandaged face. Her inert form no longer crackled with negative black-light energy. Mr. Bones lay in pieces upon the broken pavement, his skeletal features making it look like he had already died years before. A lit stogie smoldered on the ground a few inches away from his fleshless skull. An opportunistic mutant crow picked one of Count Vertigo's eyes from its socket. Corpses were frozen in agonized contortions, hinting at the use of some vile nerve agent. Justifiers in gas masks prowled the battlefield, looking in vain for survivors. A toxic yellow haze hung over the postapocalyptic wasteland.

Dozens of feet below, in the underground bunker, Turpin witnessed the carnage via an elevated view-screen. The captive ex-cop was held fast to a mechanical throne by a web of plastic tubing, wires, and catheters. Electrodes monitored his vital signs. Stripped to his waist, he slumped upon the throne, barely able to hold up his head, which felt unbearably heavy. Feverish, he felt his body drying from the inside out. Rivers of sweat failed to cool his baking flesh. The ghastly images on the screen made it even harder to combat the despair flooding his soul. Death and devastation seemed to be winning on every front.

Don't give up, he thought stubbornly. *There's always hope.*

Godfrey Good marveled at Turpin's struggles. "The superhumans huddle in their holes, afraid to face us. Yet this 'ordinary' maggot battles on alone against Anti-Life infection." The sinister preacher looked like he had aged fifteen years since they had first arrived at Command-D. Deep wrinkles creased his haggard face. His sweaty robes hung loosely on his withered frame. He leaned heavily on a walking stick. Rheumy eyes regarded Turpin with concern. "The incubation phase demands the ruin of a powerful, noble spirit, but if the mortal continues to resist?" He dabbed at his brow with a damp handkerchief. "The bodies we wore in the Fourth World before its Fall were fit for Prime Celestials. But this . . . this rotting, wheezing engine of meat?"

He coughed into the handkerchief. Blood spotted the cloth.

Mister Simyan growled in response. A monocle magnified the ape-man's baleful left eye.

"Well said," Mokkari addressed his hirsute colleague. Smeared makeup defaced his epicene features. Dried blood stained his dingy lab coat. "Zealots of the Cult of Simyan and Mokkari toil without rest on Evil Factory production lines across the planet, building brave new bodies for the Fifth World!"

"So?" Good objected. "*My* night-missionaries spread the Gospel of Anti-Life to every living soul! My devotees far outnumber *yours*." He snorted at his rivals. "As if Darkseid will favor you filthy wretches when he finally incarnates!"

Mokkari shrugged languidly and took a drag on an imported cigarette. "Who knows?" He had the unconcerned air of a dissipated Prussian aristocrat. "Maybe he'll favor Granny Goodness, now spreading our contagion to the stars. Let us not forget, the cosmic Power Battery of the Guardians of the Universe is within her grasp, Godfrey." A low growl intruded on the debate and Mokkari nodded at a bestial figure at the other end of the laboratory. "Or Kalibak here, the savage son of Darkseid, in a new body bio-figured to reflect his barbarism."

The Tiger-Man raised his shaggy head at the mention of his name. Gleaming blue armor covered his herculean torso and wrists, and a furry paw clutched a massive steel mace. He growled loudly as he chewed on the severed arm of a dead Green Lantern. The rest of Opto3O9v lay at Kalibak's feet. The alien Lantern had foolishly infiltrated Command-D in hopes of clearing Hal Jordan's name. That had proved to be a fatal mistake.

Turpin averted his eyes from the gruesome sight. He strained against the infection inside him. In his day, he'd fought monsters and gangsters and super-creeps, but nothing like this. *I've never backed down,* he thought. *Never asked for help. But Lord help me now.* Someone *help me!*

He stared at his own reflection in a mirror mounted to the side of his throne. His craggy face was growing ever more gray and ossified, its deep lines etched into tissues that looked more like stone than flesh. Suppurating fissures cracked open his dry, crumbling skin, and a reddish film coated his eyes. His hair had all fallen out days before.

"Look!" Good rejoiced, drawing comfort from Turpin's steady desiccation. "Humanity's descent into the Forever Pit has begun!" He gazed rapturously at the suffering detective. "Bring on your glorious nativity, Great One! Hallelujah!"

Turpin's own gaze drifted back to the bloody battlefield. His heart sank.

How can I keep on fighting, he despaired, *if there's nothing left to fight for?*

WASHINGTON, D.C.

"I ran into Black Lightning on his way here," the Tattooed Man revealed, "but the Justifiers got to him." He glared sullenly at the heroes gathered in the Justice League conference room. "You want more, you can drop the cop attitude."

Green Arrow leaned upon his bow, one leg up on a chair. "Stick to the story, wise guy."

"'Wise guy'?" Richards bristled. "Screw you!" A tattooed pit bull bared its fangs upon his forehead. He shook his head in disgust, as though furious at himself for letting things get so out of hand. "We all should've seen it coming, back at the 'Dark Side Club.' The boss and his bad dreams, getting weirder every day, until it seemed like he was harder . . . older. . . ."

More like an evil god? Oracle surmised. *Dark Side equals Darkseid?*

"That was only the beginning," she said, leaning forward in her wheel-chair. "They've wounded our people, our minds, our planet, in ways we can barely imagine. We're disoriented, out of our depth, and whatever we think this appears to be, it's *worse*." Her voice was grave. "I only saw a fragment of the Anti-Life Equation before I killed the Internet. . . . I only experienced it for a few moments. . . ." Her face paled at the memory. She hadn't slept well in days. "But it's a mathematical proof that Darkseid is the rightful master of everything in existence."

"My foot!" Ever the rebel, Green Arrow scoffed at the notion. "There's no Anti-Life a little narrow escape can't cure."

Oracle admired his spirit, but feared that he underestimated the apparent hopelessness of their situation. "Oliver, we're surrounded. There's no way out. No power." The mob outside the Hall of Justice had multiplied at a geo-metric rate over the last few hours. The force field was on its last legs. She could hear the Justifiers pounding against the reinforced promethium blast doors. The emergency lights were dimming. "And they know we're here."

"We get it, okay!" Linda Park snapped. The Flash's wife comforted her children, who looked spooked by Oracle's bleak assessment of their odds. "But we're not giving in now. Not us. Not you."

Little Iris clung to Joan's side. "I'm scared, Mrs. Garrick." She looked anx-iously at Ray Terrill, who was standing by a communications console. The sunny glow radiating from his body seemed to reassure the girl a little. "Ray, you're not scared, are you?"

"A little scared is pretty normal," he said gently. His golden helmet rested on the conference table behind him, revealing the face of a handsome blond man in need of a shave. He shone more brightly to combat both the figura-tive and literal gloom. "I don't just deliver the news, though. I can ride light beams around the world seven times a second. I'm a human power genera-tor." He laid a glowing hand onto a deactivated control panel. "Think how easily someone like me could set up a worldwide video link."

"No! Don't!" Oracle blurted. She rolled forward to stop him from power-ing up the console. "They're in the system! They monitor *everything*!"

Ray ignored her protests. Power flowed from his fingertips to light up a series of monitors along the wall, and dead circuits hummed back to life.

"The system I'm using was abandoned." The glare of his being forced Oracle to back away and place her right arm before her eyes. "Did you know the super-criminal fraternity had its own secret Internet, the Unternet?"

Startled looks answered his question.

"Yeah, neither did we," he admitted, "until a highly placed source in Libra's Secret Society told us how to get in." He gazed up at the central screen. "Watchtower 1! Are you there?"

"Well, I'll be a mindless slave of the corporate machine," Green Arrow murmured as a fuzzy image resolved upon the screen. A familiar face appeared on the monitor.

"Ray! You did it!" Mister Terrific said. He peered long-distance at the glowing hero. "This is Watchtower 1: Switzerland. The siege has gotten worse since you were here, but the Castle is still holding."

Checkmate HQ occupied a medieval castle hidden away in the Swiss Alps. Frantic technicians could be seen manning their posts behind Mister Terrific. A separate screen lit up, revealing an exterior view of the fortress. Its imposing stone walls and battlements were under assault by an army of European Justifiers, including several converted super-villains. The heroes in D.C. watched from afar as Hawkgirl defended the Castle from the Silver Swan, one of Wonder Woman's old enemies. Flames licked the fringes of Hawkgirl's feathery wings, but she kept on soaring. Her spiked mace struck her winged adversary in the face, sending the Swan's Justifier helmet flying. Metallic silver pinions kept the Swan aloft, however, and she retaliated with a piercing sonic cry to rival Black Canary's. Her curly brown hair had been flattened against her scalp by the mind-controlling helmet. Crazed red eyes revealed that she was still under Darkseid's sway.

Explosions detonated in the sky around the aerial combatants as antiair-craft guns mounted in the castle's turrets targeted the combat choppers straf-ing the stronghold. Red Tornado hurtled through the air, his android body propelled by a whirlwind of his own creation. His whirling arms generated a vortex that brought down an attacking gunship. But his heroic efforts drew fierce opposition in the persons of Bolt and Halo, both of whom wore Justi-fier helmets upon their heads. Bolt, a former special effects technician turned professional assassin, teleported past the Red Tornado's whirlwind to zap the android elemental with a powerful high-voltage blast, even as Halo hit the Tornado from behind with a concussive burst of bright orange energy. The artificial hero went into a tailspin before crashing into the alpine slopes below. Oracle hoped he hadn't been damaged beyond repair.

So much for Swiss neutrality, she thought bitterly. A moody twilight sky reminded her that the battle at the Castle was taking place a good seven time zones away. Apparently no place was safe from this ultimate crisis. *We're all in this together.*

On the central screen, Michael Holt held a walkie-talkie up to his ear. His patented T-Spheres orbited his head; the baseball-sized computers used holographic displays to provide him with a constant flow of fresh data. "Mister Terrific online for Checkmate Global Peace Agency. Stand by all Watchtowers. I'm handing you over to the Green Lantern."

The image shifted to a view of Alan Scott standing before an illuminated status board tracking the availability of nearly every superpowered champion on Earth. Oracle was distressed to see that Superman, Batman, Wonder Woman, Cyborg, Blue Devil, Black Lightning, Dr. Fate, the Flash, Starfire, and several other heroes were all listed as "MIA." Others, such as the Enchantress and John Stewart, were listed as "INJURED." The Martian Manhunter, of course, was now "DECEASED."

Wonder how many of us will end up in that final category? Oracle recalled the fragment of the Anti-Life Equation she had glimpsed before and a shudder worked its way down to her waist. *Could be worse. I think I'd rather die than become another one of Darkseid's brainwashed slaves. . . .*

"Friends, defenders of the Earth, ladies and gentlemen," Alan Scott addressed the Resistance. "Listen up and listen good. We only have moments before our enemies intercept and corrupt this transmission." He stood proudly before them, his back straight like the old soldier he was. His purple cloak was draped somberly over his shoulders. Emerald flames flickered around the mystical ring on his left hand. "Our world has become the target of gods, with powers and abilities we've never encountered before. They have access to experimental genetic technology in the Blüdhaven Command-D facility. They can splice people and animals to create hybrid soldiers. Their living presence deforms time and distorts our minds. . . ."

Not much of a pep talk so far, Oracle thought. *I hope he's got something more up that puffy red sleeve of his.*

"But it's not over yet," Scott insisted. "We've gathered superhumans, crime fighters, and refugees in five great Watchtowers, in a ring around the world. This is the first moment we've all shared since our foes made their move. And this is my last chance to say, have courage." His voice rang out defiantly, just as it had against Hitler's tyranny generations ago. "You are not alone!"

One by one, the other Watchtowers checked in:

"Watchtower 3 online!" Supergirl declared from another screen. "The Fortress of Solitude."

The crystalline pillars behind her reflected the alien architecture of the planet Krypton. Dozens of survivors were crowded into Superman's arctic refuge, including the Metal Men, Tawky Tawny, Liberty Belle, Hourman, and Blue Beetle. Civilians in winter gear, including Lois Lane, Jimmy Olsen, Perry White, and what was left of the staff of the *Daily Planet*, mingled with the costumed heroes and robots. A pair of scared urchins clung to Supergirl's side as Streaky rubbed its head against her leg.

"We're holding fast," she reported. "Awaiting orders."

A similar report came from the jungles of Africa. "Watchtower 4!" King Ulgo reported from Gorilla City, a hidden realm of super-intelligent primates first discovered by Barry Allen years ago. To Oracle's horror, she saw that the gleaming spires of the city were under attack by shaggy black apes wearing faceless silver helmets. *God help us,* she thought. *Are those* gorilla *Justifiers?*

Ulgo's elite simian army battled to defend their home, aided by a handful of African heroes such as Freedom Beast, Kid Impala, and Congorilla. Freedom Beast, wearing nothing but a loincloth and a traditional tribal mask, leapt deftly among the brainwashed gorillas, lashing out with his bare hands and feet. The sacred mask, along with a mystical elixir, heightened his strength and senses to superhuman levels. He fought back against the invaders just as fiercely as he had once battled apartheid in his native South Africa. Congorilla, a large golden ape housing the mind of a legendary African explorer, beat his chest with his fists as he stood over the limp body of a fallen Justifier.

Their younger colleague, Kid Impala, was faring less well. Despite his super-speed, the teenage Zulu warrior was struck down by a psychic blast from Gorilla Grodd himself, now under Darkseid's control. Not even Kid

Impala could outrun the speed of thought, it seemed. Overpowered by the powerful apes, the youth was unable to stop Grodd from placing a Justifier helmet onto his head. *We just lost another hero to the enemy,* Oracle realized, heartsick at the loss of the young man's free will. *Who's next?*

"Holding!" Ulgo declared perhaps a trifle optimistically. Gorilla City looked like it was facing extinction.

Another screen lit up. "Watchtower 5!" August General-in-Iron, the commander of the Great Ten, China's own government-sponsored team of "super-functionaries," reported from their hidden base within the Great Wall of China. His rust-colored biometal hide resembled a segmented suit of armor. His teammates, including Accomplished Perfect Physician, Ghost Fox Killer, and Immortal Man in Darkness, stood behind him. Explosions sounded in the background as dust rained down from the ceiling. "Holding."

But for how much longer? Oracle worried.

KAHNDAQ.

Alan Scott's transmission had also been intercepted by a view-screen in the imperial throne room of the royal palace of a small Middle Eastern kingdom. Black Adam, the once and present ruler of Kahndaq, sat grimly upon a forbidding stone throne. The skulls of his enemies were piled high around him. Dusty tapestries hung upon the walls. Green Lantern's call to arms accompanied a tense encounter between two longtime enemies.

"I fought my way here, Adam," Shazam said. Once known as Captain Marvel Jr., Freddy Freeman's superpowered alter ego had recently adopted his magic word as his codename. His new costume resembled that of the original Captain Marvel. A golden thunderbolt was emblazoned on the chest of a cherry red uniform. A white cape with golden trim hung from his brawny shoulders. No mask or hood concealed his square-jawed features. A mane of thick black hair gave him the look of a modern-day Samson. He stood before Black Adam, facing the scowling tyrant. "Do you intend to brood upon your throne until the sky falls in, or will you rejoin the Marvel Family at last?"

Teth-Adam had been the first of the wizard's champions, back in the days of the pharaohs. But when tragedy hardened his heart, turning him from justice to vengeance, Mighty Adam had become the dreaded Black Adam—and a relentless adversary of all who later claimed the power of Shazam.

"The ancient deities who lend us their powers have been overthrown by these New Gods of Apokolips," Adam pointed out. His dark hair narrowed to a widow's peak above his saturnine features. His silk costume was black where Shazam's was red. A golden sash encircled his waist. Tapered ears heightened his demonic appearance. "We are at our weakest. Outnumbered. *Doomed.*"

"You've survived over four thousand years," Shazam challenged him. "Don't tell me you mean to surrender now." He nodded at the broadcast from Checkmate HQ. "Listen to the man."

The transmission was starting to break up, but the gist of Alan Scott's vital message came through:

"Sources confirm Blüdhaven . . . entry point into this world . . . everything we've got . . . bridge at Blüdhaven . . . dawn . . . our last stand . . ."

"Hmm," Black Adam stroked his chin, reconsidering. A bloodthirsty gleam came into his dark eyes. "Sounds like my kind of battle."

CHAPTER 20

WASHINGTON, D.C.

"Calling all super hero—!"

Green Lantern's stirring exhortation was cut off by a final burst of static. The screens upon the wall all blanked out.

"They're gone," Oracle realized aloud. "We're on our own again."

Green Arrow figured they'd heard enough. "Blüdhaven," he spat. "I knew that place was brewing trouble."

"So what do we do now?" Linda Park asked.

The Tattooed Man spoke up. "Black Lightning told me this was important, but he didn't say why." He peeled off the remains of his shredded tank top, revealing a muscular chest liberally embellished with snakes, knives, and scorpions. A new design began to surface from beneath his skin, displacing the earlier tattoos, which swam out of the way. "So don't ask me what it means."

This better not be some sort of trick, Green Arrow thought warily. He drew a fresh arrow just in case.

"He called it a circuit," Richards elaborated as a gleaming silver pattern formed upon his head and chest; the design did, in fact, look like a sophisticated circuit diagram. "And he said to keep it safe." He shrugged casually, looking vaguely embarrassed to be cooperating with the Justice League of all people. "The man put his life on the line for my family, or I wouldn't be here, understand." The mysterious sigil glowed like phosphorous upon his flesh. "I kept it hidden where they'd never find it. Right here on my skin."

The pattern looked oddly familiar to Green Arrow, but it took him a moment to place it. *Isn't that the same design Metron used to sport?* He had been reviewing the League's files on the New Gods ever since this crap first hit the fan.

He wasn't the only person to recognize the circuit. "That looks like those crop circles that just sprouted up in England," Oracle pointed out.

"And those cave paintings they found in the subway tunnels," the Ray observed.

What the heck? Green Arrow thought. He wished to God that Black Lightning himself had made it to the Hall to explain, instead of the Tattooed Man. *Where is Jefferson anyway?*

An electrical blast, coming from the front gates, shook the headquarters. The emergency lights shorted out, throwing the conference room into shadow. Sparks erupted from screens and consoles, and a loud zapping noise made the hairs on Green Arrow's neck rise.

"That sound!" Black Canary exclaimed.

Green Arrow spun toward the entrance. "That's the shield popping! They're through!" He looked worriedly at Linda, Joan, and the kids. "We have civilians!" He fitted an explosive arrow to his bow before turning to his wife. "Any ideas?"

"The Hall of Justice has a teleport system." She peered quizzically at the Ray, who flared up to replace the burnt-out lights. "How about you transform into a teleport carrier wave and use the transmitter array to carry us out?"

Ray put his golden helmet back on. "It could work. I can transform to any wavelength on the electromagnetic spectrum, which *should* include teleport carrier waves."

Should? Green Arrow got the distinct impression that Ray had never tried anything like this before. *That's not exactly reassuring.*

The Tattooed Man sounded equally dubious. "You really think you can do this? Just like that?" He swore under his breath. "You guys are nuts!"'

"It's the only way," Black Canary said decisively. "No arguments!"

She herded everyone out the door toward the transporters. The Ray pushed Oracle's wheelchair, and the Flash kids ran alongside their mom. Black Canary helped Joan Garrick along; thankfully, the elderly woman was fairly spry for her years. Green Arrow wished he knew where Iris Allen was; unfortunately, Barry Allen's "widow" had insisted on staying behind in Central City to wait for her husband. He heard the blast doors crashing open only a few rooms away.

We're cutting this pretty close.

Racing for the teleporters, they took a shortcut through the League's spectacular trophy room. The exotic mementos on display celebrated the JLA's past victories over the forces of evil and honored the champions—both living and dead—who had risked their lives to defend the Earth from unimaginable perils. Oversized playing cards bore mug shots of the infamous Royal Flush Gang. Coruscating bits of "dark matter" were suspended in a vacuum chamber. A holographic portrait gallery displayed rotating images of every past and present member of the League, from Ambush Bug to Zatanna. Kanjar Ro's Gamma Gong, Amazo's robotic head, artificial kryptonite, Aztek's helmet, Wandjina's battle-axe, the Key's skeleton key, and other weapons were safely locked away in transparent display cases. An alien starfish clung to the sides of a bottle-shaped aquarium. Miniature robot duplicates of the JLA, built by the Toyman and Abra Kadabra, pounded on the walls of their unbreakable dollhouse. A tiny Green Arrow, the size of an action figure, kicked irritably at his cage. The real thing barely gave the trophies a second glance.

This was no time to reminisce.

Leaving the trophy room behind, they quickly reached their destination. The transporter array consisted of a row of upright transparent containment tubes, each large enough to hold three or four individuals. Power couplings and sensors paneled the extraterrestrial apparatus capping each tube. Quarantine step pads in the base of the tubes sterilized all transmissions. A control kiosk faced the tubes. Blinking lights warned of imminent power failure.

Green Arrow waited outside while the others piled into the cylinders. He shoved his wife in ahead of him, then slammed the tube door shut behind her.

"Oliver, no!" she shouted through the clear plastic. "What are you doing?"

He could hear the bad guys heading this way. The baying of the hell-hounds echoed through the corridors outside.

"They'll come right after you, you know that," he said, spelling it out as bluntly as he could; there was no time to soften the blow. "Justifiers never stop. But if I wreck the teleport navigation controls after you've gone . . ."

Dinah pounded on the cylinder from the inside. "No, *no!*"

"Watchtower teleports are offline." Green Arrow held the door shut. "You're the leader of the Justice League. T-Man's rocking the voodoo tattoo. Ray's the carrier wave, and the Flashes will kill us both if anything happens to their families." His mind was made up. "Nowhere on the planet is safe, but I have an idea."

"Don't do this," she pleaded. "I can't lose you."

"I worked out the angles," he lied. Their hands pressed against each other, cruelly divided by a curved sheet of Thanagarian crystal. "They won't get me. I'll use the anti-Anti-Life arrow." Despite his bravado, his throat tightened at the prospect of being separated from Dinah, possibly forever. "Pretty bird."

She reluctantly accepted the inevitable. Her lips pressed against the interior of the sterile tube. "Ollie. My beautiful Robin Hood."

The Ray powered up the teleporters, then vanished in a burst of light. A pinkish energy flux filled the cylinders, and its occupants faded into the glare. The ambient matter was instantly teleported to waiting receiver modules. Green Arrow watched sorrowfully as the love of his life, along with the others, vanished from sight, leaving only a smudge of lipstick behind. Dinah was gone.

Good-bye.

With no time to lose, he fired the explosive arrow into the control kiosk. The console burst into flame. A moment later, an evil cavalry burst into the room. Justifiers mounted on rabid hellhounds crashed through the door. "Destroy!" the lead rider bellowed. The dogs' massive paws trampled the broken door into splinters. "Anti-Life justifies our actions!"

"Is that so!" Furious at being torn away from his wife, Green Arrow welcomed the opportunity to take out his frustrations on the invaders. He unleashed a volley of razor-tipped arrows. "Well, my absolute hatred of dog-riding totalitarian storm troopers justifies this!"

The arrows, fired one after another in rapid succession, slammed into the first wave of giant mastiffs. Yelping in pain, the beasts stumbled and crashed to the floor. Justifiers tumbled headfirst from their saddles onto the hard ceramic tiles. Arrows pierced their wrists, forcing them to drop their weapons. Skewered kneecaps downed more Justifiers, but Green Arrow deliberately avoided any kill shots. *Those are innocent people behind those goddamn helmets!*

A rope arrow erected a wall of netting between Green Arrow and the invaders. The lead Justifier rose to his feet on the other side of the barrier. Metallic gold lightning bolts adorned his disturbingly familiar black and blue uniform. A steel helmet hid his face, but not his identity.

"Ah, crap!" said Green Arrow, recognizing his missing teammate. "Jefferson!"

"I live for Anti-Life," Black Lightning said. Crackling blue electricity flashed around his body. "I die for Anti-Life."

Green Arrow refused to accept that his friend was gone for good. "I know that's you in there, Jefferson! Fight it!" He held off launching another arrow, praying he could get through to the hero beneath the helmet. "Whatever they're feeding you, fight it!"

"Freedom is surrender to Darkseid!"

Lightning jumped from the Justifier's fingers. The bolt burned through the netting, striking Green Arrow in the chest. Another powerful jolt knocked the archer off his feet, and his bow flew from his grip. Black Lightning and his fellow Justifiers ripped down the rope barrier and charged across the teleport room. While nameless dog soldiers subdued Green Arrow, Black Lightning strode over to inspect the empty tubes. He cocked his head at the smoking control panel.

"They've left no trail to follow," he informed the other Justifiers.

Shaken, but still defiant, Green Arrow relished his victory. "You didn't get them! You'll never get us all, you bastards!" The soldiers hauled him onto his knees. His entire body was shaking, and his beard was singed, yet he took comfort in the knowledge that Dinah and the others were safe for the time being. "And we'll fight to the last, we'll—"

A metal helmet was pressed down onto his head. The Anti-Life Equation poured into his ears.

Loneliness + alienation + fear + despair . . .
Oliver Queen fell silent.

THE WATCHTOWER.

"Ollie."

Two hundred miles above the Earth, Black Canary gazed down on the spinning blue globe from the observation deck of the JLA's orbital Watchtower. A bright emerald radiance shone through the airtight picture windows. Thankfully, the planetary quarantine established by the Alpha Lanterns had not cut off the satellite from the embattled world below; the glowing green bands were farther out. The Ray, Oracle, and the other survivors kept their distance, allowing her a moment of privacy.

Her eyes teared as she recalled her husband's heroic sacrifice. She wondered if she would ever see him again.

Then her responsibility to the League—and to humanity—asserted itself. Oliver had stayed behind to ensure that the rest of them could keep on fighting. *I'll be damned,* she vowed, *if I let him down now.*

"Okay." She turned to face the people in her care. Her eyes and voice were hard as steel. "Station weapons review. *Now.*"

"Yes, sir!" the Ray said, snapping to attention.

Even the Tattooed Man got the message.

CENTRAL CITY.

Located across the river from Keystone, Central City had once been a thriving Midwestern metropolis, slightly more urbane and sophisticated than its more industrial sister city.

No longer.

Iris Allen trudged numbly through the desolate streets of a city transformed. Her shift at the Evil Factory done for the day, she shambled back toward her home alongside her fellow drones. Soot and sweat rendered the mindless men and women almost indistinguishable from each other. Newly erected chimneys belched smoke into the churning red sky. Police cars, with freshly painted omega symbols on their doors and windows, cruised the dirty streets. Rotting bodies hung from the streetlights as examples to others. Loudspeakers, mounted to telephone poles, bombarded the cowed populace with the brutal wisdom of Apokolips:

"Work! Consume! Die!"

A police car pulled up to a curb, and armored Justifiers exited the vehicle. Snatching a female Lowlie at random from the sidewalk, they threw her to the pavement and started tearing off her clothes. The woman's mate foolishly mustered the will to protest. The Justifiers turned from the female and proceeded to beat the male into submission. No one in the vicinity, including Iris, batted an eye. The omnipresent loudspeakers told them all they need to know.

"Judge others! Condemn the different! Exploit the weak!"

Iris reached her residence unscathed and entered the dimly lit apartment. Every muscle in her body ached from hours of tedious labor, but she accepted her exhaustion without complaint. To die on the job was to die for Darkseid.

She planted herself on the couch in front of a flickering TV set. A scarlet omega dominated the screen. She let the television's relentless message wash over her, just as she had every night since she'd accepted the Equation.

"Anti-Life makes it right," the TV chanted. "All is one in Darkseid."

A whoosh of air heralded the arrival of two Scarlet Speedsters. Loose wrappers and napkins fluttered to the floor. Iris distantly registered the presence of the intruders, but lacked the energy to care. Her blank red eyes remained fixed on the television set as its words swept away her will.

"Self = Darkseid. Self = Darkseid. Self = Darkseid."

"Hi, honey!" Barry Allen said. "I'm home."

His voice roused her from her stupor. She staggered to her feet and backed away from the Flashes in alarm. An inarticulate whimper escaped her lips.

Condemn the different.

Barry was taken aback by her reaction. "Iris?"

"It's Anti-Life," Wally reminded him. He sounded sick to his stomach. "I don't think there's anything we can do for Aunt Iris."

Barry disregarded his nephew's warning. "She's still my Iris." He approached her slowly, trying his best not to frighten her. She surrendered meekly to her fate as he leaned forward to kiss his wife. "It feels like I've waited a thousand lifetimes to do this."

His voice stirred something deep inside her, something she barely remembered. A name surfaced from her memory, slipping past the Equation echoing endlessly in her brain. She toyed nervously with the ring upon her finger.

Barry?

Their lips met and a spark of electricity arced between them.

BARRY!

Life and love flooded back into her soul. The incarnadine glow faded from her eyes. No longer frightened, she returned his kiss and embraced him with all her strength. Tears of joy leaked from the corners of her eyes.

"Hey, you," Barry said softly, after their lips finally pulled apart. "Sorry I was late."

A bittersweet smile lifted her lips. Back when they were courting, the Fastest Man on Earth had never been on time. "Barry . . ." She rested her head on his shoulder, drawing renewed strength from his familiar presence. "It's going to be all right now, isn't it?"

"You bet," he promised.

CHAPTER 21

THE SWISS ALPS.

The assault on the Castle continued. Night had fallen, but the stormy red sky made that a moot point. Alan Scott joined the Castle's defenders in the air above the besieged fortress. Emerald flames, fueled by his own indomitable willpower, carried him aloft, where he found Hawkgirl still battling valiantly against the oncoming horde.

"Where's our backup?" Kendra Saunders called out anxiously. A beaked metal helmet gave her face an avian cast. The Nth Metal in her belt, along with the artificial wings strapped to her back, allowed her to defy gravity. She swooped through the night sky like her predatory namesake, wielding a spiked metal mace. The reincarnation of a murdered Egyptian princess, she had a natural affinity for ancient weaponry. "When does it end?"

Alan wished he knew. Fleets of enemy choppers came soaring over the mountaintops, along with an even more alarming threat: Super-Justifiers. Some were villains, recruited from the Secret Society, while others, disturbingly, had once been heroes. Despite the Justifier helmets hiding their faces, Green Lantern recognized far too many of their attackers: Halo, Man-Bat, Killer Moth, Bolt, Firestorm, Typhoon, Donna Troy . . .

"Dear God," Alan murmured. "Some of them are our own people!"

The relentless onslaught forced them to retreat to the Castle ramparts.

Antiaircraft emplacements provided temporary cover, but for how much longer? Green Lantern felt his strength and determination waning; the emerald flames around his ring began to sputter and die. "We can't stop yet," he said stubbornly, as much to himself as Hawkgirl. "We have to protect the Castle until the Omega Offensive is ready."

Troops were already massing for the dawn assault on Blüdhaven, but they still needed a few more hours to prepare. There was too much at stake to go off half-cocked.

"Can you feel it, Kendra?" he said in hushed voice. "The world of the gods, colliding into ours." Crimson lightning flashed overhead, and a driving rain began to fall. A cold wind blew against his face. "As if we're at the end of everything."

Hawkgirl looked up at the sky. "Alan, this rain . . ." She held out her hand. Crimson droplets pooled in her palm. "It's *blood*." Sticky red rivulets streaked her upturned helmet. "It's raining blood. . . ."

BLÜDHAVEN.

"The birth struggle is almost over!" Reverend Good rejoiced. Gasping, he leaned upon his cane. "Hurry with his crown before my own wretched flesh disintegrates."

Mary Marvel sauntered into the laboratory bearing a blue-steel helmet upon a black velvet cushion. Her broken elbow had long since been healed by the dark magic flowing through her veins. Turpin recognized the corrupted heroine from the alien memories taking over his brain. *I did this to her . . . or rather* he *did. . . .*

The defeated cop slumped hopelessly upon his throne of pain. He had tried to fight back, show them what humanity was made of, but wrestling with Darkseid was like trying to beat back the ocean. Good and the others crowded around him, transfixed by his ungodly transformation. Mokkari tittered evilly, and Simyan peered through his monocle. Kalibak gnawed on a bloody bone.

"Hosanna!" Good preached. "We live another day! Give us a sign, Great Darkseid!"

A spark of defiance flickered inside Turpin. His petrified gray face twisted in contempt. "K-kiss . . . kiss my . . ."

Mary Marvel lowered Darkseid's crown upon his head.

"Thumbs-up for the triumph of the human spirit," Good asked mockingly, "or thumbs-down to summon a day of holocaust that will never end?"

A solitary tear ran down Turpin's face. *Like I really have a choice!*

THE SWISS ALPS.

"T-Spheres say we have incoming!" Mister Terrific shouted. The levitating globes projected the UFO's trajectory before his eyes. His motto, "FAIR PLAY," was printed in block letters upon the sleeves of his black leather jacket. "Incoming from nowhere!"

Thunder clapped inside the vaulted stone command center of the castle. A Boom Tube opened up at the far end of the chamber. Mister Terrific threw up an arm to shield himself from the sudden glare and concussion as a flying car zoomed out of the vortex to skid to a halt across the scuffed tile floor. Checkmate personnel dove for cover as the silver sports car came in for a hard landing, smashing through empty cubicles and monitoring stations. Sparks flew from the undercarriage of the vehicle. A convertible top popped up, revealing a gaggle of Asian teenagers inside. Mister Terrific immediately identified them as Japan's celebrated Super Young Team.

Had they been brainwashed by Darkseid too?

A pair of grown-ups accompanied the teenagers. One of them leapt to his feet in the front of the car. He wore a garish red and yellow costume. "Don't shoot!" he shouted, yanking off his mask. His anxious face was familiar from dozens of top-rated TV specials. A distinctive pattern had been painted on his face with makeup. "I'm Mister Miracle, super escape artist!"

This did nothing to reassure the Castle's stressed-out security officers, who had seen the Castle under attack by former heroes for hours now. Sharpshooters targeted the Wonder Wagon and its passengers. Frightened analysts and technicians ran for safety.

"Don't shoot!" Mister Miracle threw his hands in the air. "We can save the world!"

It was the wrong time to ask for restraint; the guards were already on edge from the daylong siege, and the Wonder Wagon's explosive entrance was easily mistaken for an attack. Before Mister Terrific could order the troops to hold their fire, an overeager guard squeezed his trigger. A shot rang out.

No! Mister Terrific thought. *Wait!*

The bullet hit Shilo Norman in the chest. He toppled backward like a dead man.

BLÜDHAVEN.

"Freedom's spirit falls!" Reverend Good exulted, growing more ecstatic by the minute. "A sign, Great One!"

Darkseid's acolytes gathered around Turpin, praising him.

"Devastator!" Mary Marvel cooed. "Lord of Woe!"

"Eternal Ruler!" Mokkari added, shamelessly currying favor. "Master of Creation!"

Simyan grunted. Kalibak snarled.

"Show us your will!" Good pleaded.

Alone upon his throne, Turpin realized the choice was simple. Because, here at the end, there was no choice at all. Only Apokolips and Darkseid forever.

His left arm rose of its own volition.

I can't fight him anymore, Turpin thought. *I give up.*

His thumb pointed downward for all humanity.

CHAPTER 22

OA.

Hal Jordan stood on trial at the center of the universe. His arms and neck weighed down by luminous emerald shackles, he faced his accusers in the meeting hall of the Green Lantern Corps, in the Guardians' vast citadel on the planet Oa. His fellow Corps members filled the bleachers and galleries, while all nine of the Guardians hovered above the proceedings. Alpha Lantern Boodikka stood guard over Hal, her twin rings generating his bonds. The enormous Central Power Battery, from which all Lanterns derived their strength, loomed in the background, glowing brightly upon its pedestal. Fashioned in the shape of a giant lantern, the great Battery was over fifty feet tall. Molten green plasma churned within its core.

Malet Dasim, an alien Green Lantern from Sector 183, presided over the trial. Wriggling tentacles dangled from his stocky torso as he levitated above the floor. A flowing green robe fit his current duties as prosecutor. A bristling brown beard carpeted his venerable countenance, and twin metallic horns sprouted from his cranium. His power ring was embedded in his forehead. He was the master district attorney on his home planet of Dlist. His deep, resonant voice echoed throughout the hall.

"Hal Jordan of Earth. Green Lantern 2814.1. You stand accused of deicide and conspiracy to overthrow the laws of Oa." A gloved tentacle pointed at an intimidating figure standing a few yards away. "Your accuser, Alpha Lantern Kraken. She has uncovered evidence that you have become host to a malevolent psychic parasite. By order of the Book of Oa, an Alpha Lantern's judgment is said to be infallible."

The Book of Oa, composed by the Guardians themselves, laid out the rules by which the Corps enforced peace and justice throughout the cosmos. As such, it was the ultimate authority.

"There's no such thing as infallibility in this universe," Hal retorted. "I'd have noticed." He remained confident that the truth would ultimately clear his name, despite the worrisome blanks in his memory. His finger felt naked without his power ring. "But I can't seem to account for my whereabouts." He glanced over at Kraken. "If you can prove . . ."

She eagerly testified against him. "Observe the scar on his head where the god Orion struck in his death throes. I submit that this Jordan, once so easily possessed by Parallax, now plays host to a murderous god of Apokolips!"

Hal winced at Kraken's reference to the time he spent possessed by Parallax, the living embodiment of fear. That dreadful ordeal remained a blot on his record, and his conscience, that he might never live down. *But I'm not guilty this time,* he thought. *I'm sure of it!*

"Jordan is a valued officer," one of the Guardians observed. Her inscrutable blue face bore a neutral expression. Her hands were tucked into the sleeves of her scarlet robe. "We must examine your evidence carefully."

"What of his fellow Lanterns?" a second Guardian asked. "Sent to Earth to question Lantern John Stewart? Can anyone speak in Jordan's defense before we enact judgment?"

A hush fell over the meeting hall, and, for a long moment, Hal feared that he was on his own. Then a brilliant emerald flash heralded the arrival of Kyle Rayner and Guy Gardner, a pair of human Green Lanterns who had joined the Corps after Hal. The two men now served as Honor Guards on Oa. They phased through the domed ceiling before touching down on the floor of the meeting hall between Hal and Kraken.

"Hold it right there!" Guy shouted. He was a brash, redheaded brawler who had never been accused of tact or decorum. His abrasive manner belied his years of service to the Corps. "There's a reason for that scar on Hal's head! And a reason he can't remember how it got there!"

"Honor Lanterns Gardner and Rayner," a Guardian addressed the new-comers. The immortal being frowned at the unseemly abruptness of their entrance. "What is this?"

"We couldn't get near Earth," Kyle explained. The dark-haired young artist had taken Hal's place as Green Lantern when Hal was possessed by Parallax. Although inexperienced at first, he had proven himself a valuable member of the Corps—and a trusted friend to Hal. "But we think the scar on Hal's head is hiding an implant. A suppressor field chip!"

Guy pointed an accusing finger at Kraken. "*That's* why she's been staying close to him! She put it in there when he was sleeping and it's been hiding her from detection!" Emerald sparks, leaking from his ring, attested to his volatile temperament. "Alpha Lantern Kraken is hosting one of the evil gods of Apokolips! She tried to murder Green Lantern John Stewart, and we ain't having it!"

"Impossible!" Kraken protested. Green flames crackled up and down her left arm. "No Lantern escapes the Alpha Lanterns!" She sneered at Guy and Kyle. "The Earth Lanterns are in league."

A Guardian's brow furrowed. "An Alpha cannot be compromised. That was the very point of their creation."

"Infallible," one of his peers agreed. She peered at Kraken. "Is there any truth to these charges?"

Kraken shrugged. "What can I say?" An evil glint shone in her eyes. "That it was folly to underestimate the power and craft of Darkseid?"

That sounds like a confession to me, Hal thought. Torn between relief at his vindication and dismay at the revelation of the traitor among them, he recalled that the real Kraken had once incurred the wrath of Darkseid by rescuing another Green Lantern from Apokolips. Was this the evil god's revenge?

"Have you any idea how easy it is for a god to hollow out a living mind and hide in this bleeding shell?" Kraken gloated. She walked boldly toward the giant lantern. "As easy as it was for me to reach the Central Power Battery!

Providing the raw energy for the rings of the Green Lantern Corps . . . the deadliest weapons in the universe!"

Kyle and Guy instantly moved to block her. Vicious green centipedes leapt from her twin rings, attacking the Honor Guards, who defended themselves with emerald constructs of their own. A former cartoonist, Kyle willed a suit of manga-inspired armor around him, while Guy generated a bulked-up caricature of himself to wrestle the centipedes into submission. Plasma flared as the artificial constructs battled furiously against each other. Kraken threw out her arms, directing her lethal creations.

The Guardians themselves took action. "Protect the Battery at all costs!" Their delicate fists made stabbing motions as they hurled their willpower at Kraken, and coruscating green fire flashed in their eyes. "It must not be corrupted!"

Their attack hurled Kraken across the hall—into the very lens of the cosmic lantern. A burst of emerald energy exploded around her, revealing the outline of the skeleton beneath her mortal carapace. She crashed into the plinth at the base of the Battery.

Undefeated, she rose to her feet once more. Her mask flipped up, revealing the robotic face beneath. The cybernetic countenance resembled that of the mechanical Manhunters the Guardians had employed in the distant past, long before the creation of the Green Lantern Corps. "Imagine it!" she taunted the hovering immortals. "Darkseid's unstoppable will in command of all this power!" She cackled in anticipation of her triumph. "I'll be his favorite once more!"

Ignoring Hal and the other Lanterns, she launched a direct assault on the Guardians themselves. A pair of giant centipedes struck out at the very Guardian who had insisted on the Alphas' infallibility only moments before. The emerald insects coiled around the immortal's dwarfish body. Venomous stingers stabbed the Guardian over and over again, while his peers looked on in shock; a physical attack on a Guardian was practically unheard of. Bright blue blood sprayed from the victim's lips.

The other Guardians instantly threw up defensive shields around themselves. Dozens of Green Lanterns targeted Kraken with their rings, only to find their weapons surprisingly ineffective. Naught but a few feeble sparks and flames sputtered from their rings. Alien eyes, antennae, and other sense organs regarded their weapons in confusion.

What on Oa was happening?

The Guardians realized their mistake. "We gave her the power to drain the rings!" Crystalline emerald walls protected them from the possessed Alpha Lantern. "Initiate Krona Protocol before it's too late!"

Turning her back on the chagrined immortals, Kraken gazed up at the giant lantern. Loose energy spilled from its shattered lens. "Is this the ultimate technology Metron pointed them toward? A deadly plasma that responds to the dictates of pure will?" She started to draw the released energy into her own chest-battery, even as it began to fade from sight. "It belongs to Granny now!"

No! Hal thought. He strained against his crumbling shackles.

"ALPHA RING POWER AT THIRTY PERCENT," Boodikka's rings reported, as Kraken siphoned their energy away as well. "FIFTEEN PERCENT—"

That was just what Hal wanted to hear. With Kyle and Guy still fighting for their lives against the swarming centipedes, it was up to him now. Ring or no ring, he wasn't about to let Kraken claim the Battery's power for Darkseid. *Not if I have anything to say about it!*

A Green Lantern's greatest strength was his willpower. Hal proved that by exerting his muscles to their utmost. The disintegrating chains finally snapped apart, and he lunged at the distracted Alpha Lantern. "I'm sorry, Kraken," he said, clenching his fists. "I know it's not really you!"

"Jordan!" She glanced back at him over her shoulder. "Your will is no match for—"

He didn't give her a chance to complete her threat as he tackled her to the floor. Her head smashed against the huge jade pedestal. "Rings only work if you can *think*!" he reminded her as he pounded her senseless with his fists. Gloved knuckles slammed repeatedly into Kraken's face and chest as he knelt atop her, pinning her to the floor. Metal gears and components sparked beneath his pounding blows. She had two rings and he had none, so he couldn't let up for a second. If she got the slightest chance to concentrate, he was a dead man. . . .

Her robotic face crumpled into pieces and her body went limp, but Hal kept on hitting her, just in case she was playing possum. The other Alphas raced forward, their own masks flipped upward to reveal the Manhunter beneath. They quickly leeched Kraken's stolen powers away from her.

"Cease and desist!" Boodikka ordered, pulling Hal off the fallen Alpha Lantern. Kraken did not get back up. Varix and the other Alphas aimed their rings at their battered comrade. "That will be enough, Green Lantern 2814.1!"

"Lower your rings, Alphas!" an imperious voice called out. Floating above the fray, the surviving Guardians tended to their stricken peer. Foul black bile dripped from the casualty's gaping wounds. Startled gasps erupted from the bleachers as the assembled Lanterns reacted to the unthinkable. "An immortal is injured!"

Breathing hard, Hal stepped back. His knuckles ached from hammering them into Kraken's cybernetic chassis. He glanced up to check on the great Battery, and was startled to discover that the giant lantern was nowhere to be seen. Only a wisp of green smoke swirled above the pedestal. His eyes widened behind his mask. "What did they do?"

"Krona Protocol," Guy explained. With Kraken defeated, her deadly centipedes had dissolved into the ether. "Come DefCon 1, when the Battery itself is up against the ultimate threat, the Guardians hide it until the all-clear."

This was news to Hal. Such a drastic stratagem had never been employed in all the years he had served in the Corps. *Are things really that bad this time?*

"Get her sedated and into a sciencell!" Salaak pointed at Kraken. The four-armed Slyggian was the keeper of the Book of Oa. His large pink head was canoe-shaped and covered with rough, bony protuberances. "See if we can determine the specific god-consciousness she's harboring."

Hal spared them the effort. "It calls itself 'Granny Goodness.'" Back on Apokolips, the evil crone had ruled hellish orphanages devoted to turning innocent young minds into unquestioning slaves of Darkseid. He wondered whether even Oa's maximum-security sciencells would be able to hold her for long. "And you can strike *infallible* from the rule book."

"Hal, it's hard-core," Kyle informed him. He and Guy fell in beside their teammate. "Space-time around the Earth just crumpled like it was crushed in a fist. Weeks smashed into days."

"They couldn't have known what hit them," Guy agreed. "We couldn't get close to the gravity sink without being sucked in."

A male Guardian confirmed the men's dire report. "The destructive emanations which have fastened themselves to planet Earth are power-classified: New Gods." His somber tone impressed the severity of the situation on the Lanterns below him. "They have word-weapons capable of enslaving souls. Machines that can rewrite the laws of being and bring entire civilizations to their knees."

The Green Man, the new leader of the Alpha Lanterns, entered the hall. A large amphibian humanoid with mottled chartreuse skin, he came from a planet on which individual names were unheard of. His power battery shone within his broad chest. "Even worse, Sector Scanning indicates that Earth is at ground zero of a Doomsday Singularity. The impact of Darkseid's fall is causing cracks to form through all space sectors."

"What'd I tell ya!" Guy said with snort. He turned toward Hal. "John Stewart's still down there. Darkseid's dragging all our friends into hell with him!"

"Then I say we go after him," Hal replied. "You, me, Kyle, and anybody else who wants to. And we kick his ass."

Salaak stepped forward. His upper right arm held out a familiar green artifact. He dropped it into Hal's palm. "Your ring, Jordan."

"Cleared of all charges," a male Guardian pronounced. Along with his surviving peers, he gazed down at the vindicated hero. With the Central Power Battery in limbo, the Lanterns' rings held only a solar day's worth of energy. "You have twenty-four hours to save the universe, Lantern Jordan."

Hal slipped his ring back onto his finger.

So what are we waiting for? he thought.

THE SWISS ALPS.

"Castellan Draper informs us that Castle defenses will fail within the hour, but we are not without resources or a plan, Ms. Montoya." Colonel Khalid escorted Renee through the medieval architecture of Checkmate's alpine fortress. A pair of armed goons maintained a discreet distance behind them, just in case Renee felt like making a break for it. "We brought you here, at great expense, for a reason."

Lucky me, she thought. Her Pseudoderm mask was wadded up in the pocket of her jacket, but she still had plenty of questions. "Which is?"

"I'll let Miss Waller explain," Khalid said, deferring to his colleague.

Amanda Waller met them at the bottom of a sweeping marble stairway. A heavyset black woman in her late forties, she was infamous in intelligence circles as a ruthless and Machiavellian mastermind who seldom let humanitarian concerns get in the way of national security. Formerly Secretary of Meta-human Affairs under the Luthor administration, she now served as the White Queen of Checkmate.

Renee disliked her on sight.

"So what did you think of Overgirl?" Waller asked.

Renee recalled the Aryan Supergirl who had crashed to Earth in Manhattan. "She was almost cute, until I got to the swastika."

"She arrived from a parallel Earth, Ms. Montoya," Waller stated bluntly. "And she left a trail." She fixed her steely eyes on Renee. "We believe it's no coincidence that she found you."

Was she serious? "Look at me," Renee said. "I'm a health nut with a hat and survivor's guilt." As both a cop and a super hero, she had outlived at least two partners. "I don't do science fiction."

"Try science *fact,*" Khalid challenged her. "I suggest you read up on M-theory, higher dimensional branes, and the bulk."

Renee was familiar with the basic idea, that the entire universe was a vibrating membrane inside a higher-dimensional realm known as the bulk. And that separate branes, containing alternate dimensions and realities, sometimes impacted with our own.

"I did," she admitted. "So there's somewhere out there where I never became the Question? Great." She glanced around the main hall of the Castle, which looked more like a historical relic than the top secret base of an international counterterrorism agency. Embroidered tapestries hung upon the walls. Crystal chandeliers dangled from the vaulted ceiling. A stone fireplace was large enough to house a small family. "How did I end up in this dump?"

"You're here because we have something to show you," Waller said.

The silhouette of a black chess piece—a knight, to be precise—was embossed on a pair of large double doors at the end of the hall. The doors swung open at their approach, revealing a high-tech laboratory the size of an airplane hangar. Going from the palatial hall, with its dark age trappings, to the futuristic lab was like traveling through time. Renee felt like she had just stepped from Camelot into the World That's Coming.

"Jeez," she murmured, looking around. "You've got to be kidding me."

Technicians in all-body clean room suits, of the sort worn by workers employed in the manufacture of microchips, were unpacking pieces of artificial people from foam-filled aluminum cartons. Prefabricated heads, legs, and other appendages, all of the same basic design, were removed from the crates. A stoic male face, complete with a bristling blue-steel Mohawk, was wedged between two folded legs, the better to utilize the packing space most efficiently. Each carton appeared to contain all the components needed to put together one complete android.

With some assembly required.

"These are prototype kit super-soldiers with seven-day life spans," Khalid informed her. "Generation zero biomacs." He gestured proudly at the buzzing activity. "Checkmate was created to be the last move in the human game."

Renee didn't know whether to be impressed or appalled. "For real?"

"Do we look like the sort of people who wouldn't have a plan for the day the super heroes failed to save us?" Waller planted her considerable girth in front of Renee. Her beefy hands rested on her hips. "We want you to be part of it, Renee."

Waller didn't sound like she was going to take no for an answer.

BLÜDHAVEN.

Little trace of Dan Turpin remained. Now Darkseid sat upon his blinking steel throne, a blue-steel helmet framing his craggy gray face. Hinged metal calipers supported his legs, and tubes fed into the veins of his ossified limbs.

Crabbed hands gripped the cold metal armrests. Zealous acolytes, their mortal frames deteriorating rapidly, knelt at his feet.

"The cult of Simyan and Mokkari has achieved miracles in your name!" Mokkari proclaimed, prostrate upon the floor. Greasy makeup failed to conceal his gaunt, withered countenance. He looked like an aristocratic junkie in the throes of withdrawal. "We prepared an Earth body fit for the god above gods!"

"Don't listen to him!" Reverend Good squeezed past Mokkari. "It was I, Glorious Godfrey, who spread the Gospel of Anti-Life!" He held out his palsied, liver-spotted hands in supplication. Sweat dripped from his ashen features. "Don't let me perish, Great One!"

Simyan grunted loudly, his sloping forehead pressed against the floor tiles. The ape-man's shaggy mane had gone gray. Cataracts clouded the eye behind his monocle.

". . . populations robbed of their own volition," Mokkari wheezed, talking over his rivals' pleas, "to become Hands of Darkseid, Eyes of Darkseid, limbs of the Night-Lord! Yours is the impulse, they exist only to carry out the deed!"

A gravelly voice emerged from Darkseid's petrified face. "You have accomplished only as *I* will it." He spoke haltingly, as though every word was an effort. "The hour . . . of Apokolips . . . is upon us."

His incarnadine eyes peered past his dying servitors, seeing beyond them to the Spartan barracks elsewhere in the bunker, where his Female Furies prepared for battle. Wonder Woman strapped her beast-mask over her face. Ugly welts crisscrossed her muscular back, a legacy of Mary Marvel's loving discipline. Catwoman pulled on a high purple boot. Batwoman, her face pale and vampiric, holstered her pistols. Giganta crouched within cramped barracks, her mammoth head scraping the ceiling. Giant mastiffs, stabled in nearby cages, awaited their riders. They gnawed on bloody bones and entrails.

"Heed my voice," Darkseid exhorted them. "Ride out, rabid angels . . . my plague goddesses . . . my Furies . . ."

The women mounted their canine steeds, save for Giganta, who loped after them, her knuckles dragging on the floor. Wonder Woman raised her spear. Catwoman cracked her whip. Batwoman gripped the reins of her dog between her teeth as she drew her guns with both hands. Giganta beat her chest. All four Furies hastened to carry out their master's command.

"End it all."

CHAPTER 23

THE SWISS ALPS.

Tracer fire streaked the sky above the Castle. Explosions blossomed as anti-aircraft fire brought down attacking Justifier gunships. Checkmate soldiers, toting bazookas and missile launchers, scrambled atop the fortress's towers and ramparts as flying heroes and villains battled overhead.

Her wings aflame, Hawkgirl crashed onto the battlements from above. She grabbed onto a bullet-scarred stone merlon to keep from toppling over the edge, then rolled onto the floor of the rampart. The smell of burning feathers filled her nostrils. Dancing flames scorched her back, and she cried out in pain.

Tempest, once known as Aqualad, came to her rescue. Atlantean magic conjured up a spray of seawater, which he used to douse Kendra's burning wings. The black and red colors of his skintight wet suit honored the flag of a lost undersea colony. A mystic tattoo was inked upon his lean white face.

"I'm fine, Garth!" she shouted at him. She pulled herself up onto one elbow. "Never mind me! Help Alan!"

Dozens of feet above, Alan Scott was outnumbered. Flaming green falcons and dragons failed to drive back the endless horde of Super-Justifiers. Bolt and Halo held his arms fast, while a third Justifier flew toward him, holding out an empty helmet before her. Stars sparkled upon her inky black leotard. Her silver bracelets and armbands had been forged on Paradise Island.

"Primary target acquired," Donna Troy said mechanically. The former Wonder Girl had grown up to become a heroine in her own right, at least until the Anti-Life Equation stole her mind. Amazon training allowed her to soar upon the wind currents. "Superhuman designate: Green Lantern."

Fighting to free himself, Alan tried to get through to the brainwashed Titan. "Donna, it's me! Don't—!"

Bolt's arm, locked around Green Lantern's throat, choked off his entreaty. Microcircuitry in the villain's dark blue costume hit Alan with a powerful electric jolt. An emerald crossbow evaporated as Alan's concentration faltered. Halo, a brainwashed heroine whose range of powers covered the entire visible spectrum, held him in place with an indigo tractor beam. Green Lantern thrashed hopelessly in his captors' grip.

"There is no struggle with Anti-Life," Donna promised him. She held out the faceless steel helmet.

No! Hawkgirl thought, watching from below. *Not Alan too!*

Before Donna could shove the helm onto Alan's skull, however, a winged figure came swooping out of the sky. A spiked mace knocked the helmet from Donna's grasp, then swung back to smack her own helmet in the side. A metallic clang rang out as the impact sent her tumbling backward through the smoky sky.

"Life, on the other hand," Hawkman objected, "is all struggle!"

The studded leather straps of his wing harness stretched across his bare chest, and his winged helmet was fashioned in the image of a bird of prey. A medieval broadsword hung from his belt of Nth Metal, and his feathered wingspan was at least twelve feet in length. His brawny sinews hammered the mace into first Bolt, then Halo, freeing Green Lantern from their clutches.

"Condor! Starman!" he shouted gruffly. "Take us home!"

The Winged Avenger led a phalanx of airborne heroes into the fray. Black Condor, Starman, and various members of the Teen Titans, the Freedom Fighters, and the Justice Society came charging through the sky, providing much-needed reinforcements. Stargirl walloped Man-Bat in the skull with her gravity-defying Cosmic Rod. Cyclone cancelled out Typhoon's whirlwind with a self-generated tornado of her own. Argent, coasting upon a slide of silver plasma, shielded the Castle from enemy fire with a shimmering silver umbrella. Blue Beetle dived after the helmet dropped by Donna Troy, then blew it apart with an energy-blast. Chopper fire bounced off the Bulleteer's impervious steel skin; she tore through a copter's rotors like a living missile.

The heroes' timely arrival rallied Green Lantern's spirits. A fresh burst of green flame carried him into the heat of the battle. Still grounded, Hawkgirl snatched an automatic rifle from a fallen Checkmate agent and gave him cover with a blistering hail of lead.

Maybe this fight isn't over yet, she thought.

CHECKMATE HQ.

"You have thoughtlessly gunned down a global megastar!" Most Excellent Superbat accused the command center's defenders. He and the rest of the Super Young Team piled out of the Wonder Wagon. Superbat pointed indignantly at the soldier who had just shot Mister Miracle. The escape artist's body lay sprawled across the back of the Wagon. "How will you explain yourself to this man's fans?"

Dozens of guns targeted the invaders. Their crashed vehicle was surrounded by rubble. "Put the guns down!" Mister Terrific shouted at the guards, even as he feared that the situation was already spiraling out of control. He couldn't tell if Mister Miracle was alive or not. Holding his hands in the air, he tried to force his way through the gun-toting security officers. He called out to the Super Young Team. "How did you get through the Castle's defenses? This is a secure location!"

A tiny winged girl, whom Michael Holt identified as Shy Crazy Lolita Canary Girl, flew toward the guards. Alarmed by the weapons turned upon her friends, she let loose with an ear-piercing cry that sounded like every teenage shopgirl in Tokyo screaming, *"Summmiimmmmmmassennnnn!"* as loud as they could, at the highest pitch possible, at the very same time. Mister Terrific and the guards staggered backward, clutching their ears. He feared for his eardrums. Guards collapsed onto the floor, their weapons slipping from their fingers. A stained-glass window exploded.

And I thought Black Canary's cry was bad, he thought. *Not to mention Silver Banshee.*

He had to wait until the pixie's wail died out before he could try to take charge again. "Stop!" he ordered, clambering back onto his feet. "Everybody calm down!"

"You shot Mister Miracle!" Lolita Canary chirped.

Well-Spoken Sonic Lightning Flash cradled the celebrity's body in his lap. "We came through time and space and everything to save you!"

"I'm sorry," Mister Terrific apologized. "A doctor's on his way for your friend." A peculiar pinging noise caught his attention; he saw that Sonny Sumo appeared to be scanning him with some sort of handsized device. "How does that . . . thing know I'm here? I'm invisible to machines."

The wrestler, whose face was painted with the same pattern sported by his adolescent companions, held up the device. "Motherboxxx is more than a machine. If gods made iPods that were alive? *Way* beyond that."

New Gods technology? Mister Terrific was intrigued. *That might be just what we need right now!*

"Ow!" Mister Miracle startled everyone by sitting up. Wincing, he massaged the smoking bullet hole in his chest. "A Boom Tube," he explained. "She called it a Boom Tube. A door to everywhere. It brought us here. . . ."

Sonny's jaw dropped. "It's true what they say. He can't be killed."

"Yeah, definitely not when I'm wearing my impact-proof vest," Shilo said wryly. He pulled his mask back on and reclaimed Motherboxxx from Sonny. "Which is always."

"Nobody's going to try anything like that again, Mister Norman," Mister Terrific said. "You have my word as White King." He reached for the supersmartphone. "Maybe you should let me take a look at that box of yours." His T-Spheres discreetly scanned the device, but found it impervious to their sensors. "You say it brought you here?"

Mister Miracle clipped the box to his shoulder pad. "She won't talk to you." Detaching a pair of antigravity Aero Disks from his belt, he then climbed onto them and was lifted above the debris surrounding the Wonder Wagon. "She survived a cosmic war, but she's not alone. She says the Time of Change is here. Everyone has to choose sides. The Fifth World is coming down hard."

Fifth World? Mister Terrific was aware that the New Gods had claimed to represent a metaphysical Fourth World, which had supplanted three previous generations of supposed divinities. An atheist himself, Holt took such claims with a grain of salt. *Gods . . . aliens . . . the labels don't matter now. Only the threat they pose.*

A technician, who had valiantly stayed at her post despite the tumult, called out from across the room. "Generator power and shields at thirty-five percent! Overload and breakthrough imminent!" She stared anxiously at an array of visual displays. "Oh my God, this can't be right. . . ."

Mister Terrific trusted Checkmate's castellans to maintain their defenses for as long as possible. He turned back toward Mister Miracle and his allies. "You've obviously managed to stay clear of the Anti-Life Equation. We'll take any help you can offer. You should know, however, that we've deliberately made the Castle a target to draw enemy fire."

A T-Sphere dutifully projected the time. "We're trying to give our people in Blüdhaven a chance to cut this thing out at the root. But you heard that report: Our shields will fail in fifteen minutes." He trudged back toward his post before the monitor screens. "I'm afraid you got here just in time for humanity's last stand."

The pale-faced tech looked baffled by the data before her. "Can somebody check this before we lose generator power? Radar says the Swiss border just got . . . farther away?"

"Listen to her," Shilo said grimly. "The war broke time and space. A fallen devil-god is dragging us down with him into a deep, dark hole in time, with no light, no hope, and no escape."

"Shields at fourteen percent!"

Mister Miracle looked down from his floating disks. "That's where I come in, Mister Terrific. You see the pattern we all painted on our faces? Tell your people to do the same."

Face paint? Michael Holt gave the escapist a puzzled look. *That doesn't seem like much of a miracle.*

Or was it?

CHAPTER 24

BLÜDHAVEN.

Cats rode dogs, as was only proper.

Kalibak and a tribe of newly created Tiger-Men sat astride their giant mastiffs as the hellhounds padded across the desolate landscape outside Command-D. Products of the Evil Factory, the Tiger-Men were both armed and armored. Their striped fur stood out colorfully against the blackened ruins.

"All quiet," a young lieutenant named Tuftan reported. He sniffed the air. "No smell."

"They will come," Kalibak promised. He brandished a metal club in his massive paw. "I will lead you to the slaughterhouse of men!"

Razor wire and artillery faced the bridge into Blüdhaven. Concrete bunkers and rotating gun towers housed an army of Justifiers. A greenish fog hung over the wasteland as a crimson sun dawned. *Daily Planet* newspapers, dropped from the sky in the wee hours of the morning, blew in the wind. A banner headline heralded "THE BATTLE OF BLÜDHAVEN."

A rumble came from across the river. Tuftan's ears lifted. His whiskers twitched. "That roar, like a storm approaching."

"Their soldiers come!" Kalibak snarled. "Just as my father foresaw!"

Engines revved loudly in the distance. Vague figures, dimly glimpsed in

"Adam, no!" Shazam landed behind him and pulled Adam away from Mary. "You'll kill her!"

"Exactly," Adam spat. He struggled to break free of Shazam's hold. "Look at her! You can see a leering old man in her eyes! She's possessed!"

So she is, Kalibak thought. *By my father's most sadistic servant.*

While the two men tussled, Mary scrambled to her feet amidst a smoking crater. An overturned city bus lay nearby, and she effortlessly hoisted it above her head. Lightning crackled along the bus's length as she flung it at the men with titanic force. The bus hit them like a missile, its gas tank exploding on impact. Black Adam took the brunt of the blast, which nonetheless hurled both men across the lifeless wastes. An enormous fireball scorched Adam's silken garments. The power of the old gods had diminished in the face of the interlopers from Apokolips. Clearly, Earth belonged to a different, darker pantheon now.

"Mary!" Shazam staggered to his feet. He tried foolishly to reason with his longtime friend. "If there's anything left of what you were . . ."

"Just enough to scream," she replied mockingly. "Mary has new gods. Mary's learned a new magic word. A blasphemous name of power!"

She dragged Black Adam from the flames. He murmured weakly, "Kill her . . . kill . . ."

Mary tossed the dazed villain at Shazam, knocking Earth's Mightiest Mortal flat onto his back. Lightning sparked and thunder boomed as the rival champions collided. Mary pounced mercilessly on Shazam, her claws raking his face.

"Adam has the right idea," she taunted, slamming his head into the pavement. "But you wouldn't dare hurt me, would you, Freddy? Soft little Freddy?" She straddled the fallen hero and tugged his cape away from his face. "Mmm. You're hot." Licking her lips, she writhed lasciviously atop him. "Wanna be bad? With a dirty magic word like mine?"

Shazam tried to throw her off. "I'm not Freddy anymore," he warned her. "Not just a junior Captain Marvel . . ."

Salvation came from an unexpected quarter as Tawky Tawny descended from the air. A sputtering silver jet-pack lowered him to the ground. His plaid jacket and cheery red bow tie looked out of place amidst the devastation. "Mary!" He aimed an oddly retro-looking rifle at the renegade Marvel.

It looked like a 1950s sci-fi version of an antique flintlock. Subatomic energy seethed within its flared muzzle. "This Quantum Blunderbuss was confiscated from Professor Sivana. Step aside and say your word!"

"Tawny! Get away!" Shazam shouted. Mary had him pinned to the ground, her hands about his wrists. He wriggled helplessly beneath her, his face full of scratch marks. "It's not Mary! She's gone mad! She'll kill you!"

"She won't have to!" a new voice growled. Kalibak galloped into battle at last, leading his tribe of feline warriors. He swung his mace at Tawny. "Die, you traitorous cat!"

Tawny's yellow eyes widened as he found himself outnumbered by his own kind.

"Oh dear!"

METROPOLIS.

"Wait there, scum!"

The Justifiers tossed Nick into the filthy holding cell. He landed on his hands and knees, scraping his skin on the rough concrete floor. His sketches and notebooks, which he had zealously guarded since his arrest, went flying across the room. Blood dripped from a fat lip. A black eye was swollen half shut. The faceless storm troopers had not been gentle with him.

He sat up and looked around. It took his eyes a few moments to adjust to the dark, but eventually he made out the stark brick walls and dingy tile floors hemming him in. Dried brown splotches smeared the masonry. A flashing red light was mounted above the door, throwing a grisly red radiance over the dismal chamber, which looked like it used to be a meat locker. The cold and damp raised goose bumps on Nick's arms. Another prisoner shared the cell: a handicapped man sitting in a wheelchair. The rank atmosphere smelled of sweat and piss and blood. Belly Burger was paradise by comparison.

"Where?" he wondered aloud.

The crippled stranger stirred. A battered trucker's hat rested atop a mop of brittle white hair. His contorted face and limbs hinted at some sort of neurological disorder, possibly cerebral palsy. "This is where they bring all the people Anti-Life can't affect," he informed the boy. His grimy fingers toyed with a Rubik's Cube. "The crazy ones, the ones wired differently . . . before they dissect them."

Sounds like me, Nick thought bitterly. He had always felt like an outsider even before the whole world went crazy. The Justifiers had tried sticking one of those tin cans on his head, but it hadn't taken; the Equation had just sounded like gibberish to his ears. He wondered what was worse: turning into a zombie like everyone else or ending up here. *Did he say . . . dissected?*

He stared at the old guy in the wheelchair. The man's lowered eyes did not look up from the Rubik's Cube. Nick hadn't seen one of those plastic puzzles in years. "What's with the toy?"

"Did you know there are a minimum number of moves you need to solve a Rubik's Cube?" the old man said. "They call it the Number of God. No one has ever done it in less than eighteen."

"Like I give a crap." Nick rose unsteadily to his feet. He spit a mouthful of blood onto the tiles. "There are no gods except Darkseid. It says so on the billboards."

The stranger leaned forward in his chair. With difficulty, he lifted one of Nick's notebooks from the floor. "The time of gods is done, to be sure. This is a time for something *different*! Something unforeseen!"

Great, Nick thought. *I'm locked up with some kind of nutcase.* He was sore and cold and hungry and scared. The last thing he needed right now was a bunch of mystical rambling. "Leave me alone, please. . . ."

"But *you* summoned this," the stranger insisted. His eyes remained hidden beneath the visor of his baseball cap A palsied hand held open the sketchbook, exposing that odd pattern Nick kept seeing everywhere. The old man nodded at Nick. "You made this moment with the power in you. Isn't that what your kind do?"

"What kind?" Nick wiped the blood away from his lip. Countless small cuts and scratches scarred his face. His skinned palms stung like the blazes. "Don't you get it? We're all gonna die and the super heroes can't save us this time. They're as useless as my stupid drawings!"

The stranger flipped through a notebook. "If your super heroes cannot save you, maybe you can think of something that can." He glanced briefly at a colored doodle of a Nazi Supergirl, complete with a swastika on her chest. "If it does not exist, think it up. Make it real."

"What's the point?" Nick protested. He stared at the floor. "We're all going to die in pain for no good reason. They're coming to get us right now!"

The other man shrugged, like that didn't concern him. He leafed through the sketches until he came across a portrait of a beautiful woman. Rows of braided black hair graced her smooth pink dome. Striking green eyes gazed up from the page. "What's this one?"

Nick glanced sullenly at his own work. "She's a drawing. A girl from another universe I dream about sometimes . . ."

Pretty much every night, to be honest.

"Was there ever a word you tried to imagine?" the stranger prompted. "The sort of word that could remind you who you truly were inside? Maybe it's more than a word. . . . It's a face, a scent, a voice. Like a memory of a place where someone truly cared for you. A name."

How does he know this? Nick thought. He felt uncomfortable and embarrassed, like the old man could see into his very soul. "She's not real. . . . She's . . ." He stared at the haunting face on the paper, the lovely face he saw whenever he closed his eyes. All at once, her name sprang to his lips. "Weeja Dell?"

The door banged open and three of Darkseid's goons marched in. The greasy makeup on the first man's face marked him as a follower of Mokkari. The cultist was flanked by two armored Justifiers carrying metal truncheons and cattle prods. "Up!" one of the guards ordered the prisoners. "Up!"

"No time for talk," the Mokkarite sneered. He wore a bloodstained butcher's apron. "Time to show you what happens to the different. The strange. The ones who refuse to fit in."

A cryptic smile appeared on the face of the old man in the wheelchair. He raised the Rubik's Cube, which was almost solved. Lucid blue eyes glowed like TV screens, the irises square instead of round. There was an electricity in the air, like the calm before a storm. Hair stood up on the back of the guards' necks.

"Wait!" one of the Justifiers blurted. "Something's not right!"

The old man solved the cube. It pinged as each of its faces achieved a uniform color of its own.

"Seventeen," Metron said.

A blinding white flash filled the holding cell, driving back Darkseid's blindsided followers. Their garments were shredded by the blast. Justifier helmets were cracked open, revealing the frightened mortal faces underneath. Blood leaked from the Mokkarite's eyes and ears, causing his ghoulish makeup to run like tears. Loose papers from Nick's notebooks blew about wildly, burning at the edges. Sketches of imaginary heroes and villains from dozens of alternate Earths wafted down like volcanic ash. Overman, Doc Fate, Captain Adam, Brunhilde, Leatherwing, Sister Miracle . . .

Weeja Dell.

Metron's voice rang out:

"Something *new* is born. The Fifth World dawns in flame and thunder. The battle is joined."

Amidst the tumult, Nix Uotan stepped forward, transformed by the knowledge of his true self. He remembered who he was now, and what he could become. His ragged clothes and injuries had vanished along with the false identity of poor, helpless Nick. The tail of a black frock coat snapped in the breeze. Golden trim zigzagged across the front of his mod-looking uniform. Tight black cornrows ran in parallel across his unblemished brown dome. Circling his head like a 3-D halo was a glowing sphere composed of over a dozen miniature closed-circuit TV screens, allowing him to see anywhere on Earth through any camera at any time.

"Behold," Metron proclaimed. "The Judge of All Evil is here."

BLÜDHAVEN.

Batman writhed within the confines of the iron maiden. Tubes and cables stretched from the needles embedded in his skull, and a crown of syringes concealed the top of his cowl. His jaws were clenched, but a defiant growl escaped his gritted teeth.

"See how he struggles against the Psycho-Merge," Mokkari gloated. He and Simyan observed their captive with keen interest. "Now do you understand why his superior physical prowess, his strategic acumen, and courage make him unique?" Mokkari smirked at his hirsute colleague as they monitored Batman's vital signs. The captured hero resisted their every attempt to break him. "These are traits we must steal, duplicate—and mass-produce!"

Rows of tube-shaped incubators lined the walls of the laboratory. Naked clones were suspended within the transparent cylinders, floating in pale green amniotic fluid. Bubbles aerated the liquid. Batman's Utility Belt rested on a counter nearby. Simyan shambled over to examine it, moving more stiffly than once he had. Mortality was taking its toll on them all.

The ape-man grunted.

"Exactly," Mokkari agreed. "With this template we will build an assembly line army of mindless 'batmen' to fight and pillage and die in the name of our dark empire. His mind will yield up all his secrets to our clones." He leaned against the counter as he took a drag on his cigarette. The addictive fumes provided a welcome distraction from the aches and pains bedeviling his flesh. He looked admiringly at the clones in their tanks. "When they're done, we'll gut Batman for parts . . . without anesthetic, I think. And that, Mister Simyan, will be that."

No doubt Darkseid would reward them for their success, perhaps by granting them newer and stronger bodies to replace their rapidly deteriorating mortal shells. The advent of their cloned batmen would prove beyond a shadow of doubt that he and Simyan were worthiest of the master's favor. *Let vainglorious Godfrey and that hag Granny top* this!

"N-no!" Batman snarled. He strained against his bonds, and a flicker of apprehension undermined Mokkari's confidence. Surely no mere mortal could escape their clutches and yet . . . the Batman's fearsome reputation extended all the way to distant Apokolips. Perhaps there was cause for concern?

The clones began to stir in their tanks. Their eyes snapped open, and they clenched their fists and bared their teeth.

Eureka! Mokkari thought. He looked away from Batman to the new-and-improved copies coming to life before his eyes. A whole new breed of Dark Knights, with all of Batman's indomitable drive, but none of his pathetic morality. The perfect honor guard for the god of all gods.

Then everything went wrong.

The clones started convulsing inside the incubators. Their faces contorted in agony, as though they couldn't bear the intensity of the memories burning into their artificial synapses. Violent spasms rocked their bodies. Mokkari backed away from the tubes in shock.

"They're clawing out their own eyes!"

Simyan barked in alarm. He looked to his partner for answers.

"The Psycho-Merge is killing these weaklings," Mokkari realized, aghast. Monitors charted the clones' vital signs. Their heartbeats and adrenaline levels were spiking catastrophically. Mokkari stared in horror at the appalling readouts. "How does Batman process this degree of stress?"

Sparks erupted from the monitors as equipment shorted out all over the lab. The flailing clones smashed against the walls of their tanks, shattering the glass. Torrents of sticky green liquid flooded the floor, almost knocking Mokkari off his feet. Smoke rose from exploding consoles as the dying clones twitched upon the floor like fish out of water. Amniotic fluid gushed from their lungs.

"No!" Mokkari gasped. "We were so close to success. . . ."

There was no salvaging the experiment, which was coming apart all around him. He splashed unsteadily across the slick floor, terrified of falling and breaking a hip. Perhaps once he might have possessed the strength and vigor to try to regain control of the situation, but not anymore. In his present debilitated state, retreat was the only option.

I'm getting too old for this, he thought bitterly. *And so is Simyan.*

The ape-man fumbled with Batman's Utility Belt, perhaps looking for some sort of miracle within its myriad compartments. A phlegmy cough shook his stooped body. His arthritic fingers failed him, and the belt fell to the floor. His bones cracked audibly as he bent to recover it.

"Leave the belt!" Mokkari wheezed. "Leave everything! Seal the laboratory and let's get out of here!"

They scuttled toward the emergency exit. Crystal fragments crunched beneath their feet. Pausing in the doorway, Mokkari glanced back over his shoulder at Batman. Sparks flared from within his steel sarcophagus as its mechanical locks malfunctioned. Batman twisted inside the iron maiden. Leather restraints snapped loudly, punctuating the fading breaths of the scattered clones. The moribund batmen jerked through their death throes, unable to cope with whatever demons fueled the Dark Knight.

Mokkari could not believe his eyes. What kind of man could turn his own life memories into a *weapon*?

He slammed the door shut behind them, cutting them off from the site of the debacle. The defeated scientists limped down the hall toward Darkseid's throne room. Mokkari's heart pulsed feebly within his breast. Every breath was a painful rasp. He could only pray that the master would forgive their failure—and shield them from Batman's wrath.

Provided they did not drop dead first.

CHAPTER 25

METROPOLIS.

Gallows had been erected in Centennial Park, where once a statue of Superman had stood. The toppled monument now lay in the dirt behind the scaffolds, its bronze skin chipped and tarnished. Banners bearing the omega symbol flapped at either side of a large raised platform. Limp bodies hung from nooses. A large crowd of Justifiers and Lowlies had gathered to witness the mass executions. Gunships patrolled the sky.

Libra presided over the spectacle, accompanied by Lex Luthor and Dr. Sivana. The evil evangelist had gone public after the release of the Anti-Life Equation and was now the cloaked face of the new regime. He pointed his scale-topped lance at the latest victim being escorted to the gallows. "And here's the crawling vermin who thought he could betray us to the Resistance!"

Noah Kuttler, alias the Calculator, was the super-villain community's version of Oracle, a hacker and information broker supreme. Dragged away from his precious keyboards, however, he was nothing but a frantic middle-aged man in rumpled office attire. "Libra, I swear I didn't do anything!" he shrieked as the Justifier hauled him up the steps. His voice was hoarse from shrieking, and sweat soaked his face and garments. A pair of broken glasses dangled precariously upon his bloody nose; one of the lenses was cracked. Wide eyes gaped at the looming gallows. "It had to be somebody else!"

"It would take a savant to get around your encryptions," Libra observed. "So unless *someone* steps forward and admits to the deed, you're facing a very public demise." He looked knowingly at Luthor, who was once again garbed in his metallic green battle-suit. "They used the Unternet to coordinate an attack strategy against our lord's birthplace. Can you believe it, Lex?"

Luthor looked away, unable to meet the Calculator's eyes. He shuddered as Libra dropped his hand upon Lex's shoulder. "But now we have their best and their brightest *exactly* where we want them," Libra gloated, twisting the knife. "We're thinking about having you lead the rearguard action against the Blüdhaven bridge."

"An honor, I'm sure," Luthor forced himself to reply, nearly choking on the words. Bile crept up his throat. He would have sooner pinned a medal on Superman than kowtow to Libra like this, but Darkseid had changed all the old rules. A pained grimace revealed his true feelings.

"Don't antagonize him," Sivana whispered. The stunted mad scientist shuffled nervously beneath the scaffold. Coke-bottle lenses magnified his squinty eyes, and his wizened face bore a sour expression. His rumpled white lab jacket looked like it hadn't been cleaned or ironed in years. "I value my brain."

Luthor bowed his head.

"Heh," Libra chortled. Having asserted his authority, he turned his back to the subservient arch-criminals. "If you prove willing, Lex, I might even let you be first in line with Supergirl. . . ."

Lex's stomach turned.

BLÜDHAVEN.

A force field surrounded Command-D. Rubble had been cleared away to expose the reinforced concrete roof of the underground bunker. Supergirl blasted the field with her heat vision, while John Stewart willed a massive emerald earthmover into existence. They attacked the shielded compound from hundreds of feet in the air.

"I think we need more firepower, Mister Stewart," Kara said. Twin beams shot from her eyes. The air rippled around the crimson rays. "I just can't find a weak spot!"

The glowing steam shovel scraped at the unyielding force field. "Right about now," Green Lantern said, "I wish I knew what happened to your big cousin." According to Lois, Superman was assisting the Legion of Super-Heroes in the future, but he was supposed to have gotten back to the present by now. "Goddammit, what's wrong with my ring?" The emerald earthmover flickered in and out of reality. "Hasn't been right since I dragged myself out of that hospital bed!"

Supergirl's eyes widened. "This is terrible, Mister Stewart. I can see a massive energy source building inside the bunker. It's like a brain sending signals to a gigantic nervous system. . . ." She glanced over at Green Lantern, who appeared preoccupied with his malfunctioning ring. "Mister Stewart?" He didn't appear to have heard her. *Right,* she thought. *Not everybody has super-hearing. . . .*

She opened her mouth to raise her voice, only to be tackled in midair by a rival heroine who came diving out of the sky like a falling star. Supergirl spun around to find herself grappling with a crazed young woman she barely recognized as Mary Marvel. Lightning arced around the girls as they plunged together toward the ground below. Mary's left hand squeezed Kara's throat, her sharpened claws digging into the Maid of Might's invulnerable skin. Mary drew back her right fist to strike a blow, but a burst of heat vision from Supergirl set Mary's dyed pink hair bunches aflame. She shrieked in fury as she put the flames out with her hands.

Supergirl couldn't believe the change in her peer, whose revealing new outfit was astonishingly immodest. She blocked Mary's latest brutal punch with her forearm.

"Mary!" she shouted over the wind rushing past their ears. "There's still time to talk!"

SPACE.

"My God," Kyle Rayner exclaimed. "Look at it."

Hal Jordan led a squad of Green Lanterns toward Earth. No longer shielded by the Alpha Lanterns' orbital barrier, the defenseless blue planet was disappearing into a funnel of curved space. It was like staring into the mouth of a cosmic whirlpool. Ghostly images of alternate Earths were embedded in the swirling walls of the vortex. A crimson radiance spilled from the ripples, evidence of the Bleed that ordinarily separated parallel universes from each other. Earth and all its myriad counterparts were falling into an endless hell where everything was Darkseid.

John Stewart's voice emanated from Hal's ring. Static muddled his desperate SOS. "Get me some backup . . . pronto!"

"Hang on, John!" Hal replied, uncertain if his embattled partner could even hear him. An emerald aura shielded his body from the vacuum. "Help is on the way!"

"POWER AT TWENTY PERCENT," his ring reported ominously. They were running out of time and energy. "NINETEEN PERCENT."

Guy Gardner flew up beside him. "We're using up juice to maintain hyperspace velocity," he pointed out. They had been flying at superluminal speed since leaving Oa. "I'm just saying."

Hal felt the vortex tugging on him. "We don't need to fly anymore," he realized. "Power down to life support only. We can free-fall into the singularity." He fearlessly dived past the event horizon into the spinning maw of the whirlpool as Earth pulled him in. "Get ready for time distortions!"

Mere seconds later the other Lanterns followed him into hell.

WASHINGTON, D.C.

The president of the United States sat behind his desk in a supposedly secure location. The secret command center was intended to allow the executive branch of the government to continue functioning in the event of a major disaster or enemy attack, but no one had ever imagined a doomsday scenario like the one unfolding right now. The president slumped in his chair, a defeated expression upon his haggard face. His necktie hung in disarray. And he needed a shave. Bloodshot eyes stared bleakly at the pistol in his lap.

"The Justifiers have found the bunker, sir!" Father Time reported. The dapper head of S.H.A.D.E. hefted an automatic rifle as he guarded the door to the Oval Office. Secret Service agents paced restlessly around the perimeter of the room. Nothing in their training had prepared for a threat of this magnitude. How do you shoot back at an Equation?

"This can't be happening," the president murmured. He sounded like he was in a state of shock. The first lady sat weeping on one of the room's sofas. "The scale of it, the *speed* of it . . . not in my lifetime . . . not like this . . ."

Darkseid was the commander in chief now.

BLÜDHAVEN.

"POWER AT THREE PERCENT . . ."

John Stewart touched down on the blackened and debris-filled floor of the battlefield. He couldn't risk flying anymore, not with his power leaking away at such an alarming rate. He didn't understand what the matter was; he had recharged his ring before joining the Offensive. It was like there was something wrong with the Central Power Battery on Oa, but that was impossible.

Wasn't it?

"Ring!" he demanded. "What the hell's going on?"

The battle raged all around him. He looked for Supergirl, but her airborne struggle with Mary Marvel had already carried the brawling super-teens out of sight. Human Defense soldiers, who had followed the super heroes into Blüdhaven, fired from behind the stacked bodies of their fallen comrades. An energy-cannon sprouted from the shoulder of Blue Beetle's living armor; he used it to blow open a concrete gun turret. Hourman, his superhuman strength good for only sixty minutes at a time, hurled one Justifier at another, knocking a mounted soldier off his hellhound. A bomb blast went off in the sky. The cables supporting the Blüdhaven bridge began to snap.

Everything's going to hell, John realized. *Literally.*

A gang of Justifiers spotted him. They stomped toward him, brandishing Tasers, spears, and clubs. Green Lantern visualized an emerald wall between himself and the enemy, but the construct refused to cohere. All the sputtering ring could manage was a few disconnected rods and grids that quickly dissolved from sight, like a blueprint washed in the rain. His ring dimmed, and a wisp of green smoke rose from the dying weapon.

"POWER AT TWO PERCENT AND FADING . . ."

John Stewart realized that he was in serious trouble. He wondered if he was going to be crucified again. The scars still ached from the first time.

Blood began to rain down from the heavens.

METROPOLIS.

Carrion birds circled above the park. The Calculator was dragged kicking and screaming toward the waiting gallows. An army of zombies numbly awaited his demise. The Calculator's legs went limp with fear. Justifiers held him up as a wire noose was lifted above his head.

Luthor averted his eyes. He had no illusions regarding the cheapness of human life, but this was just ugly. The Calculator was a man of intelligence and talent. He deserved better than this.

Sorry, Noah, he thought. *It's you or me.*

A rumble of thunder interrupted the execution. Lex looked up to see a burst of strange black energy spreading across the bloodred sky. The very fabric of reality seemed to warp and fray high above their heads as coruscating dark matter shredded the heavens.

"He's *here!*" Libra exulted. He turned his masked face upward, basking in the hellish glow of the unnatural fireworks, and slowly raised his arms. "The age of Darkseid has begun! The night that lasts forever!"

Luthor gritted his teeth. *Where the hell* are *you, Superman?*

BLÜDHAVEN.

Darkseid's acolytes were dying at his feet.

"Mokkari has failed you, great one!" Reverend Good croaked. Unable to stand, he crawled across the floor of the bunker toward Darkseid's throne. Mokkari and Simyan lay upon the floor as well, gasping their last breaths. They had collapsed only seconds after stumbling back into the throne room. "Batman killed the clone army these fools tried to build!"

The exiled gods, their mortal bodies combusting around them, pleaded for deliverance. They reached out with trembling fingers. Simyan grunted accusingly.

"Traitor!" Mokkari snapped at his onetime partner, who refused to accept his share of the blame for the Psycho-Merge disaster. He clawed at his own chest. Pain twisted his face. "Forgive me, Lord Darkseid! Let me live. . . ."

"Hallelujah," Good wheezed, only a few paces away. He struggled to lift his head from the floor. His mummified face looked over a hundred years old. His withered body was lost within the folds of his unwashed clerical robes. "Halle . . . luh . . ."

His voice gave out and he sagged onto the tiles.

Darkseid looked on impassively as, one by one, the three gods expired. Simyan pitched forward onto his face. Mokkari sucked one last drag on a cigarette before joining his colleagues in death. Wisps of dust rose from their desiccated throats as their labored breathing gave way to silence, until only Darkseid remained alive within the somber throne room. Crimson eyes burned beneath his craggy brow.

"It is over," he declared. "No living thing can resist me now. All flesh will be Darkseid's body." Memories of his past battles with Earth's champions were pushed to the back of his mind. "They have only ever faced the *idea* of a god before. Now has God Incarnate come among them." He raised his left arm, tearing it loose from the tubes and drip feeds that had sustained him during his emergence from Turpin's mortal shell. His apotheosis was complete. He clenched his fist in triumph. "All is one in Darkseid!"

He rose from his throne. Every movement was a torment, but the stiffness of his petrified flesh only fueled his boundless disdain for all existence. He donned the royal regalia his slaves had prepared for him before they'd outlived their usefulness. The omega symbol was emblazoned on his indigo surcoat, and matching omegas were embroidered on the backs of his thick leather gloves. Metal braces supported his thick legs. His ponderous tread echoed in the sepulchral silence of the hidden lab.

His mind reached out to all who had succumbed to the heartless logic of the Equation. His gravelly voice burrowed into their captive souls.

"I am the New God. This mighty body is my church. When I command your surrender, I speak with five billion voices." He squeezed his fingers together. "When I make a fist to crush your resistance, it is with five billion hands."

All across the globe, in Centennial Park and elsewhere, his mindless drones raised their own fists. Darkseid felt their strength at his command. Billions of voices spoke in unison, mouthing his words.

"When I stare into your eyes, when I shatter your dreams and break your heart, it is with ten billion eyes!"

He heard his own litany shouted to the heavens. The deafening roar of the harnessed voices penetrated even the impregnable walls of Command-D. In distant Metropolis, Luthor listened to the zombified masses in horror. Dr. Sivana plugged his fingers into his ears, but could not block out the roar of the crowd. Libra held out his staff in benediction.

"Nothing like Darkseid has ever come among you. Nothing ever will again. I will take you to a hell without exit, and there I will murder your souls! And make you crawl and beg . . . and *die*!"

The whole world chanted with him, rejoicing in its own damnation.

"Die for Darkseid!"

CHAPTER 26

METROPOLIS.
THE THIRTY-FIRST CENTURY.

"Hurry, Superman!" Brainiac 5 said breathlessly, his disheveled blond hair flapping in the breeze stirred up by his fast walking. "I calculate we have exactly 72.4 seconds before time breaks down and this sentence becomes meaningless."

The clubhouse of the Legion of Super-Heroes was housed inside an inverted rocket ship, which extended several levels beneath the streets of the city. Inspired by the heroic example of Superman and his twenty-first-century contemporaries, the Legion were the foremost heroes of this future era. Superman had first encountered the time-traveling Legionnaires as a young boy. He had frequently visited their own time, although seldom under such dire circumstances.

"What's this all about, Brainy?" he asked. "What's so important you had to drag me here in such a hurry?"

They descended a helix-shaped staircase through the Celestial Chamber, which featured floating holographic models of all the myriad worlds the various Legionnaires hailed from. The phantom globes orbited through an illusory starfield. Superman spotted Colu, Durla, Saturn, and Braal among many others, including Earth and Krypton. The Legion was a shining example of interplanetary unity and cooperation.

Tremors shook the headquarters, something that should have been impossible in the thirty-first century; seismic engineering had long since eliminated the possibility of random earthquakes. Yet the winding stairway shuddered beneath their feet, and windows rattled throughout the city of the future. Superman lifted off from the steps, preferring to fly the rest of the way, and kept watch over Brainiac 5 just in case the brilliant super-genius lost his balance. Looking out for the people around him was second nature to Superman.

At the same time, he couldn't stop worrying about what was happening back in his own time. "Lois is still in danger," he reminded Brainy. "You promised you could return me to the exact instant I left!"

"That was before," the alien youth hedged. Despite the flight ring on his finger, he held on tightly to the stair's handrail. His golden belt generated a personal force field. "The Crisis in your era is of absolute magnitude, threatening all of reality." The holographic globes flickered in and out of existence. "Time and space are fracturing around us, as you'll shortly become aware."

Superman did not like the sound of that. He knew from experience that Brainiac 5 was not prone to exaggeration. He contemplated the tremors rattling the clubhouse. What kind of disaster could send shock waves into the future a millennium later?

They reached the bottom of the stairs, Sublevel 2, where a checkerboard design of green and black floor panels stretched before them. "Excuse me, Superman," Brainy said. "It's vital that I remember the exact sequence of tiles to reach the arsenal."

He stepped carefully across the floor, as though navigating a minefield. One wrong step would trigger the clubhouse's formidable security measures, which had been designed to keep out the likes of Mordru and the Fatal Five. The last thing they wanted was to get snared by those defenses, especially with time running out.

"What are we doing here?" Superman asked impatiently. He floated behind Brainiac 5. "How do I get back home in time to stop this?"

"Listen carefully," Brainiac said tersely. On the opposite side of the checkerboard, a bright red keypad was mounted on the wall beside a reinforced steel bulkhead. Arsenal was inscribed in Interlac above the sealed doorway. His fingers stabbed the keypad, and a series of electronic beeps was almost drowned out by the rumble of the earthquake. "In 2960 the Controllers—a renegade offshoot of the Guardians of the Universe—discovered a way to refine the Guardians' will-powered technology to create the final machine. The ultimate technological artifact. A device that turns thoughts into things."

The bulkhead receded into the floor, allowing them access to the arsenal. The cavernous underground chamber held a vast collection of futuristic weapons acquired from the Legion's assorted allies and enemies. Superman recognized a Dimensional Blaster, a huge turbine-shaped Energy Concentrator, a concussive force field projector, and even one of the transparent Time Bubbles the Legion used to travel through history. He half expected Brainy to climb into the Bubble, and was surprised when the youth walked past the spherical time machine without a second glance. Apparently, this was all about some incredible wishing machine instead.

"Why are you telling me this?" Superman asked. "If a device like that exists, why can't we use it to protect ourselves *now*?"

"I'm afraid it's not that simple." Brainy broke into a run to reach an imposing steel vault at the far end of the arsenal. Dust rained down from the ceiling. A steel girder shook loose and plummeted toward Brainy, only to bounce off his protective force field. He didn't even lose his train of thought. "When we realized the horrific potential of a single stray thought to completely alter reality, we switched the device off . . . permanently."

Superman wondered how the Legion had taken custody of the machine. No doubt there was an amazing adventure involved; he regretted that there was no time to hear it. *Maybe later,* he thought. *If the universe survives.*

The vault door swung open, and an ominous red light lit up the sanctuary beyond. The heroes stepped out onto a metal gantry overlooking what appeared to be an empty steel chamber. Then the floor opened up, its halves folding up like wings. A huge gray cube, the size of an industrial cargo container, rose from a trapdoor beneath the vault. Steam vented from the broken seals.

"We sealed the machine for all time in a block of inertron," Brainiac 5 explained. The rare metal was the densest, most impervious substance in the known universe. "Very few people know of its existence, and the only person I'd trust to even look at it is *you*."

The metal cube unlatched. Sectioned panels snapped loose, then peeled away to unveil the gleaming contents of the cube. A brilliant blue radiance flooded the vault.

"Do you understand what I'm saying, Superman?" There was no mistaking the urgency in Brainiac 5's voice. This was obviously a matter of life and death. "I'm about to show you the God-Weapon."

"Make it fast," Superman said, distracted by the sight of his own arm *turning faintly transparent*. It fritzed out for an instant, like an image on a dying TV screen. He reached out with his other hand, which passed through the phantom limb as though it wasn't even here. He was obviously losing his grip on the thirty-first century, fading back into history. Becoming nothing more than a memory . . . or a ghost.

Brainiac took this unnerving development in stride, as though he had been expecting it all along. "Do you understand?"

Superman tore his gaze away from his own progressive insubstantiality to inspect the object Brainiac 5 was so determined to show him. Exposed upon its platform, the device was surprisingly old-fashioned in appearance, like something Nikola Tesla might have designed in the latter years of the nineteenth century. Sparks arced between tall vertical electrodes as the elaborate mechanism powered up automatically. Whirring dynamos spun ferociously. Interlocking gears, which seemed to be composed more of energy than matter, rotated coils of blazing plasma. Jeweled lenses focused coruscating amethyst particle beams while crystalline vacuum tubes hummed and sizzled. A luminous circuit diagram imprinted upon the face of the machine reminded him of those puzzling crop circles the *Planet* had been reporting on lately. A whiff of ozone teased his nostrils. The device glowed like a newborn sun.

"Great Krypton," he whispered.

Brainiac 5 gazed at the invention in awe. "In the language of the Controllers, its name is *Geh-Jedollah*-the-Absolute. There's no translation that really makes sense." His voice was hushed. "We call it the Miracle Machine."

Rao knows we need a miracle, Superman thought. *Right now and a thousand years ago*. He took off from the elevated catwalk, intent on claiming the device, only to find himself dissolving into the past like a specter banished to the Phantom Zone. Immaterial hands groped uselessly for the Miracle Machine. "I can't reach it!" he exclaimed. "I'm fading . . . !"

"You don't need to touch it," Brainiac shouted. "Look at it, Superman! *Just look!*"

Superman got the message. His eyes glowed brightly.

And then he disappeared.

THE WATCHTOWER.
NOW.

The Tattooed Man gazed down on Earth from the space station's observation deck. "Never thought I'd get to see Earth from space," he admitted. "Sure is a beautiful thing." He sighed and shook his head. "Pretty pathetic that it took the end of the world to show me what's right."

He looked over at Black Canary, who was also contemplating the endangered planet below them. A profound realization came over him. "What I have . . . this tattoo thing I took for granted, this power . . . it's a *gift*."

"It's what you make it, Mr. Richards," she replied solemnly. The tough blonde chick was holding up pretty well, he thought, considering that she had left her husband behind to face an army of Justifiers single-handed. Her jet-black outfit made her look more like a widow than a bride. Her smoky blue eyes never left the spinning globe they had barely escaped. "As chairman of the Justice League, I'm making you an honorary member as of now, with full privileges *and* responsibilities."

"Crap," Mark Richards murmured. He hadn't seen that one coming. "Honorary Justice League?"

"Yeah," she said. "So now you're taking orders from me." Thinking aloud, she assessed their situation. "We have civilians and kids on board, and we need to get Ray back to Earth with that circuit of yours. . . ."

Before she could lay out her plans any further, they were interrupted by excited squeals from the Flash kids. Iris and Jai came running toward them, followed by their mom and Joan Garrick and the Ray. The two women toted futuristic rifles that looked like props from a sci-fi movie. The kids' beaming faces reminded Richards of his own son and daughters, still stuck back on Earth. He prayed that they were okay.

"Hi, guys." Black Canary turned away from the window. "Find anything cool in the armory?"

"Lots of weird stuff," Iris West enthused. "But Mom found a sting-gun from the planet Korll."

The planet what? Richards thought.

A blinding light suddenly flooded the deck, coming from outside the Watchtower. Joan looked past Black Canary and the Tattooed Man in alarm. She raised her rifle. "Dear God, no!"

A trio of modified space shuttles approached the satellite. Torpedo ports, missile launchers, and other armament bristled upon the ships' hulls. The omega symbol was painted on their prows. Harsh white spotlights targeted the startled heroes and civilians as proximity alarms sounded throughout the station.

Figures, Richards thought, squinting into the glare. The cobra on his biceps reared up defensively. Vampire bats fluttered around his shoulders. *Ever since I became a damn super hero, peace went out the window.*

Jai clutched his mother's side. "Mom?"

Black Canary cursed under her breath. "Ray, you have to leave!"

"But I can't ditch you guys now," he protested. His finned helmet failed to conceal his distress. He flared up brightly. "I just can't!"

"Now!" Black Canary barked. "That's an order!"

CHAPTER 27

BLÜDHAVEN.

"Admit it, Supergirl!" Mary Marvel giggled. "You're *loving* this!"

Locked in combat, the grappling super-teens spun through the sky above the battlefield. Mary squeezed Supergirl's throat with both hands, her claws digging into Kara's skin. Her legs were tangled around Supergirl's own slender limbs. The Maid of Might fired back with a fresh burst of heat vision, and Mary's garish pink hair bunches burned like torches once again.

She thinks this is fun? Supergirl thought, repulsed. She fought to break free from Mary's vicious embrace. Her hands tugged on the other girl's wrists. Mary's gleeful eyes and demented grin made her skin crawl. *Yuck!*

Momentum carried them downward toward the ruined city. They smashed through the roof of a multistory parking garage, plunging through level after level of solid concrete, before crashing into the garage's subbasement. The jarring impact loosened Mary's grip, and Supergirl wrested a leg free long enough to kick the crazed ex-heroine off her. Mary went flying backward, smashing yet another gaping hole in the garage's roof. Falling chunks of concrete bounced harmlessly off Supergirl as she took off after her foe, the entire parking garage collapsing behind her.

Thank goodness this city was already a graveyard!

Mary ploughed through a deserted office building, raining steel and glass onto the streets below, before crashing back down to Earth. The pavement cracked and cratered beneath her. Derelict cars and buses were thrown into the air by the force of her landing. Scowling, she crawled out of the crater on her hands and knees. An enormous shadow fell over her. Mary looked up in time to see a massive semitruck descending toward her. She caught a glimpse of a bright red cape above the semi and hissed venomously.

"Slut."

The truck hit her head-on, crumpling like an accordion as it flattened her into the shattered pavement. Bright electric sparks erupted as a furious Mary Marvel blasted out from beneath the mangled metal with murder in her eyes, deadly shrapnel flying in all directions. A look of utter hatred replaced the sadistic glee she had been flaunting before. Her clenched fists preceded her, and a demonic rage contorted her face. She wasn't playing around anymore.

"*You?*" Supergirl responded from high above the wreckage. She eyed the tacky cutout exposing Mary's absurdly enhanced cleavage. "Calling *me* a slut?"

Fiery red beams shot from Supergirl's eyes. The unleashed solar energy drove Mary backward. Engulfed in flames, she plummeted to the ground, not far from where she had left Black Adam and Shazam lying, dazed and demolished, amidst the debris. An overturned taxi blew up beneath her. A blazing fireball marked her landing. Billowing clouds of thick black smoke rose into the sky.

The explosion roused Black Adam. Grimacing in pain, he lifted his head from the pavement. His saturnine countenance was bruised and scratched. He dragged himself across the rubble toward the burning cab, muttering darkly to himself:

". . . powers fade . . . my gods far from here . . . but I can hear the voices of these cursed New Gods . . ." His dark eyes zeroed in on Mary as she rose and shook the flames from her hair. Oblivious to Adam's approach, she glared up at Supergirl, who hovered far above the fray. Black Adam crawled nearer. ". . . sneering, shrieking . . . over and over in her head . . ."

Mary started to launch herself at Supergirl, only to feel a powerful hand clamp onto her ankle. Startled, she glanced down at Adam's battered face. She tried to tug her foot free, but the prone warrior refused to let go.

"Desaad!" he shouted up at her, demanding answers. "What name is this?"

Super-hearing carried the exchange to Kara's ears. *Desaad?* Supergirl recognized the name. *Wasn't he Darkseid's chief torturer and majordomo back on Apokolips?* Supergirl recalled a gaunt, ugly skeleton of a man in a hooded purple robe that was usually stained with the blood of his captives. *Why would Adam be hearing Desaad's voice in Mary's head?*

Unless . . .

"How you doing, honey?" Liberty Belle called out to Hourman. Along with the other heroes, they were busy defending the bridge from wave after wave of hostile Justifiers. A bright red liberty bell was emblazoned on her blue tunic, despite her torn and scuffed jodhpurs. A peal-like sonic blast repelled a squadron of Justifiers. Patriotic zeal imbued her with super-strength; her family had been fighting for freedom since the American Revolution. She knew how vital it was to secure the bridge. The Omega Initiative depended on reinforcements being able to pour into Blüdhaven until victory was achieved.

"Got about a half hour of Miraclo juice left in me!" Hourman shouted back. The hourglass dangling around his neck measured how much longer his superpowers would last. He hoisted a Justifier above his head and hurled him back across the enemy lines. The armored storm trooper knocked over a row of his comrades. Hourman turned and blew a kiss at Liberty Belle. "Looking good!"

Jesse Chambers feared her husband was being overly optimistic. Granted, his "flash-forward" vision sometimes allowed him to peek an hour into the future, but did he really think this battle was going to be wrapped up before his Miraclo pill wore off? The Battle of Bunker Hill, in which her distant ancestor, Miss Liberty, had fought, had lasted for hours. *Let's hope we can hold out as long. . . .*

"What is this, Tyler?" Wildcat barked at Hourman. Once the heavyweight champion of the world, the grizzled ex-boxer wore a tight black cat costume, complete with whiskers, that would have looked ridiculous on anyone else.

"*Romeo and Juliet*?" His bandaged knuckles dented a Justifier's helmet. "Shut up and hold the line!"

Their opponents seemed equally determined to reclaim the bridge, or perhaps destroy it. Not far away, Magenta, her features obscured by a Justifier helmet, used her magnetic powers to tie Iron of the Metal Men into a knot, even as the robot's shape-changing teammate, Platinum, wrapped herself around the mind-controlled villainess. The animate steel coil ensnared Magenta, who was identifiable only by her purple cape and metallic silver bodysuit. A bona fide nutcase, who had once dated the Flash before her powers drove her insane, Magenta probably hadn't been too hard to brainwash.

Elsewhere, G.I. Robot mowed down the enemy with a barrage of rubber bullets. J.A.K.E., the Jungle Automatic Killer-Experiment, was literally built for this sort of heavy-duty combat. Liberty Belle was glad he and the other robots were on their side, as they needed all the help they could get.

"Let go of me!" Mary Marvel snarled. She savagely kicked Black Adam with her heel, breaking his jaw. His fingers surrendered their grip, allowing Mary to pull her ankle free. He flew backward, blood and teeth spraying from his mouth. She spat at Adam as he struggled to collect himself. "You pigheaded excuse for a Marvel! We should have wasted your sorry Egyptian ass *years* ago!"

Not wanting to let Adam's efforts go to waste, Supergirl swooped down from the sky. She wrenched a rusty streetlight from its moorings and swung it at Mary like a gigantic baseball bat. Moving with preternatural speed, Mary dodged the attack and lashed out at Supergirl with her claws. She snared Kara's hair and yanked her closer. Supergirl gasped as she felt her long blonde tresses being pulled out by the roots. Dropping the streetlight, she grabbed onto Mary with both hands. The heavy metal pole clattered loudly beneath them as Supergirl tried to pry Mary's fingers from her hair.

"That's it!" Mary hissed. Spittle sprayed from her lips as she jerked Supergirl's head toward her. Her knee rose to meet Kara's face. "You and me. Together!"

Supergirl's head snapped back, Mary's knee-jab loosening her teeth. She tasted her own blood in her mouth. She tumbled backward through the air, leaving a handful of blonde hair in Mary's grip.

No more of that, Kara decided. *Never mind who she* used *to be. Mary gets the full bad-guy treatment now.*

Halting her headlong flight, she righted herself dozens of feet above the battlefield. Mary came zooming at her like a latex-clad missile. Supergirl took a deep breath to clear her head, then retaliated by blowing Mary backward with her super-breath. A cyclonic gust of wind propelled Mary into the ground once more. The hurricane-force gale also sent scattered debris flying across the desolate landscape. Airborne refuse bombarded the Justifiers besieging the bridge. Knocked off their feet, the faceless troopers grabbed onto fractured posts and building foundations to keep from being blown into the river.

Mary was unimpressed. "Is that the best you've got?" She laughed manically over the squall. Planting herself securely on the ground, she leaned forward into the wind, her scorched hair and cape streaming behind her. She slashed fiercely at the wall of air holding her back, as though she could slice it to ribbons with her claws. "I always knew you Kryptonians were full of hot air!"

"Supergirl!" Shazam shouted at her over the roaring wind. The World's Mightiest Mortal got up on one knee, his face bruised but determined. The golden thunderbolt on his chest was a poignant reminder of the heroic legacy Mary Marvel was now despoiling. He lowered his voice so that only she could hear him. "It might take the last of my strength, but I think I can stop her!"

Kara listened closely.

"What *are* you?" Kalibak demanded. Crimson droplets fell from his metal mace. He stood over the prone body of Tawky Tawny, whose very presence seemed to perplex and annoy him. He gnashed his fangs impatiently. "Tell me before I smash your brains out!"

Severely beaten, Tawny sought to retain his dignity. He lifted his feline face from the ashes. His fur and whiskers were matted with his own blood. His discarded jet-pack lay atop a heap of rubble a few paces away. He spit a chipped canine onto the ground. "My friends, sir, call me 'Tawky.'" He coughed hoarsely. "My name in my own tongue translates as 'Tawny,' but don't let my cultured tones deceive you. . . ." He took a moment to catch his breath before pouncing at Kalibak with his claws extended. His bestial jaws opened wide, exposing a mouthful of ivory fangs. "Tawny *bites*!"

"And Kalibak is a god!"

The feral son of Darkseid met Tawny's challenge with a swing of his mace, but Tawny lunged past the strike to sink his fangs into Kalibak's shoulder. His powerful jaws punched through the New God's armor, causing Kalibak to roar in pain. Taken aback by the unexpected ferocity of Tawny's attack, Kalibak stumbled backward, tripping over a capsized fire hydrant. Fur flew as the tiger-men rolled across the blasted landscape, snapping and clawing at each other. Tuftan and the rest of the Tiger Tribe cheered on their commander, their pony dogs rearing up beneath them. A bloodthirsty tiger-man galloped forward, eager to join the fracas, but Tuftan called him back.

"No!" the feline youth insisted. "No help! Strong must win!"

Kalibak's mace connected with Tawny's skull, dislodging the other tiger-man's jaws. Tawny's bloody maw came away from Kalibak's shoulder, tearing loose strips of torn metal and meat. "I'll beat you till your bones are paste!" Kalibak growled, gaining the advantage once more. He drew back his mace. His other paw ripped a slice out of Tawny's tufted right ear. "Kalibak will beat you and beat you and beat you blind!"

A bone-jarring blow from the mace felled Tawny. He splashed face-first into a greasy puddle. Kalibak rose triumphantly above his fallen foe. Blood dripped from his wounded shoulder. He shook his club at the turbulent heavens.

The other tiger-men leaned forward on their mounts. Yellow eyes glowed avidly.

They waited expectantly for the kill.

Moving at super-speed, Supergirl pounced on Mary Marvel, knocking the other girl onto her back. She snatched up the heavy metal streetlight from where it had fallen moments before and pressed it down across Mary's throat.

She crouched atop the squirming villainess, pinning her to the ground. Mary thrashed violently beneath her.

"Knock it off!" she admonished Mary, her jaw still smarting where Mary had kneed her. The pain frayed her temper somewhat. "Don't be too sure I won't just break your neck!"

That pervy grin returned to Mary's face. She tittered smugly beneath Supergirl, obviously pleased at having gotten under the Maid of Might's skin. She leered up at Supergirl like . . . Desaad!

"Goody-goody-goody," she cackled. Her fiendish eyes lit up in triumph as she peered past Supergirl at something behind the kneeling heroine. Pounding footsteps came charging toward them. "Great Darkseid, spare your servant!"

A brick hit Supergirl in the back of the head, startling her more than hurting her. More missiles followed: broken bottles, cans, rocks, cement, bones. Looking away from Mary, she risked a glance back over her shoulder. To her dismay, a horde of ordinary people were scrambling out of the haze, their eyes glowing red as hellfire. The possessed mob clambered over the rubble, waving metal pipes, jagged lengths of rebar, and whatever else they could lay their hands on. They fell upon Supergirl en masse. Futile blows rained down on her invulnerable form.

"No!" Supergirl pleaded with the entranced rioters. "I don't want to hurt you!"

"*But I am Darkseid!*" her attackers chanted in unison. Dozens of relentless hands pulled her off Mary. Supergirl was unable to fight back, for fear of injuring the fragile humans. They pummeled her with their fists and feet and weapons. "*I will break your soul!*"

Forget it! Kara thought. *No way am I going to end up like Mary.*

"Supergirl!" Shazam flew over the mob toward Mary, who was already lunging at Supergirl. Diving past the crowd with the Speed of Mercury, he tackled Mary to the ground. The titanic interception rippled the pavement, scattering Darkseid's mind-controlled minions like tenpins. Shazam's muscular arms held on to Mary Marvel with the Strength of Hercules. "Leave this to me!"

Mary thrashed wildly, frantic to break free. "You again?"

"Un-huh," he said. "And this time I'm counting on my magic lightning to be strong enough to transform *both* of us." Holding on to his squirming prisoner, he invoked the powers of the gods. *"Shazam!"*

A tremendous thunderbolt lit up the battlefield, momentarily turning the murky haze to brightest day. The flash was so bright that even Supergirl was forced to look away for a second. Her remaining attackers halted their assault, struck dumb by the dazzling spectacle. The lightning dispelled the mob, who retreated in fear. It was like Eternity itself had called a time-out.

But for how long?

Standing over Tawny's abused body, his gore-smeared mace poised to deliver the killing blow, Kalibak was distracted by the stupendous thunderbolt, which struck the earth only a few yards away from the site of his victory. The glare of the lightning bleached out his face as it briefly bathed the ruins with a heavenly radiance. He looked away from the defeated tiger-man at his feet. A bloody forepaw shielded his eyes.

"Look!" Tuftan shouted in awe. The rest of the Tiger Tribe backed away from the overpowering incandescence, tugging on the reins of their pony dogs. Static electricity caused their fur to crackle. "It blazes like the sun!"

So it does, Tawny thought. The familiar thunderbolt restored his spirits. He lifted his swollen muzzle from the filthy puddle. His tie was askew. A torn ear stung like the very dickens. Crafty yellow eyes spotted his jet-pack a few feet away. As he recalled, there was still a little bit of a "tiger" left in its tank.

He reached stealthily for the pack.

"Have no fear!" Kalibak snarled at his kin. He sneered at their cowardice. "Darkseid owns the lightning!"

"I beg to differ," Tawny replied.

Once more fitted snugly across his back, the jet-pack ignited. Tawny rocketed at Kalibak. His claws swept out in a devastating arc, gutting the shocked New God where he stood. Entrails spilled from Kalibak's sundered midsection. His mace went flying from his claws. He dropped to his knees, clutching his abdomen. His paws clumsily tried to hold in his liberated bowels. Whimpering in agony, he looked to his Tiger Tribe for succor.

"Help . . ." he mewed. "Help me. . . ."

The mounted tiger-men kept their distance. Tuftan shook his head.

"No 'help,'" he said gravely, just as Kalibak himself had taught them. "Strong is only."

Kalibak toppled forward. His plaintive whimpers ceased. The son of Darkseid died as he had lived.

Without mercy.

The glare from the lightning faded, leaving behind two shaken teenagers sitting atop the rubble. Freddy Freeman cradled Mary Batson in his arms. The dark-haired young girl, whose kinky black costume had been replaced by a rumpled white T-shirt and khakis, wept uncontrollably as she recalled the atrocities committed by her depraved alter ego. All because she'd let Darkseid tempt her into embracing his power.

"What have I done?" she sobbed. "Oh God, I didn't mean this. I didn't mean *any* of this."

"Sssh," Freddy comforted her. His crutch lay across the debris next to him. "It wasn't you, Mary."

Wasn't it? she agonized. That insidious voice in her head, the one that had kept urging her on to ever more unspeakable acts, seemed to have fallen silent at last, but how could she be certain that it was gone for good? What if it was still lurking somewhere in her soul, waiting to seduce her to the dark side once more? The obscene magic word it had taught her lingered at the tip of her tongue. One careless breath and she would be Mary Marvel once more.

"I can never say it again." She shuddered in Freddy's arms, clinging to him as though he was the Rock of Eternity itself. "Never say the word. Never say it ever again."

Supergirl gazed down on her in pity.

Tawny faced the assembled might of the Tiger Tribe.

He touched down on the ground, his jet-pack exhausting the last of its fuel. Kalibak's lifeless body lay in a pool of his own blood. The mounted tiger-men surrounded Tawny. Dozens of lambent yellow eyes gazed at their commander's killer. Tawny realized that he was both out of tricks and severely outnumbered. The jet-pack slipped off his shoulders, and he straightened his tie.

"Legendary tiger tea," he offered by way of explanation. "Confers the strength of ten. At least for a little while."

A sudden weariness overcame him, but he maintained a civilized posture. He greeted the feline cavalry with all the dignity he could muster. "I'm sorry we had to meet under such appalling circumstances, but . . ." A low growl cleared his throat. "Do your worst, gentlemen."

He was prepared to meet his end without regret, grateful that he had lived to see Mary freed from whatever malignant spell had held her in its grip. He closed his eyes in anticipation of the Tiger Tribe's fatal charge. With luck, it would be over quickly.

But nothing happened.

Puzzled, he opened his eyes. Expecting to see fangs and claws descending upon him in a predatory frenzy, he was astonished to discover that the tiger-men had dismounted instead. They knelt before him in a semicircle, their heads bowed low. Tawny blinked in surprise.

"Oh my."

The battle was turning the heroes' way at last. Fallen Justifiers littered the ground, while their comrades fled in disarray. Hourman hugged Liberty Belle, lifting her off her feet. S.T.R.I.P.E. crushed a Justifier helmet between his huge robotic gauntlets, then hurled the crumpled metal onto a heap of equally totaled headgear. Fused circuitry sparked and crackled uselessly. Mister America leaned against the torched remains of an old tollbooth, taking advantage of the lull to lower his bullwhip. Patriotic stars trimmed his tattered red cape, and his slick black hair and pencil mustache gave him the dashing look of an old-time matinee idol, despite the bruises and scrapes. Wildcat raised his fists above his head, like he was celebrating a knockout in the ring. Red Arrow restocked his quiver and smiled to himself.

S.T.R.I.P.E. used the electronics in his helmet to report back to headquarters. Once the Star-Spangled Kid's sidekick and bodyguard, Pat Dugan now fought evil from inside an immense suit of mechanized body armor. His codename stood for Special Tactics Robotic Integrated Power Enhancer. "Tell 'em we secured the bridge. Bring up the second wave. . . ."

His electronically amplified voice trailed off as a thunderous roar approached from the east. A gigantic female figure emerged from the mist, preceded by a quartet of mounted figures. The racing paws of enormous mastiffs stirred up clouds of dust and ash in their wake.

"Algo se acera," Iman gasped aloud. His own cybernetic exoskeleton was badly in need of repair. A dented green helmet turned toward the threatening riders. Anxious blue eyes could be glimpsed through his shattered visor. *"Como el sonido de unde caballos."*

Hourman knew enough Spanish to get the gist:

Something coming . . . like the sound of horses.

CHAPTER 28

THE SWISS ALPS.

Mister Terrific brought Mister Miracle and his allies up to speed. "You arrived via your Boom Tube, so you may not have seen what it's like out there."

He called the newcomers' attention to a large flat-screen monitor that depicted the scene outside the Castle, where an endless throng of possessed Swiss civilians was scaling the walls of the fortress. Moving as one, as though controlled by a single malignant intelligence, they clambered over each other's heads and shoulders in their monomaniacal determination to breach the stronghold's defenses. A crimson glow rendered their eyes incarnadine, and their soulless faces lacked any trace of individuality. They even *breathed* in unison.

"This is the last redoubt," Mister Terrific continued. He eyed Shilo Norman skeptically. "Notwithstanding the fact that there are potentially no more than three billion free humans still alive on this planet, you say you can help with a solution?"

Mister Miracle pointed at the unusual glyph painted on his face. "You can start with this. The same pattern appeared everywhere all at once. Crop circles. Cave paintings. Before all this." Shilo claimed to have encountered Boss Dark Side and his minions before, prior to the Crisis. That gave him some authority on the subject. "I have reason to believe that it's a letter from the alphabet of the New Gods. A living symbol that means 'freedom from restriction.' And protection against Anti-Life."

"Hmm." Michael Holt scratched his chin, wishing he could accept the other man's theory at face value. It was almost too good to be true.

"White King," a castellan addressed Mister Terrific. He stepped forward to deliver the news. "The shields are history. Countdown has begun."

Holt realized time was running out. "Guess I'll have to get back to you on that, Mister Norman." Whatever intel the escape artist might possess had just become academic. "Black gambit status," he informed Castellan Draper before turning back to Shilo Norman and his friends. "Did I tell you about Checkmate's endgame if the super heroes failed, if hope expired?"

That day had come.

The Super Young Team were spread out around the crashed Wonder Wagon. Shy Crazy Lolita Canary fluttered nervously as Mister Miracle quietly conferred with Sonny Sumo. "We've never been in a real fight," she chirped. "Most of our powers are cosmetic!"

"Not mine," Shiny Happy Aquazon said bravely. She fingered the harpoon launcher at her hip.

Big Atomic Lantern Boy admired her courage from the other end of the car. "This is it!" he whispered urgently to Well-Spoken Sonic Lightning Flash. "I have to tell Aquazon how much I love her, Keigo." He gazed at the beautiful merwoman rapturously. "Tell her I've *always* loved her, like the tree loves to grow, like the sun loves the day. . . ."

"Doomsday is coming, ten minutes tops!" Sonic Lightning Flash shoved his large friend toward the fish-girl of his dreams. "Tell her yourself. Make a date!"

Lantern Boy wondered if he truly dared.

Across the room, cut off from the boys by the Wonder Wagon, Aquazon confided in her tiny winged friend. "Oh, this is terrible. I can't seem to tell Sonic how I feel about him." She snuck a glance at the laconic speedster, who was checking the wires on his oversized boots. They lit up encouragingly. "I'm still too shy!"

"Wait until we've saved the world," her tiny winged friend advised. "*Then* tell him!"

Mister Miracle spared Aquazon any further debate by rounding up the teenagers to give them a pep talk. They gathered around him, the girls on one side, the boys on the other, except for Most Excellent Superbat, who was busy rummaging through the trunk of the Wonder Wagon. Aquazon stood stiffly at attention, determined to impress Shilo. Hero worship shone in her limpid aquamarine eyes.

"So, team." Mister Miracle looked over the adolescent heroes, one by one. "Lantern Boy, you've got that ray thing coming out of your chest. Canary, you can scream yourself raw. Sonic, you can break every speed limit. Aquazon, you can swim like nothing else." He glanced over at the teenagers' leader. "Superbat, you never told me what *your* power was."

Superbat lifted his head from the trunk. "I have the *greatest* power of all, Mister Miracle." He grinned confidently as he hoisted an armored version of his mask from the rear of the Wonder Wagon. The rest of an awesome-looking power suit, in bright primary colors, could be glimpsed inside the trunk. "I'm so rich I can do anything!"

BLÜDHAVEN.

The Female Furies galloped into the ranks of the dumbfounded heroes, who were taken aback by the sight of Wonder Woman leading the charge. Her boar-mask denied her humanity and shocked her former allies. The debased Amazon princess leaned back in her saddle, her arms spread wide in perverse exultation. Clouds of vile green vapor exuded from her open palms. Hourman clutched his throat as he choked on the fumes. In theory, he had several minutes of power left, but the foul contagion seemed to counteract the Miraclo in his system. He felt his enhanced strength and agility slipping away.

Some sort of germ warfare?

The Omega Initiative broke apart before the Furies' assault. Catwoman cracked her whip, the lash flaying Wildcat's mask from his face. Ironically, it had been Ted Grant who had first taught the young Selina Kyle how to fight. Now he was trampled beneath the heavy paws of her rabid hellhound. The mastiff foamed and frothed at its bit.

Giganta stomped her foot, the seismic tremor knocking the coughing heroes off their feet. Her giant fists scooped up S.T.R.I.P.E. and Iman and slammed them together. Batwoman fired energy-pistols from both hands, their rapid-fire blasts melting the Metal Men. The vampiric-looking Fury drooled at the carnage she was creating.

This is a full-fledged nightmare, Hourman thought. He tried to hold his breath, but the poisonous vapors invaded his lungs anyway. Unable to stand, he collapsed into the mud, along with the rest of his teammates. Lightning crackled across the crimson sky of the battlefield. The air smelled and tasted like blood. Barely able to lift his head from the gory muck, he saw Liberty Belle gasping for breath only a few feet away. Trembling fingers reached out for his wife, only to fall a few inches short. He felt sick and feverish. *This just keeps getting worse and worse!*

Undaunted, the Furies rode roughshod over the stricken heroes.

THE WATCHTOWER.

"Submit," Green Arrow ordered. "Or we gut the brats."

The Justifiers had taken command of the satellite. After boarding the JLA's orbital refuge, they had rounded up everyone they found, separating the heroes from the civilians. Now Black Canary and the others found themselves surrounded by enemy soldiers on the observation deck. That her husband and Black Lightning were among the invaders tore at her heart.

"No, no," she pleaded. "Ollie! Jefferson! Don't do this!"

Helmets hid the brainwashed heroes' faces. Armed Justifiers menaced little Jai and Iris. Stripped of their weapons, Linda Park and Joan Garrick watched helplessly, clinging to each other for support. Oracle looked like she wanted to lunge from her wheelchair at their merciless captors. Black Canary knew exactly how she felt.

"You saved my family!" the Tattooed Man reminded Black Lightning. Tattooed scorpions and tarantulas crawled across his skin. "Show me that guy!"

"All is one in Darkseid," Jefferson Pierce replied. A bolt of lightning dropped the Tattooed Man to his knees. "Accept Anti-Life and see. *Submit*."

A nameless Justifier forced a helmet onto Mark Richards's head as Green Arrow came forward with a helmet for Black Canary. A pair of Justifiers held on tightly to her arms. "All is one in Darkseid," Green Arrow promised.

She just couldn't believe that her husband had fallen victim to this plague. Oliver Queen was the most infuriatingly stubborn and opinionated man she had ever known. "Don't!" she urged him, hoping to get through to the hero behind the helmet. "It's *me*, Oliver! I love you!" Her throat tightened and her eyes stung with tears. "I love you so much!"

"Love is pain," he recited like an automaton. "Anti-Life is the anesthetic." He lowered the helmet toward her, while the other Justifiers kept her still. Their gauntlets dug into her arms hard enough to leave bruises. "Submit."

"No!" The Tattooed Man wrenched the helmet from his head. That mysterious glyph glowed like silver upon his face. "You let her alone, you hear!"

Spitting cobras sprang from his shoulders, striking Black Lightning in the chest. Their venomous fangs pierced his dark blue uniform. Spiders leapt from Richards's outstretched hands. They scuttled across the floor at the other Justifiers. Bats and flaming skulls flew through the air.

The surreal distraction was just what Black Canary needed. Kicking off from the floor, she flipped backward between her two guards, twisting free from their grip, while simultaneously kicking the helmet off Green Arrow's head with the sole of her boot. He staggered backward, reeling. His dislodged helmet clattered across the floor. Sparks flared from the circuitry inside.

Sorry, Ollie, she thought. *You'll thank me later.*

"Station! Voice activate!" The Watchtower's automated systems were programmed to accept her commands. "Black Canary! Gravity off!"

The station's artificial gravity disappeared, leaving the flummoxed Justifiers floundering in the suddenly zero-gee environment. Green Arrow tumbled weightlessly, still dazed from a much-needed kick in the head. Needing no gravity, the Tattooed Man's cobras snaked through the air to strike Black Lightning again and again. Sparks flared wildly from the wounded hero, but apparently you couldn't electrocute a tattoo. Oracle pulled herself along a safety rail, out of the line of fire. A veteran of countless zero-gee training drills, Black Canary expertly slammed the heads of her former captors together. The clanging helmets made a satisfying racket.

That's *more like it,* she thought.

The Flash kids got into the action, using their unique abilities. Jai accelerated his metabolism, bulking up his muscle mass until he looked like a pint-sized version of Gorilla Grodd. He elbowed the disoriented Justifier standing guard over him, flinging him into the solid promethium wall behind him. Jai ricocheted in the other direction with equal and opposite force. Meanwhile, Iris vibrated her molecules to intangibility, so that her own guard *fell through her* into a solid gut punch from her mom. Joan Garrick kicked the guard in the ribs for good measure.

Black Canary silently thanked Batman for insisting that the League add weightlessness to its training regimen. She elegantly shoved off from the ceiling in a move she had practiced hundreds of times before. Her momentum carried her right where she wanted to go: straight toward Green Arrow.

She snagged onto the floating Emerald Archer. A punch to his chin got his attention. Although his helmet was gone, glowing red eyes still glared at her from behind his green domino mask. He fought to get away from her. His zombified expression made her sick to her stomach. It was like he didn't even know who she was—or what they meant to each other.

"Look at me, Oliver Queen!" she shouted into his face. "Look at me and fight, damn it!" Tears leaked from her eyes as she shook him violently in midair. "Snap out of it!"

"Anti-Life . . ." he mumbled uncertainly. The red glow in his eyes began to fade, but not fast enough. He groped for one of the arrows in his quiver. "Anti-Life's so easy. . . ."

Black Canary never wanted to hear the word *Anti-Life* again, not from Ollie, not from *anyone.* An open-hand strike, taught to her by Lady Shiva, the world's greatest martial artist, cut off his creepy catechism. She didn't have time to be gentle about this. *"Now!"*

Outside the satellite, the sun began to dim. Space-time warped, catching the station in the swirling eddies of a powerful vortex. The moon was stretched out of shape, its silvery image distorted by the bizarre phenomena.

Hemispheric bulges protruded through the ruptured fabric of the universe, offering fragmentary glimpses of alternate Earths, all impinging on this reality. The Watchtower was tugged from its orbit, circling in toward the shallow curve of Earth's horizon. Its gleaming underside struck sparks off the atmosphere.

They were going down.

CHAPTER 29

THE SWISS ALPS.

The Castle's facilities seemed to go on forever. Leaving Amanda Waller behind to supervise the assembly of the biomacs, Khalid led Renee on to an elevated catwalk overlooking what appeared to be an advanced physics lab. Technicians in white lab jackets manned a series of linked terminals. A Cray super-computer hummed in the background. The phosphor glow of the monitors lit up the tense faces of the staff, who looked like they hadn't slept in days. A pair of super heroes, in matching red and blue uniforms, looked over the technicians' shoulders. The lab smelled of sweat and copious amounts of caffeine.

"Welcome to Checkmate: Omega, Ms. Montoya." Khalid gestured at the hubbub below. "Professors Palmer and Choi are preparing to ride the graviton highway to another universe."

Is he serious? Renee waved at the costumed scientists. "Hi, guys. Better you than me."

The older of the two heroes looked up from his work. He waved back at her. "Ray Palmer," he introduced himself. "The Atom."

An auxiliary member of the Justice League, Palmer had been the first man to harness the power of a white dwarf star to explore microscopic realms. Although normal-sized now, he was capable of shrinking to any size, no matter how minuscule. Overlapping atomic orbitals were printed on the forehead of his light blue cowl. He nodded at his young Asian protégé, who had taken over for him during Palmer's recent sabbatical. "Professor Ryan Choi, also known as the Atom."

"Ray, I need a new name," Choi protested, blushing. The atom emblem was embossed on the buckle of his metallic golden belt. He pulled on his own cowl to hide his flushed cheeks. "This is embarrassing."

Renee wondered if she'd feel the same way if the original Question came back to life. Stranger things had happened, especially lately.

Khalid escorted her out of the physics lab into a long corridor lined with locked steel doors. Windows embedded in the doors offered glimpses of the various operations underway at this crucial juncture.

"Here in Room 90," he explained, "our psychics are attempting to purge the human mass consciousness of the Anti-Life Equation. With mixed results, I fear."

Renee peeked through the window. Rows of people, of all ages and ethnicities, were seated on chairs like students in a classroom. Unknown civilians mixed with costumed telepaths like Miss Martian, Mento, Brainwave, Faith, and Mindgrabber Kid. Anxious medical personnel hurried between the distraught psychics, who looked like they were suffering the torments of the damned. Blood leaked from the ears of a wizened old black man in a tweed jacket. Bulging veins pulsed across the shaved cranium of a trembling ten-year-old boy. Tears streamed down the ashen cheeks of a cute South Asian girl in an orange silk sari. Sweat drenched drawn and twitching faces. Nosebleeds were epidemic. Mindgrabber Kid, a D-list former teen hero who mostly worked the convention circuit these days, hawking his autograph to super hero groupies, clutched his skull in agony, before toppling off his chair onto the floor. Violent convulsions attracted the attention of a nurse, who barely got to him in time to keep him from biting off his own tongue.

"Make it stop!" Miss Martian shrieked. She pulled out handfuls of her bright red hair. Paramedics attempted to inject her with a tranquilizer, but the needle snapped against her indestructible green skin. Now that J'onn J'onzz was dead, she was the last surviving Martian on Earth. "Make it stop!"

Renee was suddenly very glad that her own brain was of the conventional variety. *What the hell are they hearing inside their heads?*

They moved on to the room across the hall, where some kind of séance seemed to be going on. Zatanna, the Justice League's foremost sorceress, hovered above a round oak table, her booted legs crossed in the lotus position. Dr. Occult, Madame Xanadu, John Constantine, the Enchantress, Doctor Fate, Black Alice, Sebastian Faust, Traci 13, Ibis the Invincible, Manitou Dawn, Sargon the Sorcerer, Raven, and Jakeem Thunder sat around the table, holding hands. The mystics' eyes were closed in mediation, their heads tilted upward toward the higher planes. They chanted softly. Strange unearthly shadows, seemingly disconnected from the bodies of the creepy coven, danced across the walls.

"In here," Khalid stated, "our mystics attempt to contact the Spectre in the afterworlds."

Tiny hairs stood up at the back of Renee's neck. The Spectre was a ghostly apparition of unparalleled power, said to embody the very Wrath of God. The vengeful spirit of a murdered cop, bonded to an elemental entity dating back to the dawn of Creation, the Spectre had both menaced and rescued the world on various occasions. By invoking them, the assembled sorcerers were playing with fire. Renee wasn't sure that was such a good idea.

"So what's over here?" she asked. Anxious to leave the uncanny séance behind, she quickly moved on to the next door. Her eyes widened as she spotted the lifeless body of Overgirl stretched out on a metal slab on the other side of the door, while pathologists in surgical scrubs analyzed her remains. Articulated scanners, resembling mechanical praying mantises, rotated around the cadaver. Glowing monitors displayed X-ray and MRI images of her internal structure and organs. A determined medical examiner attempted to take a sample of the girl's blonde hair, using a high-speed circular saw, but its teeth splintered against the indestructible tresses. Sparks flew and the foiled pathologist jumped backward. Dissecting a Supergirl, even a Nazi one, was apparently no easy matter. Renee wondered what Checkmate hoped to learn from her corpse.

She recalled Overgirl's final moments, after the battered Aryan teenager crashed to Earth in New York. *Mine was probably the last face she ever saw,* Renee realized sadly. She felt a twinge of pity. Nazi or not, the doomed girl had died in pain and far from home. *Is anybody out there missing her?*

"Never mind that," Khalid said hastily. He steered her away from the autopsy toward a pair of double doors at the end of the hall. A pair of armed sentries stepped aside to let them pass. "Through here, Ms. Montoya."

They entered a large circular chamber that Renee instinctively guessed was the end of the tour. Curved steel walls surrounded an enormous golden sphere half submerged in a gaping mechanic's pit. A circular porthole gave the igloo-sized dome the look of a giant Magic 8 Ball. A stainless steel iris covered the porthole, concealing the sphere's contents for the time being. Renee wondered what Khalid had in store for her next.

What's the point of all this show-and-tell?

Five towering inhuman figures stood guard over the mysterious globe. A blue ceramic glaze coated the stationary bodies of the OMACs, short for Observational Meta-human Activity Constructs. Mohawklike fins crested the tops of their hairless craniums, the better to receive and transmit cybernetic instructions. Solitary red lenses occupied the centers of their smooth, featureless faces, which reminded Renee of her own faceless alter ego. Gauntlets loaded with lethal weaponry weighed down their wrists. A graphic representation of an unblinking human eye was emblazoned on their chests. Each over twelve feet tall, the intimidating cyborgs were Checkmate's most infamous creations, designed to police both super heroes and super-villains alike. Renee thought they had all been destroyed a few years back. Apparently, she was mistaken.

"This is where the Black Gambit will be played," Khalid revealed. "The Omega Offensive." He gestured at the humongous sphere. The metal iris opened to reveal a disembodied human brain floating in an amber-colored nutrient solution. "I'd like you to meet Lord Eye."

Not to be confused with Brother Eye, Renee guessed. The artificial intelligence that had previously controlled the OMACs had gone all HAL 9000 on the human race during the Infinite Crisis, forcing the Justice League to blow it to bits. *Looks like Checkmate is taking a more organic approach this time around.*

She wondered *whose* brain it was.

"What the heck?" she groused. "Enough of this goddamn sensory overload." She was tired of being led around like a petting-zoo pony. What did Khalid think he was playing at? "There's nothing out there in the world. In case you hadn't noticed, it's all over for the home team!"

An eerie electronic voice emerged from Lord Eye's tank. "We live within a Multiverse of possibilities, Ms. Montoya." The brain's throbbing lobes turned toward her, as it somehow examined her without benefit of eyes. "The choices we make decide worlds. You have unprecedented levels of law-enforcement experience, with particular regard to meta-human crime-fighting activities, Renee."

That's one way to look at it, she admitted. Working the Major Crimes Unit in Gotham, then fighting the Religion of Crime as the Question, had certainly given her an interesting resume. *But what does that have to do with the end of the world?*

"You are the template for something new," Lord Eye stated.

A circular trapdoor opened in the floor between Renee and the porthole. Swirling chemical fumes, which Renee immediately identified as the binary compound she used to turn into the Question, accompanied a hydraulic platform that lifted four newcomers into view. Renee's jaw dropped at the sight of uniformed agents whose featureless blank visages mimicked the Pseudoderm mask she wore as the Question. Black leather jackets further added to the resemblance.

Renee fished her own mask out of her pocket. *I wonder if I can sue for copyright infringement.*

"We have already identified a target Earth into which we will make our retreat," Lord Eye informed her. "If Professors Palmer and Choi are successful, we will core through the bulk into a parallel universe. We want you to lead the Global Peace Agency that will establish the remnants of this world on another."

"Wait a minute," Renee protested. This was a lot to absorb all at once. "Say that whole bit again."

Khalid stood off to one side, awaiting her answer.

METROPOLIS.

The Calculator twisted in the wind. Gravity tugged on his hanging body, stretching his throat, as the noose slowly choked him. He dangled from the gallows, the cords of his neck standing out painfully, his bluish complexion evidence of slow asphyxiation. A strangled gurgle escaped cracked and bleeding lips.

"Amazing," Luthor marveled. "He's kept him alive indefinitely."

He and Sivana stood on the scaffold, gazing up at the Calculator's endless execution. Lex wondered how long Libra intended to let Noah Kuttler suffer for a crime he hadn't even committed. Luthor understood the necessity of making an example of an underling occasionally, but this struck him as excessive. Not even Superman deserved this kind of brutality.

Well, maybe *Superman . . .*

Sivana leaned toward Lex. "I hate you, Luthor," he said sourly, keeping his raspy voice low. "Don't ever forget that. But when they made my own dear daughter submit to the Equation, that was the last straw. The very last straw."

Luthor found it hard to imagine that the gnarled old mad scientist had ever sired children, but his file confirmed that was the case. Beautia Sivana was quite a fetching young woman, in fact. Clearly, she took after her mother.

Sivana looked about furtively. "Listen close. Libra's right behind us." He sneered at the Justifiers accompanying Libra. "The helmets are Mad Hatter design. Practically medieval." He took out a pocket watch from inside his rumpled white lab coat. "I converted my watch into a short-range signal jammer."

"Good," Luthor murmured, pleased by Sivana's ingenuity. "They finally allowed me to power up my war suit in anticipation of today's 'battle.' " He consulted the diagnostic readouts on his gauntlet. All offensive systems were fully armed. "Charitable of them."

Libra climbed the wooden steps leading to the scaffold. An honor guard of Super-Justifiers attended him. Luthor recognized the Human Flame, Talia, Deathstroke, and Mirror Master among the evangelist's unthinking acolytes. "Calculator will die there forever," Libra decreed, "protesting his innocence, begging forgiveness."

"Ready?" Sivana whispered.

More than you can imagine, Luthor thought.

"It was you, wasn't it?" Libra accused him. By now, Lex despised the very sound of the man's voice. "Given the honor of leading an army of villains

against the last of the super heroes, you chose treason instead." He came
up behind Lex and beckoned to his entourage. The Human Flame marched
forward, bearing an empty helmet. Deathstroke held a helmet for Sivana as
well. "You'll never choose again, either of you."

Luthor nodded at Sivana. "Impress me."

"Easy," the aged scientist muttered, twisting a knob on the pocket watch.

The effect on the Justifiers was instantaneous. They reeled about, clutching the sides of their helmets. The extra two helmets dropped onto the
wooden floor of the scaffold. Caught off guard for once, Libra took Darkseid's name in vain. He hefted his pointed staff, the same one he had used
to impale the Martian Manhunter, and aimed it at Luthor. The metal scales
jangled discordantly as the spearhead glowed red-hot.

Lex was unintimidated by the display. "Libra, the man who became the
sock puppet of the gods." Covert investigations had finally revealed that
Libra was actually an overambitious criminal scientist named Justin Ballan-
tine, whose attempt to achieve godhood by tapping into the cosmic energy of
the galaxy had apparently brought him under the sway of Darkseid. Luthor
raised a metal gauntlet, palm forward. "I'll show you balance. . . ."

Red-hot plasma shot from Luthor's gauntlet. The blast blew right through
Libra, leaving a gaping exit hole in the lackey's back. Luthor relished his victory for a moment, until he realized that the indigo costume was now *empty*.
The vacant outfit collapsed and crumpled to the floor, completely losing the
definition of a human form. Smoke rose from the back of the scorched yellow
cloak.

"Hmmph," Sivana snorted. He nudged the empty costume with his foot.
"That's a classic 'We haven't heard the last of him!' if I ever saw one."

Although disappointed, Luthor took Libra's cowardly vanishing act in
stride. A second blast seared through the rope holding the Calculator aloft,
and the hanging villain crashed to the floor of the scaffold. Not the gentlest
landing in history, but preferable to choking for all eternity, Lex figured. He
knelt to undo the noose around Noah's neck. Ugly purple bruises mottled
the gasping hacker's throat.

"This is a war against life, Sivana." Luthor stood up and tossed the noose
over the edge of the platform. The Calculator moaned weakly at his feet. "I'm
somewhat fond of life, for all its ups and downs."

"Meh. Sentimental hogwash." Sivana handed the pocket watch to Lex. "They'll hear your voice as the voice of Darkseid if you speak into this." Deprived of their leader, the addled Justifiers crouched before Luthor, their heads bowed. Sivana crankily advised Lex to be careful. "Don't shout, or you'll break it."

Luthor had no intention of doing that. No intention at all.

CENTRAL CITY.

Ever the scientist, Barry Allen expounded on the nature of the cosmos.

"At relativistic speeds, as you know, time, space, light . . . it all runs together and becomes one thing. Beyond the superluminal barrier, matter converts to pure information."

Wally took his uncle's word for it. A police mechanic, he was nowhere near the brain Barry was. He perched on the arm of the living room couch, next to Aunt Iris, who gazed adoringly at her newly returned husband. The TV set, which had been broadcasting the Anti-Life Equation nonstop, had been switched off faster than the average person could find the remote. Jay Garrick had joined them in Iris's apartment. A canvas *Daily Planet* bag rested at his feet, half-full of the latest edition.

"I was sent back from beyond *knowing* things," Barry explained. He had peeled back his scarlet cowl to expose the neat blond crew cut underneath. It was good to see his familiar face again. "I know what I have to do to stop Darkseid this time. And I need your help." He nodded at his illustrious predecessor. "Now that Jay's here, we're ready."

The original Flash tipped his silver cap at Barry and Wally. He looked tired, but determined. "My God, it's good to see you boys."

"You too, Jay," Wally replied. They had been forced to leave Jay behind before, when they'd broken the time barrier to get away from the Black Racer. Wally was relieved to see that the older hero was still in the game.

Barry shook his mentor's hand. "Jay, I know I can trust you to take care of Iris until we get back." He looked lovingly at his wife. "And we *are* coming back."

Jay sat down on the couch, resting his weary legs. "I've run holes in my boots from Watchtower to Watchtower," he recounted, "until one by one they fell to the Anti-Life Equation. I searched the country upside down for Joan and Linda and the kids, and I finally followed your trail here." Despite everything he had gone through already, he placed a protective arm around Iris. "Just tell me what you need me to do."

"I know you'll find Joan soon," she said. Thankfully, no trace of Darkseid's influence remained in her compassionate brown eyes. She was her old self again. "We'll all be reunited."

Wally prayed that wasn't just wishful thinking. He couldn't help worrying about his own family, whom he hadn't seen since he and Jay had started snooping around that strip club in Keystone City. He told himself that the fact that not even Jay could find them was a good sign, that it meant that Darkseid's minions probably couldn't find them either, but he wouldn't really breathe easy until he knew for sure that Linda and the kids were safe. *Take care of yourselves,* he urged his missing loved ones silently. *Wherever you are.*

Barry looked at his onetime sidekick. "If I can't make this work, Wally, it's up to you." A worried look came over his face. "The Black Racer didn't just give up chasing me. He won't stop until he catches me."

A chill ran down Wally's spine as he recalled the ominous black knight skiing through the air after them. He felt a twinge of déjà vu. "Barry, I think I met this guy before when he was called the Black Flash." He remembered a skeletal doppelganger chasing after him like the Grim Reaper a few years ago. "I outran him."

Barry chuckled proudly. "I'll bet you did." He looked abruptly to the west, as though sensing something beyond the others' perceptions. Wally shivered as a cold wind seemed to invade the apartment. Was it just his imagination, or did he hear something whooshing toward them from outside?

Like skis?

"Places, everybody!" Barry said urgently. "Here he comes!"

Wally jumped up off the couch. Jay stood in front of Iris, who tried to look brave. She swallowed hard.

"We're going to use him," Barry stated. He pulled on his cowl, becoming the Flash once more. "Darkseid is sitting at the center of his own personal singularity, beyond the reach of light. To get to him, we'll have to run faster than we ever have before." He dropped into a runner's stance, like a track star at the starting line. Wally got into position alongside him. "On your mark, Wally. Get set . . .

"*Go!*"

The two Flashes took off at lightning speed, vibrating straight through the walls of the apartment. The breeze generated by their departure whipped Iris's hair about. She started as she felt her husband kiss her good-bye faster than the eye could see. In a heartbeat, Barry and Wally were gone. An icy wind chased after them.

Iris clung to Jay for support as she stared off in the direction the two Flashes had departed in.

"Godspeed," she whispered.

CHAPTER 30

BLÜDHAVEN.

Batman crept through the bowels of Command-D. The unmistakable sounds of a major military operation, going on somewhere overhead, penetrated the concrete walls of the bunker. It sounded like World War IV was being fought in the bombed-out ruins above. Batman hoped the right side was winning.

Escaping that modern-day iron maiden, and the flooded laboratory, had been a challenge, but nothing beyond his abilities. He had long ago mastered the techniques of the world's greatest escape artists, including the original Mister Miracle. This was hardly the first time he had circumvented some diabolical predicament. The Joker could teach these New Gods a thing or two about building a proper death trap.

A flickering red light at the end of the corridor drew him on. Moving as silently as a ninja, he approached an arched steel doorway. He heard someone breathing with difficulty beyond. He paused outside the crimson glare, taking stock of the situation. The fetid atmosphere reeked of rotting human remains.

"I wondered when you would show yourself." A deep voice rendered his stealth superfluous. "Stop skulking in the shadows. Accept that the Equation is proven. Come out. Embrace Anti-Life and be whole."

"Darkseid," Batman said, scowling. He stalked forward in response to the evil god's summons. Behind the opaque white lenses of his cowl, his bloodshot eyes zeroed in on a hulking gray figure seated upon an imposing metal throne. "You look like I feel."

The onetime master of Apokolips had clearly seen better days. He slumped upon his throne like an invalid. Open sores pitted his petrified flesh, and IV tubes dangled limply around him like jungle vines. Every breath sounded like a herculean effort. His stiff, arthritic hands chopped and punched the air before him, like a conductor leading an invisible orchestra. The desiccated bodies of his acolytes lay sprawled at his feet. They resembled shriveled mummies.

Batman wasn't in much better shape. His cowl was punctured in dozens of places where syringes had been simply punched into his skull, and bloody scabs caked his scalp. His clenched jaw needed shaving. His mouth tasted like something had died in it. Every muscle in his body ached, and his head throbbed. He hadn't felt this queasy since the last time Poison Ivy kissed him.

His chapped lip curled in disgust as he glared at the inhuman architect of this latest Crisis. He knew he was looking at the ultimate enemy of humankind. If he squinted, he could almost see Darkseid's immortal essence hovering above the calcified husk before him, like a tribal mask composed of writhing alien biotechnology. The disturbing image was superimposed over the seated figure like a mirage. "You shouldn't have shot Orion."

"It was Orion's destiny to fall in the Final Battle," Darkseid rumbled. "Splintered like light in a prism through an infinite number of deaths."

"And on the way he wounded you beyond repair, didn't he?" Batman contemplated the crippled ruin before him. "A rotten carcass of a god, crawling into a sewer to die." He reached beneath his midnight cloak to draw out a futuristic pistol he had salvaged from the flooded lab. The exotic weapon was clearly extraterrestrial in origin; he recognized Apokoliptian technology when he saw it. "I made a very solemn vow about firearms, but for you, I'm making a once-in-a-lifetime exception." He raised the pistol. "A gun and a bullet, Darkseid. *Your* idea."

The pistol felt strange, unnatural, in his grip. Ever since a gun had claimed the lives of his parents so many years ago, the Dark Knight had always shunned firearms. But this was a special case—and a very special bullet.

"Radion. Toxic to your kind," he elaborated. "I sealed the bullet that killed Orion in my belt for inspection." He had confiscated the unique projectile back at the Hall of Justice, intending to subject it to further analysis back at the Batcave. It seemed, however, that Fate had a different plan.

Darkseid halted his grotesque manipulations and leaned forward on his throne. "But—"

"*Do I make myself clear!*" Batman interrupted. He aimed the pistol at Darkseid's head, and his finger tightened around the trigger. The very sensation appalled him.

"Little man," the god chuckled, unafraid. His volcanic red eyes flared brightly. "Can you outrace the Omega Sanction? The Death that is Life?"

"Try me," Batman said.

He squeezed the trigger, the recoil jarring his arm. At the very same moment, a pair of coruscating violet rays shot from Darkseid's brimstone eyes. The theotoxic bullet blasted into Darkseid's upper chest, knocking him to one side, even as the lethal Omega Beams veered away from each other, then converged on Batman from opposite directions. The Dark Knight hurled the empty gun away from him in disgust as Darkseid clutched his wounded chest. Slimy black ichor splattered against the back of the throne.

"Gotcha," Batman said, a split second before the zigzagging Omega Beams struck both sides of his head simultaneously. He opened his mouth to scream out in pain.

The last thing he saw was a blinding flash of light.

Then darkness.

METROPOLIS.

Nix Uotan surveyed the unraveling of the world. A sphere of holographic monitors rotated before his eyes, allowing him to view events all around the imperiled planet, far from the squalid prison cell he now occupied. The myriad images formed an unsettling collage of an Earth on the brink of utter damnation.

The Fortress of Solitude: Angled crystalline pillars dwarfed Jimmy Olsen and Lois Lane as they took refuge in Superman's arctic stronghold. Jimmy activated his signal-watch; a microchip beacon inside the watch emitted a hypersonic alarm audible only to Superman. Lois watched the sky above the Fortress expectantly, Supergirl's orange tabby cradled and purring in her arms. "He'll hear us, Jimmy," she promised, although her worried expression betrayed a trace of doubt. Only a few faint bruises remained as souvenirs of her former injuries. Miraculously, she was fully recovered, the Bleed having done its work. "Wherever he is, I know he'll hear us!"

Perhaps, Nix thought. He admired Lois Lane's faith in her husband. *But will he return to this plane in time?* The attentive Monitor turned his attention elsewhere.

The Swiss Alps: Hawkman and Hawkgirl strode through the shaking corridors of Checkmate Command, their feathered wings folded inward to allow them to traverse the halls unobstructed. Reincarnated lovers, whose death-defying romance dated back to the bygone days of the pharaohs, they had lived and died together many times before.

"Did you feel that?" Hawkman asked, as the Castle's ancient walls shuddered around them. He faced the end with the grim-faced stoicism of a classical warrior. "I brought my people through fire and terror. I saved the best of them."

Hawkgirl turned toward her avian partner. "Is this the end . . . again? Are we going down in flames one more time?" Unlike Hawkman, she had no memory of their previous lives together, and had stubbornly resisted the idea that they were fated to love each other through all eternity. "It's too soon."

"Don't you understand?" He took hold of her shoulders and turned her toward him. Smoldering eyes gazed out from behind his beaked helmet. "I'd rather die and be reborn in a new life. Maybe then you'll love me again . . . like you always have before."

She looked away in confusion. "That's not fair."

Nothing is fair, Nix thought, *where Darkseid is concerned*. The Anti-Life Equation left no room for love or desire. Hawkman's frustrated longing for his eternal paramour raised painful memories of Weeja Dell and their own torturous parting. Nix wished he could grant the Hawks the blissful reunion they deserved, but he feared that not even death could bring them together this time around. Darkseid's triumph would mean the end of all things, even the eternal cycle of reincarnation. For the Hawks, true oblivion beckoned at last. *If they are among the lucky ones.*

A new location took its turn before his surveillance-vision.

Outer space: Hal Jordan led an emerald cavalry toward Earth. The Green Lanterns dived headfirst down the gravity well after the retreating planet. A swirling vortex threatened to swallow the planet before their eyes. Alternate Earths blistered the bulging red walls of the space-time whirlpool. The three Earthmen took the lead, ahead of dozens of their alien comrades. Guy Gardner let out a war whoop. His ring transmitted the bellicose howl through the airless vacuum. "What a rush!"

"It never seems to get any closer!" Kyle Rayner exclaimed. Frustration tinged his voice. "No matter how far down we go!"

"RING POWER AT NINETEEN PERCENT," his ring announced. "RING POWER AT EIGHTEEN PERCENT."

Hal's own power ring was similarly depleted. He ignored its insistent warnings; with the Central Power Battery still in hiding, there was no way to recharge the rings. "Keep going, Kyle!" he urged the younger Lantern. He kept his eyes fixed on the precious blue planet falling into hell below them. "Even if we burn out, even if we die trying, we will not abandon our people to that!"

The Green Lanterns accelerated into the bottomless void.

Such courage, Nix thought, *and willpower.* He understood now why the Green Lantern Corps was essential to this universe's safety. But could even their emerald light dispel the blackest of nights as it descended upon reality?

Blüdhaven: Supergirl stood atop a heap of rubble, watching protectively over the huddled forms of Freddy Freeman and Mary Batson. Darkseid's remote-controlled mob kept their distance, spying at the young people warily through the sickening yellow fog. A hush fell over the battlefield, the only sound Supergirl's bright red cape flapping in the wind.

"Everything's gone so quiet," she observed. She knew this was only a momentary respite; even now the possessed horde was silently creeping toward them with malevolent intent. The eerie stillness reminded her of the eye of a hurricane. Broken buildings stabbed at the roiling red sky like jagged fangs.

"If only Billy was here," Freddy said, as Mary helped him to his feet. He leaned upon his tarnished metal crutch. "If only he could see us now." The crippled youth faced the advancing mob bravely. He'd tried to change back to Shazam, but his magic word hadn't worked. Darkseid had cut them off from the ancient gods and immortals who usually empowered him. "We won't give in."

Billy Batson, the original Captain Marvel, had been forced to take up residence in the mystical Rock of Eternity after the wizard Shazam died in the last Crisis. Charged with guarding the Seven Deadly Sins for all time, he seldom appeared on the earthly plane anymore. Supergirl wondered if Captain Marvel could see them through the terrible red storms that shrouded the planet. Was Earth now beyond the reach of Eternity?

"We can make him proud," Mary said. She picked up a broken length of pipe to defend herself with and stepped protectively in front of Freddy. It was hard to believe she was the same girl who had been clawing at Supergirl's face only a few minutes ago. Amazing the effect one little magic word could have!

Too bad they were out of tricks now . . .

Nix struggled to assimilate the disparate images orbiting his head. "Metron, I can't coordinate this! It's all happening at once." He shook his head in bewilderment. "I know I was exiled with these germ-people for a reason, but this . . ."

The sheer extent of the catastrophe overwhelmed him. One Earth had already perished under his watch. Was he now doomed to look on helplessly as all of Creation became one with Darkseid?

"Nix Uotan," Metron addressed him. No longer trapped in the body of a spastic cripple, the enigmatic New God was revealed in all his glory. An opalescent sheen clothed his lean, ascetic form. A distinctive pattern, familiar to Nix from mortal dreams and newspaper headlines, was etched in silver upon Metron's brow and skintight raiment. He looked strangely transparent, almost glasslike, as though a mere touch might shatter him, yet also stronger and more enduring than a mountain. His slender fingers toyed with the solved Rubik's Cube. The decrepit wheelchair had been replaced by his fabled Mobius chair, restored to Metron at last. A sublime glow lit up the corners of the dismal prison cell.

"Observe," he continued. "Your rebirth inaugurates the Fifth World.

The age of men as gods. These new humans will face a greater menace than Darkseid should they breach the Bleed Wall protecting this Earth from the rest of the Multiverse."

A greater menace than Darkseid?

Nix knew Metron could only be referring to one unspeakable evil. The young Monitor's immortal blood ran cold.

No! he thought fearfully. *Not him!*

CHAPTER 31

BLÜDHAVEN.

A mobile hospital unit had been set up across the river from Blüdhaven, where a refugee camp used to be. Dr. Mid-Nite, the Justice Society's resident physician, desperately performed triage on the soldiers and super heroes retreating from the battlefield on the other side of the bridge. The Female Furies had completely broken the ranks of the Omega Initiative. Feverish casualties, infected by whatever foul contagion Wonder Woman had spread, were laid out on scattered cots and stretchers, while frantic medics valiantly tended to their injuries. Canvas tents provided minimal protection from the howling wind and almost nonstop lightning. Tanks and jeeps rumbled past the tents on their way to defend the bridge. It was unclear how much longer they could hold off the Furies.

"It's a mutated strain of the *morticoccus* bacteria," Dr. Mid-Nite diagnosed. The genetically engineered plague was believed to be extra-dimensional in origin; according to a top secret report filed by the Challengers of the Unknown, a variant of the disease had already devastated a parallel world designated Earth-51. Pieter Cross leaned over the supine body of his ailing patient. Hourman moaned upon his cot. Dr. Mid-Nite checked the hero's pulse, which fluttered alarmingly beneath his fingers. "People are losing their powers and dying."

His own throat felt sore and raw. Despite his infrared goggles, his night-vision began to fade. True darkness encroached on his sight. He coughed up blood. Chief Man-of-Bats, the Native American medicine man who was assisting Cross, gazed at the stricken doctor with concern. A ceremonial feathered headdress crowned his midnight black cowl. A beaded bat-totem was embroidered on the chest of his fringed buckskin tunic. He reached out to steady his fellow healer.

Hourman writhed in agony. Following standard super-hero medical protocol, his yellow cowl remained in place to protect his secret identity. The hourglass around his neck was running out of time. "I need to get back to my wife," he gasped haltingly. His fist closed around Dr. Mid-Nite's wrist, but he lacked even the strength of an ordinary adult male. He tugged on the physician's arm. "Please . . . I *promised*. . . ."

Dr. Mid-Nite didn't know what to say. He knew too well that Liberty Belle was only a few cots away, herself on the brink of death. Was it worth trying to move them closer together?

Explosions and energy-blasts echoed from the front lines, which were getting nearer every moment. Ebony lightning flashed outside, like a photo-negative of a less-unnatural electrical storm.

"Nobody can stop this," Dr. Mid-Nite realized. There was no point in trying to evacuate the casualties; no place on Earth was safe from this literal apocalypse. He gently disengaged Hourman's hand from his wrist. As a doctor, he knew that some cases were hopeless. The Earth was a terminal patient now. "We're powerless. This is the end of the world."

Man-of-Bats hugged his son and sidekick, Raven Red. The strapping Sioux youth wore an angular scarlet helmet. The silhouette of his namesake was printed on his short-sleeved red shirt. The boy gave his father a worried look. "Dad?"

THE SWISS ALPS.

Alan Scott felt the world coming apart. A sudden wave of nausea swept over him. Standing upon the ramparts of the Castle, trying to hold back the mind-less zombies scaling the walls of the fortress, he grabbed onto a flaking stone merlon to support himself. His mystic connection to the raw magical power of the universe let him know exactly what was happening. He kneaded his furrowed brow as the emerald flame around his power ring sputtered out. A few stray sparks rose like soap bubbles before blinking out of existence. "Darkseid's poisoned the root. He's broken the world."

Blue Beetle rushed to the aid of Green Lantern. The inexperienced young hero called out to a Checkmate medic. Chitinous azure armor shielded Blue Beetle from enemy fire. "Can we get some help over here?"

Alan appreciated the boy's efforts but feared they were wasted on a lost cause. The sun had gone black, and a red sky whirled dizzyingly overhead. Blood rained down on the battlements. They needed more than just backup.

They needed a miracle.

BLÜDHAVEN.

The mob surged toward Supergirl, Freddy, and Mary like a tidal wave. Supergirl pursed her lips, preparing to blow them back with her super-breath, but wondered how much longer she could defend Freddy and Mary from the brainwashed refugees and soldiers without actually hurting any of Darkseid's innocent pawns. She weighed her options, which seemed to be shrinking faster than the bottled city of Kandor.

What would Superman do at a time like this?

A sonic boom caught everyone by surprise. The earth-shattering bang rattled what windows remained in the blighted metropolis. Supergirl gasped out loud. Even Darkseid's unthinking army halted their inexorable advance. Startled, they lifted their infernal red eyes toward the turbulent heavens.

Supergirl did the same. Her super-vision penetrated the roiling scarlet clouds. Her blue eyes widened in amazement. She pointed excitedly at a sudden flash of red and blue.

"Look, up in the sky!"

Superman came hurtling down from clouds, his heat vision blasting ahead of him. Faster than a speeding bullet, more powerful than a locomotive, he carved out a gaping trench between Supergirl, her teenage allies, and the relentless mob. She swept up her cape to shield Freddy and Mary from the flying debris, even as her cousin zoomed past them like a supersonic missile. The shock wave generated by his passage hurled the zombie army off its feet. Supergirl dropped her cape, and hope lit up her face.

"Kal-El?"

She had never seen him so intense, so furious before. Brilliant coronas surrounded laser-bright eyes which glowed as fiercely as Krypton's red sun as he tapped the full destructive potential of his heat vision. At the same, his mouth was wide-open, unleashing a devastating sonic assault that sounded like Black Canary times one hundred. Supergirl clapped her hands over her own indestructible ears. Glass and masonry exploded in his wake, and melted skyscrapers collapsed into heaps of rubble.

Look at him go! Supergirl thought. Her heart nearly burst with pride. *He's pulling out all the stops this time.*

She took to the air after him. Her telescopic vision tracked his progress as he tore through Blüdhaven toward the Command-D bunker. Wonder Woman and her Female Furies were blown off their giant mastiffs by the incredible concussive force of his flight. Pavement rippled and snapped apart. Cracks forked across the broken asphalt. Concrete foundations were uprooted. Entire buildings were knocked over on either side of him. The sheer devastation was awe-inspiring.

I wouldn't want to be Darkseid right now, Kara thought. *My cousin is* pissed!

The force field shielding the underground bunker was no match for the Man of Steel. His heat vision exposed the blazing contours of the invisible dome. His ear-piercing cry cratered its surface, causing it to cave inward. A fragmented energy grid briefly flashed into view, then disintegrated before Supergirl's amazed gaze. The force field, which had previously resisted both her and John Stewart's attempts to breach it, surrendered before the irresistible force that was Superman. The Last Son of Krypton had returned to save his adopted planet, and there was hell to pay. Supergirl tried to catch up with him, but he was flying too fast.

The piled ruins atop the bunker were the next to go. A power dive carried Superman straight through Darkseid's hidden lair, turning it into ground zero. A cataclysmic explosion hurled Supergirl backward as the entire structure was obliterated in the space of a heartbeat. Columns of vaporized debris ascended into the sky, laying bare the guts of the subterranean compound . . . and a shocking discovery.

Great Rao! Supergirl clapped her hand over her mouth. *Is that* Batman?

Superman touched down on the floor of one of the exposed sublevels. The cleansing fire in his eyes dimmed slightly as he bent to lift a smoking corpse from the ground. The charred remains of an unmistakable black cape and cowl were fused to the skeletal remains. A bat emblem was seared into its chest, a golden Utility Belt had melted into slag. No heartbeat could be heard within the limp and lifeless form as Superman cradled the body in his arms. Sorrow showed upon his chiseled features as he realized that he had lost one of his closest friends and allies.

The Dark Knight was dead.

"Darkseid!"

Superman cradled Batman's smoldering remains in his arms. It was hard to believe that Bruce was really gone, but the evidence was impossible to deny; Darkseid, it seemed, had succeeded where the Joker, Two-Face, Rā's al Ghūl, Poison Ivy, and so many other others had failed. As Superman faced his friend's murderer, a profound anger grew within him.

"You turned your back," Darkseid gloated, "and I wrecked your world." He rose, with obvious pain and effort, from his throne. Muscles and leather creaked loudly as he straightened his legs. IV lines and cables fell away from him. Viscous black ichor oozed from his wounded chest. "I robbed your people of their powers, their hopes, their futures, themselves." The crimson sky poured through the broken ceiling. "What will you do when your friends, your lover, are all Darkseid? When there is only one body. One mind. One will. One life that is Darkseid." An evil laugh emanated from his wheezing lungs. Bloodred eyes glowed with sadistic mirth. "Will you be the enemy of all existence then? What irony will *that* be, son of Krypton!"

Superman had encountered Darkseid in the past, but the evil god seemed more repellent and vile than ever before. "Monster!" Superman placed Batman's body aside at super-speed, then surged forward and wrapped his fist around Darkseid's throat, yanking the New God off his feet. His bright red cape was lifted by the blinding speed of his attack. "What have you done?"

"Kill me, Superman," Darkseid taunted him. "Kill the frail old man upon whose soul Darkseid fed and fattened!"

What? Superman thought. He peered at the villain dangling in his grasp; upon closer examination, it was clear that Darkseid had indeed possessed and mutated the body of an ordinary human being. Superman scanned his captive's DNA—and was shocked by what he discovered. *"Turpin? Dan Turpin?"* The tough old cop had once been a mainstay of Metropolis's police department. Superman recognized a vestige of Turpin's bulldog face beneath the cracked and agonized visage of Darkseid. But why Dan Turpin of all people? Superman loosened his grip on Darkseid's throat, trying to understand. "You could have chosen Batman. . . ."

"He would have resisted longer than I wished," Darkseid explained. "Turpin struggled just enough to nurture me before he surrendered." He peeled Superman's fingers away from his neck. His boots dropped back onto the rubble-strewn floor of the throne room. His petrified arms clasped behind his back, he smugly defied Superman to destroy him. "Now what, Superman? How can you hurt a foe made of people?"

What are my options here? the Man of Steel debated. *Is there any trace of Dan Turpin left?*

Before he could resolve his dilemma, the situation got even worse. Hundreds of ordinary men, women, and children, enthralled by the Anti-Life Equation, invaded the ruined bunker. They fell upon Superman like sharks in a feeding frenzy, assailing him with sticks, rocks, knives, guns, and their bare hands. They clawed uselessly at his invulnerable face and skin. Swamped by the unreasoning horde, Superman was dragged away from Darkseid, who observed his predicament with bleak amusement.

"Kill them," Darkseid dared Superman. "Kill me and you kill *every-thing!*"

Hunched and limping, the dying god bent to retrieve the gun Batman had stolen from the bunker's armory. He gesticulated with his left hand, controlling the mob keeping Superman from him. He winced in pain as he dug the radion bullet from his chest. "The sun has set forever," he declared. "There is a black hole where my heart should be." An army of minions stationed themselves between Darkseid and Superman, turning themselves into human shields. Darkseid's voice emerged from dozens of lips as the eyes of every single slave began to glow purple. "Now, Superman. Are you prepared to join Batman in oblivion? Can even you outrun the Omega Sanction?"

Superman's keen ears alerted him to a whooshing sound racing toward Blüdhaven at stupendous speed. "Maybe I won't have to," he replied from behind the wall of innocent puppets. He recognized the sound of the fleet heels of the Fastest Men Alive. On the horizon, there was a slim glimmer of light below the boiling red and black sky. "You didn't get all of us, Darkseid. It's not over yet."

All at once, it was as if the sun had risen in the west, as if the dawn was made of lightning, and the approaching thunder became the roar of a gunshot yet to be. . . .

The Flashes came sprinting into Blüdhaven, running faster than they ever had before. Space and time warped behind them, distorting the macabre scenery, as they zoomed across the river. Their superhuman pace carried them across the surface of the water. The Speed Force, the arcane energy from which the Flashes derived their hypervelocity, flared and crackled all around them.

"Death's hot on our heels!" Wally called out to his uncle, who was a few crucial paces ahead of him. "He's gaining on us!"

Sure enough, the Black Racer came swooping down out of the sky after them. The armored figure was bent low across his ebony skis like a gold-medal skiing champion leaning into a jump. He scythed through the air, only a few yards behind the Flashes.

"Faster, Wally!" Barry Allen urged his protégé. "We can't let him catch us! Not yet!"

They rushed toward the ruins of Command-D.

Darkseid loaded the radion bullet into the gun. His own black blood smeared the translucent casing of the bullet. A modified version of *morticoccus* swarmed inside the glowing purple shell. Crafted to kill a god, it was none the worse for having been fired by Batman a short time ago.

"The time vortex opens as foretold." He peered at the warped space opening up across the battlefield. "From here, where he no longer exists, Orion cannot see me. As all time becomes one time, the hour has come to strike." He raised the gun and aimed it at the approaching radiance. "My son's doom begins now."

This is it, Barry realized. *Darkseid is using the time warp we're creating to kill Orion in the past.* A twinge of guilt tweaked his conscience, but he knew that he had to let Orion's murder play out just as they had witnessed before. *If he doesn't fire the bullet, then John Stewart won't find it, and Batman won't be able to use it against Darkseid. . . .*

Distance receded infinitely ahead of them. Orion's imminent death was distorting space itself. They'd have to break through the light barrier to get to him. "Relativity," Barry muttered under his breath, "I hate you sometimes."

They raced down shattered streets lined by brainwashed humans under Darkseid's control. The teeming zombies formed a gauntlet along the Flashes' path. The crowd's eyes glowed brightly as they simultaneously unleashed a volley of violet Omega Beams at the Scarlet Speedsters. Zigging and zagging above the blasted landscape, the death rays pursued the Flashes in concert with the relentless Black Racer.

"Good God!" Wally exclaimed. Putting on an extra burst of speed, he caught up with Barry. He glanced behind him long enough to see the lethal beams streaking behind them. "You see that?"

"Those Omega Beams will follow us until they connect!" Barry kept his eyes fixed on their destination. "At light speed, time stops. Flash fact." His leg muscles burned. A stitch in his side stabbed him like a red-hot poker, but he kept on running. For Iris, for his family, for the whole damn world. "We're approaching a never-ending instant. The ultimate stop sign." He sucked in the noxious air. He barely had enough breath to speak. "Have to reach superliminal velocity!"

He started to fall behind. A cold wind blew against the back of his neck. He could practically feel the Black Racer's armored fingers reaching out for him, only a few inches away. The Omega Beams nipped at his heels. "I can't keep up!" he gasped. "Save yourself, Wally!"

"No way, Barry!"

Wally reached out and pressed his hand against the other Flash's back. Barry accelerated as he felt a sudden burst of energy quicken his weary legs. The stitch in his side evaporated. It was like he had suddenly been granted a second wind. The deathly chill lightened.

How?

"I can transfer speed now!" Wally explained. "A little trick I learned while you were . . . away." He flashed a grin at his uncle as they continued on, side by side. "Think I'd leave you to do this on your own? Together, Barry!"

Barry smiled back, proud of the man Kid Flash had become. "We're going in together," he agreed, "and we're coming back together!"

"No matter what!"

Darkseid squeezed the trigger. The muzzle of his pistol flared and the deadly bullet zipped past Superman's head at the same time that the Flashes zoomed past him in the opposite direction. Expecting to see Jay and Wally, Superman was stunned by the sight of the familiar figure racing alongside Wally West. The second speedster was an old friend he had never expected to see again.

"Barry Allen?"

Darkseid enjoyed a split second of victory, savoring the retroactive demise of his rebellious son, before he spotted his downfall speeding toward him beyond the speed of light. The Flashes, the Black Racer, and a barrage of unleashed Omega Beams came rushing at the dying god. He stared aghast at the Black Racer.

"No!" he gasped. For perhaps the first time in untold eons, fear contorted his stony countenance. He threw up his hands to protect his face. "Not you!"

The Black Racer spoke. His visor took on a hellish red glow. A sepulchral voice echoed off the crumbling walls of the exposed bunker:

"The terminal moment is here. I come to all. Even *you!*"

Achieving light speed, the Flashes *vibrated through* Darkseid like the world's fastest phantoms. They outran death, but Darkseid was not so fortunate.

The Black Racer reached out to touch the horrified god, at the very instant that Darkseid's own Omega Beams struck their maker. He let out a bloodcurdling cry as a phosphorescent glow lit up his hulking body, briefly exposing his very skeleton. Moaning feebly, he collapsed onto his hands and knees. Oily black vomit spilled from his jaws, and his wounded chest bled anew.

His mission complete, the Black Racer skied away into the void, swiftly vanishing from sight. The Flashes themselves were long gone. There was no way death could catch up with them now.

They did it, Superman realized. *They finished what Batman started.*

The mob of people holding him back collapsed as well. They dropped limply onto the rubble. For an instant, Superman feared for their safety; what if their link to Darkseid had doomed them as well? His super-hearing and vision, however, quickly confirmed that they were simply stunned into unconsciousness. With luck, they would remember little of what transpired while Darkseid was manipulating their bodies.

". . . in us," the defeated god moaned, or was Dan Turpin in there as well, breathing his last? Black blood flowed like tears from Darkseid's eyes. He crawled across the rubble like dying roadkill. ". . . in all of us . . ."

Superman strode over to the fallen villain. He gazed down soberly at Darkseid. He feared it was too late to save whatever remained of Turpin's life, but he hoped that the possessed detective would soon find peace. *He was a good man*, Superman thought. *He deserved better than this.*

Unlike Darkseid.

"John Stewart found the bullet that you fired backward in time," Superman said, putting it all together. "Batman used it to mortally wound you." He shook his head sadly. "This was suicide, Darkseid."

But would the moribund god take the rest of the Multiverse down with him? Glancing up, Superman saw that the sun was still black, the sky still red and turbid. The new dawn briefly heralded by the Flashes had faded with their meteoric departure. By now, he guessed the Flashes were halfway around the world if they hadn't sped onto a higher plane of existence altogether. Superman scanned the sky with his telescopic vision. Beyond the roiling crimson atmosphere, a swirling vortex tugged voraciously on the imperiled planet. All of creation was being swallowed up by an inescapable event horizon.

This isn't over yet, Superman realized. *Not by a long shot.*

Galloping paws stirred up the poisoned dust outside Command-D. The floor of the throne room vibrated from the tread of gargantuan boots. Superman turned away from Darkseid to discover that they were not alone.

The Female Furies, astride their rabid canines, posed atop the heaped rubble overlooking the open bunker. Wonder Woman, instantly recognizable despite the boar-mask hiding her face, raised a bloody spear high. Giganta's colossal shadow fell over Superman. Batwoman and Catwoman flanked their Amazonian leader. Superman was shocked to see Diana leading the enemy forces.

"Darkseid is order," Wonder Woman declared. "Darkseid is peace." Her words made a mockery of everything that the transformed heroine had ever fought for. "On your knees. *Submit.*"

Not likely, Superman thought. *Not to Darkseid, and not to you.*

She pointed the tip of her spear at the sky above them. The heavens filled with the sight of dozens of brainwashed super-villains, all wearing identical chrome helmets. It looked like the entire Secret Society was descending on Blüdhaven.

"Behold! The army of Libra has arrived."

CHAPTER 32

Checkmate went down fighting. Prefabricated biomac warriors battled Super-Justifiers in the drafty corridors of the Castle, but were unable to hold back the tide of invaders storming the fortress. Enemy flamethrowers swept the halls, setting fire to priceless medieval tapestries. The combined forces of S.H.A.D.E., Checkmate, and what remained of the Justice Society fell back toward the main labs, which now offered their only hope of escape. Super heroes guarded the rear of the exodus, steadily losing ground against the endless Justifiers overrunning the Castle. Frightened technicians, communications specialists, and intelligence analysts were herded toward a newly assembled steel archway that seemed to lead to nowhere. Swirling nothingness filled the yawning mouth of the portal. Blinking lights flashed along its curved metal sides. Exposed wiring and circuitry gave it an unfinished look. Frantic engineers hastily applied last-minutes fixes and solders. Huge silver clamps, cast of solid promethium, anchored the archway to reality.

Humanity's own homemade Boom Tube was almost set to go.

But would it be ready in time? The sounds and shocks of furious combat rocked the Castle, drawing ever closer to the besieged laboratories. Renee Montoya, flanked by a squadron of faceless Global Peace Agents, watched anxiously as Checkmate's scientific whiz kids raced to complete their efforts.

Could they, and the Atoms, get the interdimensional escape route up and running before Darkseid's army burst in, guns blazing?

Hurry it up, guys, she thought. *Apokolips is banging at the door.*

"Professor Palmer!"

Ryan Choi, the junior Atom, floated weightlessly in the quantum foam as the microscopic heroes bounced between fraying atoms and molecules. Dislodged electrons and subatomic particles flew like shrapnel; Ryan ducked his head to avoid being tagged by a wild quark. Ionic tremors buffeted him. He let go of a beeping piece of hardware that resembled a modern communications satellite, only thousands of times smaller. "The nano-beacon's in place," he shouted over the primordial chaos. "But the tunnel between the universes can't take these stresses." Fluctuations in the strong nuclear force started pulling him down into the seething core of a splitting atom. He paddled helplessly against the pull of the blazing nucleus. He could feel its radioactive heat against his back. "*I* can't take these stresses!"

"We did our part!" Ray Palmer assured him. He grabbed onto his protégé's hand and dragged him to safety. They clung together like paired electrons. "Now it's up to Lord Eye to handle the computations!"

Ryan hoped the floating brain was up to the challenge.

"The Black Gambit is failing!" a disembodied voice announced over the loudspeaker. An unmistakable note of panic could be heard in Lord Eye's electronically amplified warnings. "Inter-brane escape tunnel integrity is diminishing!"

Renee realized they couldn't wait any longer. "The tunnel's collapsing!" she shouted. "Everybody out!"

Darkseid's forces were at the gate, held back only by a handful of outnumbered super heroes, including a sumo wrestler, a celebrity escape artist, and a bunch of costumed Japanese teenagers. The untried Boom Tube was the only way out. Panicked people stampeded into the lab, fleeing the fighting in the hallways outside, yet the endangered personnel hesitated before rushing into the churning vortex inside the portal, which led to God knew where. The survivors were trapped between the devil and the uncharted sea that was the Multiverse. Who knew what kind of Earth, if any, waited on the other side of the portal? For all they knew, the portal led only to oblivion.

Talk about a leap of faith, Renee thought. Looking at the frightened faces of the teeming evacuees, who were in danger of trampling each other to death, she saw that somebody was going to have to go first before anyone else entered the archway. So who was going to take the plunge? *That's the Question, isn't it?*

"What the hell," she muttered. She ran fearlessly toward the glowing emptiness. "Last one in is Darkseid's lap poodle!"

For the first time in years, she wished she hadn't quit smoking.

The Super Young Team, their hour come at last, defended Checkmate's retreat. Their backs to the gaping portal, they held the line against a seemingly inexhaustible army of Justifiers.

"Let me show you what money unleashed can do!" Most Excellent Superbat declared, now encased in the most sophisticated armored exoskeleton his fortune could buy. Lacquered ceramic plating mimicked the borrowed colors and design of his postmodern super-hero costume, so that he resembled a robotic cross between the Dark Knight and the Man of Steel. He assumed an elegant fighting stance. A blast of artificial heat vision fired from the opaque white lenses of his spiked helmet. He plucked a bat-winged throwing star from the Utility Belt slung across his chest. The explosive *shuriken* detonated in the doorway ahead, hurling a pack of Justifiers back into the hallway outside.

Not bad, Sonny Sumo thought. Maybe these cocky club kids could hold their own in a brawl after all. His own plain black T-shirt hung in tatters upon his robust frame as he fought to keep the enemy away from Mister Miracle and, perhaps more important, Motherboxxx. Affixed to Shilo's shoulder, the living computer was pinging madly. Sonny sensed that Motherboxxx was somehow key to humanity's survival. *Maybe that's my role in all this. To keep her safe . . .*

Hefting a captured Justifier above his head, he flung the storm trooper at the other Justifiers, bowling them over for at least another minute or two. An enemy sniper was knocked off his feet. His shot went wild, missing Mister Miracle by inches. Motherboxxx pinged in relief.

Shy Crazy Lolita Canary Girl was not so lucky. The blast nailed the diminutive pixie, who let out a super high-pitched cry before spiraling toward the floor, where she was sure to be stomped to death beneath the boots of the invaders.

"Lolita Canary!" Well-Spoken Sonic Lightning Flash exclaimed. Spying his teammate's jeopardy, he sprinted across the lab almost as swiftly as his American namesake. His outstretched palm caught her seconds before she hit the floor. "Got her!"

Holding on to her was going to be tricky, though, as a slew of fanatical Justifiers came charging at him. How could he protect the unconscious Canary and defend himself at the same time? He looked around desperately for someplace safe to put the tiny winged girl.

"Over here!" Shiny Happy Aquazon called out to him. She tossed her empty harpoon launcher aside and cupped her hands in front of her. Despite her name, she looked anything but happy over the danger they were in. "Give her to me!"

A faceless Justifier, whose sparkling black leotard ID'd her as Donna Troy, lunged at Sonic Lightning Flash. With no other choice before him, he lobbed Lolita Canary over the heads of the frenzied combatants toward Aquazon's waiting hands. His electrified sneakers twinkled brightly as he ducked out of the way of the brainwashed Amazon's silver bracelets. Anxious eyes tracked Canary's trajectory as she arced above the fray.

"I have her! I have her!" The winged casualty landed safely in Aquazon's open palms. The green-skinned mergirl jumped for joy. She gazed adoringly at the teenage speedster. "I love you, Sonic Lightning Flash!"

Big Atomic Lantern Boy looked liked he had just been sideswiped by a radioactive dinosaur. "But I love *you*," he whispered, his lovesick anguish all but lost in the furious melee. The emerald beam emanating from his chest porthole wavered slightly.

Poor kid, Sonny thought, noting the exchange out of the corner of his eye. He swung a metal chair into Donna Troy's helmet, denting it on one side. *Too bad he has to get his heart broken on top of everything else.*

The adolescent romantic triangle was the least of their worries right now.

Churning plasma flared brightly inside the glowing archway as thunderous booms rocked the Castle. Circuits shorted out along the metal archway. Flames and smoke filled the lab, followed by an intense white light.

Mister Terrific's levitating T-Spheres could not cope with the unnatural data flooding their sensors. Static crackled loudly. Bright blue sparks arced between the spheres. They crashed to the floor. "What the hell?" he exclaimed. "What's happening?"

"Time! Space!" Atomic Lantern Boy shouted. His blazing heart flashed in sequence with the storm inside the gateway; he seemed attuned somehow to the interdimensional energies cascading within the escape tunnel. "Everything is splitting up! Shredding!"

That doesn't sound good, Sonny thought.

Motherboxxx pinged frantically.

Lord Eye was losing it.

"What year is this?" the bodiless brain asked. "Is this a test?" Its frontal lobes throbbed inside its nutrient bath. "Initiating emergency shutdown . . ."

"Eye's having a breakdown and closing the tunnel!" Hawkman shouted at Hawkgirl, even as he fought his way toward the huge golden globe containing the brain. His spiked mace sent Justifiers flying from his path. He glanced over at the evacuees pouring into the Boom Tube. "Those people will die if I don't stop him!"

His gray feathered wings carried him over the fighting into Lord Eye's circular chamber. Stationary OMACs sprang to the brain's defense. Ruby laser beams shot from the cyborgs' cyclopean visages. Hawkman's wings burst into flame.

"Damn you, Carter!" Kendra swooped to his defense. She blocked the OMACs' attack with her own wingspan. The smell of burning feathers filled her nostrils. She felt her flesh burn and blister. "You can't do this alone!"

Heedless of the blaze engulfing his body, Hawkman drove his bare fist through the transparent porthole in the large steel globe. Amber fluid gushed out, dousing the flames. He ripped Lord Eye out of its sanctuary and crushed the pulsing gray matter in his fist. The emergency shutdown terminated abruptly. The OMACs froze in place. Their searing eye-beams blinked out of existence. Hawkman threw the pulped brain at his feet. He squashed it beneath his boot, just to be safe. Cerebral juices spurted across the floor.

Gross, Hawkgirl thought, *but effective.*

She shrugged off her torched wings and stumbled toward him. Agonizing second-degree burns scarred her skin, but she had no regrets. They had survived once more.

Their next lives would have to wait.

"C'mon, you crazy hawk," she whispered hoarsely. Leaning against each other for support, they staggered from the flooded chamber, past the eerily immobile OMACs. The glow of the Boom Tube lit up their scorched helmets. "We've got a whole new world waiting for us . . . again."

Then they joined the exodus.

CHAPTER 33

BLÜDHAVEN.

"Submit!" Wonder Woman demanded. Slobber dripped from the jaws of her drooling hellhound. The dog's red eyes were the same incarnadine hue as her own. The Female Furies loomed behind her. The stormy sky was filled with brainwashed villains. Superman spotted Luthor leading the enemy reinforcements, clad in an all-too-familiar blue and green war suit. The Man of Steel shook his head. *I should have known Lex would side with Darkseid.*

He braced himself for the fight of his life.

But before Wonder Woman could lead Darkseid's army into battle, an unusual combatant entered the fray. Frankenstein came riding across the battlefield atop an enormous wolfhound. The immortal monster galloped through the ranks of the startled Furies, swinging an immense broadsword and firing his antique steam-pistol. The wolfhound bounded into Wonder Woman, knocking her from her saddle, even as Frankenstein's sword slashed down to decapitate the giant mastiff. The dog's head tumbled across the ruins as its upset mistress crashed to Earth. The other hellhounds reared up in panic, all but throwing Catwoman and Batwoman from their seats. The Furies tugged on the reins, fighting to bring their canine mounts under control. The unruly dogs slammed into Giganta's oversized ankles. The giantess stumbled awkwardly, trying to avoid tripping over her sister

Furies. Her simian mask made her look like a distaff version of Titano the Super-Ape.

Superman was surprised by Frankenstein's unexpected intervention. His aerial reconnaissance earlier had revealed that every hero still free had been laid low by the *morticoccus* plague. He scanned Frankenstein with his X-ray vision, but found no trace of the lethal bacteria in the famous monster's patchwork anatomy. *Of course,* he realized, *the germ would have no effect on a living dead man!*

He welcomed Frankenstein's aid, but feared they were still severely outnumbered. Already Wonder Woman was scrambling to her feet, while Luthor descended from the sky at the head of a veritable legion of arch-villains. Doctor Sivana was at Lex's right, riding a multilegged robot that resembled a cross between an octopus and a giant tarantula. Justifier helmets hid the faces of the other villains, but Superman spotted Deathstroke, Mirror Master, the Human Flame, and Lady Shiva in the forefront of the onslaught. Dozens of extra villains massed behind Lex.

"You see, Superman," Darkseid wheezed. The dying god rose to his feet like a fighter in the ring, barely able to hold himself up, but refusing to go down for the count. The gaping black hole in his chest sucked in the light around him. "Libra has spread my gospel to all your enemies."

"Libra?" Sivana chortled. He wiped a speck of dust off his glasses. "Heh."

Luthor stepped forward. "Libra *was* the Anti-Life Equation. Now he's not." He smirked at the Man of the Steel. "Need a little help, Superman? I just happen to be in charge of an army of mind-controlled super-criminals."

To Superman's surprise, the villains charged *against* the Female Furies. Lady Shiva, possibly the world's greatest martial artist, leapt atop Catwoman's pony dog and flipped the latex-clad cat burglar out of her saddle. Catwoman lashed out with her razor-tipped whip, but the Human Flame incinerated it with a blast from his flamethrower. Deathstroke lunged at Catwoman, stunning her with an open-palmed strike before she even hit the ground. Selina Kyle's feline agility was no match for Slade Wilson's superhuman reflexes. The master assassin had Catwoman out cold in a matter of seconds. Lady Shiva rendered the riderless mastiff unconscious with a few deft blows to its pressure points. The beast slumped to the ground beside its insensate mistress.

Batwoman didn't fare any better. She fired at Luthor's forces with twin laser-pistols, but Mirror Master reflected the beams back at the enthralled heroine. Batwoman let out a bloodcurdling shriek before toppling off her hellhound. Webs sprayed from the stainless steel mandibles of Sivana's robotic spider, snaring the writhing Fury. Lady Shiva kicked her in the jaw. Artificial fangs flew from Batwoman's mouth. Superman watched carefully to make sure that none of Luthor's minions went too far.

Guess I underestimated Lex, he realized. *And so did Darkseid.*

"Not a single word, Superman," Luthor said smugly. Secure in his armored war suit, he took his place beside his arch-foe. "We'll just call this an historic alliance between the forces of 'good' and 'evil.' And I'll take the credit for the win."

"Whatever you say, Lex." Superman wasn't about to turn down any assistance at a time like this. "But I'll be keeping one eye on you until this is over."

Over sixty feet tall, Giganta towered over Luthor's army. One stomp of her mammoth boot sent a throng of villains flying. She snatched Frankenstein from the ground and shook him above her head in what looked like some bizarre outtake from *Frankenstein Meets the Bride of Kong.* The monster struggled to extricate himself from her giant grip as Giganta beat her chest with her other fist. A growl escaped from behind her bestial mask.

"You know, that's really not a good look for you." Supergirl zoomed down from the sky. Her fist collided with Giganta's prognathous snout. The ape-mask shattered into a million pieces. Broken fragments rained down on the heads of Luthor's soldiers. "No charge for the makeover!"

The colossal woman teetered precariously. Alert villains ran for cover as she crashed to the ground like a fallen redwood. The battlefield quaked. A huge cloud of dust blanketed the wasteland. Supergirl caught Frankenstein in the air and safely lowered him to the ground. "Anyone ever tell you that you look a lot like Bizarro?" she asked him. "No offense."

"None taken," the monster croaked.

Superman was proud of his cousin. One by the one, the Furies were falling.

Only Wonder Woman still posed a threat. A mob of super-villains piled onto her, but she effortlessly shook them off. Silver bracelets deflected heat-rays and bullets. Her boar-mask had a chipped tusk. She reclaimed her spear from where it had fallen amidst the dust and ash. She took to the air, above the heads of Luthor's army, and aimed at Superman. It dawned on him that they had never really determined which of them was faster.

"Kill him!" Darkseid commanded. "Slay the Last Son of Krypton!"

THE WATCHTOWER.
FALLING FAST.

The space station plunged toward Earth. Its outer panels glowed red-hot as it began to burn up in reentry. Communications antennae and sensor arrays melted into slag.

Black Canary floated weightlessly inside the endangered outpost. Unconscious Justifiers and dented steel helmets drifted past her, while Oracle and the others clung to safety railings. The Flash kids held on to their mother and each other; Jai's supercharged musculature had melted back to normal eight-year-old proportions. The Tattooed Man lashed himself to a pylon with an inky length of barbed wire. Illustrated imps and reptiles squirmed in discomfort atop his sweaty skin. The colors ran together in the heat. Joan Garrick looked like she was on the verge of passing out; Oracle grabbed onto her to keep the older woman from drifting away. Emergency klaxons blared. The temperature was unbearably warm. The air was growing thinner by the moment.

"OXYGEN AT TEN PERCENT," an automated voice reported. "LIFE SUPPORT CRITICAL . . ."

"Ollie," Dinah whispered, gasping for breath. Perspiration soaked through her torn black leathers and fishnet stockings. Her lungs burned; she doubted she could muster a Canary Cry even if she wanted to. She reached out for Green Arrow, who was floating, dazed and incoherent, only a few feet away, but, maddeningly, her outstretched fingers fell short by only an inch or two. She choked back an anguished sob. "I think we did it."

The clear expanse of the observation window was spread out beneath her, so that she could see the rim of the Earth rushing toward them at alarming speed. A bright golden glow streaked across the cyclonic red storms cloaking the planet. She watched in excitement as the beam traced a distinctive pattern atop the entire world. It was the same design gleaming upon the Tattooed Man's face.

"Look, Ollie!" she urged him. "Ray made it. He did it." Despite their impending doom, she felt a fierce surge of triumph. In theory, the magical pattern would counteract the Anti-Life Equation all over the planet. "We rule. . . ."

"You bet, pretty bird." Green Arrow smiled back at her. His own fingers found hers at last. He squeezed her hand as they pulled themselves into a passionate zero-gee embrace. No trace of Darkseid remained in his loving green eyes. "I always knew you'd come through for me in the end. You were my secret weapon."

Tears leaked from Dinah's eyes as she got her husband back at last. Her voice was husky with emotion. "Don't you ever forget that, Oliver Queen!"

Locked in each other's arms, they watched the Ray free the Earth.

BLÜDHAVEN.

Wonder Woman drew back her spear. At the back of her mind, a horrified voice cried out in protest, but the insidious teachings of Apokolips drowned out her conscience. Darkseid was peace. Slavery was freedom. All was one in Darkseid.

Superman must die.

But before she could release the deadly javelin, a sudden golden radiance penetrated the seething red clouds above her. She looked up in surprise— and found her gaze captivated by a glowing sigil that seemed to be traced across the sky by the very finger of Apollo. The heavenly sign was new to her, yet seemed strangely familiar as well, as though it touched some ancestral memory dating back to the dawn of time.

By the gods . . .

A lock came undone within her mind, and the chains fell from her soul. She tore the beast-mask from her face, revealing the timeless beauty of a true Amazon princess. Angry blue eyes gazed in disgust at the hideous disguise that had denied her humanity. Darkseid had turned her into an animal, just as Hercules had once enslaved her mother and Amazon sisters in the dark days before the founding of Paradise Island. Wonder Woman's silver bracelets were eternal reminders of that past subjugation, which her people had cast off so long ago. Her stomach turned at the realization that history had repeated itself.

No more, she vowed. She shattered the mask in her hands. *Never again.*

Flinging the bloodstained lance away from her, she glided toward Darkseid upon the wings of the wind. Superman and Luthor spied the determined look on her face and wisely got out of her way. She unfurled the Lasso of Truth from her hip and hurled it over the evil god. Sorely tempted to choke the life from Darkseid with the golden noose, she found the strength to simply draw its enchanted links tightly about him instead, binding his arms to his sides. He fought to break free of its unbreakable grip.

"Now you too know the bitter sting of bondage," she decreed. The righteous wrath of the oppressed informed her royal judgment. "Face the Truth, Darkseid. You are already dead!"

"Nooo!"

The golden lasso drove Darkseid's malignant spirit from the mortal form it had unjustly usurped. Like an oily black shadow, a demonic face oozed away from the contorted features of its tortured host. The god's impotent fury echoed off the walls of the demolished bunker as the shadow disappeared into the murky underworld beneath the ruins. The foul darkness of his presence was lost in the tenebrous gloom of a modern-day Tartarus.

Wonder Woman stood proudly once more.

Good to have you back, Diana, Superman thought.

Her magic lasso had done what he could not: free Dan Turpin from Darkseid's possession. Still enmeshed in the lasso's coils, the wounded detective collapsed onto the floor. Superman used his heat vision to cauterize Turpin's wounded chest, then scanned the man from head to toe. Turpin was still breathing, but comatose. His skin was gray and pitted. Superman guessed that the violated ex-cop would be a long time recovering from his ordeal, if he ever did. Turpin was tough, though. That had to count for something.

At least he's still alive, thanks to Diana.

Then Superman heard something falling high above the Earth. Peering up through the clouds, he was dismayed to see the JLA Watchtower plummeting from orbit. From the look of things, it was only moments away from burning up in reentry.

"Kara!" he called out urgently to Supergirl. "Heads up!"

The two Kryptonians sprang into the air, rapidly leaving Blüdhaven behind. They zoomed upward through the storm to meet the plunging space station. Working together, they caught the Watchtower with their bare hands, halting its deadly descent. They held on tightly to the red-hot steel. Molten metal squished between Superman's fingers.

That was a close one, he thought. His X-ray vision quickly confirmed that the satellite's inhabitants were still alive. Prying open an intake valve, he replenished the station's oxygen supply with a gust of his super-breath. Black Canary, Green Arrow, and the others begin to stir inside. Kara cooled the station's exterior with her own super-breath.

Kryptonian muscles held the Watchtower aloft. Supergirl glanced over at her cousin. "Now what?"

Good question, Superman admitted. They couldn't return the satellite to its usual position; beyond Earth's orbit was a violent maelstrom that was degrading the very fabric of time and space. Alternate Earths could be glimpsed through the cascading red-black torrent, impinging on reality as they spiraled into the same voracious darkness that awaited Earth. Darkseid's black soul was still pulling all of creation into his own endless demise. *This is the Final Crisis Brainy warned me about,* Superman realized. *It's not over yet.*

"Head for the Fortress," he instructed. The Watchtower would be safer in the Arctic than in space, at least for the time being. "We'll make our last stand there."

CHAPTER 34

ELSEWHERE.

The escape tunnel led only to desolation.

Renee gazed bleakly at the postapocalyptic wasteland surrounding her and the other refugees. The lifeless landscape made Blüdhaven look like a party town. Thick gray ash coated weathered rubble badly eroded by time and the elements. Nothing grew in the dry, brittle soil. No birds filled the sickly yellow sky. A dead sea lapped at a barren shore; the corrosive brine blistered the skin of anyone foolish enough to touch it. Checkmate's scientists had already pronounced the water too acidic to support life, never mind being drinkable. Whatever life had once flourished on this parallel Earth was long gone.

What the hell happened here? Renee wondered. She felt like Charlton Heston in *Planet of the Apes*, minus the talking monkeys. *And where do we go from here?*

"At least we're somewhere," Mister Miracle commented. "That's something."

He had a point. There had always been the possibility that the untested portal would be a one-way trip to nowhere. Renee had half expected to find her atoms scattered between universes, or to end up floating in the vacuum of space somewhere between Earth and Thanagar. *Could be worse,* she admitted. *But not by much.*

In the end, roughly seventy people had escaped the Castle via the Boom Tube. Most of them were now milling about aimlessly, with shell-shocked expressions on their faces, although Mister Terrific had already organized a search party to survey the area. Medics tended to the wounded, like Hawkman and Hawkgirl, whose nasty burns were painful souvenirs of the fighting back at the fortress. Renee felt a twinge of envy as she watched the couple comfort each other. She couldn't help wondering what had become of Kate back on Earth. Rumor had it Batwoman had already succumbed to the Anti-Life Equation.

Renee prayed that wasn't so. *We never even had a chance to say good-bye.*

First aid supplies were already running low. Armed sentries guarded a meager stockpile of emergency rations. Hungry survivors huddled around campfires. Renee's own stomach rumbled. Her mouth was as dry as the Kahndaqi Desert back home. *Now I know what the Donner Party felt like,* she thought grimly. *How long before things get* really *ugly?*

A cold wind chilled her to the bone. She zipped up the front of her scuffed leather jacket, then fished a balled-up wad of Pseudoderm from her pocket. Gloved fingers found the hidden switch on her belt buckle. Binary gases billowed from the buckle. The swirling fumes smelled like baby powder and cardamom. She smoothed the artificial flesh over her face, letting the chemical mist bond the Pseudoderm to her skin. Renee Montoya's face disappeared beneath the featureless mask of the Question.

What the heck, she thought. *It's not like I'm going to be eating anytime soon.*

With luck, the mask would keep her face warm.

"Holy cow!" Shiny Happy Aquazon exclaimed, pointing at the faceless detective. She elbowed the speedy boy with the snazzy sneakers. "Look, Keigo! It's the Question!"

Sonic Lightning Flash gaped at Renee. "The new one?"

Guess I've got a fan club, the Question thought. *Too bad the green-skinned cutie is a little too young for me.*

She gazed out over the lifeless harbor. A toppled monument, the size of the Statue of Liberty, lay on its side across a small rocky island. Rust and acid rain had eaten away at its features, but there was no mistaking the corroded green S on its chest. The fallen statue was a gigantic memorial to Superman. Or rather *a* Superman.

Guess he didn't save this world, the Question thought. *Just our luck.*

Electronic pings intruded on her reverie. The annoying racket came from some sort of PDA gadget affixed to Mister Miracle's shoulder. Renee remembered watching his HBO special years ago, before the world went belly-up. He had supposedly escaped from a black hole, live and on the air. She'd always figured there was some sort of trick involved.

Not that it really mattered now.

"What's with the wacky ringtone?" she asked wryly. "You expecting a page or something?"

The world-famous escapist detached the gizmo from its pouch. The Japanese heroes gathered around him in excitement. "Motherboxxx says something is coming!" He pointed at the sky. "Up there!"

Is he serious? This new Earth was a ghost town. *Face it, we're on our own.*

Her skepticism was dispelled, however, by the astounding vessel that broke through the smog overhead and came gliding in toward a landing. The streamlined airship was the size and shape of a submarine and soared through the sky despite having no visible means of propulsion. Its dazzling golden hull was amazingly bright. Strips of polished ruby trimmed its molded nacelles and rampant turret. The brilliant reds and yellows were almost too vivid to be real; there was something almost psychedelic about it. The ship shimmered in the air as though descending from a higher plane of reality. Its graceful contours were those of an advanced and elegant civilization. Prismatic rainbows rippled in its wake. Chords of ineffably poignant music serenaded its passage.

Renee wasn't sure she had ever seen anything so beautiful.

All eyes turned upward to track the ship's progress. Mouths dropped open in awe, yet no one panicked or showed signs of fear, not even when the vessel passed directly over them, casting no shadow on the rapt survivors. The more religious among them crossed themselves. Others gazed at the heavenly ship with hopeful expressions. Surely nothing so sublime could possibly be of Darkseid.

Who? the Question wondered.

The ship touched down softly on an arid plain several yards away from the refugees' camp. Curiosity overcoming caution, Renee ran to greet the ship. Mister Miracle, Sonny Sumo, and the Super Young Team were right behind her, followed by the braver of the survivors. Motherboxxx pinged enthusiastically.

"What is it?" Sonny asked Shilo Norman. "Is it the New Gods?"

Mister Miracle shook his head. "No. This comes from a realm above even them!"

Above the gods? The Question wondered if she'd heard him right. *Who or what is above the gods?*

Apparently, they were about to find out. A bell-like chime of crystalline purity rang out from somewhere inside the vessel. A seamless gold bulkhead parted in the middle to form a narrow egress. A flexible ruby ramp unfurled on to the inhospitable terrain. A slim female figure appeared in the doorway. She stepped into the harsh sunlight.

Braided black cornrows streaked the woman's smooth pink cranium. Numinous green eyes gazed out at the gathered refugees. Tall and slender, she wore an elegant amethyst gown topped by ornate gold shoulder pads. A scarlet cloak was clasped around her swanlike throat by a silver collar. A jeweled belt girded her waist. Priceless gems sparkled upon her golden boots and wristbands. Delicate filigree adorned her ornaments. The scintillating fabrics rustled silkenly as she descended the ramp.

The woman's unearthly glamour took Renee's breath away. Like her wondrous vessel, there was something almost hyperreal about the alien beauty. Renee had once met Wonder Woman in the flesh, yet she felt positively starstruck in this woman's presence. She blushed behind her blank mask.

"Wh-who are you?" the Question asked, uncharacteristically tongue-tied.

"I am Weeja Dell, Monitrix Earth Designate-Six." Her musical voice was tinged with sorrow. "Lover of Nix Uotan, exiled long ago to the germworlds within the Orrery. My people are the Monitors of Nil. Masters of the Overvoid."

Uh-huh, Renee thought, understanding maybe a third of that. She had heard of the Monitors, though. They were supposed to be a race of godlike immortals who presided over the Multiverse. Crazy conspiracy theories blamed them for various cosmic Crises.

"Earth-Six," she repeated, trying to make sense of Weeja Dell's pronouncements. She gestured at the charred wasteland surrounding them. "Is that where this is?"

The self-described Monitrix shook her head. "No. This is Earth-51, blackened heart of the graveyard universe. My lover was unjustly blamed for its devastation, but he was merely the scapegoat in a dark design. I suspect the foul hand of Mandrakk, the Eater of Life, behind my dearest Nix Uotan's cruel banishment." A solitary tear glistened like a diamond upon her flawless cheek. "I was searching this cosmos for proof of his innocence when I heard your distress signal."

The Question struggled to keep up. "Signal?"

"Motherboxxx!" Sonny Sumo realized. The device pinged in response. "I knew she was important!"

"Indeed." Weeja Dell nodded at the device. "She called out to me across this blighted universe." She walked among the refugees like an angel in their midst; Renee felt a pang of jealousy every time the lovely Monitrix spoke of her long-lost lover. "This haunted Earth is no fit habitation for your people. If you wish, I can transport you in my god-ship, the *Ultima Thule*, yet I fear that soon there may be no safe harbor for you anywhere in the Multiverse. Mandrakk stirs within the eternal sepulcher to which he was cast down in eons past. The Dark Monitor rises, crawling up from Blackness to feed upon the Light. . . ."

Great, Renee thought sarcastically. *Things just keep getting better and better.* "Can't your people do something about this? Isn't that supposed to be their job?"

"Alas," Weeja Dell replied, "my fellow Monitors are lost in denial, or else have already fled into hiding. They cannot face the awful truth that Mandrakk's prophesized moment has come round at last." A shudder shook her regal frame. "The Circle of Monitors has failed its sacred trust. Fifty-two universes lie undefended."

The Question let out an exhausted sigh. "And we thought Darkseid was bad," she muttered. An eyeless face scanned the bleak horizon before them, searching for some glimmer of hope in a darkening reality. Her inquisitive gaze fell upon the decaying statue in the harbor, a forgotten tribute to this Earth's version of Superman. Her blank brow furrowed in thought. A crazy idea occurred to her. She looked urgently at Weeja Dell.

"Did you say there were *fifty-two* Earths?"

CHAPTER 35

THE NORTH POLE.
LATER.

Watchtower Omega was humanity's ultimate refuge. Cobbled together from Superman's Fortress of Solitude, the Hall of Justice, Titans Tower, and the JLA's dislodged space station, it floated in a timeless void, defying the voracious darkness that already engulfed the rest of the planet. The bloodred glow of the final sunset streaked its patchwork towers and ramparts. An endless night, filled with ravenous red eyes and gnashing fangs, filled the sky. When space-time had folded down, the solitary structure was all Earth's heroes had managed to salvage. Beyond the Watchtower's hastily fortified walls, there was nothing left that wasn't Darkseid.

Months had passed since that final battle in Blüdhaven, yet despite Batman's tragic sacrifice, doomsday had only been postponed. Earth continued to spiral into the empty heart of Darkseid. Heroes stood guard upon the ramparts twenty-four hours a day, watching out for crumbling shards of parallel universes. Days past, if the word *day* meant anything in this unending twilight, one such fragment had collided with the Watchtower, carrying with it the Metal Men of Earth-44 and their human leader, "Doc" Tornado. Cybernetic replicas of the Justice League, the robots had been driven berserk by

Earth's distorted magnetic field and attempted to commit technocide inside the Watchtower. The Trophy Room had been wrecked, irreplaceable mementoes lost forever, before Supergirl, Frankenstein, Starman, Blue Devil, and the other sentries managed to deactivate the crazed androids.

Just another day at the end of time, Lois Lane thought wryly. She watched as the final edition of the *Daily Planet* rolled off the presses. The Metal Men's destructive rampage hadn't even made the front page, having been relegated to a sidebar on page A-17. A giant Lincoln penny, rescued from the Batcave, loomed over the printing presses.

The fresh ink came off on her fingers as she inspected the newspaper. "EARTH ENDURES" read the banner headline, above her byline. Jimmy Olsen had provided the front-page photo of the Watchtower. Batman's obituary began below the fold. Clark had insisted on writing it himself, despite everything else he had on his plate. Out of respect for his friend, he had declined to reveal Bruce's true identity in the piece. Lois admired Clark's ability to resist scoring one final scoop, so that the legend of Batman could retain its mystery. *That's my husband for you.*

She walked across a spacious hangar to where a missile-sized rocket rested at an angle upon a tilted launching pad. The rocket, of basic Kryptonian design, resembled the outer-space craft that had transported Superman to Earth so many years ago. Its colors were those of Superman himself. A polished blue hull tapered at the nose. Bright red fins sprouted from its tail. Jimmy, Supergirl, Freddy Freeman, Mary Batson, and others were gathered around the ship, placing precious souvenirs of Earth into an open hatch. Lois reverently laid the newly printed paper inside the hatch, alongside Batman's Utility Belt, Jimmy's signal-watch, a Martian Manhunter action figure, a scroll from Paradise Island, a fragment of the Rock of Eternity, a copy of *Action Comics*, singed hawk feathers, and other artifacts. Her throat tightened.

"That's it," she said, maintaining a brave front. She shut the lid on the time capsule. "Put it to bed."

Supergirl cradled Streaky in her arms. The cat purred happily. Kara sealed the hatch shut with her heat vision. "Everybody step back." She offered a remote control device to Lois. "Would you care to do the honors?"

Lois shook her head. "You do it, Jimmy."

"Okay, Ms. Lane." The carrottopped photographer stepped forward to accept the remote. His bow tie bounced atop his Adam's apple as he swallowed hard. "Here goes."

He pressed the button. The tail of the rocket flared brightly as it hurled up the launch ramp toward an open skylight. Lois craned her neck back as she and others watched the rocket disappear into the oppressive darkness beyond the Watchtower. "Call it a message in a bottle," she murmured. "The story of the world we loved, who we were, and how we fought for what we believed until the very end."

"You think anybody will ever find it?" Jimmy asked.

"Maybe, Jimmy." She lowered her gaze. "I hope so."

The small crowd dispersed, and Lois went looking for her husband. Clark had not been able to attend the launching; he was too busy with his big project. He was spending most of his time in his private lab these days, seated in front of his drafting table in the Mobius chair the Flashes had rescued from the Secret Society. Lois overheard people speculating about Superman's plans as she made her way through the crowded corridors of the Watchtower. Idle super heroes roamed the halls. Marching OMACs patrolled the citadel on alert for any breaches in the fortress's structural integrity. Cracks, leaks, and power outages were becoming more common. Lois stepped around a puddle of melted crystal.

"So what is it?" an intelligent gorilla asked. "What are they building?"

"I hear it's some kind of omni-computer," his companion answered. The doll-sized yellow humanoid, who hailed from a miniature city in the Amazon jungle, perched on the ape's shaggy shoulder. "Something that can calculate the Life Equation."

A mermaid in a nearby aquarium joined the discussion telepathically. "It's a super-communications device, like a cell phone to the gods. Or so I'm told. . . ."

The same conversation was going on throughout the Watchtower. People were obviously desperate to believe that Superman could still save them. Listening in with a reporter's ears, Lois knew exactly how they felt. *This would be a good human-interest story*, she mused, *if there was still a paper to write for.*

"It will be okay," Wonder Girl insisted to her fellow Teen Titans. The fit blonde teenager was dressed casually in a belly shirt and blue jeans. The eagle-shaped emblem on her shirt paid tribute to her Amazonian mentor. "Kara says Superman found a way to shrink and bottle the whole universe for protection."

"That's just a precaution," Kid Devil maintained. Horns sprouted from his scarlet forehead. He spit flames as he spoke. "He's got something else up his sleeve too. A weapon. *The* weapon." He crossed his arms confidently atop his lobster-red chest. A pointed tail poked from the rear of his tight black trousers. "In Superman we trust."

Farther down the hall, Lois spotted John Stewart conferring with Iman. "A will-powered machine that makes the Guardian's power ring tech look like a slide-show projector." He slid his emerald ring off his finger and handed it to Lois. She noted that the scars on his palms had nearly healed. "If my ring can help, here it is."

"*El va a arrancar el tiempo, esto es lo que me han dicho,*" Iman said hopefully. His pale green armor was scorched and pitted. Lois's high school Spanish was a little rusty, but she caught something about "jump-starting time." "*Vivir en el mundo con un hombre asi.*"

"*Gracias,*" she answered before moving on.

Her path led through a cluttered laboratory where the world's greatest minds, both good and evil, labored over blueprints provided by Superman himself. Luthor and Sivana worked side by side at a long stainless steel counter. A few feet away, Will Magnus, the eccentric inventor of the Metal Men, conferred with Niles Caulder, the wheelchair-bound mastermind of the Doom Patrol. Magnus, a tweedy academic type, puffed on his pipe while keeping one eye on the criminal scientists nearby. Clearly, he trusted Luthor and his cronies just as much as Lois did.

"Outrageous," Lex exclaimed. He eyed the blueprints with a little too much enthusiasm. "Too bad we're only permitted to work on one section, Sivana. This looks to me like something capable of rewriting the laws of physics."

Sivana was unimpressed. "Meh."

Lois hoped Luthor wasn't getting any ideas.

EARTH-?.

"The End Is Nigh!" read the hand-painted sign outside the White House gates. A scruffy-looking protestor, wearing a tattered sackcloth robe, paced back and forth in front of the spiked iron fence. His sandals trudged along the pavement. Penitent ashes were smeared upon his unshaven face. He held his ominous sign aloft. Security cameras dutifully tracked his progress. "Repent!" he shouted hoarsely. Seething red clouds added credence to his warnings. Flashes of pitch-black lightning punctuated his jeremiad. "Judgment Day is upon us!"

Wonder if he knows something we don't, the president thought. The leader of the free world turned away from the window. A flock of anxious aides, advisors, and Secret Service agents hurried to keep up as he strode briskly through the West Wing. Framed portraits of his predecessors hung upon the walls of the long, carpeted corridor. A tall African-American man in his early forties, the president wore a dark blue bespoke suit. His athletic physique had inspired a generation of voters to renew their gym memberships. He couldn't help pondering what Lincoln or JFK or McGovern would have done at a moment like this. *Lana Lang's probably glad she was impeached.*

"Sir!" Courtney Knight, his chief science advisor, came up beside him, clutching an armload of manila folders. The brunette young woman's IQ was far more impressive than her age. "Updates on the Red Skies Crisis." He listened attentively as she brought him up to speed. "Justice League data has been confirmed by independent reports from the Large Hadron Collider. The latest disturbances have been traced to graviton impacts." She leaned closer and lowered her voice. "Er, gravitons are—"

"I actually do know what they are," he informed her, "and what it means, thank you." A pair of hand-carved oak doors guarded the Oval Office. The president stepped inside and turned to face his entourage. "Thank you all. Now, if you'll excuse me, ladies and gentlemen."

He firmly shut the doors behind him, so that he had the office all to himself. A swift scan assured him that he was not under observation. Banishing all recording devices from the Oval Office had been one of his first executive orders. He tugged on his necktie as he stood upon a shag carpet adorned with the Presidential Seal. His deep voice addressed the seemingly empty chamber. "Brainiac: Vathlo Prime!"

"Affirmative," the artificial intelligence responded. Brainiac's hard drive was concealed within the purple kryptonite paperweight on his desk. "Megasonic alarm recorded at 4:45 P.M."

"I heard it," the president said. The telltale ringing still echoed in his ears. "Cover for me: One hour."

"Affirmative."

The president undid the buttons of his starched white shirt. "I have business to attend to . . . at my other job."

He pulled open his shirt to reveal the bright red S-shield underneath. The commander in chief could not do America any good right now.

This was a job for Superman.

Brainiac opened a phase-window in the ceiling. Raising his fist above his head, the Man of Steel took off into the sky, faster than the White House's security monitors could ever cope with. Brainiac would protect his secret identity until Earth was safe once more. And if he didn't return . . . well, Vice President Wayne would have his hands full then.

Graviton impacts, Superman mused as he soared above the nation he had sworn to protect. *That's a bad sign.*

Within seconds, he had crossed the Pacific. He descended swiftly through turbulent scarlet clouds toward a hidden island off the coast of Africa. A dense white fog, conjured up by the island's high priestesses, concealed it from the rest of the world. Strange, unearthly music drew him downward to a marble temple atop a granite peak. A statuesque black woman in a star-spangled leotard posed atop the temple. A jeweled tiara crowned her billowing charcoal hair. Her skin gleamed like polished mahogany. She held a conch-shaped horn before her lips. An embossed eagle spread its wings across her gilded breastplate. The sacred Girdle of Erzulie cinched her waist. Her silver lasso rested against her hip.

"That music!" Superman exclaimed. "Great Krypton, Nubia!" He didn't need super-hearing to feel the mystic chords vibrating the very fabric of reality. "The entire universe is shaking!"

Nubia lowered the horn, yet the music kept on playing. "The Wonder Women of Amazonia bring only antiwar technology into the world." She flew upward to meet Superman. "But the Wonder Horn was a gift from the Universals in mythic time before time, to be used only once when all else has failed."

Upon closer examination, Superman saw that the Horn was composed not of shell, nor any other kind of mundane matter, but of molded sunlight itself. It shimmered like the Golden Fleece. Musical notes evanesced visibly in the air. The intoxicating aroma of ambrosia filled Superman's lungs. He heard the storm clouds part above them.

"Whatever it is," he realized, "*something*'s responding."

A sparkling aureate radiance bathed the island in light. A celestial choir joined the fading echoes of the Wonder Horn. The stirring melody swelled triumphantly.

"What is that music?" Superman asked once more. "Like I've known it all my life: so sad, so hopeful, so brave . . ."

Not even the bygone anthems of time-lost Krypton had ever touched him so.

"The Music of the Spheres," Nubia said knowingly. "The sound of the tides of the Infinite breaking upon our mortal strand." She drew him aside as a magnificent airship broke through the clouds above, trailing rainbows in its wake. Its sleek golden hull defied his X-ray vision. "And bearing a vessel, surging on a foam of gravitons like some new Argo. Its cargo not gods, perhaps. Not monsters. But heroes."

The ship cruised gently to a landing atop Amazona's fabled Elysian Fields. Superman and Nubia alighted upon the grassy meadow next to the mysterious UFO. The temples and palaces of the Wonder Women rose proudly in the background. A doorway opened in the vessel's pristine hull. A ramp extruded toward the lawn. A snarky female voice emerged from the ship.

"Super heroes? I don't freakin' believe this." A faceless woman in a black leather jacket stepped out onto the gangplank. A rumpled fedora was perched atop her mussed brown hair. "A whole goddamn Multiverse and they all look like you guys?"

Superman shared a bemused look with Nubia. *This wasn't exactly what I was expecting.*

His eyes widened as an astonishing parade of Supermen poured out of the ship after the sharp-tongued enigma. Of every race and nationality, they projected a strength and confidence he recognized from his own mirror. Many of them wore variations on his own celebrated uniform, while others wore less familiar costumes. He spotted white, Asian, Hispanic, Native American, and Bizarro Supermen, clad in every color of the rainbow. Some wore masks, most had capes. Their hairstyles ranged from flowing blond manes to monklike tonsures. While some had the S-shield on their chest, others sported different symbols like O or V or the Greek letter alpha. There was even, disturbingly, what appeared to be a Nazi Superman, complete with swastika on his chest. *That's just wrong,* Superman thought. *In more ways than one.*

"By my ancestors, Kal-X," Nubia whispered in amazement. "I think they're *you.*"

"Well, sort of." A broad-faced champion with a distinctly boyish demeanor eased past the faceless woman. A golden thunderbolt was emblazoned on his bright red double-breasted tunic. Golden rosettes trimmed his short white cape. A golden sash circled his waist. He cleared his throat. "Minus the swearing," he said, with a sideways glance at the woman. "Name's Captain Marvel, from Earth-Five. We're here to recruit the Supermen of the Multiverse on a life-or-death mission of cosmic proportions."

The masked woman was unapologetic about her cussing. "I like swearing when the situation demands." She stepped forward to introduce herself. "The Question. Global Peace Agent."

This was getting more surreal by the minute. The only Question Superman knew was Guru Sage, the occult Zen master of Hub City.

"I think you're going to have to explain, miss. . . ."

THE WATCHTOWER.

Rows of ordinary men, women, and children were lined up at the far end of a cavernous crystal sanctuary, each person individually sealed in large plastic capsules. Minute air filters kept them from suffocating. Superman heard them whispering to each other, offering last-minute prayers and good-byes, as Wonder Woman angled the shrinking ray toward them. Brainiac, the alien computer tyrant, had once used the same technology to capture and bottle entire cities. *How grimly ironic,* Superman thought, *that I find myself forced to resort to the same methods—for the good of humanity.*

He and Supergirl looked on as the phosphorescent turquoise beam shrank the civilians and their capsules to the size of vitamin pills. The miniaturized people were sorted into trays, each compartment carefully labeled with a microscopic tag. Supergirl retrieved the trays and gently carried them to a waiting cryogenic chamber, where hundreds of other trays were already stacked one atop another. Each tray contained over a hundred micro-humans, frozen in suspended animation. The vault itself held over six billion capsules. Nearly the entire population of Earth, preserved on trays in a freezer. Frozen super-villains were kept in a separate repository, safely locked away from the rest. An embossed red S marked the door of the vault. Supergirl added the new trays to the collection.

"It feels like we've been at this forever," she commented. "How long has it been anyway?"

Wonder Woman adjusted the lens of the shrinking-ray projector. More human-sized capsules automatically rose from the floor. One last assortment of refugees, mostly composed of the JLA's friends and family, filed into the spacious chamber and took their places inside the tubes. Superman spotted Alfred Pennyworth, Jim Gordon, Linda Park, Joan Garrick, and the Tattooed Man's wife and kids. Although visibly nervous, the gathered refugees placed their lives and futures in the heroes' hands.

"It's impossible to say," Diana replied. "What used to be time is slowing to a stop. What was once meaningful and significant is losing importance. History and memory are fading into myth." She powered up the projector once more. "Or so it feels to me."

Supergirl shivered. "I don't think I've ever felt anything so strange, like everything's all broken up from one minute to the next. . . ." She hugged herself. "There *has* to be a way to fix this."

I'm working on it, Superman thought.

Lois came forward from the crowd, after wishing Jimmy and Perry good luck. Superman had saved his friends and loved ones for last. Martha Kent blew him a kiss from inside her capsule, not wanting to intrude upon her son's final moments with his wife.

Superman took Lois in his arms. "I promise I'll restore you all when this is over." He still had a daunting task ahead of him. "Brainiac 5 allowed me to look at the Miracle Machine for no more than a few seconds. I tried to memorize every nut and bolt and circuit."

"Hey, I trust you," she assured him, as beautiful now as the day they first met. No ray on Earth could truly shrink her spirit. "And you'll get the big kiss when I'm back from the fridge, Smallville."

"I'm going to hold you to that," he said with a smile.

EARTH-?.

President Superman and Nubia listened in amazement as the mysterious Question related a bizarre tale of how she and various others had fled the imminent damnation of another Earth. The impromptu briefing sounded disturbingly similar to the Crisis now threatening the world on which they stood. The faceless woman seemed to find her own story hard to believe.

"... at the exact moment our Earth fell into the Abyss, Mister Miracle's Motherboxxx secured a Boom Tube connection to a nearby universe and we made the great escape." The Question sighed and shook her head. "Listen to me. Every time I talk about my life lately, I sound like a schizophrenic." Chemical fumes escaped her belt buckle. She reached up and peeled off a layer of artificial skin, exposing the somber features of an attractive Latino woman. "After we save the Multiverse, I'm out—for sanity's sake."

"Incredible," Superman said. "We've long suspected the existence of parallel universes, but this . . ." He scoped out his myriad counterparts. There were at least four dozen of them. "Multiple Supermen?"

Renee Montoya snorted. "Welcome to a mind-bending world I still feel ill-equipped to deal with."

The Nazi Superman came forward. He regarded the displaced detective with what looked like genuine sympathy. A heavy black cloak was draped over his muscular Aryan frame. A German accent tinged his voice. "And yet you volunteered to accompany the champions of almost fifty worlds on a voyage with perhaps no return."

Renee shrugged. "I have a lot of friends back on my Earth. 'Earth-Zero,' Weeja Dell calls it. I wouldn't want to let them down." She shifted uncomfortably, and took a deep breath before lifting her gaze to look him directly in the eyes. "Overman, I think I met your cousin and . . . I'm so sorry. . . ."

He knew at once what she meant to tell him, and grief contorted his face.

CHAPTER 36

THE WATCHTOWER.

"Almost done," Superman murmured to himself.

His heat vision welded two components together as he smoothed his hand over the polished surface of the Miracle Machine, applying the finishing touches. It had taken all of Earth's resources, the accumulated knowledge of an entire culture, to fashion this crude facsimile of the device he had briefly glimpsed in the thirty-first century. The machine resembled the one buried beneath the Legion's headquarters, only slightly smaller. The distinctive circuit diagram on its face, which he had since learned was the Metron sigil, symbolized the universe's last hope. Silent and inert, the device was not quite operational yet. There was still one piece missing.

Weeks had passed, or had it been years, since Lois and the others had gone into the deep freeze. Time was warped beyond comprehension these days. Only a handful of super heroes had remained to guard the crumbling citadel while he labored in his private workshop. The crystal pillars above him shuddered as, elsewhere in the Watchtower, a portion of the makeshift structure slid into oblivion like a collapsing ice shelf. Greasy fluid dripped from the ceiling, and entropy ate away at the building's foundations. Metron's abandoned Mobius chair sat in the corner of the workshop.

"The walls are coming down around you, Superman," a gravelly voice gloated from the encroaching shadows. Darkseid's restless spirit, in the form of a demonic death mask composed of writhing Apokoliptian biotechnology, manifested above the Machine. Webs of vaporous circuitry spread like lichen around the fringes of the ghostly visage. Malignant red eyes burned like hellfire. A satanic grin mocked Superman. "It's over."

"You're right about that," Superman said, not at all surprised by Darkseid's return. He had been expecting the disembodied entity to show itself eventually. He turned his back on the fearsome apparition. "But you're long dead, Darkseid. Wonder Woman drove you from your body. Batman wounded your soul. The Flashes lured you to your doom in Blüdhaven."

Darkseid's oily tendrils caressed the Miracle Machine. "You've constructed a cargo cult Mother Box capable of a single operation." Brimstone eyes gleamed in anticipation of the havoc such a device could wreak. Black blood seeped from the translucent walls of the workshop. Pools of slimy ichor spread across the floor. "How could I ask for a better gift to destroy you with?"

Or the perfect bait to lure you from hiding, Superman thought. He smiled grimly. It was time to spring the trap. *This is for Batman. And the Martian Manhunter.*

"The worlds of the Multiverse vibrate together, Darkseid, and make a sound like an orchestra. Everything's just vibrations, really. Even *you*." He turned to face Darkseid once more. "And counter-vibrations cancel them out."

His mouth opened wide, unleashing a single musical note that crashed against Darkseid like a sonic tidal wave. The eldritch death mask shattered into pieces. Jagged fragments of Darkseid shredded Superman's cape before boiling out of existence. An apocalyptic bolt of jet-black lightning blew out the walls of the Watchtower. The ceiling caved in, exposing the oppressive black void beyond the citadel. The crimson eyes and teeth haunting the endless night evaporated, so that only impenetrable darkness remained. Rubble rained down on Superman, bouncing harmlessly off his invulnerable physique. The thunder of Darkseid's passing hurt the hero's ears. So did a god end his existence.

Darkseid never liked music. . . .

The Man of Steel stood alone in the ruins. Smoldering flames singed his tattered cape. Only the Miracle Machine and the Mobius chair had survived the cataclysm. Everything in sight had been reduced to wreckage by Darkseid's explosive demise. Superman feared for the safety of the cryogenic vault several stories beneath him. Silence fell over the wreckage. Darkness closed in on him. Even dead, the weight of whatever Darkseid was kept dragging the world into hell.

"Superman here," he whispered, recording a final message for posterity. His vocal cords had been strained by the chord that had undone Darkseid. "Losing my voice . . ." He peered up at the Stygian chaos overhead. No stars or moons relieved the utter emptiness, which stretched farther than even his eyes could see. He had hoped that the darkness would be dispelled with Darkseid, but apparently the time-space continuum was too badly damaged to recover on its own. "It's still not over. . . ."

A faint ticking sound, like a heartbeat, attracted his attention. The inexplicable pulse came from the discarded Mobius chair, which had once belonged to Metron, the most enigmatic of the New Gods. Superman strode toward the throne. Crystalline splinters crunched beneath his boots. Even with his super-hearing, he would have never heard the throbbing but for the absolute silence.

A panel in the contoured back of the chair glowed like the moon. Superman reached into the panel and drew forth a palm-sized artifact that twisted and shimmered in his grasp. It appeared to be in a constant state of self-creation, coiling and unfolding like a serpent devouring its own tail. Impossibly delicate and fragile, it flickered weakly as though about to die out. Its feeble glow illuminated Superman's face.

"I think it's Element X," he said in a hushed tone. "The fire of the gods. The Philosopher's Stone. The Worlogog." The protean artifact, which was said to be a fractal map of space-time from the Big Bang to the ultimate End Point, had been instrumental in defeating Darkseid once before. "It can take any shape . . . become the last part of a jigsaw. . . ."

He carried the miniature object across the floor to the embryonic Miracle Machine. Opening a hatch, he placed the divine spark into the heart of the mechanism, like a pilgrim offering a votive candle at an altar. It fit perfectly, as though it had always been destined to end up there. The Miracle Machine was finished. All he needed to do now was power it up.

"Have to give my vocal cords a moment to heal." He knelt before his creation, depleted and alone. Weeks of silence and solitude weighed heavily upon him; he couldn't remember the last time he had spoken with a friend or loved one. "A moment's silence . . . to prepare for cosmic midnight . . ."

Something rustled in the shadows. A sinister chuckle emerged from the tenebrous gloom.

"Exhausted. Isolated," a sepulchral voice taunted Superman. "Your father failed to save his world, Last Son of Krypton. Now it's your turn."

Who?

Superman rose to his feet. He turned away from the Miracle Machine. At first, he feared that some vestige of Darkseid had survived, yet the macabre figure that emerged from the murk was something else altogether. Over fifteen feet tall, the cadaverous entity resembled some sort of gigantic extraterrestrial vampire. Feral red eyes glowed with the sunken sockets of a skeletal red face. Batlike nostrils flared above a mouthful of jagged fangs. Pointed ears protruded from his skull. Tapered swaths of slick black hair striped his naked cranium. Bristling muttonchops framed his hollow cheeks. A ragged, vermin-infested black cloak was draped over his hunched, emaciated figure. Dry, vermillion skin stretched like parchment over his bony frame. Throbbing veins stood out beneath his shriveled hide. Long black nails curled like scimitars at the ends of his gaunt, elongated fingers. Blood dribbled from distended jaws that opened wider than seemed humanly possible. He reeked of death and decay.

The Man of Steel faced the intruder. "And you are?"

"I am Mandrakk," the ghoul proclaimed. "The Dark Monitor. The Outcast. The Eternal Enemy of All That Is." He crooked his arm across his chest, so that his threadbare cloak hung before him like a rotting curtain. "The dying god left your universe wounded, broken, defenseless, alone in the endless abyss . . . where Mandrakk dwells. Here at the end of all stories."

Of course, Superman thought. He saw now the creature's resemblance, although hideously distorted, to the godlike Monitor he had encountered years ago during the so-called Crisis on Infinite Earths. He sensed instinctively that he was in the presence of the ultimate predator.

"What do you want, Mandrakk?" he demanded.

The vampire cackled mirthlessly. "I have waited a long time to meet you,

Superman. To destroy you and all you represent." He beckoned to Superman with his ribbonlike claws. "Come closer. I need to eat you raw—as I fed on the very 'Wrath of God.' "

He drew back his cloak to reveal a shocking sight: the drained husk of the Spectre sprawled at Mandrakk's feet. Clad in a ragged dark green shroud, the Ghostly Guardian appeared even more deathly pale than usual. His tortured face was that of Crispus Allen, a Gotham police detective slain in the line of duty. Ectoplasm oozed from a gaping wound in his throat. He moaned piteously.

"Behold Creation's defender." Mandrakk wiped the Spectre's blood from his slobbering mandibles. His hinged jaws opened impossibly wide. "Bled dry. Meaningless."

Superman was taken aback by the unsettling tableau. The Spectre was one of the most powerful entities in the universe; he was to ordinary ghosts what Superman was to mortal men . . . and then some. If Mandrakk could overcome the Spectre, then he was truly a force to be reckoned with.

Nor was he alone. Another Monitor, somewhat less fiendish in appearance than Mandrakk, slunk out from behind the looming space vampire. Futuristic sci-fi armor was stained and tarnished. His ruddy face was flushed with excitement. His glazed white eyes were those of a true fanatic. He clung to Mandrakk's shadow like a jackal attending upon a lion.

"You see, master!" the nameless Monitor crowed. "It is as I promised. Only this insignificant germ stands between you and your revenge." He plucked a squirming yellow maggot from Mandrakk's cloak and popped it between his jaws. Drool trickled from the corner of his mouth. "Nix Uotan would have fought against us, but I saw to his banishment. Now will the Ultimate Prophecy be fulfilled. Slake your unholy thirst upon the Multiverse!"

Mandrakk patted the obsequious Monitor on the head. "You have done well, Rox Ogama, my good and faithful servant. You will be rewarded with a place at the blood-feast, beginning with your delectable prize."

Superman was dismayed to see Supergirl slung limply over Ogama's shoulder like a caveman's unwilling bride. Kara was out cold, her long blonde hair dangling toward the floor. Her bare throat was unviolated so far. Superman let out a sigh of relief; Ogama had not fed on Supergirl yet. Nevertheless, his skin scrawled at the sight of Kara in the Monitor's grasp.

You've got another thing coming, Superman thought, *if you think I'm going to let you or Mandrakk eat my cousin.*

His eyes darted toward the Miracle Machine, only a few feet away.

Mandrakk guessed his intentions. He dismissed Superman's plan with a wave of his claw. "There is no light, no spark here to power your empty weapon." He stalked closer to Superman, until the Man of Steel could feel the vampire's fetid breath upon his face. "Come, die screaming and writhing in the arms of your master!"

"I've got to say, I've had better offers. I'm a living solar battery," Superman reminded Mandrakk. "I store light in my cells." He turned his back on the approaching revenant. "I'll use it all if that's what it takes to activate the Miracle Machine."

Superman's eyes glowed like twin suns, and the Miracle Machine hummed to life. The Metron sigil flared neon-bright. Crackling silver plasma surged between twin electrodes. Dynamos kicked into motion. Ozone tickled Superman's nose. A holographic map of the universe rose from the surface of the machine. It swirled counterclockwise before Superman's radiant eyes. He reached out to touch it.

A miniature Big Bang lit up the ruins.

"No!" Mandrakk shrieked. He retreated from the pure white light, holding up his cloak to shield his eyes. His undead flesh sizzled in the glare. "What have you done?"

"It's simple," Superman said. "I made a wish."

SPACE.

A golden submarine came zipping past the Green Lanterns. It dove into the never-ending vortex consuming Earth, swiftly leaving the startled Corpsmen behind. Hal Jordan's eyes bulged behind his green domino mask. Unearthly music filled his ears. A rainbow spectrum of colors rippled around the astounding vessel.

Where did that *come from?* Hal thought. *And whose side is it on?*

He led the exhausted Lanterns onward. His power ring flickered weakly upon his right fist. The twenty-four hours were almost up.

"What the hell?" Guy Gardner exclaimed, right behind him. "What *is* that thing?"

Kyle Rayner struggled to keep up. Hundreds of alien Green Lanterns flew in formation behind their human comrades. Kyle shot his predecessor a worried look. "Hal?"

"I don't know," Hal admitted. A drastic idea popped into his brain. "But whatever it is, it's our way in!" An emerald grappling hook fired from his ring as he latched onto the rear of the amazing vessel. With luck, the ship would tow them beyond the event horizon.

The other Lanterns swiftly followed his example. A sudden burst of acceleration sent them hurdling toward the planet below . . . and the black hole that threatened to devour it. For the first time in what felt like forever, Hal and the others actually started gaining on the endangered world. Earth grew ever larger before their eyes. The entire planet was shrouded in darkness, except for a single spark of light at the top of the world.

There was no turning back now. The black hole's ravenous pull was too intense. They were going down, one way or another. A veteran test pilot, Hal Jordan had been in this situation before.

"Let's hear it!" he shouted to his fellow Green Lanterns. "In brightest day . . . !"

The entire Corps picked up the Oath:

> *In Darkest Night,*
> *No Evil Shall Escape Our Sight.*
> *Let All Who Worship Evil's Might,*
> *Beware Our Power!*
> *Green Lantern's Light!*

THE WATCHTOWER.

Nix Uotan realized his moment had come. His true enemy had revealed itself. Thanks to Metron's intervention, and Superman's timely activation of the Miracle Machine, he was now free to act in his capacity as a multiversal Monitor. With a snap of his fingertips, he transported himself to the ruins of the Watchtower, arriving just in time to preside over the last stand of this universe's remarkable creatures. He marveled that he and his kind had once dismissed these heroic beings as inconsequential, mere microbes infesting the celestial workings of the Orrery. Beneath consideration.

How wrong we were, Nix thought. *I see in them now the glory Metron saw so long ago.*

He materialized between Superman and the corrupted Monitors. "Superman," he said. "Your signal has been received and understood." He looked to the sky, where a scintillating golden aurora abruptly broke through the darkness. "Help is on the way."

Accompanied by a triumphant fanfare, the Supermen of the Universe swooped down en masse. Captain Marvel, President Superman, Overman, Supremo, Savior, Cyclo-Man, Principal, Guardsman, Alpha the Unimaginable, Hyperius, Icon, Mr. Might, and over forty other alternate incarnations of Superman came soaring to the rescue, theirs capes flapping bravely behind them, their mighty fists extended before them. A medieval Superman in plate armor, a Super-Demon with a Gothic S upon his chest, a geriatric Superman with a receding hairline, and the raven-haired Superwoman of Earth-11 joined forces with the teenage Son of Superman from Earth-16 and the communist Red Son of a world where the hammer and sickle flew over all mankind. Despite their differing origins and ideologies, all were united in their common mission to fight for truth, justice, and life itself. Typically confused, Bizarro Superman flew in the opposite direction.

Nix glimpsed the *Ultima Thule* soaring above the reinforcements. His heart soared. *Bless you, Weeja Dell. Is it any wonder I love you so?*

"Beware, Mandrakk!" he proclaimed. "You face the Supermen of the Multiverse: a legion of heroes so incredible it can be assembled only once against the absolute enemy!"

Rox Ogama snarled at the Supermen. "Let me kill them, master!" He hurled Supergirl away from him. "She can wait!"

But not even a Monitor could stand against the cumulative might of the Men (and Woman) of Steel. Nearly fifty pairs of eyes lit up like blazing supernovae. A barrage of heat vision targeted Ogama, who instantly burst into flame. Whimpering in pain, he crawled on all fours toward his unholy master. Baked flesh flaked away from his agonized countenance. Blistered hands clawed at the floor, searching in vain for shelter from the Supermen's solar beams. Nix felt a twinge of pity for the treacherous Monitor, then recalled what had become of Earth-51, thanks to Ogama's covert machinations. An entire universe had perished just to deflect blame onto Nix. The murderous villain was now paying the price of his perfidy. Nix made no move to save him. Too long had Rox Ogama plotted in the shadows. *Let the sun shine in.*

"Save me, master!" Ogama pleaded. Smoke rose from his burning cape. His metal armor melted, fusing to his scarred flesh. It was clear that some of the multiversal Supermen had no compunction against killing. Super-Demon scorched the crawling Monitor with a fearsome blast of cosmic hell-fire. The medieval Superman's heat vision skewered Ogama like a red-hot lance. Mandrakk's lackey grabbed onto his master's ankle. "Spare your loyal servant!"

But the cold-blooded vampire was concerned only with his own survival. Snarling in irritation, he tore himself free from Ogama's grip and kicked the burning irritant away from him. A burst of poisonous green energy shot from Mandrakk's eyes, disposing of Ogama once and for all. The worthless Monitor died screaming at his master's feet. His blazing body fell still.

None would mourn him, least of all Nix Uotan.

The young Monitor turned his attention to Mandrakk himself. "Turn back," he commanded the vampire. "Slink home to your tomb. An emerald dawn arises."

A faint green spark appeared in the heavens, high above the *Ultima Thule*. The spark fell to Earth like a falling star before revealing itself to be an entire battalion of Green Lanterns, led by Earth's own native wielders of the most powerful weapons in the galaxy. The interstellar police force descended from space, staging an all-out raid on the heart of darkness.

Fear and confusion showed on the death's-head visage of Mandrakk. He stared in bewilderment at the steadfast young Monitor. Recognition flared in his feral red eyes.

"Nix Uotan? My *son*?"

Sorrow leavened Nix's victory as he contemplated the abomination his father had become. Once, Dax Novu had been the best and brightest of the Monitors, until his investigations into the myriad life-forms of the germ-worlds had infected him with an insatiable hunger for the very stuff of existence. No trace of Dax Novu's former virtues remained in the parasitic monstrosity that was Mandrakk. Nix steeled his heart to endure what must be done. The sacred words of a legendary oath served as the ideal lyrics to sublime music emanating from the god-engines of the *Ultima Thule*. The verses fit the melody perfectly. "Let all who worship evil's might . . ."

The Green Lanterns took up positions around Mandrakk. Their protective auras blinked erratically. Lacking the power to defy gravity any longer, they touched down on the cracked and splintered floor of the Watchtower. Shocked expressions took in Mandrakk's grotesque appearance.

"Holy crap!" Guy Gardner blurted. The brash Green Lantern held up his power ring as though to ward off the space-age nosferatu. His lip curled in disgust. "What the hell am I looking at?"

"Rings can't handle this, Hal!" Kyle Rayner warned. His own ring sputtered like a dying flame. "Our twenty-four hours are up!"

Hal Jordan was undaunted. He flashed a devil-may-care grin. "Gimme one last team effort!" He aimed his ring at Mandrakk. His fellow Green Lanterns did likewise. "All together now, let's spike this vampire!"

Their combined willpower produced a huge glowing stake that plunged into Mandrakk's fetid heart. The Dark Monitor exploded into a tornado of fiery ashes that rose into the sky like a pillar of fire before crumbling back to Earth. Fierce winds whipped the ashes, scattering them to oblivion. A cheer rose from the assembled Supermen and Green Lanterns, who hugged and high-fived each other. Clark Kent, Kal-El, the quintessential Superman of Earth-Zero, helped his young cousin to her feet. Supergirl shook off the daze Ogama had left her in. Her slender fingers hurriedly checked her throat, but came away unbloodied. She embraced Superman.

"It's almost over, isn't it?" she asked him. "You did it."

"We *all* did," Superman corrected her. "Every one of us."

Nix Uotan left them to their celebrations. He walked across the exposed workshop to Rox Ogama's charred remains. A blackened skeleton was all that remained of the sinister Monitor, whose duplicity had led to Nix's exile, cruelly tearing him from the arms of his beloved Weeja Dell. Ogama had foolishly assumed that only another Monitor could oppose Mandrakk's diabolical ambitions. Like the rest of the Monitors, he had sorely underestimated the resourceful denizens of the myriad worlds they oversaw. *The*

Multiverse has natural defenses, Nix Uotan realized now, *that none of us could have ever imagined.*

He grabbed onto Ogama's fleshless neck and yanked the skeleton to its feet. Carbonized bones, held together only by dry, brittle sinews, rattled inside Ogama's scorched armor. Nix stared into the empty sockets of his betrayer's skull. Rox Ogama had gotten what he deserved.

"Nobody screws with the Judge of All Evil."

CHAPTER 37

THE CITADEL OF NIL.
NEXUS OF REALITIES.

"The damage caused to the Orrery of Worlds by Darkseid's fall is under repair," the Prime Monitor reported to the Council. With Mandrakk dead, and his dire prophecy averted, the Monitors had resumed their august deliberations. Hermuz now presided over the conclave, the aged Tahoteh's confidence and authority having not survived the recent Crisis. "As it ever was done, so shall it be done again . . . with apologies to Monitor Nix Uotan."

Nix faced his peers once more, but this time he was not on trial. He stood at the base of the Orrery itself, gazing up at the assembled Monitors who were seated in the curved galleries overlooking the levitating dais holding Nix aloft. He stepped forward to offer a fuller account of the epochal events he had witnessed with his own eyes. Holographic images were projected before the Council as he spoke. A rolled-up scroll was tucked beneath his left arm.

"The germ-creatures themselves reestablished the symmetry of the Orrery," he stressed. "I've never witnessed such industry, such intelligence. . . ."

An image appeared of Earth-Zero being towed free of Darkseid's black heart by the combined efforts of the Supermen of the Multiverse. The flying champions tugged on emerald chains generated by the Green Lantern Corps. In an astounding feat of strength, the Supermen literally pulled Earth safely beyond the event horizon to its rightful place in the cosmos. The Superman of Earth-Zero was at the very head of the grand endeavor. The Metron sigil shimmered luminously above the outlines of Europe and Asia.

"I marveled at the white-hot passions that drive them. Passions powerful enough to trigger catastrophic changes in beings of pure thought such as ourselves."

The projection zoomed in on a jubilant street scene in Metropolis. Brightly colored balloons rose in celebration as freed humanity eagerly dismantled the billboards and monuments erected during Darkseid's hellish reign. Construction workers labored to repair the Daily Planet Building; an elevated metal crane carefully lowered the newspaper's trademark golden globe back onto the skyscraper's roof. A dump truck hauled away a huge granite bust of Darkseid. Jeering citizens hurled trash and old shoes at the idol as it passed. The sun shone brightly in a clear blue sky.

In the foreground, the Flashes were reunited with their families. Barry Allen embraced his former widow. Wally West knelt to hug his children, while Linda Park wiped away a tear of joy. Jay and Joan Garrick held hands like the old married couple they were. For once, the Flashes could slow down long enough to enjoy some quality time together. Nix Uotan was deeply moved by their obvious love for one another. He snuck a peek at Weeja Dell, who gazed proudly at him from her place in the gallery. Bittersweet emotions swept over the young Monitor. Alas, their reunion was fated to be short-lived.

"For this reason," he stated firmly, "I advise immediate withdrawal of all contact with the germ-worlds, and no further interference with their destinies."

The Prime Monitor brushed aside Nix's suggestion. "Your concerns are noted. Please, just continue with your report, sparing no details."

Nix let the matter drop, if only for the moment. "Well, now we know why there's an enormous black hole at the center of Creation. It's where Darkseid fell through existence to his doom. Leaving hell deserted."

The floating image shifted from Metropolis to the dismal landscape of bleak Apokolips, former abode of the evil New Gods. Once-volcanic Fire Pits were cold and silent. Forbidding prisons, palaces, and factories had fallen into ruin. A cracked and arid wasteland stretched to the horizon. Orion's fabled astro-harness hung limply atop a chiseled stone tombstone.

Yet amidst the desolation, a single white flower blossomed at the foot of the grave. The parched air shimmered and rippled as Metron materialized above the bloom. No longer bound to his Mobius chair, the silvery god hung suspended in the air. Behind him, vague figures could be glimpsed coming into being: a white-maned elder bearing a crooked staff, a luminous youth seemingly composed of rays of purest light, an armored warrior woman of Amazonian physique, a band of adolescent free spirits whose bohemian attire defied convention and authority, a miraculous escape artist in gaudy carnival garb, and others. The indistinct apparitions multiplied quickly, gradually gaining flesh and substance. . . .

"So begins the myth of a new creation. Apokolips reborn as New Genesis. The New Gods returned to guide the destiny of a new world." He unrolled the scroll, revealing an elaborate map worked out in painstaking detail. Far-flung oceans and continents were delineated by hand. An amazing new world waited to be explored. "And here: the plan I used to reconstruct Earth Designate-51, destroyed by Rox Ogama's treachery . . ."

The scene from Apokolips was replaced by a view of Earth-51. A blond-haired stripling, who had once been confined to Darkseid's dungeons in Blüdhaven, now sat atop a pile of rubble. A wild yellow mane tumbled past his bare shoulders; only a pair of faded denim cut-offs protected him from the elements. A toppled Statue of Liberty lay half buried beneath the sandy dunes behind him. Tuftan and his Tiger Tribe gathered attentively around the human boy, attending to his words. The tiger-men sat astride their pony dogs. They too had been relocated to Earth-51.

"I saw the world remade with my own eyes," the boy told the tigers, who were transfixed by his story. "With pieces of other times, other places. I delivered an urgent message to my own distant ancestor, at the dawn of another world. All in a vision that came to me in Command-D."

Nix rolled up the map. "Designate-51 lives anew. Repairs were accomplished, time anomalies corrected, coherence and harmony restored." Weeja Dell had assisted in the relief efforts, he recalled, transporting the Question and her fellow refugees back to Earth-Zero via the *Ultima Thule*. The Supermen of the Multiverse had each been returned to their respective Earths as well. "This all but concludes my report."

In the gallery, a venerable figure rose unsteadily to his feet. "The Orrery was almost lost," the decrepit Monitor murmured weakly. Age and infirmity enfeebled him. His wrinkled face and snowy beard were equally drained of color. His quavery voice trailed away. "Our story has become toxic, beyond our control. . . ."

"Forgive Monitor Tahoteh's encroaching senility." Hermuz appeared embarrassed by his predecessor's ramblings. He coaxed the elder Monitor back into his seat. "Your exile is over, Nix Uotan. You are invited to rejoin the Circle of Monitors with full honors."

Perhaps you should listen more closely to the old man, Nix thought. Even with his wits addled by age, Tahoteh appeared to have a better grasp of recent events than Hermuz and the others. "Prime Monitor," he replied respectfully. "If I may decline any such honors as essentially meaningless, there are more critical matters to attend to."

Startled gasps greeted Nix's rebuke, but the young Monitor was not deterred by the Council's scandalized reaction. His floating platform ascended until he was face to face with the Prime Monitor. He gestured boldly at the celestial Orrery behind him. Fifty-two individual Earths revolved upon the towering helix, moving with clockwork precision. Earth-Zero rotated at the basis of the Orrery, the fulcrum upon which all the Multiverse balanced. Mandrakk and Ogama had almost wrecked that balance beyond recovery, while the rest of the Monitors had averted their eyes from the danger, willfully looking the other way. In the end, the Multiverse had been saved *despite* the Monitors, not because of them.

"We almost destroyed this beautiful living thing in our midst," he said with conviction. "This Multiverse of life deserves its freedom from our interference." Memories of Earth-51, once rendered lifeless by Ogama's machinations, passed through his brain. His decisive tone made it clear that his mind was made up; he dared any of his weak-willed peers to oppose him. The Judge of All Evil had rendered his verdict. "Make your peace."

"All the lovely clockwork is erased from the sky," Weeja Dell observed from the very balcony where once she had mourned her lover's banishment. She gazed out at the twilight of their world. Oblivion, as blank as an empty page, was already nibbling at the horizon. A sense of profound melancholy washed over her. "The searing emptiness of the Overvoid draws ever closer." She heard footsteps behind her. "The hour grows late, Nix Uotan."

He joined her upon the balcony. Rosy daylight sunk beneath the surface of a shrinking copper sea. "They couldn't make me forget you," he affirmed. "*You* brought me back, Weeja Dell. You were my dream girl, from a world I thought I could never reach."

She turned toward him. His voice and tone were both familiar and oddly strange to her ears, the inflections and idioms more Earthly than Monitor. She eyed him nervously. "You sound . . . different."

"I lived among them," he reminded her. "I saw the damage we were doing to them and what we'd have to sacrifice to save them." His soulful eyes pleaded for her understanding. "I won't forget you."

They faced each other awkwardly, like any ordinary mortal couple at the beginning . . . or the end. Weeja realized how much he was giving up for the sake of his convictions, and that he asked the same of her. The empty whiteness closed in on them, the familiar vistas dissolving at the periphery of her vision. The skeletal frames of shattered towers lost their outlines, melting away into nothingness. Soon naught would remain but a blank and featureless void. Only a single sunset was left to them.

"Then this really is the last day."

"I think so." He took her in his arms, sheltering her against the end of eternity. His strange new garments carried the scent of humanity. They embraced urgently, for the first time, for the last time. "The final crisis is ours, Weeja Dell."

So be it, then, she thought. *If this is what you think is best.* Resigned to her fate, she rested her head against his chest, taking comfort in the warmth and solidity of his embrace for what little time remained to them. "It was good to have a face, and to love and be loved." Her mind raced back over the momentous events that had brought them to this unforeseen passage. A question occurred to her. "Tell me one last thing before we part, Nix Uotan. What *was* Superman's wish upon the Miracle Machine?"

"He's Superman. He wished only the best for us." He lifted her chin to gaze lovingly in her eyes. His gentle lips kissed her brow. "Close your eyes."

The void was all around them now, wiping away the world like a watercolor in the rain, so that all that was left was just the two of them, clinging to each other for a few shared heartbeats. The vast and timeless civilization of the Monitors—the ancient spires and temples, the towering basalt cliffs and surging waves—were no more. Weeja Dell felt her own existence, her memories and identity, begin to evanesce into the unknowable. The last thing she heard was her lover's voice whispering in her ear.

"He wished for a happy ending, Weeja Dell."

METROPOLIS.

Nick Ustan sat upright in his bed, confused and disoriented. His clock radio blared loudly from the dresser. A memory of whiteness, endless and eternal, was pushed aside by the mundane reality of his cheap apartment. Dirty laundry littered the floor. The radiator hissed and rattled. Honking horns and car alarms, coming from outside his bedroom window, competed with the peppy good cheer of the morning deejay.

"You've just joined WGBS," the radio informed Nick, "on a beautiful day in the Big Apricot! With more on those newly discovered parallel worlds and how can they could change our lives forever!" Nick stared at the ceiling. He listened in wonder to the sound of his own breathing. He felt a mortal heart pounding in his chest. Mystic dreams receded as he rejoined the waking world. The radio enthusiastically promised a brand-new day. "This is one story that's only just beginning. . . ."

EPILOGUE

NORTH AMERICA.
40,000 YEARS AGO.

Many summers had passed since the shining god had given Anthro the gift of fire, yet the dancing flames still filled his soul with awe. He sat before his campfire, older now than Ne-Ahn the Brave had been when the Blood Tribe slew him. The god's sign was painted upon Anthro's wrinkled visage. Age weighed heavily upon the shaman's bones. Knotted gray hair fell over his bony shoulder. A hollow log supported his weary frame. He fingered the delicate shell necklace around his neck; his mate had long ago gone to dwell among their ancestors. Anthro knew he would soon join her.

Stars filled the deep purple sky above him. The moon was reflected upon the shimmering surface of the great salt water. A rocky cliff overlooked the lonely beach. Waves lapped at the shore. Not far away, nestled between the slopes of two sandy dunes, a gleaming blue arrow, larger than a mammoth's tusk, was embedded in the earth. The arrow had crashed down from the heavens at the dusk, as thrown by the gods. Its polished surface reminded Anthro of the shining god's bright throne. Its tapered nose was buried deep in the ground. Fins the color of flame sprouted from its tail.

One last miracle in a lifetime of wonders.

The old man rose from the log, leaving the secrets of the sky blue arrow for younger hunters to discover. He plucked a burning brand from the fire and held it above his head. Leaning heavily upon a stick, he made his way to the base of the cliff. Shadows filled the gaping mouth of a sacred cavern Anthro had first discovered many seasons past.

His torch drove back the darkness as he entered the cave. It was his wish to refresh the stories before he took his rest. As he trod once more upon the holy ground, he thought of the shining god and the burning bush in the long-ago now. The bright light of memory shone in his eyes. The old man had carried the strong fire from place to place, learning all its urgent lessons. He had made with his hands things first glimpsed in the swift and subtle heart. Where new thoughts are born in a furnace.

The god's sign was painted upon the wall of the cave, the colors faded with time. Anthro mixed bowls of paint, blending earth, ash, and animal fat to create the colors, then used his gnarled fingers to retrace the pattern on the enduring stone. Safely hidden from the wind and rain and sun, the mark might last until the end of the world . . . and beyond. He thought of the blond boy who had once appeared to him in a vision. Was this the weapon the youth had pleaded for when Anthro himself was but a boy?

Perhaps.

The old man's skull was filled one last time with brilliant flame. Content, he laid himself down upon the bumpy stone floor of the cavern. He put aside his fading torch. In a halo of blinding light that seemed to complete everything, Anthro passed like a dream.

Like smoke.

Silence fell over the cavern—until a stranger emerged from the shadows. Boot steps echoed softly inside the cave. A man whose name was still unknown to history bent low over the departed shaman. Shadows concealed the man's face. His bare chest was broad and muscular. Strong hands laid a golden belt, with many sealed pouches, atop the old man's chest. Winged mammals rustled amidst the stalactites overhead. In the light of the sputtering torch, he picked up the paints and began to trace a new symbol upon the limestone walls of the cavern: the scalloped wings of a bat.

The fire kept on burning.

END.

ABOUT THE AUTHOR

GREG COX is the author of three previous DC Comics novelizations: *Infinite Crisis*, *52*, and *Countdown*. He has also written the official movie novelizations of such films as *Daredevil*, *Death Defying Acts*, *Ghost Rider*, *Underworld*, *Underworld: Evolution*, and *Underworld: Rise of the Lycans*. In addition, he has authored books and short stories based on such popular series as *Alias*, *Batman*, *Buffy the Vampire Slayer*, *CSI*, *Fantastic Four*, *Farscape*, *The 4400*, *The Green Hornet*, *Iron Man*, *The Phantom*, *Roswell*, *Spider-Man*, *Star Trek*, *Terminator*, *Xena: Warrior Princess*, *X-Men*, and *Zorro*.

He lives in Oxford, Pennsylvania. His official website is www.gregcox-author.com.